■   ■   ■

By the time Gabe and Lucerne reached the mascot's side, it was lying quite still, facedown. Lucerne dug a pencil flashlight out of her bag, swept its beam over the fuzzy back.

"Jack," Gabe said hoarsely, "if this is a joke…" He dropped to his knees to help Lucerne, who was already tugging at the body.

■   ■   ■

WATERBROOK
PRESS
COLORADO SPRINGS

MARIGOLDS FOR MOURNING

PUBLISHED BY WATERBROOK PRESS

5446 North Academy Boulevard, Suite 200

Colorado Springs, Colorado 80918

A division of Bantam Doubleday Dell Publishing Group, Inc.

Scripture quotations are from the *King James Version* of the Bible. All
epigraphs are from *The Winter's Tale* by William Shakespeare, act 4,
scene 4. "Condolences" by Dorothy Parker, copyright 1926, renewed
© 1954 by Dorothy Parker, from *The Portable Dorothy Parker* by
Dorothy Parker, introduction by Brendan Gill. Used by permission of
Viking Penguin, a division of Penguin Putnam, Inc.

ISBN 1-57856-054-3

Printed in the United States of America

1998—First Edition

10 9 8 7 6 5 4 3 2 1

*To all the storytelling knights-errant
of the Mercer Writers' Round Table,
my brothers and sisters of the Grail*

THE THYME WILL TELL MYSTERIES

THE HARGROVE FAMILY TREE

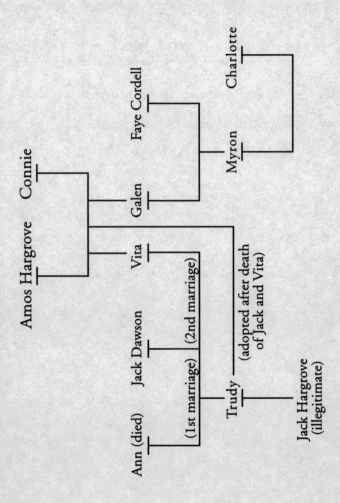

CHAPTER 1

■ ■ ■

Sir, the year growing ancient,
not yet on summer's death, nor on the birth
of trembling winter. . .

Often that fall Regan dreamed of drowning. She, who had always lived in the peaceful backwaters of life, would wake panting, struggling up from dark, tugging depths.

Regan's father had been murdered and she arrested in early summer. It had been June when the real killer pinned her underwater. A last-minute rescue and the killer's indictment should have ended it. But there had been no ending, happy or otherwise, just a headlong forward rush.

In a matter of weeks, Regan had assumed control of an herb farm, welcomed her formerly hostile half-sisters and niece home, returned her four-year-old foster daughter to Eastern Europe, and accepted a marriage proposal from the police chief she scarcely knew. Momentum had kept her afloat thus far. The wave of publicity surrounding Alden Culver's murder had tripled business at Thyme Will Tell. The fall shipping season, usually slower than spring, had surged.

Only in sleep was there time to be afraid—to sink.

■ ■ ■

The bitter scent of autumn flowers clung to Regan's hands— musky, acrid, a smoky foreshadowing of winter fires—long after

1

the quarrel. She had been toying with the bouquet on the mantel while awaiting Matt's arrival.

A big, muscular man in his thirties with craggy features and watchful eyes, Matt did not seem, when he came, any different than usual. Thinner maybe. Before her father's murder, he had been developing a slight paunch from too much diner food. There was no sign of it now. When he was busy or worried, he often forgot to eat. He apparently had found no time to change from his police uniform.

"Very lady of the manor-ish," he said of her apricot wool sweater and tweed skirt as he followed her into the living room. "And these, I suppose," he added, eyeing the lush arrangement over the fireplace as he handed her a plastic-wrapped bouquet, "are like coals to Newcastle."

There may have been an edge to his tone that hinted at something more than teasing. If so, she chose not to hear it. She smiled and kissed him. "You can never have too many flowers." If his lips were cold, it was just the chill of an October evening.

She did not reprove him for his lateness, just as she never complained when his beeper interrupted their times together. Everything was okay as they chatted about the high school homecoming, which was imminent, then got down to discussing their wedding, which was scheduled for June of the following year.

Suddenly everything was *not* okay.

They were sitting on the couch, she leaning against his shoulder. His arm was around her, making her aware of the instant he stiffened. She had just said, "When you move in here—"

She stopped and looked up at him. "Is something wrong?"

"When I move in here?" he repeated. "I thought we were moving out to my place."

"Oh, no!" she said, then realized she had said it too quickly. "I mean," she fumbled, "it's a nice place, but it's not..." She stopped.

"Comparable?" he suggested.

She was bewildered by the abruptness with which she had stumbled into this quagmire. "No," she denied hastily. "That isn't what I meant. I meant you haven't had your place very long, so it isn't really home. This is home to me."

It sounded lame even to her and did not help. He was retreating further though physically still so close. He didn't speak.

"The others have offered to move out," she plunged on, "if that's what's bothering you. Though I really don't think it's necessary. This is a big house." And, plaintively, "Matt, *what's wrong?*"

"You don't get it," he said. "You really *don't* get it, do you?"

He spoke quietly and went as quietly, simply rising and walking out. She, still leaning, had to put a hand down hard on the cushions to catch herself. She was staring at the doorway when her niece, Diane, poked a blond head in.

"I was just making popcorn when I heard him go, so I brought you a bowl as consolation. What was the emergency this time?" At her aunt's expression, she added, "Uh-oh, *not* an emergency?"

Regan shook her head. "He just walked out. It all happened so fast, I don't…" She twisted the engagement ring on her finger. Because she did not like diamonds, Matt had bought her a jade puzzle ring. It came in three pieces, and he had warned her not to take it apart because the dealer didn't have the solution to it. So she had always been cautious when she had to remove it, handling it delicately, almost tentatively.

"It was about the house, about living here, I mean. I had just assumed that we would. But I've always been careful not to mention our difference in…"

"Income?" her niece finished for her. Diane crossed to set the bowl of popcorn on the coffee table and joined Regan on the couch. They were the same age and had, after years of wary politeness, become friends over the summer. "It was bound to come up, Regan. You couldn't ignore the issue forever. You shouldn't have to be that careful with the man you're going to marry. I suspect it's obvious to him every time he comes here."

"But even when he was always late, I never complained," Regan protested.

"'No, and it was perfectly infuriating,'" Diane quoted, "'the way you *didn't* complain.' T. S. Eliot. It probably made it seem like you didn't really care that much. Don't forget that Matt must be exhausted too. He's had a lot on his plate recently."

Regan thought briefly about the mess on Matt's plate. The deaths of some farm animals in July had sparked the usual rumors about satanic cults. When school opened in September, it had quickly become apparent that someone was dispensing big-city drugs to Hayden's small-town kids.

Also, Gabe Johnson had decided to join the football team in his senior year. An unfounded rumor was circulating that Gabe was going to replace the quarterback, a popular blond giant named Jack Hargrove. Since Gabe was black, that gossip had stirred up some latent racism. Matt, who coached the team, was caught in the middle.

Yes, Matt was exhausted, but didn't exhaustion force out the true feelings that a person no longer had the energy to suppress?

"Matt is a very controlled sort, you know," Regan said quietly. "He would only walk out like that if he was on the verge of revealing too much. So what was he afraid he would say?"

"Don't look like that," Diane said. "He loves you. He'll call."

But he didn't.

■ ■ ■

"What's with the chief?" Gabe Johnson had chosen carefully the moment to ask that question. He was setting up folding chairs while Regan arranged calendulas in a bowl at the front of the classroom.

After Gabe's belated entry into the drama of her father's murder, Regan had offered him a job as her assistant. She no longer had time personally to oversee the planting of the gardens she designed. After several months of working with her, Gabe thought he knew her pretty well, or as well as anybody could.

She was always nervous before giving a speech and prone to fidget without being fully aware of what her hands were doing.

He had hoped to catch her off guard for once. By her exaggerated—almost guilty—start, he knew he hadn't succeeded.

Regan smiled blindly in his direction without meeting his eyes. "What do you mean?"

"So," he said, "you *are* the one who's got him in this funk. C'mon. What did you do?"

She shot him her most freezing look. "Is it any business of yours?"

"It is if it costs us the state championship. We have one of our toughest games coming up tonight, remember? If you must play with the guy's mind, can't you wait a few months?"

She turned back to her flower arranging without answering.

Gabe began to gather up boxes. Once she started to ignore him, there wasn't much use in persisting.

He stepped to the back of the room to assess the display of potted plants and cut flowers crowding the table and the floor around it, nodding his approval. Between the fields and greenhouses at the farm and Regan's own greenhouse and garden, they had dug up quite a variety. They also had ordered some out-of-season types from a florist.

In Hayden, homecoming was a community event. The school hosted an open house, locals were invited to give lectures, and most of the town turned out along with students and alumni.

Regan's topic this year was the Victorian language of flowers. She was not optimistic about its reception. She had asserted that teens were not interested in plants, except possibly the kind they could smoke, and had complained that the guy down the hall, who was giving a live demonstration on the efficacy of honey-bee venom, would draw a bigger crowd. She was just happy that she wouldn't have to compete with the snake handler, who wouldn't perform until three.

Gabe had let her ramble. Stage fright was about the only thing that made her vocal. He knew from experience that monkeying with the plants would expend some of her nervous energy, and she would be okay once she got started. Most people thought her a serene type because that was what showed on the surface. She never yelled or, worse yet, cried. But she was, in Gabe's opinion, strung much too tight.

Gathering up a tall stack of empty boxes, he went out into the hall. He needed both hands to steady his teetering load, so when he reached the main doors he turned to nudge one open with his hip. At the same time, someone on the outside pulled the door wide, and Gabe, expecting resistance, lurched out onto the sidewalk and had to take several quick backward steps to catch himself. The top cartons tumbled forward.

"A running back should have better footwork than that." Jack Hargrove reached to gather the scattered boxes.

"A quarterback should have better brains than that," Gabe grouched.

Jack grinned but remained quiet, seeming preoccupied as they crossed the parking lot to Gabe's truck and dumped their loads in the bed. "Did you talk to Miss Culver?" Jack asked.

"Yeah." Gabe sat down on the tailgate. "For all the good it did. She's as tight-lipped as the chief. They deserve each other."

"I was out here waiting for my mom," Jack said, lounging beside him. "She's a plant lover, so I talked her into coming to hear your boss. Do you think that suicide runs in families?"

Gabe shot him a startled look. They were both tall and

athletically built, but any resemblance ended there. Fair-skinned and blond, Jack had always been light in all the places Gabe was dark, both in complexion and outlook.

Although Gabe had heard about the old Hargrove scandals, he and Jack had always avoided discussion about their families. Resentful of this breakdown in their tacit understanding, Gabe said shortly, "I have no idea."

Jack was usually quick to sense discomfort in a hearer and to change the subject. But today, although there was a certain amused comprehension in his sideways glance, he persisted. "My mother's been talking about her real father lately. She wasn't the one who brought up the subject, but she can't seem to let it go."

Gabe felt exquisitely uncomfortable. Trudy Hargrove had, strangely enough, named Jack after her real father. Considering what Jack Dawson had done, Gabe thought she should have wanted to forget the man as soon as possible.

"And?" he said.

"Why now?" Jack asked. "She watches me a lot lately, like she's worried about something."

Trudy, like her father, had very early in life made a spectacular wreck of it. Only in her case the wreck had been literal and, some said, not accidental. She was now a paraplegic and seldom left her home.

With a family history of disaster, it was not surprising that she should worry about her son. But it was in Gabe's opinion unnecessary. Jack was the most balanced person he knew.

"Hey," Gabe said lightly, "you're a teenager. She's required to worry. You should hear my aunt. If I get home late, I'm taking up with bad company. If I get home early, I'm not popular enough. If I sass her, I'm headed for trouble. If I'm polite, I'm repressing and I'm headed for worse trouble. You can't win, believe me. I tell her she needs to get a life of her own."

Jack's sympathetic grin died. In the case of Trudy Hargrove, Gabe supposed, that last remark hit too close to home.

"I'd better get back." Gabe looked at his watch and slid off the tailgate.

Inside the halls were thronged with people returning from a covered-dish lunch in the cafeteria, and Regan's classroom was filling up fast. Gabe viewed the large turnout with pride, but no surprise. Part of it, he supposed, could be due to Regan's recent notoriety. But she was an interesting speaker, and she knew her subject.

Gabe, who still felt obscurely guilty about brushing off Jack's confidences, took special notice when Jack wheeled Trudy Hargrove into the room. She sat as erect and impassive as ever, her face like a mask. Some of her facial nerves had been injured in the accident. As a result, she had no wrinkles. A small woman, she looked much younger than she was, almost as if she had been frozen in time. Only a few strands of gray in her dark hair betrayed the passage of years.

Trudy's adoptive father, Amos, walked beside the wheelchair. Way back in the thirties, Amos Hargrove had built a sanitarium out on Speedwell Lake. Intrigued by the teachings of Jethro Kloss of *Back to Eden* fame, Amos had espoused natural healing treatments like herbs, nutrition, and hydrotherapy long before they became popular. He had lived long enough to see his methods, scorned and ridiculed for years, gain grudging acceptance and finally faddishness. His snowy hair, bright as a halo, seemed to make his face glow. Or perhaps that glow could be attributed to something else. Many considered the old man a saint.

The Hargroves found seats in the back row where Trudy's chair could be inserted with the least amount of bother. Amos caught Regan's eye and waved. Her tense, preoccupied expression melted into a warm smile.

It was a compliment to her that he had come—or perhaps to

his friendship with her late father. Though robust for his ninety-some years, Amos seldom strayed far from his home or the Speedwell hospital, where he still worked when he felt up to it.

Gabe waited until the class bell shrilled outside the door, causing many of the alumni to jump and exchange jesting remarks, before he looked for a seat at the end of a row. Only one was open, and as he drifted toward it, he saw Matt Olin come in and lean against the back wall with his arms crossed. Gabe dropped into the vacant chair, watching Regan to catch her reaction to Matt's arrival.

She had turned to face the class, and Gabe saw her stiffen, come fully alert. Well, *that* would put her on her mettle anyway.

She kept her gaze studiously averted from the back corner, looking in Gabe's direction instead. He gave her a reassuring grin and a surreptitious thumbs-up. Although he was vaguely aware of movement next to him, he didn't pay any attention.

■ ■ ■

Gabe may not have noticed the disturbance, but Regan did. She saw with dismay that the teenager had sat beside Emmett Vinson, the most notorious racist in town. At once, Emmett jumped up and pushed his way out of the row, stepping on feet and snarling something that Regan couldn't make out.

Don't let this happen. Regan had been firing off asides to God ever since she was a little girl, and he had served as her invisible friend. Those communications had become increasingly terse as of late.

A teenager named Lucerne Abiel had just seated herself on the other side of Emmett. The school eccentric, Lucerne sported straight, glossy black hair, dead-white makeup, purple finger-nails, and tall boots with the latest clunky heels.

She promptly reared up and screeched after Emmett, "Hey, I didn't want to sit by you either, cretin!" She flounced into the seat next to Gabe's and sulkily sniffed, "Some people are so utterly pedestrian!" She clearly meant to imply that Emmett's aversion was directed at her.

It succeeded only because Gabe hadn't noticed the incident. He gave Lucerne a quelling look. In the row behind him, Jack had also lunged to his feet and glared after Emmett, as though to pursue him. Matt straightened, took Emmett by the arm, and pushed him out the door, pulling it quietly shut again. Jack, seeing Betony Scion standing awkwardly alone in the back, motioned her to the now empty seat in front of him.

Regan firmly said, "Good afternoon" and drew everyone's attention to the front of the room. Without preface, she plunged in, picking up a wrapped bouquet from the table beside her. "Has any woman here ever received yellow roses from her sweetheart?"

There were some enthusiastic nods. "Just last night," one alumnus piped up proudly, nudging the embarrassed man beside her.

"My condolences," Regan said dryly. "The yellow rose stands for waning affections."

The audience rippled with laughter at the woman's startled expression. "Though I can almost guarantee," Regan reassured her, "he didn't know that. But a prudent Victorian gentleman would have refrained from sending his sweetheart a yellow flower of any type. Almost all of them had unfortunate meanings. Yellow tulips stood for hopeless love, yellow mums for slighted love, buttercups for ingratitude, Saint Johns wort for animosity, and evening primroses for inconstancy. But the sunny flowers weren't the only ones with unpleasant associations."

She laid aside the bouquet and picked up a potted plant. "This is the mandrake. Though used as a fertility drug since Old Testament days, it is also one of the most feared plants in history. John Gerard, who published his *The Herball or General Historie of Plantes* in 1597, said, 'There hath beene many ridiculous tales brought up of this plant, whether of old wives or some runnagate Surgeons or Physicke-mongers, I know not.'" The indignantly querulous tone Regan had adopted earned her chuckles from the audience.

"That probably explains why, in the language of flowers, mandrake stands for horror. Though Kate Greenaway illustrated the most popular flower dictionary in 1884, I assume that most of the definitions can be attributed not to her imagination but to tradition. Some of them go back hundreds of years. Shakespeare's Ophelia knew that pansies stood for thoughts and rosemary for remembrance."

Regan added, "The latter has come to have new meaning in this decade, when rosemary is showing promise as an antisenility herb. Rosemary may not only stand for memories, but it also may keep you from losing yours."

She plucked the blossom of a forced paper-white. "The reasoning behind much of the symbolism is pretty obvious. It's not hard to grasp why a narcissus like this should stand for egotism or lemon for zest. Those of you who know your Scriptures won't be surprised to hear that hyssop represents cleanliness and the sycamore, curiosity."

Spilling some tan pellets from a spice jar into her hand, she continued, "Cilantro is a stinking herb, but coriander, its seed, is surprisingly sweet smelling. So coriander epitomizes hidden worth. Mignonette, a plain little thing, has a heavenly scent and will say to a woman, 'Your qualities surpass your charms,' a message which, I clue you in, gentlemen, you do *not* wish to send. It is an unfortunate aspect of feminine nature that most of us would far rather be praised for our charms than for our spiritual qualities."

More giggles. Everybody was always a bit giddy at homecoming.

"As for the more ominous plants," Regan said, after waiting for the giggles to fade, "they usually attained their bad reputations by being either poisonous or putrid or both. Henbane is a loathsome weed, which understatedly denotes imperfection. One of the worst hallucinogens, it induces a sensation of rising and falling, which is probably what gave certain dubious females the impression that they could fly. As you can see, drug abuse is nothing new."

She paused again and scanned her audience, as if gathering attention, before she continued into the uneasy silence. "I don't like to preach, kids, but I'm a plant professional, and I wouldn't take the chances that some of you are taking. Henbane contains a toxin called hyoscyamine, which is similar to atropine. And I imagine that some found out the hard way that the only place it would fly them was straight to hell."

■ ■ ■

Lucerne had ignored Gabe's cold stare as she pulled out the drawing pad that was her constant companion. She began to sketch Regan and the flowers on the table. The girl was always drawing, even in class while others were taking notes. It seemed to be a compulsion, although it didn't affect her grades, which were consistently good. She had moved to Hayden in early spring and already vied with Gabe for top of the class.

"Belladonna, also being poisonous, stands ominously for silence," Regan continued. "It once was used, I understand, by foolhardy women who wished to impart an interesting pallor to their complexions."

Several members of the audience glanced significantly in Lucerne's direction.

"So I don't follow the general predilection for an unhealthy tan," Lucerne muttered. "Because I don't oil and roast myself like a Thanksgiving fowl, *I'm* the odd one?"

"If you *will* insist on looking like a mime," Gabe replied crushingly, "you must want people to comment."

Most of Lucerne's female classmates didn't like her. They

thought she was too ostentatious. Of course, much of that might be attributed to jealousy. Lucerne's mother, a famous artist, remained in New York most of the time, and the girl, chaperoned only by an indifferent housekeeper, could pretty much do as she pleased. She buzzed around town at all hours on her motorbike and did her sketching, gloveless, in the chilliest weather. Perhaps that was why her hands always appeared chapped.

Now she dropped her pencil and dramatically but silently simulated a wound to the heart. People around them were looking—and grinning.

Lucerne snapped out of it in an instant, as if flipping off a switch, picked up her pencil, and frowned over an intricacy of her sketch. "A mime? Is that the *worst* you can do, Johnson? I'm disappointed in you. Actually, I imagine people would be surprised to learn how conventional I am. Religiously anyhow. Though these days," she added wryly, "some might find my orthodoxy more scary than its alternative. My mother is a pagan, by the way. We all react against our parents one way or another."

Gabe, who lived with his aunt, didn't respond. He hadn't had any parents for a considerable time. He had hoped that ignoring the girl would halt her chatter, but she ran on, regardless, just as the sketch ran on under her hands. "The nice thing about having a fixed point morally is that it frees you up in other areas. God *likes* variety, in case you hadn't noticed."

Having finished her sketch, she flipped over a page, turned toward Gabe, and began to draw him. From the seat beyond her, Betony stared at him solemnly with muddy eyes magnified by thick glasses. He flushed with embarrassment and increasing irritation.

At the conclusion of her talk, Regan invited everyone up to make bouquets. Lucerne snapped shut her sketch pad and made a beeline for the front of the room.

She snipped off a paper-white narcissus blossom and tossed

it at Gabe, who had followed more slowly. "He's kind of stand-offish, isn't he?" she said to Regan. "I mean, people are always nice to him because they don't want to seem racist, but I'd say a jerk's a jerk in any color, wouldn't you?"

Regan smiled, and the girl wiggled herself up to sit on the edge of the table. "Somebody told me once that lucerne is a kind of plant. Is it something exotic?"

Regan's smile widened. "I'm afraid not. Alfalfa."

"I might have known." The teenager appeared resigned.

"On the positive side, it stands for life."

"Life. I like that. I like your jade ring, too, by the way. Does it come apart?"

Gabe saw Regan's smile stiffen. "It's supposed to. I haven't tried it. Not too many people recognize jade."

"Yes, well…" Lucerne seemed uneasy. She flipped open the sketch pad to change the subject. "You like?"

Jack had accompanied Betony to the front and, with a courtly bow, presented her with a gentian for beauty—an optimistic evaluation, Gabe thought sourly. Betony showed little response beyond a slight irritable tightening of the frown lines in her forehead. She was a drab little thing, one of the new students. Her father, who had not attended the lecture, now shuffled up to regard her and Jack with a sardonic smile.

Gabe guessed that Betony adopted such a boring style in rebellion against her father's aging hippie persona. Raven Scion—Gabe would bet that the name was one the man had adopted himself—wore his dead-black hair long and swept back in a headband. He must have come back to nature late because he also sported the latest hemp clothing, which Gabe had heard cost a pretty organic penny. Not to mention a white leather jacket with a mean-looking blackbird appliquéd on the back.

Most of the townspeople didn't like Scion. The drug scourge had begun at about the same time he had appeared.

Also, gossip still revolved around the possibility of a local satanic cult, with most of the population disinclined to distinguish between the New Age and an old evil. In rural areas, crows were *not* a favorite bird.

Now Raven ambled up to plant himself squarely in front of Regan. "Sorry to miss your talk, Miss Culver." Regan looked up with a smile that appeared to falter at his nearness. Raven always stood too close and stared with that constant grin. Since he also sported mirrored sunglasses, all Regan would see was her own distorted reflection.

Lucerne began to swing a booted foot significantly. Raven did back off a step or two then. Regan returned to her study of the girl's drawings.

"Hi, Mr. Scion," Jack said. "Coming to the game?"

Jack was like that, the type who was always trying to make sure everyone was included and having a good time. Adored by the misfits and the popular crowd alike, he had contrived to convince them all it was much more fun to travel in groups than pairs. So a typical Friday night would find a disparate bunch—jocks, wallflowers, nerds, and beauty queens—rubbing elbows in booths at a fast-food restaurant or around a campfire on the beach.

All good clean fun too. Jack quietly but firmly disapproved of drugs and alcohol. No wonder parents adored him.

Matt remained near the door as people began to drift out.

Regan's niece, Diane, accompanied by some old school friends, hissed at Gabe as she passed, "Get rid of the girl!"

Gabe didn't have to ask which girl was meant, or why Diane wanted her removed. He grabbed Lucerne by the arm and pulled her off the table. "Come on. We're going to miss the snakes!"

"So what?" she snarled as he propelled her toward the door. "I don't mind missing the snakes. In fact, I was counting on it."

Regan, in whose hand Lucerne's sketch pad had been left, had to smile as the girl's final threat floated back. "If any of those snakes get loose, I'm going to climb you like a sycamore, Gabe Johnson!"

"Great talk, Miss Culver." Jack had begun, quietly and without embarrassment, to put together a bouquet, which he now handed to his mother. She accepted it without any noticeable change of expression. "Standing room only. You draw a crowd."

"Thanks," Regan said. "I was afraid I wouldn't be able to compete with the thrill of seeing people get stung."

He winced. "Not a thrill for me. I'm allergic." He patted a plastic case in his shirt pocket briefly. "Have to carry this all the time. What are these?" He was looking at the large bowl of calendulas.

"Marigolds." She had spoken automatically, all too keenly aware of the man in the back corner, though she wasn't looking at him. At Jack's puzzled expression, she shook her head, said, "Sorry. They're not the same flowers we Americans call by that name. They're calendulas here, but to the Europeans they're pot marigolds."

"I was just thinking," Jack responded, "that they could represent our school colors. Do you mind if I take the rest of these and pass them out?"

"Be my guest." She picked up the bowl and handed it to him. "But I must warn you that they stand for grief—and death."

Jack grinned the tolerant smile of favored youth knowing itself distant from such things. "Here, folks. Stand up for your school." He began to toss the flowers, one at a time, to those remaining in the room. People caught them with smiles; Jack always made people smile.

Regan's own smile remained fixed though she knew Matt had gone.

CHAPTER 2

*The fairest flowers o' the season
are our carnations and streak'd gillyvors...*

Lucerne returned about an hour later, leaning on the arm of a reluctant Gabe Johnson and carrying one of her boots. The heel was broken.

"I want you to know," she said gravely to Regan, "that I played the part of the old-fashioned fainting female wonderfully. I screamed at all the appropriate places, didn't I, Gabe?"

"And some that weren't," Gabe added grouchily. "Have you ever considered just taking off the other boot?"

"He is not the chivalrous sort," Lucerne mourned. "He's lucky I didn't make him carry me." She tugged off the good boot and padded about in her stocking feet, helping Regan pack away plants as Gabe began to fold up chairs. "So this is the fearsome mandrake," she said, eyeing one specimen. "We were just reading about it in Shakespeare the other day."

"Yes, it's an expensive plant. I caught one desperate woman trying to make off with it. She muttered something about having tried everything else. I had to explain to her that mandrake can be poisonous."

"A wonder Rachel didn't expire of it then," Lucerne said,

"or was that Leah? I was always on Leah's side, myself. I think I'm more the Leah type—a confounded nuisance, in other words."

"Oh, by the way, Gabe," Regan called to him. "Somebody left a bouquet here for you. You must have a secret admirer."

He did not look enthusiastic, advancing to accept the bundle of greenery and flowers with a suspicious glare at Lucerne.

"Hey, don't look at me," she protested. "You had me under your beady little eye the whole time."

He glanced briefly at the torn piece of notebook paper wrapped around the stems, on which was scrawled in block letters *Gabe Johnson.* "Okay," he said in a resigned tone to Regan, "you're the expert here. What does it say?"

"Well…" She poked at the stems. "Narcissus is, of course, for egotism. Snapdragon for presumption. Let's just forget it, Gabe. Obviously, it's somebody's idea of a joke."

"No," he said. "Go on."

"If you must." She rattled off in what she hoped was a matter-of-fact tone, "Pinks for aversion. Lobelia for malevolence. Oleander means beware." She began to falter. "Basil stands for hatred. Really, Gabe, this is ridiculous."

Under his implacably waiting gaze, she stumbled on. "Tansy, I declare war against you. And cypress, death."

"Well," he said. "That wasn't so hard to interpret, was it? Somebody doesn't like me very much." He tossed the bouquet at the green metal wastebasket, and the flowers wafted in with barely a rustle of sound. Gabe turned back to the chairs he had been folding.

Lucerne, still on her knees, watched him as she muttered to Regan, "Emmett hasn't been back here, has he?"

"No, I would have noticed him." Regan reached into the basket, detached the paper from the bouquet, smoothed it out, and put it in her pocket. "That was very nice—what you did earlier, by the way. Pretending it was you that Emmett didn't want to sit next to, I mean."

"Well, actually," Lucerne whispered, "Emmett probably dislikes me quite as much now. He showed up at the snake thing, too, being openly offensive. I think he wanted Gabe to hit him. So he could file assault charges, you know. But Gabe couldn't hear a thing above my screams. His ears are probably still ringing. My vocal cords were feeling the strain, though, so I finally stumbled and stomped on Emmett's instep. That's how I broke off the heel of my boot. After that he gasped a few nasty things about me and limped away. He suspects me of being Hispanic, I think. At least he's an equal-opportunity bigot."

"What *are* you," Regan said, "if you don't mind my asking? I never believed in violet eyes outside of books, but yours are close."

"My mother's folks were Scandinavian." Lucerne seemed to be taking unnecessary care with tucking a daphne plant into a space in her box. She patted its leaves automatically as she finished, as if consoling it. "She was never quite sure who my father was. We could be talking a melancholy Welsh poet or a ruddy English duke."

Regan thought quickly back over what she had heard of Ruby Abiel's checkered past. The artist apparently got bored easily because she never stuck with one man for long. Most of her lovers had been equally well known. If Regan remembered correctly, the Welsh poet had blown his brains out a few years back, and the English duke had fallen overboard in a yacht race.

"Since they're both dead," Lucerne said almost defiantly, raising her head to meet Regan's sympathetic gaze, "the point is moot."

"I think I'd opt for the Welshman myself," Regan said, "with your black hair."

"It's dyed." Lucerne spoke automatically then jerked her

head as if in irritation at herself and looked sideways at Regan. "Don't tell anybody that, okay? Vanity, you know," she added with an unconvincing laugh.

"Okay," Regan said. "I wanted to talk to you about these sketches. Diane and I have been thinking about commissioning a line of note cards for the shop. Pen-and-ink drawings. Flowers, first, I think, and if those sell, maybe a set with herbs too. Would you be interested?"

Still kneeling beside the box, Lucerne stared up at her. "Wow. Really?" For once, she seemed at a loss for words.

"Really. I imagine you already have plenty of preliminary sketches to work from. I've seen you around the farm a lot this summer. I was thinking maybe Apothecary Rose, foxglove, violet, narcissus, lilac, and pot marigold. Of course, that isn't set in stone," she added as Lucerne didn't respond. "If you think any of those are going to be too difficult—"

"No, no." Lucerne scrambled up. "That's fine! I mean, I *suppose* it is. I don't know the names of flowers very well," she explained sheepishly. "City kid, you know. But I always copied them down from those little copper labels your people put out. You really fancied the sketches then? They're not at all like my mother's."

"I prefer yours." With a paper towel, Regan swept fallen leaves and petals from the table into the wastebasket. "I'm not into abstract art, and it certainly wouldn't work for botanical drawings. That's settled then? I would suggest you make etchings. They still have the press here, don't they? Then we could sell framed prints in the shop as well as the cards. I'll want a set to hang in my office too. Talk it over with your mother or your art teacher. They'll know better than I what you should get for things like that. Though we would have to price them well below what your mother commands, of course."

"Wow," Lucerne repeated. "I'll go home right now and look

at my drawing pads. I have stacks of them. Thanks. Thanks a lot, Miss Culver."

Gabe came up in time to catch the end of the conversation just before Lucerne scurried out. "Don't encourage her."

"Hey," Regan said, "who's the boss here? I happen to like her. And she draws like a dream. Kind of Gothic and mystical and very English. Maybe her father was the duke after all."

Jack appeared in the doorway. "Hey, Gabe, time for practice. We better not be late, considering how the Chief has been lately." He caught himself, flashed an apologetic grin at Regan. "Not that he's ever anything but right."

"Frequently, *I* would say," Regan muttered, reaching for one of the boxes.

"Never mind," Gabe said. "Jack and I'll get those. We still have a few minutes. In case you," he added significantly, "want to go and talk to somebody."

"Sure," Jack agreed. "After all, he can't complain if we've been helping Miss Culver."

"Oh, can't he?" Regan purred. "Come to think of it, I did want to talk to Lucerne's art teacher." She tossed the keys to her Land Rover on the table. "I strongly advise you *not* to be late to practice."

Out in the hall, she paused long enough to hear Jack ask, "What was all that about?"

"Just the way she is," Gabe griped. "Sweet as molasses most of the time, but push her too hard and things get sticky."

The hallway was temporarily deserted except for a lanky teenager leaning against a locker. Ken Fermin was reputed to be one of the druggies.

"Hey, Miss Culver," he drawled. "I noticed you didn't bring any of that henbane stuff along."

"I'm not entirely stupid," she said.

"I bet you could tell me about a lot of other trippin' plants too."

"In your dreams."

He remained unmoved, literally, draped like glue against the locker. "I don't see why not. It's only a matter of degree, you know. Every time you drink coffee, you're on an upper. And alcohol is a downer."

"I don't drink coffee or alcohol."

He ignored that. "What do you think of that new herbal thing—Ecstasy? All natural. You got to admit that."

She sighed. "Cocaine and heroin are natural, too, Ken. A natural poison is still a poison. And none of them is going to make you happy. There's no plant or pill or liquor out there that can do that. They all wear off eventually. Then you're just back to whatever it was you were trying to avoid, and in much worse shape to deal with it."

He looked sulky. "You don't know what it's like being a teenager these days." There was a trace of smugness behind that reply, as if it were his favorite, his ultimate, argument.

Regan's patience, limited at the best of times, had worn thin. "Ken," she said, "have you ever seen your own father lying dead with swollen lips and bugged-out eyes?"

He began to look uneasy. "No."

"Have you been arrested for murder and had to sit, chained like an animal, in front of a judge?"

He shook his head, gaze fixed on her in a kind of fascination.

"Then I suggest," she concluded in that same soft, steely tone, "that you not talk to me about misery. Because I am *not* going to be impressed."

She didn't notice the old man with the halo of white hair sitting at the end of the hall until she was opposite him. He was one of those few able to be perfectly still without fidgeting.

"Oh, Amos," she said. "I'm sorry! I didn't see you."

Folding chairs had been set up in groups here and there for

the convenience of those who wished to chat. She dropped into one now. "Was I too hard on the boy?"

Amos Hargrove shook his head and regarded her with affection. "Are you *that* miserable, Regan?"

Under his kindly gaze, her lip quivered, and she bit it. "No, not most of the time. I miss Daddy, of course, and Sasha. I took her back to Chevia in August. I'll be okay. How are you?"

He put a warm hand over hers. "Old, my dear. No matter how well you take care of a body, it eventually wears out. Soon I'll move on to better things. I'm hoping to last long enough to see Jack take my place. I'd like for you to come and see Trudy some day, if you don't mind. She wants to talk to you."

Regan's surprise apparently showed.

"She intended to speak to you after your lecture today, but I think she was too intimidated."

"Intimidated? By me?"

He smiled at her disbelieving tone. "Yes, you are famous these days. Not to mention that as CEO of Thyme Will Tell, you're one of the biggest employers in town. It's about Vita's gardens. Trudy would like you to look at them."

Regan had never thought of herself as a CEO and didn't much like the idea. She looked sharply at Amos and spoke carefully. "I had assumed that Vita's flowers would be long grown over. It has been…"

"Forty years. Yes, I suppose your father told you about her. Then you would know that I had the house closed up immediately after. But I've sent the gardeners from Speedwell down there several times each year to keep things going. They divide the perennials and the bulbs and, of course, some of the annuals self-sow. They haven't added anything new. A lot of the plants Vita had from my mother. Trudy has been hearing about your interest in heirlooms. She thought some of the flowers might not be readily available these days."

Interest warmed in Regan. "You wouldn't mind?"

His hand closed tighter over hers. "We must be careful that we only mourn our dead, my dear, not enshrine them. My daughter would have wanted her plants to go on. *Vita* is Latin for 'life,' you know. She had so much vitality. So much promise."

Too much, Regan thought silently, *for her to die violently at the age of twenty-nine.*

■　■　■

The team won the football game. Matt was terse and tight-lipped. Gabe, too, was edgy, and most of the others seemed to pick it up from him. It seemed to work for them though. They were grimly stoical in defense, hard driving and heedless in advance.

"Hey." Lucerne intercepted Gabe as he headed for his truck after the game. "You guys were like forlorn little boys trying to cheer up Coach Daddy. This is a game, remem—"

"Shut up! You don't know what you're talking about!" It came out in a snarl, and she backed off quickly.

"Okay, okay. I guess I don't."

The fans and alumni, at least, were in a celebratory mood. They had shouted and stomped and cheered their mascot, Bob the bobcat, till they were hoarse. Many of them wore the calendulas Jack had passed out. In fact, some of the cheerleaders had bravely made crowns of the flowers. But with the game's end, people had begun throwing the blooms onto the field. One player, wrinkling his nose as they jogged off, said, "Whatever happened to roses?"

■　■　■

That evening as Gabe pressed his way through a throng near the auditorium doors at the homecoming dance, he received many claps on the back. The principal, Myron Hargrove, a lanky, dark-haired man with thick glasses and a harried expression, grabbed Gabe by the arm. "Hey, what happened to our mascot? We should have him here."

"Fisher had to get back to his store."

"Oh." Hargrove seemed temporarily at a loss. "Where's the costume? Do you think you could get it and wear it around a little?"

"Okay," Gabe said. "It'll be over in the equipment shed." He angled toward a less congested exit. But Lucerne accosted him, teetering on ridiculous heels and looking more like a corpse than ever in a black dress that contrasted strongly with her white makeup and purple eye shadow. She carried some kind of feathered mask on a stick and an equally plumy fan.

"I've had enough of being a wallflower," she wailed above the stomp of the band. "Come and dance with me!"

"Can't," he said. "I have to get our mascot. Orders from on high."

Jack was just coming off the dance floor with the homecoming queen, Sylvia Laird. As homecoming king, he had changed his drooping marigold for a carnation boutonniere. He looked worried. Overhearing, he said, "I'll get it. You two go ahead."

Gabe wanted to object, but Lucerne did look awfully pathetic.

■ ■ ■

Regan had watched Lucerne's snagging of Gabe with amusement. For once Gabe was off balance. An independent, fiercely realistic type, he was a good leader, but completely at a loss in relating to someone like Lucerne.

Regan sat by herself in one of the chairs along the wall, wishing she could go home. Except for a few snatched minutes here and there, this was the first time she had been alone all day. Being constantly in crowds wore her out, physically and emotionally. But since she now represented Thyme Will Tell, she thought it her duty to be more sociable. Her recent notoriety had made her popular with alumni just returning to town for the weekend. Funny, she thought wryly, how they all implied old friendship with her when in actuality she had been such a solitary child.

A bespectacled teenager approached Myron Hargrove and muttered something shyly. A chess tournament had coincided with homecoming. This was apparently the winner, who got to challenge the principal at the final game. Poor boy. No student had been known to win the final yet.

Myron was Amos's grandson. He and his wife lived in the same house with Amos, Trudy, and Jack. As Myron headed toward a table set up at the front of the room, Regan recognized the yellow carnation he was wearing. He wasn't the only guy who had gotten a free boutonniere from her display.

She preferred the old names for the flower herself: pink, gillyflower, pagiant, even Sops in Wine, because the blossoms had often been used to flavor that particular spirit. Of course, the whopping blooms of the modern versions were a far cry from the originals. The flower apparently had a questionable reputation in Shakespeare's time, perhaps because it responded so readily to hybridization. One of his characters had compared those hybrids to illegitimate children.

Myron's yellow carnation would have, if she remembered correctly, stood for disdain. Why were the Victorians so prejudiced against yellow anyway?

Yellow mums had been in that bouquet Matt had given her on the night of their argument. Slighted love. As if her thoughts had summoned him, a man with police patches on his shoulders strolled through the doors opposite.

Hastily averting her gaze, Regan wished she were dancing instead of sitting this one out. Preferably with somebody devastatingly attractive like Dr. Howard Keegan from Speedwell. But looking his way, she saw the doctor headed for the door.

Jack was making for a different exit, stopping to accept congratulations en route.

I have never danced with Matt, Regan realized suddenly.

There had just never been time.

Those alumni approaching the police chief were, she noticed, a little wary, as if uncertain of their reception. Matt had always been an enigma to most of them. When a stuttering child from a welfare family, he had been teased; when a brawny football star and salutatorian, he had been respected but obscurely resented too. Perhaps because he had surpassed their expectations for him. Perhaps because he made no effort to fit into anybody's expectations.

He went out of his way to avoid playing politics. He also enforced the law with a stern impartiality and sometimes against the grain of public opinion. That did not mean he was insensitive to that opinion. Regan was one of the few who realized just how hurt Matt was by it sometimes. But he measured himself against some higher standard of his own and often, she was afraid, found himself wanting.

From the corner of her eye, she noticed someone was helpfully pointing her out to him. She found that amusing. Matt had probably seen her within seconds of entering the room. He was very observant. He had to be.

Send him over here, please. This is getting ridiculous.

Regan didn't notice the woman who sat down next to her until that woman spoke. "Were you waiting for someone?" It was Charlotte Hargrove, the principal's wife.

"No," Regan said with what politeness she could manage. "Just taking a breather. I notice your husband is very occupied tonight."

"Yes. I don't care much for these events myself. He doesn't either, but it's part of his job."

In her forties, Charlotte looked faded, her blond hair and blue eyes both graying. She needed vivid color to compensate, but the pastel blue she wore wasn't it. Most times Regan saw Charlotte out and about, the other woman seemed to be simply a wheelchair pusher.

"Do you ever get tired of taking care of Trudy?" Regan asked, not in the mood for light conversation.

Charlotte looked surprised, evasive. "It's all right. It's not as if I do anything else, you know. And I'm a patient person."

"Does it take patience?"

"Oh, yes. Trudy can be abrupt at times. Sullen. But I suppose if I were in her shoes—"

Regan wasn't in the mood for platitudes either. "She has Jack. A son like that must be some comfort to her."

"Yes, Jack is popular." Charlotte sounded dubious and laughed nervously under Regan's inquiring stare. "Oh, I like him. Everybody does. But he looks like his real grandfather, was named for him too, you know."

Diane had come quietly to sit on the other side of Regan. Now that the conversation seemed to have concluded abruptly, Diane said, "*And?* Am I missing something here?"

Charlotte looked at Regan. "You know what happened, don't you?"

Regan nodded grimly. "My father told me. Back in the forties, Jack Dawson was one of those pull-yourself-up-by-your-bootstraps kids. Came from a poor and shady family; his father was a drunk and committed suicide. But Jack went to medical school on scholarship, was sent to Korea in the early fifties and came marching home a war hero. His wife had taken sick while he was gone and died at Speedwell. The nurses looked after her baby, Trudy, until Jack came to fetch the child and met Amos's daughter, Vita."

Regan slowed, as more details occurred to her. "Vita was about twenty-six then. Her brother hadn't shown any interest in Speedwell, but she had just become a doctor herself. She was also an avid gardener, taking after her grandmother, her mother having died young. I imagine that Vita was named for Vita Sackville-West, a famous gardener of that era."

She stopped to sip from her cup of punch. "Did I mention that she was very attractive also, curvy and blond like Marilyn Monroe? Jack was much taken with her. After they married, he was invited to join the staff at Speedwell. By 1957, Vita was pregnant with their first child. The couple seemed to have everything going for them."

"People only say that," Diane commented, "when there's disaster waiting right around the bend."

"I've seen pictures," Charlotte said. "You wouldn't believe how much our Jack looks like him."

Regan took a deep breath. "Amos was thrilled, of course. He now had two people to carry on his work. Then one bright blue October afternoon, when Vita was eight months pregnant, Jack came home and shot her, then fled back to his hometown to drown himself." She stopped, and the rattle of cheerful voices went on around them, regardless.

■　■　■

As Gabe and Lucerne danced, she seemed to be watching someone over his shoulder. "Who are you looking at?" he asked, perversely irritated. She could at least pay attention.

She smiled and dug him in the back of the neck with the fan. "Somebody who's staring at us." She didn't look all that pathetic anymore. It had been, he suspected, a ruse. It was impossible to know with this one what was real and what wasn't.

Though on closer inspection, he had to admit she was an attractive corpse. Beneath all that glop, she had what another artist would probably call good bones. And it didn't take another artist to appreciate her figure.

"Pay no attention," he said. "Some people still don't like to see a white girl dancing with a black guy, and you are *very* white."

She laughed, squinting against the glitter of the mirrored ball overhead. "Yes, the contrast is striking, isn't it? We artists are big on contrast. It's what makes interesting pictures. Did your boss tell you I'm going to make some prints for her to sell at the farm?"

He tried not to look dismayed, but her smile vanished. "Is it just pity on her part, do you think? I know she felt sorry for me. Because if it is, I'd really rather know."

"She says you draw like a dream," Gabe said. "Literally. I don't remember her exact words, but that's what she meant."

"Like a dream," Lucerne repeated thoughtfully. "Surreal maybe and enigmatic and—"

"Gothic," Gabe recalled. "That was one of the words she used."

"Gothic." Lucerne nodded to herself. The dance had ended, and they were standing by the punch table. Gabe handed her a cup and picked up one for himself. They drifted to chairs on the sidelines to keep an eye on the chess match. They had been among the finalists themselves, but Gabe's game was too cautious, Lucerne's too impetuous.

"I like Gothic," she decided, "though it might have morbid connotations."

"It was a style of architecture, wasn't it?" He leaned back in his chair and stretched out his legs.

"Yes," she agreed. "Ornate and mystical. Just as long," she added humorously, "as she wasn't referring to the barbarians, the ones who sacked Rome."

"I know what barbarians they were," he said. "I'm the guy who's going to be valedictorian, remember?"

She set down her cup, raised her mask to peer at him with lofty incredulity through the eye holes. "In your dreams! I have a much better vocabulary than you."

"Yes, but you have a fatal weakness." He leaned close to whisper in sepulchral tones, "Algebra."

She shuddered. "There is no logic to algebra. You people make the whole thing up as you go along just to torment us right-brainers. Admit it."

"Maybe so," he said smugly. "But *I* can do it."

"Hah!" She rapped him on the knee with her fan. "But will you pass theater? You only have two expressions. Disapproving and critical."

"Whereas," he came back snidely, "your whole life is an act, and you're in stage makeup all the time."

The jesting had been friendly enough to begin with but was getting a bit warm.

Myron Hargrove peered across at them from the chess table. "Gabe, did you get that costume?"

"Jack went for it," Gabe said, still glaring at Lucerne. Tearing away to look at the principal, he added, "Why? Isn't he back yet?"

"I haven't seen him. Go check, will you?" Hargrove returned to the game.

Gabe got up, and Lucerne rose to accompany him. "What do you mean I only have two expressions?" he demanded.

"Well, you do," she persisted. "You're always a bit aloof, as if you didn't like any of us very much—as if you would much rather be someplace else. I mean, you do it even with Jack, and he's tried his best to be your friend."

"Jack is everybody's friend," Gabe said curtly.

"Yes, but did you ever think that might be a little lonesome? He's always encouraging everybody and lifting others up, but who does the same for him? I thought he was looking upset just now. Maybe it's only me, because I'm a newcomer here, but do any of you really know much about Jack, about his family or his feelings or what he wants to be?"

They had been walking down an empty hallway, footsteps echoing, to a back door. It clanged open at Gabe's shove, and they stepped out into the dark—and cold.

"Oooh." Lucerne crossed her arms. "I forgot it isn't summer anymore. Aren't there supposed to be some lights?"

"Yeah, but the switches are over there." Gabe pointed toward another el. "You had better go back in."

"Hey," she said, "I have eyes like a cat."

She stalked on with him following. "My feline sensors are detecting movement ahead. Maybe I should yowl to warn of our imminent arrival. Oops." She stopped. "That action looks awfully low to the ground. This could get embarrassing, Johnson."

"If any couple is thrashing about in the grass on a night like this, they deserve to be stumbled over." Gabe forged on. "It's probably just one of your tabby relations."

"That is one awfully big kitty," she retorted, then shrieked, "It *is* a cat! It's Bob!" And ran.

■ ■ ■

Back in the auditorium, Diane's appalled gaze shuttled between the faces of the other two women. "That's *it?* Why? What happened?"

Regan shrugged. "No one ever knew. The others were downstairs at the time, heard the shot. But they were too late to save Vita or the baby. Amos was so devastated that he had the house permanently shut up. He had made Jack and Vita a gift of the place for their wedding, had built another for Galen and himself across the lake from Speedwell. He adopted Trudy then, even though she wasn't really related to him."

"Maybe it was the war," Diane suggested. "Posttraumatic stress of some kind."

"Bad blood," Charlotte murmured. "That's what some people said it was. Jack Dawson's father killed himself, too, remember."

Regan and Diane stared at her. "Granted, depression may run in families," Regan said, "but I've never seen any signs of it in our Jack."

Charlotte shrugged. "The other one didn't show it either.

How much do we really know about genetics? Our Jack's father was no good either. Abandoned Trudy after he got her pregnant."

Diane frowned. "I can only vaguely remember her car accident. I was just a teenager at the time and not all that interested in adult gossip. So Jack's…"

"Illegitimate," Regan supplied. "Trudy drove off that steep curve above the lake, broke her back, almost drowned. It could very well have been an accident, but of course people suspected—"

"Bad blood," Charlotte repeated, as if to herself.

■ ■ ■

By the time Gabe and Lucerne reached the mascot's side, it was lying quite still, facedown. Lucerne dug a pencil flashlight out of her bag, swept its beam over the fuzzy back.

"Jack," Gabe said hoarsely, "if this is a joke…" He dropped to his knees to help Lucerne, who was already tugging at the body.

It rolled over finally and settled flaccidly into their arms. Jack was not that good an actor either. Gabe fumbled at the back of the cat's head, jerked off the hood. Something buzzed up and clung stickily to Gabe's hand. He swatted absently at it as Lucerne focused the thin beam. Jack's face was red with welts and sweaty, but even as they stared, the color began to drain away, the eyelids to droop.

Lucerne dug frantically in her bag again. She produced a small mirror, held it close to the half-parted, bluing lips. "Nothing." She stood and screamed loudly.

Then she dropped onto her knees again, tilted Jack's head, and said, "Count," to Gabe. She covered Jack's mouth with her own. Gabe looked at her stupidly, then, understanding, straddled Jack's body. He reached underneath to yank down the costume zipper, to peel acrylic fur down from a white shirtfront, to place the heel of his hand over the other teen's chest. When Lucerne had performed two breaths, he began to pump down hard, counting in a rapid singsong to fifteen, then stopping to allow her to do her part again.

There was movement in Lucerne's hair, a sluggish scramble of insects. "Bees all over you," Gabe panted, "three, four, five, six, seven…" Insect legs fluttered over his hands too.

Between breaths into Jack's mouth, Lucerne gasped. "Don't swat…cold makes them slow…won't sting if you don't bother them."

There wasn't time to flail out anyway. Gabe kept his gaze intent on the girl's pallid profile. His lips moved automatically, forming the numbers again and again in a hazy, crazy kind of chant. The bees clung tighter as his hands rose and fell. The movement was making them angry. They were beginning to buzz.

The scream had had the desired effect. People were running from everywhere. "Call an ambulance!" he shouted. "Three, four, five, six, seven…"

Matt Olin dropped on his knees beside them. Gabe made as if to move. "No, keep it up," Matt said. "You're doing fine."

He pulled out his portable radio and began to speak tersely into it. Gabe heard, "See if Life Flight's available; ask them to stand by."

Concentrating intensely on Lucerne's face, Gabe was only dimly aware of others moving and exclaiming around them. At least she showed up well in the dark. He scarcely noticed a flare of pain on the back of his hand.

"Somebody turn on the lights!" Matt was yelling. "And everybody stand back!" He focused a stronger flashlight beam on Jack's body and felt in Jack's pockets. "Where does he carry his EpiPen?"

"Plastic folder!" Gabe panted. "Shirt pocket, usually. Not there now."

It wasn't anywhere.

Some girls were crying, and a guy yelled, "Come on, Jack! Stick with us, pal! You can do it, buddy!" A few others took up the football chant. "Jack! Jack! Jack!"

The scene swirled with red, and an ambulance's headlights glared into their eyes as the vehicle pulled up a few yards away. The perimeter lights blazed on. As a paramedic and an EMT rushed up, Lucerne started to stand.

"Keep it up!" the paramedic snapped at her, nodded at Matt's terse explanation, and took the flashlight to shine it into Jack's half-open eyes. "This isn't just anaphylactic shock. Pinpoint pupils. Was he on anything?"

"No," Gabe protested. "Jack doesn't do drugs."

"That's what they all say. He wouldn't, he couldn't." The man shook his head impatiently. "I'd guess heroin. Get the chopper," he said to Matt, and to Lucerne, "All right, kid. You did good. I'll take over now." She stood.

Someone in the crowd gasped. Bees crawled over her cheeks, bumbled toward her mouth. "Stand still." It was the old bee-keeper, carrying a glass jar. He handed it to her, and she stood stoically, eyes slitted against the glare, as one by one he began to pluck the insects gently from her skin.

"*You* keep going," the paramedic said to Gabe, "and pray that his throat isn't completely swollen shut, or we'll have to trache him." While the EMT held a light, the medic pushed Jack's tongue to the left and fed a plastic tube into his throat. "Okay. Good news. I'm in." The EMT attached a bag to the end of the tube and began to squeeze it. Meanwhile the paramedic slit Jack's sleeve to the shoulder with a seat-belt cutter and, from his box, selected an ampule, broke it open, and began to draw liquid into a syringe.

To Gabe, still pumping furiously, all of the man's actions had seemed exasperatingly matter of fact and in slow motion.

Swabbing Jack's biceps, the medic drove the needle in at an angle. Almost at once, Gabe sensed a pulse leap under his hands.

The medic grinned and put fingers to Jack's throat. "Feel it, can't you? Epinephrine delivers a real jolt. Okay, you can quit now. Great job. You guys did that like pros. Had experience?"

"Once," Gabe said, holding his hands stiffly out in front of him as he got up. "In health class. Last week. With a dummy."

No one was listening. The paramedic was saying to his partner, "Let's get him into the unit so we can hook up an IV. We'll push some Benadryl and Narcan through that." To Matt, he added, "Better get some lights on in that field across the road."

Matt singled out several of the volunteer firefighters in the crowd and sent them scurrying to their vehicles while the white-clothed men rolled Jack onto a stretcher and hoisted it into the back of the ambulance. "We had better get the rest of his clothes off too," the paramedic said. "There could be some more bees in there."

In a matter of minutes, trucks and jeeps were roaring down the driveway, bouncing into the hay field to form a large circle with their headlights pointing toward the center. The ambulance followed, and most of the crowd trailed in its wake.

Regan came quietly forward to join Gabe and Lucerne. "Neither of you is allergic, are you?" she asked. "Any trouble breathing?"

"Well, my heart's going a mile a minute," Lucerne said, wincing as the old man wasn't quite quick enough with one of the bees. He used tweezers to yank the stinger from her cheek. "You okay, Gabe?"

He nodded. He was holding his hands out straight in front of him, and the insects had calmed down some. He and Lucerne heard the thwap, thwap of the chopper and turned their heads to watch it come down in the circle of light, to see the stretcher rushed across to it.

"Where did the bees come from?" Regan asked the beekeeper as he finished with Lucerne and moved on to Gabe. "Are they yours?"

The old man looked strained, subdued. "They could be. A couple of jars were missing when I went to pack up after my demonstration. I figured it was just someone who wanted to try the treatment himself in private."

"Maybe this person let them go?" Regan hazarded.

"The bees weren't on the ground," Gabe said. "They were in the hood."

They all looked at each other. The helicopter was thwapping away to the south. People were drifting back to their cars, talking in low tones.

Lucerne, arms crossed, shivered. "He's right," she said after a moment. "The bees were in the hood. And a lot of people thought you were going to be wearing that hood, Gabe."

CHAPTER 3

■ ■ ■

You see, sweet maid, we marry
a gentler scion to the wildest stock,
and make conceive a bark of baser kind...

"What do you mean?" Matt Olin's voice from just behind
Gabe made the teen start and wonder how long the chief had
been standing there. Regan, who must have seen her fiancé,
had given no sign.

Lucerne turned toward the newcomer. "The principal had
asked Gabe to get the costume. But I wanted Gabe to dance
with me, so Jack offered to go instead."

As if suddenly realizing his audience, Matt said, "I need to
talk to you two. Come along."

He trudged off across the field toward the equipment shed,
and the two teenagers trailed silently after him. Gabe noticed
Lucerne still had her arms crossed. Somewhere along the way
she had lost her mask and fan. Gabe took off his suit coat and
draped it over her shoulders. She mustered a faint smile for him.
"It is a gentleman after all."

Matt shone his flashlight along the ground as they walked.
When they were close enough to see that the door stood open,
the light picked up a cluster of two or three groggy bees.

"Keep your eyes open," Matt told the teenagers. "You might

have to back me up on this sometime." And to Gabe, "How many people heard Myron ask you to get the costume?"

"I couldn't say for sure," Gabe said. "Quite a crowd was around the doors. I wasn't really looking at faces."

"And later? Who heard Jack offer to go?"

"There was Sylvia," Lucerne said. "Jack had just been dancing with her. Ken was hanging around. And that to-die-for Dr. Keegan from Speedwell. I think he left about then. The principal's anemic wife was looking at me disapprovingly. Any one of them could have heard. As usual Jack stopped to chat with a few people on the way out, which could have given somebody time. This isn't really helping, is it?"

"Not much." The shed was dark. Standing in the doorway, shining his flashlight into all corners of the small enclosure, Matt said, "You two stay out here." He focused on the light fixture in the ceiling with its dangling chain. No bulb. "So Jack couldn't have turned that on even if he wanted to. He would have had to feel his way."

The big hook from which the costume usually hung protruded from the back wall. A bin of soccer balls stood slightly out from that wall, as if somebody had stumbled against it. A ball had rolled out into the middle of the floor, and a bee crept sluggishly up its rubbery slope.

Matt walked wide around the ball, and it stirred a little, eerily, at his passing. He stood looking up at the hook for a moment, then all around him. He aimed the flashlight's beam at the bin, pulled out a handkerchief, and plucked up something, letting the handkerchief's folds fall back to reveal a white plastic case. "This it?"

Gabe nodded.

"It's empty," the chief said. "The bees might have been aimed at you, Gabe. Somebody could have meant malice but not murder. You might have gotten stung pretty badly, but it takes a lot of that to kill someone who isn't allergic. There's still the question of why the EpiPen—if Jack had it—didn't seem to work, what he did with it, and why his pupils were contracted."

"Emmett Vinson," Lucerne said decisively. "You put him out of the room, remember, Mr. Olin, when Miss Culver was talking. He could have gone down the hall to the other lecture; he could have taken the bees."

"But was he at the dance?" Matt asked. "I didn't see him."

Lucerne looked uncomfortable. "I didn't either," she admitted grudgingly. "And *I* was watching. Oh, stop looking so mystified," she added crossly to Gabe. "You are so oblivious at times. Why do you think I've been doing the clinging vine bit all day? It certainly wasn't for the pleasure of your company. If you'd heard what Emmett was saying, you would have hit him, the chief would have been obliged to charge you with assault, and things would have gotten considerably messier than they already were. That's what's wrong with you males. You don't think things through before you lash out."

Discomfited, Gabe avoided the chief's gaze. Matt Olin must have seemed equally ill at ease because Lucerne paused and looked speculatively from one to the other. Perhaps she was recalling rumors about a battle royal between the two of them.

"I'm going to lock up this place," Matt said, coming out of the shed and yanking the door shut behind him. "Until we can get a state police forensic team out here." He reached above the lintel for the key, which he pocketed. "You were right, Miss Abiel. Things are going to get messy. I've already been lambasted for sticking to one case despite conflict of interest. Seeing that I'm Jack's coach—"

"They'll say it was me," Gabe interjected.

The other two turned to look at him incredulously, Matt tilting his light to cast uncanny upward shadows on all their faces.

"Oh, come now—" Lucerne began.

"I mean it. People are already saying I wanted Jack's position on the team. They'll think I chose this way to get it."

A tic began to throb in Matt's temple. He looked like a man who had been pushed to the limit of endurance.

"We've heard worse," Lucerne told him cheerfully, as if he had, in fact, spoken. "And before either of you get carried away with your troubles, I would remind you that I have been closer than a brother to Gabe for most of the afternoon and evening. I was sitting beside him at Miss Culver's lecture, and we went together to the snake thing. I was leaning on his arm all the way back to Miss Culver. The guy was not secreting any bees on his person, believe me. Then there was the bouquet." She turned to Gabe. "We have to tell him about the bouquet. Miss Culver kept the paper off it. Maybe he can figure out something from that. Not to mention," she finished in the same gust to Matt, "that at the time Jack left to get the costume, I was dancing with Gabe, and I stayed with him right up to the time we found Jack." She paused to breathe. "Bet you never thought you'd be so grateful for my presence, huh?" she purred sweetly at Gabe.

Looking vastly relieved, Matt said, "If I were you, I wouldn't answer that. That's a loaded question if I ever heard one. There can't be any suspicion of collusion, can there? I mean, you two weren't friendly before?"

"Anything but," Lucerne answered. "I don't know if you've noticed," she added chattily, as they started back toward the school, "but Gabe is a conservative sort. He does not approve of me. I am loud, in more ways than one, and frivolous and artsy. Now Gabe"—they both looked at him, much to his embarrassment—"is serious and ambitious and out to prove something. He cringes at my presence. He literally does. Look at him. So I think it's only poetic justice, don't you?"

"Clearly," Matt said. "What was all that about a bouquet anyway?"

■ ■ ■

Caught in another nightmare, Regan drove too fast down a narrow, torturous road where trees, in the swim of headlights, crowded in from the sides and popped up confusingly in front of her as the road bent. She was afraid to try the brakes because it had begun to rain hard.

When her father had taught her to drive, he had warned her that timidity would get her in trouble on slick roads because using the brakes was what usually sent a car into a skid. Better to slow down gradually by easing off the accelerator. It wasn't working though.

The wipers whapped back and forth frantically, and the trees blurred in the runnels of water coursing across the windshield. She hunched wide-eyed, white-knuckled. *If you would only give me a little slowing-down time, time to breathe, time to think.* It was like her drowning dream, only this one wasn't a dream.

It had all started with Matt's approach when she was standing with the two teenagers and the beekeeper. Although she had been avoiding his gaze all evening, she looked at him then, sympathetically, knowing what a case like this was bound to do to him.

The movie hadn't helped. She, Matt, their little town of Hayden, and her murdered father had made national news for at least a couple of days back in June. Fortunately, by then the case was winding down. She had been approached by several people who wanted to make a TV movie, but she had refused to cooperate. They had taken their revenge for that refusal. The movie, which was made anyway, included a highly equivocal ending, an implicit suggestion that the attractive and wealthy Regan Culver must have gotten away with *something*, and that the hick cop had been duped.

The actress who had played Regan's part was more than attractive, a beauty who played the vampy villainess on soap operas. All of this had, strangely enough, won Regan a certain respect from the townspeople. There was obviously, their attitudes suggested, much more to Regan Culver than they had realized. But it had not done Matt any good.

And tonight he had walked away with Lucerne and Gabe without even acknowledging her presence. The beekeeper gave her a speculative stare. "I wonder if anyone has thought to call Trudy," she said, to be saying something.

"She and Amos might need a ride," the beekeeper suggested. "I don't think Amos drives much anymore." Then she felt obliged to go and see.

That was how she had ended up on this road, passing high above the valley in which the lake lay. On this particular stretch, the road inclined toward the lake, giving drivers a brief, panicked notion that they were tipping sideways. Regan was not surprised that Trudy had gone into the water there, though a brief, smeary glance at that tree-studded plunge made her doubt it had been on purpose. There were much easier ways for a doctor to attempt suicide.

The jeep hissed around the final bend to the Hargrove home and then plunged into the drive without slowing. Regan brought the car to a grinding halt on the gravel, unclenched her hands from the wheel, and patted it, as if it were a horse that had brought her through safely. She waited for her pulse and the rain to slow.

Across the water on her right loomed the blur of lights that was Speedwell. Lights were on to her left, too, in the Hargrove house. Somebody was still here.

She left the Land Rover running as she jogged up the steps to the covered porch and rang the bell, shivering in the damp trench coat, which was all she had worn over her evening gown. She was relieved when no one answered. They must have left in a hurry and forgotten the lights. She turned to look across the lake at Speedwell. Big, white, and rambling with a multitude of porches and balconies, downstairs and up, the private hospital had an airy, pristine feel in good weather. Just now, it wavered aloofly like a mirage.

Warmer light fell across the porch behind her, and Trudy said, "Regan? Daddy told me you would come to see me, but I didn't expect you so soon. Won't you come in?"

She doesn't know. "Didn't they call you?"

"Call me about what?" Now Trudy was watchful, tense.

Regan's stomach churned. "It's Jack. Something's happened to him."

Trudy's fingers tightened on the hand rims of her wheels.

"He got stung," Regan stumbled on. "They've taken him to the Clearview Hospital. The paramedic thought there was something else too. Some kind of drug. I'm afraid it's bad. Gabe and Lucerne were giving him CPR."

Trudy's blankness of expression was unsettling. She shoved back abruptly, then spun the chair around and began to wheel rapidly away. "We'll have to take my van. It's in the garage through here. We should stop for Amos too. He's down at Speedwell."

Minutes later, Regan was in the driver's seat of the van, edging it around her own jeep. At least the jeep had four-wheel drive and was familiar, while this... She stopped to switch off the Land Rover, to give it a wistful glance before clambering back into the van.

"Whatever happens," Trudy said as they approached the road, "don't swerve."

Regan looked sharply across, but the other woman's gaze was on the steep curve with the lake on one side and a high, brushy bank on the other. "Whatever happens, just keep going," Trudy repeated.

Edging onto the blacktop, Regan barely touched the accelerator as they coasted into the bend. She should have moved the seat forward; everything was too far away. Although the road was arcing to the right, she already could feel the perceptible drag to the left.

It was like a certain slope in her yard at home. Even though she always had safely navigated the side of that slope on the riding lawn mower, each time she felt the sickening tilt, she experienced the irrational conviction that the mower would lose its grip and roll.

Just then a human body plunged from the bank above, straight down into the headlights. Regan gasped and jerked at the steering wheel, but it was now held in Trudy's inflexible grip. The other woman stared straight ahead at the road, her left hand turning the wheel ever so gradually to follow the curve, her profile like granite. She was very strong.

The tires thumped over the body. The van continued its relentless course until the road straightened. Then Trudy released her hold, and in a spasmodic, delayed reaction, Regan's foot stomped the brake. The van jerked to a stop.

Regan could only sit, breathing hard, staring aghast, at the other woman's mask-like face in the dim reflection of the panel lights. Then she shoved the gearshift into park, groped frantically for the door handle, and couldn't find it. Trudy's hand dropped onto her arm. "Don't worry. It wasn't a body. It was a dummy. It won't be there now."

A flashlight was clipped to the dash. Regan jerked it free, threw open the door, and jumped down to aim the beam back the way they had come. *Let her be right.* Nothing was there but the snakish twist of the blacktop. Regan ran to make sure—heart drumming to the rhythm of her feet—all the way around the curve. She stood for a moment in the chilly dark, throat hot and raw, breast heaving, looking over the steep embankment. The lights of Speedwell shone peacefully through the skewed trees.

Regan walked back, slanting the beam of the flash downward. There was little undergrowth and no body. The van waited on the inside of the curve, breathing quietly like a large animal, huddled close to the high, brushy slope. Regan opened the door, said to Trudy, "H-h-how d-d-did you know?" and realized only as her words shook that she was trembling violently.

"Because that's what it was last time. Eighteen years ago. I reacted like you did. Anybody would have. But this time I was expecting it." She leaned to switch the heater to high. "I don't want you to tell anybody about this, at least not until I have a chance to explain it to you. And there isn't time now. Get in."

■ ■ ■

Rain poured down when Matt and the two teenagers were only part of the way back to the school building. They ran, Lucerne holding Gabe's coat over her head.

"Did you come on your bike, Miss Abiel?" Matt asked as they paused, panting, under the canopy over the double doors.

At her nod, he added, "Better get Gabe to take you home then. It's a bit cold for that sort of thing." And to Gabe, "Ask Regan for that paper."

"Oh, I won't run into her as much now that the farm's closed for the winter," Gabe said firmly. "You'll probably see her before I do." He followed Lucerne down the hall.

She retrieved her black cloak from the rack outside the auditorium, and Gabe shrugged into his damp jacket. Almost everyone had gone. A few middle-aged women were gathering up paper cups, and a custodian was pushing a wide broom across the floor.

Gabe loaded Lucerne's bike into his truck, thankful it wasn't a full-sized motorcycle. She had fallen silent for once, and huddled on the passenger side with her cloak wrapped tight around her, she looked exhausted. "Where do you live?" he asked as they reached the end of the drive.

"I don't want to go home," she said. "I want to go to the hospital. And so should you. What kind of friend are you anyway?"

He was too tired to argue. At the hospital, they shuffled in the only open door, the emergency entrance. In their rumpled evening dress, they stood irresolute, blinking blearily at the brightness. A nurse said, "You for the Hargrove case? Everybody's in there," and gestured toward a waiting room.

Everybody was right. The place was packed. But a couple of people jumped up to offer Gabe and Lucerne seats, and everybody patted at them in a dolorously grateful way. Gabe wished heartily that he *had* gone home, especially after the editor of the local paper rushed up to take their picture and fire questions.

Eventually the crowd thinned, and those remaining settled in to wait, speaking only in urgent whispers, as if the lateness of the hour demanded the hush.

Lucerne had gone silent, too, still huddled in her cloak, with her head bowed and her eyes shut. When the other couple on the sofa left around one, Gabe poked her and said, "You can lie down, if you want." Several members of the football team were lying full-length on the floor, using their folded suit jackets as pillows, and he slid down to join them.

Lucerne did recline full-length on the couch then, wrapping her cloak about her like a shroud. But she didn't sleep. Under the heavy mascara of her lashes, her eyes remained fixed on the clock.

The other guys had turned eagerly toward Gabe, as if looking for some kind of leadership. "What happened to him?" Chris Colby demanded.

"It looks like he got stung," Gabe said. "Bees were all over him. We found some back in the storage shed too. It looks like somebody put them there, in the costume."

They looked bewildered. "It's a mean joke," one volunteered finally.

"That's no kind of joke!" Chris said fiercely. "Everybody knows he's allergic."

"The medic thought there was some kind of drug too," Gabe finished reluctantly. "His pupils were tiny."

They all shook their heads in one accord. There was a chorus of, "Not Jack! No way would Jack do something like that!"

"It was probably that stuff he's supposed to take for the stings," Chris suggested. "What is it? Eppa-something."

"Epinephrine," Lucerne said without moving her head. "It's just adrenaline; it wouldn't make his eyes like that."

They all gave her startled glances, looked back at Gabe as if for confirmation.

"The paramedic would have known." Gabe turned his face away. He didn't feel like talking. They gave his silence exaggerated respect by falling quiet themselves.

People thought—Lucerne had thought—that he was Jack's best friend. He had never seen it that way himself. Gabe had never really thought of himself as having any friends here. All through his high school years, he had had only one thought, to get done with this and get away. He couldn't leave any earlier than graduation; he had promised his dying mother he would stay with his Aunt Lily until then. But he had burned with resentment toward the town he considered a prison. Especially after Matt Olin had discouraged Gabe's city friends from returning to visit him.

But somehow the fight between him and Matt had changed all that. In June, Gabe had provoked the embattled chief into taking a swing at him. The brief, savage altercation that followed had drained off much of Gabe's rage that had been building for years.

He had proved the cop only too human, but somehow the proof hadn't given Gabe the satisfaction he had expected.

And when he had gone back to visit his old haunts shortly

after that, it had been with more an idea that it was something that had to be done. He had asked Jack Hargrove to go with him.

It had proved to be a mistake. Jack's blond, all-American boy-next-door looks were startlingly out of place in the black neighborhood where Gabe had grown up. There was thinly veiled hostility. The bleakness of that neighborhood, to one who had spent years in a bucolic, small town, was a shock. Gabe felt more oppressed there than he had ever felt in Hayden. Many of the guys his age already had criminal records and illegitimate children.

It was not they who had changed, he realized eventually. It was he. His mother had been right after all. If he had grown up there, he would have long ago turned as hopeless and bitter as they had.

While there, Jack was as open and friendly as always, but Gabe found himself constantly standing in front of the other, as if to protect him from the ugly looks, the loud comments.

"You're different," a cousin said to Gabe. "You've been around those white boys too long." Another, friendlier, took him aside to whisper, "Sorry, pal, but you don't belong anymore. You'd better leave."

As they were on the way home, Jack said, "You're angry, aren't you?"

"Yeah. I'm sorry about the way they treated you. If I'd known that was going to happen—"

"Don't be." Jack stretched out his long legs and hunkered down in the seat. "At least I found out what it's like to be a minority." And quietly, "So I suppose you feel like you don't belong anywhere now?"

Jack was always perceptive. When Gabe didn't answer, Jack went on, "It's always been clear you couldn't wait to get away. What will you do now?"

Jack's comment bore no hint of reproof, but the whole conversation came back to haunt Gabe now. There *should* have been reproof. His attitude had been an insult to Jack and everyone else in Hayden. Only now could he admit that most of them had treated him well enough. Many had gone out of their way to be friendly, in fact, had tried too hard, which only served to underline his difference. That had made him angry once, too, but now he could find it amusing.

Since he had come back from that trip to the city several months ago, people had been easier around him. It had taken him awhile to realize it was because he was easier around them, no longer burning with that barely suppressed anger, touchiness.

Hayden did have its racists, of course, but Gabe was coming to realize that they were motivated, deep down, by fear. He was not at all sure he would have hit the one from whom Lucerne had been trying to shield him.

But now, perhaps because of that kind of blind hate, Jack was dying. Jack, who didn't know how to hate. Jack, who must have had it hard enough himself being raised in a house where everyone was much older. Jack, who never complained. Perhaps because everybody else was too busy taking from him to bother to listen. Jack had been worried, Lucerne had said. Gabe had sensed that himself early in the afternoon when Jack had tried to talk to him about suicide.

Was Jack, under all that sunny good nature, lonely and depressed? It didn't seem possible, but wasn't that always the way in the news stories? "He had everything going for him. He was so happy and popular."

Gabe tried to push that thought away as being unworthy. Nobody would choose bee stings and heroin to kill himself. But Jack might. To spare his family the stigma of yet another suicide, he might well have wanted it to look like an accident. No! Jack had planned to go to medical school. He had talked enthusiastically of a group called Doctors without Borders.

Gabe didn't know how long he had been carrying on this inner argument when Myron Hargrove came into the room and looked down at all of them from behind his glasses. Those on the floor scrambled to a sitting position, Gabe with his back against the couch. He felt one of Lucerne's hands creep out to clasp his shoulder but didn't know whether she was giving or asking for reassurance.

"Jack's still in a coma," Myron said flatly. "They say it was a combination of anaphylactic shock and a heroin overdose."

The room vibrated with silent waves of consternation. Lucerne's grasp tightened convulsively. Myron continued, "They don't know whether he'll come out of it or not. He seems stable now. There's no point in your staying here," he continued impatiently when none of them moved. "You might as well go home and get some sleep." He turned and left as abruptly as he had come.

They looked at each other. There were spontaneous cries of "No! Jack would never…I don't believe it!"

Lucerne was trembling. She withdrew her hand, and Gabe turned his head to look up at her. Tears welled in her eyes.

Neither of them had spoken, but something in that brimming gaze told him that she shared the same awful suspicion. It didn't seem to have occurred to the others yet. They were still trying to work it out as an accident. He decided to encourage them in that. "Matt Olin thought the bees might have been meant for me."

They grasped eagerly at that. Emmett Vinson's name came up. Apparently not everybody had been as oblivious as Gabe himself.

"Even after Jack collapsed, somebody might still have thought it was you, Gabe," Chris pointed out. "If he was in that outfit, they wouldn't be able to see his skin. They might have injected the heroin just to make sure."

The idea of anyone going to such lengths just because of the color of that skin temporarily floored them, but one insisted weakly, "It *does* happen. If Vinson belongs to one of those groups, he might not like all those rumors about Gabe taking Jack's place."

They all looked at each other again, as if realizing the irony that perhaps Jack had taken Gabe's place.

"And they wouldn't realize," Chris continued triumphantly, "that the bee stings alone were enough to kill. Because Gabe isn't allergic. The stings wouldn't have hurt him as much. So they had to do something more."

Gabe felt strangely detached from this discussion of some person or persons plotting against him. Detached because he didn't believe it. It was, in a way, too neat. The large irony of a racist killing the wrong guy, the white guy. The newspapers would love it, but real life wasn't that apt, that tidy. And though the white-supremacist groups made a lot of storm and bluster, very few these days actually worked themselves up to murder.

The guys on the team were settling stubbornly back to their places on the floor; they were going to wait it out.

■ ■ ■

"There's really not much more that we can give him," the doctor said. "Except time." Trudy's expressionless face seemed to disconcert the doctor as much as it had Regan. He turned his explanation toward Amos Hargrove. "We've given him drugs to counteract what he's had. Now we just have to hope he hasn't gone so far down that he can't come back. Despite all our sophistication these days, that's what we often are reduced to."

Amos smiled faintly. "Don't worry. We are not the types to over-rely on the wonders of modern medicine. Especially since Howard, Trudy, and I are doctors ourselves." He was sitting with Trudy next to the bed, holding her hand and Jack's. Trudy had gone back to staring at her son's face. "And, of course," Amos continued, "Regan's father was a doctor. We used to call him in frequently on consultations."

The ER doctor smiled in a puzzled way. He obviously was wondering about Regan's presence. Regan smiled stiffly in response. She was wondering herself. Howard Keegan had been with Amos at the sanitarium and had come along. Regan would have been happy to let Howard see the other two up in the hospital elevator. She had planned to park the van and call Diane to pick her up.

But when she had stated her intentions, Trudy had said, "I would appreciate it if you would stay with me for a while." So now Regan waited, standing near Keegan in the background.

A bachelor in his forties, he had been brought up at Speedwell by his father, Ian, also a doctor, and had devoted most of his life to the place. He was not really a background sort of person, and obviously single by choice, not necessity. Tall, dark, and muscular, even silent he exuded a kind of leashed vitality that inclined everyone in the room toward him, as toward a power source. Everyone but Trudy, that is. She never looked at him. Howard followed the ER doctor out.

"I think only a couple of us are supposed to be in here at once," Myron said. "Charlotte and I will be in the waiting room."

Regan started to follow, but Amos stood. "If you'll stay here with Trudy, Regan, I'd like to talk to Howard. I have a lot of faith in his opinion."

He went out, too, and Regan sat down, tentatively, in the seat he had vacated.

"Amos has always been very good to us," Trudy said, "considering that we're not really family. I was only Jack Dawson's child, not Vita's."

"I know."

"My mother's name was Ann. Nobody much remembers her. She wasn't my father's great love. She was from his poor past. Vita was from his bright future. Wealthy, confident, smart, beautiful, all the things my mother wasn't. People objected when Amos kept me after the murders. Because I wasn't a blood relation. There was some idea, I think, that Jack was a graft that didn't take. That Vita's child, with the Hargrove blood, would have been okay if it had lived. Not that I've been much impressed with any Hargrove besides Amos. Vita's brother Galen was a spoiled dilettante. He always thought they should change Speedwell into some kind of cultural retreat for the wealthy, like Chataqua."

"What was Vita like?" Regan asked.

"I don't remember. They tell me that I was shy around her. Amos thought she was too overwhelming for my quieter personality. He says he kept telling her to give me some breathing room. Even then, I was more of a dreamer, I suppose, and Vita was a doer. I hear that she even came through her pregnancy glowing, making it look easy. Vita made everything she did look easy, I guess, maybe because things had always been made easy for her. Amos has never really gotten over her death."

And you, Regan thought, *believe you are just a replacement, no match for the real thing.*

"What did you mean about the dummy, Trudy? Was that what caused your accident?"

Trudy's attention did not waver from Jack's face. "Yes, a dummy thrown down in front of my car just like it was tonight. Of course, I didn't realize it was a dummy then either. It's quite clever really. With that steep bank on the right, there is nowhere to go but left, and no time to brake. And, once you're off the blacktop, that slope funnels you down. After I came around in the hospital, I tried to tell them what had happened—I thought

I might have hit the person—but they didn't believe me. There was no one hurt, no one missing. I could see what they thought, that I'd tried to kill myself and my unborn baby with me. To be kind, they pretended to accept my story. You can't argue with people when they won't argue back."

"But how, when your back was broken, did you get out of the water?" Regan asked.

"I didn't. Howard got me out. He says he was on the porch at Speedwell when it happened, saw me go in. It was a miracle, really, that the baby was okay."

"And who do you think threw the dummy? Who would want you to die? And why did they wait so long to try again?"

"I don't know. Amos was going to leave Speedwell to me. That's all I can think of. I was going to carry on his dream."

"Myron and Charlotte then? But it couldn't have been them this time, Trudy. They were both here at the hospital when it happened."

"Amos wouldn't leave them the place. He knows they wouldn't carry on his work. All that land around the lake is worth millions. He's had offers, in fact. Speedwell goes to me first, then to Jack. If both of us are dead, Howard gets it. Nobody has any motive except Howard."

"But you're not making sense, Trudy! It was Howard who saved your life. Why would he have done that if—"

"It's just what he would have done if he wanted to deflect suspicion from himself." Some color had begun to show in Trudy's face, and she turned toward Regan as if eager to convince her. "Howard is clever. Nobody would suspect the hero who bravely risks his life to have been the instigator of the accident. I was unconscious, and the water was cold. He wouldn't be able to tell if I was still alive until he got me out. By then other people were there, and he had to make a good show of it. Maybe he's just a little too clever for his own good. You said that somebody put bees in the hood of that costume?"

"There were bees, yes. But we can't be sure that someone was after Jack. It was Gabe who was supposed to fetch the mascot."

"Oh, it was planned this way. That's why he was waiting out there to get me too. There would be no point in killing Jack unless he killed me as well. He probably expected Amos to be driving..." She stopped.

"See," Regan said. "There's the big flaw in your theory. Howard knew that Amos wasn't in that van because Amos was over at Speedwell with him. And if Howard was over there, he couldn't have been out tossing a dummy from that bank."

"He still could have snatched the opportunity to get me," Trudy insisted stubbornly. "He could have dealt with Amos later, or just waited him out. How much longer can a ninety-seven-year-old live? We don't know that they were together the whole time. While you were checking the road, Howard could have made it back to Speedwell before us. He's in very good shape. Who else could it have been? Howard is the only person I know who has the nerve for something like that. He is definitely not a timid sort. We can't tell anybody, Regan. We have no proof. They'll just say it was some kid's Halloween trick. We can't afford to have people thinking we're imagining things. Not now. Shh. Amos is coming back. I don't want him to hear this. He's fond of Howard. I do need to talk to you some more though. Please stay."

Something irksome itched at the back of Regan's mind as she watched the old man give his adopted daughter a reassuring kiss on the cheek. Something else she should have asked.

"Murders," Trudy had said earlier when speaking of Vita's death. "After the murders." And she had used the plural.

■ ■ ■

It was the longest night Gabe had ever known. The group had dwindled; parents had come to take some home. But most of the team stayed, along with Lucerne and the homecoming queen, Sylvia Laird, still wearing her sash, her tiara plunked carelessly on a magazine table, her high heels kicked off, and her stocking feet tucked up under her long skirt.

Gabe could have sworn he was aware of every tick of the clock, but he must have dozed off occasionally because every now and then he would be back out in the dark, trying to pump life into a big cat.

At six, he got up and stepped gingerly over recumbent bodies to switch on the television. "...weekend news," a bright-eyed blond was chirping at the camera. "In our lead story this morning, only hours after winning a decisive victory in Hayden High's homecoming game against Clearview, Jack Hargrove, the Bobcat quarterback, was rushed to Clearview Hospital, reportedly suffering the effects of anaphylactic shock and a heroin overdose. At this hour, he remains in a coma."

Lucerne had started up violently at the sudden noise and banged one elbow on the couch's wooden armrest. Now she shook her arm dumbly as she stared at the announcer's animated face.

"Hargrove, also senior class president and homecoming king, was a popular student at the high school. Hayden Police Chief Matt Olin, who also coaches the Bobcats, refused to comment on the case at this time. He declined to speculate on what this would mean to the Hayden football program. The Bobcats were reputed to have a strong chance at the state championship this year. There has been much community concern in recent months over increased drug activity at the high school."

"Are you okay?" Gabe said to Lucerne. She was continuing to shake her arm.

"Yes. Just hit a nerve. Is it only my imagination, or was there a strong flavor of 'you just never can tell' about that?"

Gabe sat down on the edge of the couch. "They're going to

crucify Jack. People love tearing down respected figures. It's a national pastime these days." The others were sitting up also, looking dazed.

"The eternal optimist, that's you," Lucerne said dryly. "But this time, you're probably right."

"Good morning." They all turned to see Regan in the doorway. "Jack's pretty stable now, if you would all like to go out and get some breakfast or something. He could stay like this for hours. Days even. You still have that cellular phone, don't you, Gabe? I'll call you if there's any change."

Everyone looked at Gabe. In Jack's absence, he realized he had been tacitly elected their new leader. "Thanks," he said, standing and stretching, slinging his rumpled suit coat over his shoulder. "We'll bring you back something. What would you like?"

"Anything that doesn't come out of a vending machine will be refreshing."

CHAPTER 4

Here's flowers for you.

The weather should have been dreary to fit their mood, but the early morning sky was clear, the air brisk. It was going to be one of those bright days for which October was famous.

Following the two girls in the group as they picked their high-heeled way around potholes in the McDonald's parking lot, Gabe noticed that Lucerne was staring at a wan Sylvia. Becoming uneasy under that close regard, Sylvia managed a smile and said, "Have you ever noticed how tacky evening wear looks in the morning light?"

"You really care about Jack, don't you?" Lucerne blurted.

Sylvia sighed. "I've been in love with him for years. Is that so surprising? Of course, he never notices. I'd have had a better chance with him if I'd been a loser like—"

"Me?" Lucerne supplied helpfully.

Sylvia laughed. "No, I wasn't thinking of you, more of types like Betony. It's impossible to feel sorry for you."

"Thanks," Lucerne said.

The fast-food place was almost deserted at that hour, except for a couple of old men eating breakfast in a corner, who viewed the teenagers with patent disapproval.

"We are a sorry-looking group, aren't we?" Sylvia slid into a booth next to an eastern window, followed by the others. They sat in silence, waiting on Chris, who had gone to the counter to place the order.

"Hey!" Lucerne said, noticing a police car in the drive-through. "There's Chief Olin. Let's get his attention!"

And she leaned over Sylvia to wave frantically. The rest participated in more restrained semaphoring.

Matt saw them, raised a hand in return, and pulled into a parking space. As he walked toward the restaurant, the morning sun picked up the lines and stubble on his face. He met Chris at the front and accompanied him back to the booths.

"Anything new?" Lucerne demanded.

Matt shook his head. "Still in a coma." By now the old men and the servers assembling the large order on the counter were openly staring.

"You see the TV this morning?" Matt asked and, at their subdued nods, added, "Sorry, kids. That's only the beginning. Some guys from the state police task force and I got a warrant last night and went through the lockers at the school. A bag of heroin was in Jack's. Along," he said with a sideways glance at Ken, "with a bit of residue elsewhere."

"But he didn't use the stuff," Chris pled, looking from one face to another almost pitifully, *"did he?"*

"No," Ken said. "He didn't." As they all looked at him, he continued, "I would know."

"I don't suppose," Matt suggested, "you would like to tell me who did?" Ken turned his face away. "I really should hand this over to the state boys," Matt said. "But I already know what Lieutenant Brodsky thinks. In his opinion, the bees were aimed at Gabe here, and Jack got unlucky on the same night he decided to start experimenting with heroin. Brodsky is willing to concede it was a first time for Jack because there were no other needle marks on his body. That would explain his extreme reaction to the drug. But the amount of the stuff in his locker implies Jack was dealing, even if he hadn't used it before."

Ken frowned and leaned forward as if to speak, then appeared to change his mind.

"Another strange thing, which Ken here was just about to point out," Matt added dryly, "is that teens these days are understandably leery of needles. They usually snort the stuff from capsules."

"No," Sylvia said. "Jack wouldn't and didn't. Either way."

"What," Gabe demanded of Matt, "do *you* think?"

"Me? I think somebody tried to kill him." Matt held up a hand to restrain their excited comments. "By replacing his epinephrine with heroin, then making sure that he would get stung so he would have to use it. The motive possibly being that he had found out who *was* dealing. The heroin would, of course, have been planted. That will be almost impossible to prove though. Even if we do find the EpiPen, most likely only Jack's fingerprints will be on it. And they were on the bag in his locker. That's not conclusive, by the way. There could have been something else in it when he handled it. Obviously, I'm prejudiced in Jack's favor. But the Clearview police don't have enough manpower to put a guard on the hospital room."

"You have to stay on the case," Sylvia said. There were vehement nods of agreement all around. "Gabe was right. They'll crucify him. You have to stop it."

"We'll help," Chris offered. "We'll guard that room. Two of us at a time so we can watch each other too—just in case."

Lucerne looked skeptical. "Will they allow that?"

"I'll talk to the administration at the hospital." Matt stood. "Okay, kids, I'll do what I can. If you have any ideas at all about who's behind this drug activity, come and tell me. Don't keep it to yourself or try to confront anybody. Gabe and Lucerne, can I talk to you for a moment?" They followed him outside.

"There is another possibility," Matt said, looking toward the rising sun, "that I didn't mention in there, but it's bound to come up."

Lucerne nodded. "Suicide."

"So, it *has* occurred to you." He turned. "Is there any reason it did?"

"Jack is the type," Lucerne said, "who gives and gives but doesn't give away much about himself. For all we know, he could have been depressed under that cheerful exterior. He never talked about his own problems."

"Maybe he had good reason not to," Matt said. "His grandparents' death was a murder-suicide, and there have always been suspicions about his mother's accident."

"God help him," Lucerne breathed. "As if things weren't bad enough already. People are going to say that it runs in the family, aren't they?"

It was eerily reminiscent, Gabe thought, of the question Jack had asked him the day before: "Do you think suicide runs in families?" At the time, Gabe had almost convinced himself Jack was only talking about his mother's accident. But it could easily be construed otherwise. *There's no way,* Gabe promised himself, *that I tell anybody about that conversation.*

The police chief was looking at him speculatively. *He wonders why I'm so quiet. He knows that if Jack talked to anybody about killing himself, it would probably be me, and he's asking himself why I'm not objecting to the whole idea.*

"Why can't it be the good stuff that runs in the family?" Gabe plunged in truculently. "Amos Hargrove is his great-grandfather."

"I've always thought Jack took after Amos," Matt agreed. "But they aren't related by blood. Genetics only determine so much, after all. In my opinion, it all comes down to a personal decision, and I don't think this is a decision Jack would have made. He would never have abandoned his mother, for one thing. But I have a feeling we're going to be bucking the tide. People would forgive a suicide attempt; they won't forgive the heroin. Stand up for him, and they might paint you with the same brush."

"Hey," Lucerne said, "they already think I'm wild. What's to lose?"

"Ditto," Gabe agreed. "Black skin already equals druggie in a lot of minds. How about you, Chief? You *have* something to lose, your job. You really going to stick?"

Matt met that challenging gaze steadily. "Oh, I reckon I can hold out as long as you can, Johnson."

"Shades of John Wayne," Lucerne said with a sniff as the chief walked away. "Do I detect just a hint of antagonism between you two? I hear you had a real slugfest last summer. Who won?"

"That's nobody's business but ours. What did you hear?"

Lucerne smiled. "N-O-Y-B. Two can play at that game, *Johnson.*"

Going back into the restaurant, Gabe and Lucerne found the other kids drawing up a schedule on a napkin. "We're chopping it up into six-hour shifts," Chris said. "That will work for the weekend. But what do we do for the hours we have to be in school?"

"We find some adults to fill in for us," Sylvia suggested. "Do we know anybody who's free during the day?"

"Thyme Will Tell just closed for the winter." Gabe reached for the list. "Regan and Diane might be willing to help."

"I'll send my housekeeper over," Lucerne offered. "Mostly, she just sits anyway. She might as well sit there as at home."

"My Aunt Lily can sit with her." Gabe looked seriously around at them. "Though you realize we have to do more than sit. The longer he stays in that coma, the less likely he'll ever come out. We have to talk to him, read to him—something."

"Music," Chris suggested. "We bring in some of his favorite tapes. What else?"

"Pray," Lucerne said. "Let's all join hands." Then, looking around her at the alarmed expressions of the football players, she said, "Okay, okay! We'll do the huddle thing and stack them." And, as they complied, "Gabe comes out on top. That means he gets to do the honors."

Her amused look held a certain challenge. She probably suspected his relationship with God was distant at best. Although Gabe attended church every Sunday morning with his aunt, his attitude toward Deity was, "You leave me alone, and I won't ask you for any favors."

This, he realized, was going to mess up the smooth tenor of that agreement. The others had already ducked their heads and shut their eyes expectantly.

Gabe stared out the window at the blue sky and said, "Well, God, not all of us know you that well. But Jack did. So the Bible says you will look out for him. We're here to hold you to that. Jack did his part. Don't let him down." Having finished, Gabe pulled his hands out of the pile.

"Amen," Lucerne said, "though I'm not sure whether that was a prayer or a dare. They've put you and me on for the first shift from nine to three. I suggest we go to our respective homes and change clothes first. And I suggest that the rest of you get some sleep before your turns."

■ ■ ■

As Regan walked back toward intensive care, she saw Howard Keegan standing in the hallway, talking to a doctor. The doctor bustled away as Regan came up. "Anything new?" she asked Howard. It was the same place he had been standing when she had left.

It gave him, she realized, a clear view of Jack's bed, but he could not be seen by those around it. She wondered if he had been there when she and Trudy had been talking about him. He wouldn't have been able to hear them, of course, but still…

He shook his head. "Jack could stay like this for days. Months. Even years."

Regan knew Speedwell usually had at least a couple of comatose patients, those whose families thought Speedwell's brand of personal care might succeed where the hospitals had failed. Nurses at Speedwell were chosen for their kindness and patience as much as their professionalism.

"But no reason to be pessimistic yet," he added. "Every reason to be optimistic, actually. The combination of shock and overdose by all rights should have killed him. And it didn't."

Searching his features, Regan could find no hint of chagrin or disappointment.

"Tell me, Dr. Keegan," she said, "what is your opinion of Trudy? Is she the paranoid type?"

"No."

That simple, unequivocal answer told her that Trudy's opinion of Dr. Keegan had been right. This was not a timid man. *If anybody had asked me a question like that, Regan thought, I would have hemmed and hawed all around it.*

"Then you don't think she would be apt to imagine things?"

"No, why? Does she think that what happened to Jack was deliberate? So do I. I do need to get back to Speedwell though. If you'll—"

"So, *go* then." Trudy had wheeled herself out behind them so quietly Regan hadn't heard her coming. "I don't know why you're hanging around here anyway."

Her hostile stare implied she had her suspicions. Howard looked amused. "One of the doctors here has just informed me that some of Jack's friends are volunteering for guard duty. They'll be here at nine. I've been keeping an eye on things myself. But I was just going to suggest to Miss Culver that she—"

"Rather like the wolf keeping an eye on the sheep," Trudy said. "You're the only one with a good reason for getting rid of Jack. You didn't want him to eventually take over your hospital, did you? You've been top dog too long."

"Trudy," Regan interposed hurriedly, "you can't just say stuff like that."

"Why not," Howard said, "if it's what she believes? She's hardly objective though; she's hated me ever since I warned her about Lance. If I've had to become *top dog,* as you put it, it's because *you* abdicated, Dr. Hargrove. Amos sent you to medical school so you could take over management of Speedwell once he was gone. But after your accident, you decided to sit on your hands and feel sorry for yourself. Plenty of people continue their careers with worse handicaps than you have. So, Dr. Hargrove, I would advise you to either keep up or shut up!"

He had spoken in a matter-of-fact tone, seemingly with more impatience than hostility. He turned to Regan and said, "Sorry you had to hear that, Regan. I imagine that Trudy's settled on you because of your in with the police chief. Just so you're fore-warned." He nodded farewell and strode off.

Trudy was white to the lips, and her hands trembled as she tried to turn the wheelchair around.

"Let me," Regan suggested, getting behind Trudy to push. "He shouldn't have talked to you like that—especially at a time like this."

"Oh, Howard doesn't know the meaning of shouldn't," Trudy said bitterly. "He says anything he wants and gets away with it. Most of his patients hang on his words. Not only does he make them toe the line, he makes them *like* it. I always felt extraneous when I was working there. All the patients wanted him because he was sure of his diagnoses. He's been wrong his share of times, but you would never know it by his attitude."

"That's typical." Regan dropped into a chair on the far side of the bed and kicked off her high heels. "Of males in general, I mean. We women tend to be more insecure."

"He was right about Lance," Trudy said. "I have to admit that. Howard said that Lance would never be serious about someone like me and was just looking for a brief affair to entertain himself while he was stuck out here. Dr. Keegan makes the correct diagnosis yet again!"

As she took Jack's hand in her own, she went on. "I was in my midtwenties then and had never had a good-looking guy pay attention to me like Lance did. He was an actor recovering from pneumonia. I guess I didn't realize how good an actor he was. One time, and I got pregnant. Amos must have been disappointed in me. He brought me up to know better. When I tried to tell him I was sorry, he said I shouldn't apologize to him but to God. That was later though. At first, I was just angry at everybody: Lance for leaving; Myron for raising his eyebrows in that superior way he has; Charlotte for being amused; Amos for being so kind; and Howard for being his I-told-you-so self. I had a fierce argument with him at Speedwell just before the accident. Perhaps I *was* driving too fast."

The bustle of the hospital was increasing, but intensive care was disturbed only by the soughing of respirators, the relentless soft beeping of machines. Only one other patient shared the room—an elderly man watched over by an elderly woman who stared across at Regan and Trudy with a dull curiosity. *My evening dress,* Regan realized, *must look funny in the morning.*

"Howard was right about my using you too," Trudy said. "I knew that Vita's garden would interest you, and then I was going to try and work in her murder."

"You don't think your father killed her, do you?" At Trudy's startled glance, Regan added. "You might not have realized it, but you said murders—with an *s*—when you were talking about them. Of course, you could have been talking about the baby, I suppose."

"It's probably just wishful thinking." Trudy played nervously with the edge of Jack's top sheet. "It was for Jack. I was still angry when I gave him that name, you know. It was a kind of defiance, I guess. But I shouldn't have done it. It made the comparison inevitable. Because of who my father was, people have been more ready to believe the worst about me. Jack looks so much like him. I couldn't help thinking that people would watch for him to crash too. He would know it, and it might become a self-fulfilling prophecy. So I thought that, if I could prove...but I didn't expect the crash so soon. They're going to say he took the heroin himself, aren't they?"

"Some will. I doubt that Matt will." Regan stood. "Just so I'm not here under false pretenses, Trudy, I don't have any kind of in with Matt at the moment. We're not even speaking. He probably would be eager to reject any suggestion from me."

Trudy's shoulders drooped. "It was a stupid idea anyway. Amos was there; he wouldn't have believed it, if there had been any room for doubt."

"And Amos was the *only* one there," Regan reminded her gently, "who is still around today. Would there be any point in discovering a murderer who is dead already?"

Trudy's shoulders stiffened. She threw back her head. "Yes," she said. "Yes, there would! We might not be able to save this Jack either. But we can at least save his name. They wouldn't be able to use his grandfather as an excuse for their suspicions. Who needs the police? We'll do it without them!"

She scrabbled in the pocket of her wheelchair for some photos, tossed them across at Regan so that they scattered all over Jack's feet. "Those are Vita's flowers. They're mine now. And I'll give you all of them if you'll help me!"

As Regan was gathering up the photos, Charlotte entered and stood, frowning slightly, at the foot of the bed. "Since there isn't much he can do here," she said, "Myron has decided to go home and get some sleep. I'm sure that Miss Culver would like to do the same."

"Oh, no, I'm fine." Regan had sunk back into a chair, already occupied with one of the pictures. Could that possibly be what they used to call the Cinnamon Rose? Wilder described it, if she remembered correctly, as "small, flat, and tumble-headed."

"Really," she repeated finally, looking up when Charlotte didn't move. "I'm okay. You go home with your husband, if you want. I'll stay here with Trudy."

Just then Lucerne Abiel came stumping into the ward, dressed in a military-looking shirt, pantaloons, and combat boots, followed by an embarrassed Gabe Johnson. "Team one, reporting for duty," she said, clicking her heels and saluting snappily.

Regan smiled, Gabe rolled his eyes, and Charlotte raised her brows. "What?"

"Chief Olin sent us to guard Jack," Lucerne explained in a more normal tone. "Here's your breakfast, by the way, Miss Culver." She handed over a small white bag. "We brought extras in case anybody else wanted some." She handed similar bags to Charlotte and Trudy. "Egg McMuffins and orange juice."

"Oh, thank you," Trudy said. "I hadn't thought of breakfast. You're going to be watching Jack all the time? You won't leave his side?"

"Not for a minute," Lucerne assured her. "We come well equipped with lunch, snacks, and reading material, and we have been to the rest rooms. Even medical personnel will proceed with their duties only under our eagle eyes."

"Good." Trudy pushed her wheelchair back from the bed. "Because Regan and I have to go someplace for a little while."

"Trudy," Charlotte said in a reasonable tone, "how could you be thinking of those flowers at a time like this? Not to mention inconveniencing Miss Culver. How is she going to stroll through flower beds in high heels? You're not making any sense."

"No problem." Regan stood and stretched. "I'll drive by my place first to change. It really is no bother. I don't have anything else I need to do today, and if it'll help take Trudy's mind off things…"

Charlotte sighed. "All right. I admit I could use the break. We'll be back this afternoon."

After she was gone, Regan said to Gabe, "You don't take your eyes off of him at all, understand?"

"Aye, aye, ma'am." His tone was sardonic. "What have we just been saying?"

"I'll take my cellular phone with me. Call at once if there's any change."

"And," Trudy added, "Dr. Keegan is not authorized to treat Jack at all. Remember that."

"We get you," Lucerne said. "Dr. Keegan keeps his distance. Too bad. Old enough to be my daddy, I admit, but my pulse would race if he took it."

"Probably why he leaves that to the nurses," Trudy said dryly. "Just remember that Ted Bundy was cute too."

■ ■ ■

"Just keep going," Trudy instructed Regan as they pulled into the driveway of the old Hargrove home. "Past the garage. You'll be able to see some faint tracks there."

The garage was at the edge of the cleared space; beyond it were saplings and brush. The tracks led straight up to a thin spot in the vegetation. That opening seemed scarcely wide enough to admit a vehicle, but Regan gritted her teeth and aimed for the center.

They rocked through, branches clawing at the sides of the van, then dropping away. Once they were in, the lane, if it could be called such, widened, though it didn't get any smoother. Its carpet of fallen leaves hid unseen dips and jolts and, only here and there, patches of sparse gravel.

Trudy sat well back in her wheelchair and clutched the side rails. "I haven't been back here since my accident," she said. "But Amos has had it kept up for me. I did the gardens myself before that. Once I was old enough, that is. I was only three when Vita and my father died. I only have one memory from that time. I dream about it sometimes. Of being a little girl, waking up from a nap to hear people arguing in the next room. I get out of bed and walk across to a door. But I always wake up before I can turn the knob. Or maybe it's only a dream; maybe it isn't a memory at all."

They bumped across a clearer section where brush and trees thinned out, and they could look down on the lake. "Amos has never been back," Trudy said. "He says that some things are best left behind for good. As soon as the police were done with the place, he had it boarded up. Not that the police bothered to do much. With the killer dead, there wasn't any point. I never went into the house myself, even though Amos gave me the key. I think I was afraid that if I found the room in my dream, I might remember. I didn't want to complete that dream. I didn't want to know for sure that my father had done it. Can you understand that?"

"Yes." They had plunged back into a narrow space again, and Regan concentrated on weaving through clinging branches. "I didn't really want to know who had killed my father either."

"At least nobody accused him of being a murderer. Now, of course, I *can't* go upstairs. We're almost there."

To Regan, grimly fighting the wheel, that seemed unlikely, but then they lurched around a tight curve into a broad open space and sunlight. Regan tromped on the brake.

The house had grayed gracefully. With its porches upstairs and down, it must have been the model for Speedwell. But its windows were blind, boarded over, deadening the light, airy effect. There was rot here and there on the porches and the outer steps, but the house itself seemed solid.

Imaginatively, Regan thought it looked toward them with those sightless eyes, begging for release from its confinement. The lawn was high but obviously would have been much higher if it hadn't been mowed at least a couple of times this year. And on banks and terraces to the right and left of the house, flowers bloomed—mums, asters, snapdragons, and calendulas.

The drive circled in front of the house. Regan drove to the top of that circle and shut off the engine. Once the crackle of the wheels over dry leaves had ceased, what struck Regan most was the absolute silence. They were at the far northern end of the valley here, tucked up against the shielding hills.

Perhaps that was what kept vandals out. Anyone wanting to get here would have to brave those steep, brushy slopes or else pass very near the newer Hargrove house to reach the trail. Or maybe it was just that, like Regan, most people had no idea this place was still standing.

Once Trudy was out of the van, she didn't approach the house. A crab-apple tree across the drive still retained some of its leaves, and she wheeled herself into its shade.

"Sit down a moment," she said to Regan. "I want to tell you how it happened. Then you'll have to go in by yourself. These old houses were not built with the handicapped in mind."

Despite herself, Regan felt a certain anticipation as she looked at the building's shuttered exterior. She had always loved exploring old houses. She had been introduced to this precarious hobby by her mother, Rosemary, who had sought out abandoned farms, old houses, and old cemeteries in a quest for roses and other heirloom perennials. Regan had spent many happy childhood hours in such pursuits and had learned the rules. Watch your step and only take cuttings or divisions, never the entire plant. She had also learned there was no reason to be afraid of the dead. Dead people couldn't hurt you. It took the living to do that.

"It was a day just like this," Trudy said. "Forty years ago. It was unnaturally warm that October too; all the flowers were blooming late. People would insist on calling it Indian summer, but you and I know you don't get Indian summer until after a snowfall. After the wars, the number of patients at Speedwell had declined drastically. Natural medicine was considered backward. People were gung-ho for progress. Questioning the direction of that progress was considered un-American. This was the decade that enthused over DDT while the *Reader's Digest* called organic farming 'bunk.' Amos got depressed and worried—not only about physical dangers, but spiritual ones as well. There was a surface religiosity, but people were ardently pursuing materialism and conformity in direct contradiction to Christ's teachings. Actually, in October of '57, everybody was worried. There had been too long a spell of good weather, so to speak. But early in that month, the Soviets launched Sputnik I, and suddenly all the old McCarthy angst about the advance of communism reappeared. I think that Amos, like Linus Pauling, was more anxious about nuclear fallout from all those bombs our government was testing out in the desert."

Trudy contemplated the house as she spoke. "Vita had graduated from medical school two or three years earlier. She must have had courage to do that. Women who pursued any but the lowest-level jobs were considered unfeminine. Fortunately, Vita also had the lush blond good looks that were popular then. She cooked as well as she doctored, so perhaps ambition was excused in her. I've had a hard time developing a clear conception of her or my father as personalities. People just don't want to talk about the whole thing, I guess. But everybody agrees they were a good-looking pair. They were called the golden couple."

Trudy turned her head to make a wry face in Regan's direction. "It was the decade of clichés and simplistic assumptions. People didn't look much below the surface. Of course, some would hint afterward that Vita's death was partly her own fault because she had competed with her husband in the medical arena. Ian Keegan didn't appreciate the addition of Jack Dawson to the staff. Mainly because Ian felt, probably rightly, that Speedwell couldn't afford another doctor just then. Ian was a widower with a little boy, Howard. Maybe he expected to marry Vita himself, before Jack came into the picture. It might have been better. I don't see a Keegan feeling threatened by anybody.

"Galen, Vita's brother, wasn't happy either. He had been trying to convince Amos to change Speedwell into some kind of retreat for artistic types or, failing that, to sell. Even then, with the amount of acreage involved and the prospects for a resort or something like that, they could have sold it for a couple of million. They had offers, in fact. Galen was intelligent, but perhaps not quite as intelligent as he thought. Though he dabbled in the arts, he never succeeded in any of them. Many artistic types felt alienated in the fifties, but I think Galen enjoyed feeling different from—*above*—the common herd. He was the type who wrote snide reviews of other people's work but seldom put his own material on the line. He did make some halfhearted attempts at getting radio stations to air his plays. But TV had largely taken over drama by that time, and radio stations were concentrating on music. I don't think anything ever came of it; nothing came of most that Galen did."

Trudy's quiet voice lulled Regan into a drowsy torpor. "An actress named Faye Cordell had come down to Speedwell to recover from a nervous breakdown. I might as well say right off that she's the only alternative I've come up with so far—the only mental patient at Speedwell then. And I don't think she was crazy. She had a shingled hairstyle and a boyish figure that would have been more appropriate to a twenties flapper. She might have been just the type to fall madly in love with Jack and decide to eliminate his pregnant wife. But she had only been at the sanitarium a few days, hardly long enough to have developed so extreme a passion.

"You do understand," Trudy said to Regan, "that I don't remember any of this myself? It's all from what I've been told."

Regan, who now was leaning back against the tree trunk with her eyes half-closed and her arms around her knees, nodded. Trudy's gaze returned to the house.

"Faye came from a wealthy family, I understand, but they didn't approve of her being an actress. Especially since she preferred the artsy productions not calculated to make much money. I assume they paid for her sojourn at Speedwell. Ian Keegan didn't think anything was wrong with her except an overdeveloped sense of drama. Ian, as you may have deduced, was much like Howard. He always knew what he wanted, and he always got it. Or he did until Jack Dawson came along. Jack was plenty ambitious himself and not shy about contradicting Ian. I don't need to describe Amos to you, except to say he was in his late fifties at the time. I was three, a shy, dreamy child, I gather. Do you think you have the setting and characters all straight now?"

Regan nodded again. She already felt as if she had been transported back to an era that wavered between anxiety and optimism, that did not want to rock the boat of its uneasy peace.

As Trudy began to speak again, Regan closed her eyes completely to see faces on the inside of her eyelids, to envision probable conversations and undercurrents. "Vita had planned a dinner party for Saturday, the twenty-sixth, but during that afternoon, a surgeon named Reuben Bennington called to say he could make it down to Speedwell for a couple of hours after all. He was an acquaintance of Jack's and had been invited in hopes that he would invest some money in Speedwell. His coming agitated things. Vita insisted the dinner party still commence at five; she didn't like her plans upset at the last minute. Ian and Galen were both opposed to Bennington's coming at all. Ian feared he might lead Speedwell away from its naturalistic origins. Galen hoped the sanitarium's financial problems would necessitate a more drastic change."

Trudy produced a sheaf of folded papers from her wheelchair pocket. "I've typed up a fictional account of the day of the murder, which I want you to read before you go in. The facts are straight, but I've had to imagine the dialogue and thoughts. So those aren't gospel. But it should give you some idea."

CHAPTER 5

Hot lavender, mints, savory, marjoram...

The stocks were blooming. Vita had never seen them this lush before. They preferred cool weather and, unless sown very early in the spring, would simply stop growing during midsummer's heat and wait for the cool fall nights to bud. More often than not, freezing temperatures would kill them before they flowered. But now the spikes were plump with double pink blooms, exhaling a spicy fragrance to compete with the mustiness of fallen leaves.

The color of those leaves had been dull. It took frost to ignite the flaming reds and oranges, and there had been no frost. This alien pink was not a fall color.

Jack was nervous over Bennington's arrival. He felt he should be the one to show Bennington around Speedwell but had been vetoed in favor of Amos. Jack, who still wasn't comfortable with all of the healing methods espoused by his father-in-law, probably would have played them down for the surgeon's benefit.

Unworried herself, Vita was cutting mints, savory, and oregano, which had once been known as wild marjoram. She piled the herbs in baskets. It was the third crop of the year.

The poor things must be getting worn out with this surfeit of production.

Even the lavender was still sending up a few fragrant spikes. Vita planted lavender because it was a good headache remedy, and some of her patients liked it. She had never cared for the scent herself. Lavender had once been considered an old maid's herb, and the Victorians equated it with distrust.

Then, too, Gerard, the most famous herbalist of the Renaissance, had seemed to have misgivings about the plant, recommending it only for faintness and headaches and advising against its use in other illnesses. He had warned that it would "fill and stuffe the head," making the disease worse, "especially when letting of bloud, or purging have not gon before."

Of course, Gerard's qualms might now be considered as outdated as the "letting of bloud" he mentioned. But lavender was still prescribed mostly for faintness and headaches or possibly as a sleep aid. Some things didn't change.

Vita enjoyed this reflection on all the generations that had tended and commented on herbs. It tied her into a timeless cycle of planting and harvest—of production.

She would soon be producing herself. She looked down at the rounded stomach under her sleeveless cream blouse and khaki slacks. Bloom, pollination, fruit. All part of the natural order.

Taking care of a new baby and Trudy while continuing to help out at the hospital would be difficult, but Vita didn't doubt her ability to do it—all of it—not only sufficiently but also well. "You are a wonder," Jack always said.

Vita looked for Trudy to discover the little girl sitting in the sunflower house. Morning glories vining up the stalks formed the walls. The sunflowers were browning and drooping, but the morning glories still bloomed riotously, their color reflecting the October sky's blue.

Vita resisted calling the child to her. "She is a different personality," Amos had gently rebuked his daughter. "Not a small extension of yourself. You can't constantly be running her at your own pace."

No, Trudy was not an extension of Vita, not in personality, not in biology. Jack had had another life, another wife. It was the only thing that chafed at Vita's perfect content. Not that she was jealous of Ann. As if anybody could be. But it seemed so untidy somehow—so unnecessary.

"Have you thought about it?" She hadn't heard Galen approach. He was frowning down at her in his sulky, black-browed way.

"Thought about what?"

"About convincing Dad to accept Norville's offer."

Vita had forgotten her promise to think about Norville's offer. She had only promised, in fact, to stop Galen from pestering her. She had had no intention of seriously considering it. She rubbed a sprig of mint between her palms. "This Norville is only talking culture to impress you. As soon as he got the place, he would turn it into another chintzy, overcrowded campground."

"So what if he does?" Galen demanded. "At least we'll have some money out of it for once. I hope you aren't expecting this Bennington to come galloping to the rescue. He won't touch Speedwell when he sees how outlandish some of its treatments are, especially with a woman on its staff."

Vita had decided long ago not to let Galen's bluster make her mad. "Dad would never agree to that," she said. "He won't accept any investors who don't share his vision." She already was losing interest in the conversation, thinking that the mint lacked some of its usual pungency. Plants that hung on too long lost much of their original impact.

"Share his pipe dream, you mean," Galen said rudely. "Well,

never say I didn't give you your chance." He stalked off toward the house. Brothers who always harped on the same old themes, uttered the same empty threats, soon lost their impact too. Not that Galen had ever had much impact. Poor Galen. After a while you just stopped hearing him. Her father and Jack were meeting in the house to plot their strategy with Bennington. She had provided cider and snacks, then left them to it, having been not too tactfully excluded by her husband. Jack thought she would jeopardize their chances. While Bennington might smile approvingly at a pretty, pregnant woman over a well-set table, he did not appreciate female input on serious topics. She had got her way over supper though; they all would return at five.

It was best to go along with Jack on this. If the surgeon would just write a check and go away. But what if he made stipulations with that check? Straightening up with her piled baskets in her arms, Vita had the briefest stab of uneasiness. What if, for once in his life, Galen was right?

For a moment her head felt, as the old herbalist had said, stuffed, overfull. She shot the lavender a glance of active dislike then had to laugh at herself. The idea that the extraordinary plenitude of the garden—of her life—could be in danger was ridiculous. The power of suggestion. Things would work out. They always had. "Come, Trudy," she called. "Don't you want to say good-bye to Grandpa Amos?" Trudy didn't answer; she had fallen asleep.

Vita had to leave the baskets outside to carry the sleeping child in through the kitchen. The men were in the hallway, just preparing to leave. "Don't tell me you're not coming with us, Vita," Galen said mockingly.

Jack was shooting her a warning look. "She has to prepare dinner and look after Trudy. In her condition, she should really have a nap too."

Galen was opening his mouth to speak again. She quickly

forestalled him with, "Maybe you're right. I do feel tired all of a sudden. You are planning on being back by five?"

"We wouldn't miss it," Amos assured her.

■ ■ ■

Amos drove at a leisurely pace, which seemed to annoy Bennington, who, although he did not comment on it, sat forward in his seat. "Speedwell is a comforting environment for those recovering from serious illness also," Amos remarked as they approached the lake. "Especially nervous illness. Everybody comments on the serenity and the unhurried atmosphere."

"The isolation, you mean," Bennington said curtly. "What do you do if you have an emergency?"

"Most of our cases are not emergencies. Modern medicine does quite well with trauma and bacterial disease. I've always admitted that. We concentrate on degenerative diseases, autoimmunity, cancer, psychosomatic symptoms—"

"And you think you can succeed where conventional medicine hasn't?"

"Often we do. Our contention is that the mind and emotions strongly affect the body's health. The old custom of having someone in to sit with the ill person made a lot of sense. People need to be listened to, to be taken seriously. We choose our nurses for their kind dispositions and their willingness to lend an ear. Our doctors are required to spend at least half an hour a day with each of their charges."

At Bennington's skeptical look, Amos added, "They can do that because we limit the number of cases we accept. We encourage our patients to speak up rather than play the victim. We ask them what they think caused the problem and how they think it should be treated. And we listen to their answers. It's surprising how often the nonprofessionals are right! We also have an outpatient clinic once a week for locals with more minor problems. We teach them to take responsibility for their own health by making a few lifestyle changes and by learning patience. The body can usually heal itself, given time."

The long porch was fronted with flower beds, which included tall, blue spikes of the plant for which the hospital and the lake were named. On the other side of the drive, a wooden pier stretched out into the water from the beach. A woman was lying on the white sand close to the water's edge in an umbrella's shade. "Good morning, Elaine," Amos called as he got out of the car.

She flopped over onto her side to beam at him. "Good morning, Dr. Hargrove. And it's a glorious one, isn't it?"

"It certainly is."

As they turned toward the steps, Bennington said, "Polio?"

"You have a sharp eye," Amos said. "Yes. She's had it since she was thirteen. Elaine is in her forties now. Most of the year, she lives with her sister. But when the sister goes on vacation, Elaine comes to us. There's not much we can do for her condition, of course. Though she always claims she feels better after she's been here. She loves the water and the sand."

"Is accepting patients like her economically feasible?" Bennington asked. "I assume you charge her less than you would charge those patients whom you are actively treating."

"Naturally. No, we don't make much money off of Elaine, but we always feel better after she's been here too. That sunny spirit of hers is contagious. But caregivers, even of a patient as amiable as she is, need a vacation now and then if they're to maintain their own health. Elaine can be so cheerful because she accepted her handicap years ago. Acceptance is the first thing we try to teach our patients. Acceptance of God, of course, but lacking that, at least acceptance of themselves and their diseases."

"Isn't that a cop-out?"

A girl with short, dark hair and high color lounged on a porch divan, reading a magazine. She might have been on vacation rather than a hospital patient. "Faye Cordell," Amos said. "Dr. Bennington."

She looked up to nod shortly. Her bright-eyed gaze shifted to Jack. There was something coiled and tense in her tall, slender frame with its bare, sun-browned arms, something sly in the stare that dropped back to her magazine again.

"Nervous type?" Bennington asked when they were out of earshot.

"Yes. She breathes too fast and too shallowly. A common problem. You do it yourself, doctor. In answer to your question, no, we don't consider it a cop-out. Without acceptance, you expend too much energy in unnecessary stress. Calm down, and you give your body a chance to correct itself. There's a big difference between acceptance and resignation. Too many people die because they are resigned to it, because their doctors have told them there is no cure. We don't consider any disease incurable."

Amos was leading the way into a big, sunny room, furnished with comfortable couches and low tables. "We have seen amazing results in people who were supposedly untreatable. This is our lounge. Patients often congregate here in the evenings—especially in winter. You'll notice we try to keep all of our rooms as bright and airy as possible. We think the traditional closing up of the sick in dim, stuffy wards is detrimental both to health and mood. We have fresh flowers in each room from our gardens out back. We grow almost all of the food we serve. We emphasize fresh fruits and vegetables at the peak of ripeness, and freeze or can those that aren't going to be used right away. Most produce intended for grocery stores is picked before it's mature. It loses many of its nutrients that way. Local farmers grow our organic grains for us. We're fortunate to have a mill nearby that still stone-grinds flour."

Bennington said, "I can see why you're having problems. Too

many staff members for the number of patients. When you add gardeners and cooks—"

"One gardener and one cook," Amos corrected. "Our guests help us out with chores. If you'll follow me…"

He led the group along a hallway to a window at the back of the building, stood aside for Bennington to look. In the yard a kettle hung over a crackling fire. In chairs and wheelchairs, patients and nurses sorted apples. Amid much banter and laughter, they set the good apples aside in baskets, trimmed and cut up the spotty ones for the kettle.

Farther back in the orchard, others scavenged under trees for the deadfalls while a couple of the burlier types picked from ladders. "We're making apple butter today," Amos said. "It's why you'll find the place a bit empty."

They turned down the transverse hall to an open door. The man lying on the bed was stripped to the waist as a nurse applied alternate hot and cold compresses to his stomach. In a chair tipped back against the wall, a doctor scribbled on a chart. "Dr. Bennington, Dr. Keegan," Amos said.

"What does that accomplish?" Bennington asked.

"Stimulation of the kidneys and liver, helps eliminate toxins," Keegan replied shortly.

"What other cancer treatments do you use?"

"Treatment is different for each patient." Keegan consulted the chart. "Right after Mr. Drew came to us, he was given an enema to clean out his system and put on a three-day fast in which he was allowed only fruit juices and herbal teas. We also gave him some sweat baths to induce fever, followed by salt rubs and massage. Then we started him on our cancer formula and on a nutritious diet. Mostly whole grains, fruits, nuts, and vegetables, with an emphasis on sulfur-rich garlic and onions, radish, cabbage, and kale. A Hungarian doctor has been having some success with raw beets, too, so we've recently added those."

"Has any of this helped?"

Keegan turned to the patient. "Has any of this helped, Mr. Drew?" he asked dryly.

Drew grinned. "And how! The tumors are shrinking, and I feel better than I have in years. Sleep like a baby. There's nothing like a sweat bath and a salt glow to make you feel alive, doctor."

Following Amos down the hall again, Bennington said, "How much of this is a placebo effect, Dr. Hargrove—the patient feeling better because he expects to?"

Amos shrugged. "I don't know, and frankly I don't care. It's amazing how many people who think they are getting better actually do. Since we know that stressful emotions can make a person sick, why can't positive emotions help him recover? My goal, Dr. Bennington, is to stimulate the body into healing itself. It does a much better job, after all, than any of us can. We have about a 40 percent remission rate for cancer. Considering that most of those who come to us do so only after trying everything else, I think that's a pretty good average."

He led the way down a flight of stairs, pushed open a swinging door. "This is our kitchen."

Two women in wheelchairs scrubbed potatoes at the end of a long table. They beamed at the new arrivals. "Good afternoon, Dr. Hargrove."

"Good afternoon, ladies. This is Dr. Bennington. I'm giving him a tour. What's on the menu for tonight?"

Another woman, rosy-cheeked, pulled bread pans out of the oven and tipped steaming, brown loaves out onto a long board to cool. "Soybean loaf, baked potatoes, and spinach," she said, straightening to smile at them. "Plus fresh bread, of course. George says we had better use the spinach now because it won't last in this weather. He refuses to let me have the Brussels sprouts until after it frosts. Tonight we'll have apple butter for the bread."

Amos grinned at Bennington's dubious expression. "You would like it, doctor. Everything that Betsy cooks is delectable, right, ladies?"

They nodded enthusiastically. "I wish I could stay in this place forever," one said. "I've never tasted vegetables like you have here."

"When you're using homegrown stuff, you can hardly go wrong," Betsy said. "Just as long as you don't cook it into mush.

"George has been complaining about that new patient, by the way," Betsy continued. She rides the horses hard, then doesn't rub them down or put them away, just leaves them outside the barn for him to deal with. He wouldn't mind if she was really sick, but—"

"But she isn't," Amos finished. "Or not on the surface anyway. I'll talk to her. She's probably used to servants at home. George," he explained to Bennington as they went out, "is our gardener; he also looks after the stable."

They joined the apple-butter party outside, and Bennington was chatting with some of the patients when Jack came out to speak to Amos. "Galen says Vita just called, and she's really angry about something. I think he and I will drive back now and try to calm her down. Ian has agreed to row you guys across. It'll give Reuben a chance to appreciate the lake. Don't be late."

Amos raised his brows. His daughter wasn't usually prone to temper. "All right. Bennington seems like a nice enough chap."

"Rock-ribbed though," Jack said with a sigh. "He doesn't like Vita; that's plain enough. So we want to make sure she doesn't give him any more reason for that dislike."

About fifteen minutes later, Ian appeared to report himself ready. Faye was still curled on the porch divan as the three men left the hospital. When Amos delivered a mild rebuke over her horsemanship habits, she responded with a raising of brows and a flippant shrug. "Whatever you say."

The men continued down the walk and out onto the dock where the boat was tied, waving at Elaine as they passed her. When they were halfway across the lake, Ian shifted the oars to say abruptly to Bennington, "You do understand that we aren't willing to change our methods?"

"So Amos informed me."

The rest of the trip was completed in silence until they drifted up to the pier at the northern end of the lake. Jack's car was in the driveway, and they found Galen in the front room with a magazine. "Vita didn't make supper," he reported with a kind of gloomy relish, gesturing toward a tray containing pitchers and glasses. "I got us some cider out of the fridge. You all might as well sit down. Jack has been up there arguing with her about it, but you know how she is once she's made up her mind."

"Yes, I do," Amos said. "But what is she upset about?"

Galen looked at Bennington. "Well, that isn't so hard to figure out, is it? She didn't appreciate getting stuck at home with the kid and the housework. You can't blame her really."

"Well, why didn't she say something before?" Ian asked irritably. "We could have gone to a restaurant."

"Vita usually likes to entertain." Amos's tone was mild, but he looked worried.

Raised voices from upstairs interrupted them.

"You want, you want!" Vita said. "How come it's always what *you* want? When do I get my turn?"

"I don't understand what's gotten into you," Jack retorted. "You were fine this morning."

"Was I? How do you know? Because I can smile like the perfect little wife?"

Ian moved as if to switch on the radio to drown them out. "Leave that alone!" Galen snapped. "I think it's about time you all heard the truth about Vita's lovely marriage."

"Keep your voice down," Jack said, as if aware now of the listeners downstairs.

"Why? Because I might wake the child? *Your* child who has somehow become *my* responsibility? Or because somebody might hear that you don't have the ideal family after all? You're always worried about your image, aren't you? The up and coming bright young man. Wait until they find out what I did. That you're all image, hollow, a nobody, the son of a nobody, a cipher."

"Stop it!" Jack said in a thick voice. "I'm warning you—"

"Or you'll do what? Hit me? I'm sure that would prove how big a man you are. Or maybe you'd like this? Your wartime prop. You don't feel quite complete without it, do you? Go on, take it! You don't scare me one little bit. Both of us know you'd never have the guts to pull the trig—"

The crash of a gunshot drowned the final word. In the room below, the four men froze, staring at each other as the echoes ricocheted and faded into a stunning silence. Then Amos bolted for the stairs, the other three on his heels.

Overhead, panicked footsteps scuttled out onto the upper porch, rattled down the steps. Vita had fallen facedown across the bed, blood oozing from the back of her head. Amos and Bennington bent over her. The room stank of cordite. Galen had run to the open window. "There he goes!"

Ian joined him. The fleeing figure was too distant for catching now, had already reached the car. As they watched, the vehicle roared to life, lurched drunkenly into the lane. The young doctor turned back to the bed. Bennington had turned Vita's body over, was preparing to make an incision in her abdomen with a penknife. Amos was cradling the bloody blond head. "Then she's—"

"Dead," Bennington said grimly. "Come here and help me, won't you, Keegan? And you"—he looked at Galen—"see if you can find the child. Don't bring her in here, whatever you do."

Finished, Regan straightened the pages, returned them neatly to their envelope. "You've brought it to life. What happened after that?" A leaf detached itself from the tree, floated gently down into her lap.

"They couldn't save the baby," Trudy resumed. "Galen found me lying in my bed, crying. Perhaps the sound of the shot had frightened me. Within an hour or so, police had found Jack's car about fifty miles away, on a bridge over Blue Lake in Trafalgar, his hometown. A suicide note was in the car. The gun was there too. His service revolver. It's deep water, hard to search. They found one of his shoes, I think, but not his body. Corpses in deep, cold water don't always surface."

"And those left behind?"

"You can imagine the shock it was to Amos. But Speedwell survived, largely, I think, through the determination of Ian Keegan. I imagine that Galen was shaken too. He stopped trying to convince his father to sell and took up with Faye Cordell. After they married, they moved away to the city to try their luck in the theater and seldom came back. About a year after Myron was born, Faye cracked up and was institutionalized—has been, from what I hear, ever since."

Trudy shook her head impatiently as if she was depressing even herself with this litany. "Ian died in a plane crash in South America during one of his mission trips in the seventies. Galen degenerated after he lost Faye. I suppose Amos made him and the boy an allowance. Galen must have drunk because by the time he returned to Hayden, his liver had deteriorated. He wouldn't let them treat him at Speedwell either. He'd taken a turn against the place. Not long after his return, he died of a heart attack. That was around the time of my accident. Myron had a teaching degree by then. He stayed here because we were the only family he had left. Charlotte was a teacher, too, but didn't show any interest in continuing her career after they married."

Trudy raised her shoulders. "And life goes on. Amos closed up the house shortly after it happened. There hadn't been much of an investigation. No need for one, everybody figured. They all knew who the guilty party was. They had virtual witnesses, his fingerprints on the gun, the suicide note, and his flight, which implied guilt."

Regan stood, dusted off leaves. "But *you're* not satisfied."

"I have no good reason not to be. No proof of anything different. Just the hope of an orphaned child that it somehow wasn't true. It's time for me to grow up now and face things, one way or the other."

CHAPTER 6

The marigold, that goes to bed wi' the sun...

The silence lay as thick as the dust. Standing just inside the door, Regan looked around with quickening curiosity. She had once been fond of mystery novels—before she had found out for herself what real-life murder could do to a family.

But this was not her family, and this murder case was forty years old. By now, the passions that had motivated its characters were as lifeless as those characters themselves. It should be possible to treat it all as an intellectual exercise.

Did Dr. Dawson shoot his pretty, pregnant, young wife on a sunny day in October? There seemed little doubt of it. It had been, Regan remembered with a jolt, only a few years earlier that Dr. Sheppard had been arrested for murdering *his* pretty, young wife. There had seemed little doubt of that at the time either, but now...

Her footsteps echoed, but faintly, on the wood floors, as if muffled by years. It was dim but not dark. Light crept through cracks in the shutters.

In front of her, slightly to her left, were the stairs going up to the second floor. Immediately to her left was an open doorway. She walked through it.

This was what they had called the front room. A shutter had broken away from a window here, and the room was bright. Divans and armchairs, decked in white slipcovers, appeared intact beneath a layer of grime. Summer covers, which had not been changed, perhaps, because the weather had not changed. Regan had the irrational feeling that, if touched, the furniture would crumble away into nothingness. She stepped lightly to avoid jarring that brittleness.

A magazine was thrown down in a corner of the divan. A pitcher rested in a tray on the coffee table, with glasses scattered around it on the table's surface. Four men having cool drinks on a warm day, waiting for their host with that air of constraint caused by domestic awkwardness.

There was a door in the far wall between bookcases. Regan crossed to open it. The room beyond seemed darker, with a large fireplace, a crimson antique sofa, a paisley wool rug, heavy velvet drapes, a roll-top desk, barrister bookcases. This room would, she thought, have been used more in the winter when its solid furniture and rich, muted colors would be warming. Its extreme neatness indicated it hadn't been touched since that October day.

Regan returned the way she had come, passed the foot of the stairs again, and entered the dining room on the opposite side of the hall. The table was set. Vita must have done that after lunch so she wouldn't be bothered with it while she was fixing dinner.

Regan reached out, ran her finger along the rim of a china plate. The pattern was sprays of wheat with gold piping. Napkins still nestled in rings that matched the neatly laid silver. Unlighted amber candles stood tall in sticks that matched the rings.

There had also been some kind of centerpiece in a low basket. Autumn leaves and gourds perhaps. Or flowers. Whatever it was had long since decayed into a fluffy, black dirt. Compost. Regan crossed to the sideboard. Serving dishes had been laid ready there, taken from the china closet, probably. Vita had been so determined on her dinner party. A predominately male dinner party. Perhaps Vita had not been popular with members of her own sex.

After she had expended this much energy in preparation, would she have let one chauvinistic doctor bother her that much? Or was he, more likely, the last straw—Vita's quarrel with her husband the final one in a long series? Was the golden couple perhaps not as ideal as they seemed? When they were this removed from their neighbors, nobody would know; nobody would hear...

A smaller hallway connected the dining room with the kitchen. Halfway along it, a door led into a bathroom. Against the far wall, under the window, a claw-foot tub hunched in its circle of curtains with a showerhead bent over it. One would expect a constant drip from a nozzle that outdated, but this one had been dry for years. Regan lifted the lid off a glass canister, rubbed the grainy stuff it contained between her fingers. Bath salts, she decided. Holding her fingers up to her nose, she could detect just the faintest musty essence of rose, as from a desiccating potpourri.

Her own reflection moved dimly in the mirror, the only sign of life. The mirror was attached to a medicine cabinet. She opened it. Old bottles, tubes, boxes. Aspirin, iodine, razor blades.

Regan shut the door and looked at her smudgy reflection again. Just dried-up remainders of two people who had died a long time ago. Perhaps their love had died even earlier.

People were seldom as surprised as they should be over husbands and wives killing each other. It had always happened, always would happen—love metamorphosing into hate.

Maybe sometimes it was like the plant in the Bible, she thought, that sprang up quickly but withered because it had no root. She was careful not to consider whether she was thinking of Vita's love or her own.

She went out into the hallway and along to the kitchen at the rear of the house. Baskets lay in a jumble on the table there. Half-tipped into one another, they suggested carelessness and haste. Did Vita never get around to hanging those herbs? Some kind of plant detritus lay in the baskets, scattered about on the table.

If Vita was the type who believed in being prepared, she might have...Regan opened the refrigerator door. Baking dishes were lined up neatly on the racks. Any odor of decay had long been superseded by that of stagnant air. Yes, Vita had had her dinner ready to put in the oven when the time came. If Regan knew anything about fifties dishes, it was that most of them took at least an hour to cook. Surely, Vita would not have napped for long.

Something had happened, Regan decided, something drastic, and it must have occurred shortly after the men left. Something to cause Vita's extreme anger at her husband. Something which, when Jack was confronted with it, had provoked irrational rage in him.

Some men were like that. Some women, too, for that matter. They couldn't stand the imputation of guilt, of fault, and struck back violently. What had Jack done that Vita had thrown in his face?

A pantry between the kitchen and bathroom was still stocked with glass jars of tomatoes, pickles, jams, and jellies. Regan wiped away the smut on a jar of peaches to find their orange glowing brightly. Finding an answer would require cleaning away all of the innuendo that had accumulated over the years. To discover a couple who, though not as perfect as they had first appeared, surely deserved that an effort be made by somebody.

It didn't seem to have been made at the time, in kindness perhaps. People liked Amos, didn't want to expose him to more pain, thought the whole mess best buried and forgotten as soon as possible.

This house imparted something of the sense one got in an old graveyard. How can what happened here be important now? It was over and done with long ago. Let it lie.

But it wasn't done. What had happened in the fifties could still reach far enough to smudge a nineties teen. A smaller staircase lay between the pantry and the bathroom. It seemed, with its twists and turns, less intimidating than the main one. Any suggestion of loud haste, of rage run amuck, seemed unlikely now with only a faint gritting of dust underfoot and thin seams of sunlight striping the closed shutters on the landing. She turned and continued upward into the silence. No arguing voices now. She came out in a hallway about two-thirds back from the front of the house.

A doorway was beside her, leading into what seemed like an empty room. The staircase went on up; there must be an attic too.

Regan entered the empty room. It wasn't completely bare after all. Strings sagged from one wall to its opposite over screens with legs and wooden racks. This had been a drying area for Vita's herbs. With windows on two sides open, fresh air would have flowed through the room.

Walking back along the hallway toward the front of the house, Regan glanced in open doors as she passed. These big, old houses had many small rooms, a bathroom and guestroom on this side. At the front, Regan stopped to peer through a crack in the shutters at the woman under the crab-apple tree, sitting small, straight, and expectant.

Why did she choose me for this? I'm not the detective type. My mind goes off on irrelevant tangents even when I'm talking. And things that are right under my nose I'm more than likely to overlook.

Regan sighed and went back, running a hand along the railing that circled the stair space. At the front on the other side was a sewing and storage room. Next, the bedroom that must have been Trudy's, almost empty. They had taken her things before they closed up the place. Only she remained alive to need things. A connecting door would lead directly into the master bedroom. Hanging on that door was a calendar. October 1957. A blond little girl hugged a collie puppy. The calendar rustled as Regan pulled the door toward herself.

She was looking at the foot of a bed, the headboard being neatly positioned between the two north windows and the foot extending into the middle of the room. It was a bold placement. Regan's own bed always seemed to huddle against a wall. The bedclothes had been stripped off and not replaced.

The rug on the eastern side of the bed was rucked up. A small lamp table stood beside it, and a vanity was tucked into the northeast corner. Thoughtfully eyeing her shadowy image in its mirror, Regan wondered if a three-year-old had once been reflected there, peering in on a scene of carnage.

To the west, a tall dresser paralleled the wall beside the French doors, which had once opened onto an upstairs porch. On top of the dresser, an old radio was neatly centered on a lacy dresser scarf.

Regan circumvented the rug to tug open the drawer of the lamp table. There was, as she had hoped, a diary.

Tucking it under her arm, she touched the yellowed doily under the bedside lamp. It would, she thought, clean up well. There was little damage, little damp here.

Regan went out and climbed the stairs to where they ended under the attic beams. It was warm up there under the roof. She sat on the top step and looked wistfully at boards that lay across the beams and were stacked with old trunks, frames, and furniture. Much of this must have belonged to Amos's parents.

But this story was not old enough to be antique or to justify explorations up here. There had been an extra door next to the pantry in the kitchen—bolted. Regan found an empty box into which she could dump the papers from the desk and went back downstairs.

The bolt was stiff and reluctant. Once it was conquered, the door dragged, scraped against the kitchen floor as she tugged it toward herself. A rustle of movement from below stopped abruptly. Rats? But rats didn't freeze when surprised; they scuttled.

"Hello?" she said. "Is anybody down there?"

No answer, but no further movement of scrabbling paws either. If it were an animal, it would keep running.

The rough wooden steps descended to an earthen floor. That floor seemed brighter than it should be. Most old houses had outer doors to the cellar with stone steps. Those would probably be at the northern end here, since porches circumvented the rest.

A sudden rush of movement. Regan tried to slam the door, but it dragged, taking its time. She pressed against it, heart thudding, fumbling with the bolt, then realized that the sound wasn't coming toward her. Whoever, whatever it was, had headed for the outside stairs.

■ ■ ■

After questioning several of the more observant of Hayden's citizens who had attended the dance, Matt had concluded to his own satisfaction that most of the teens volunteering for guard duty were in the clear. Especially Gabe and Lucerne, who had been noticed, sometimes disapprovingly, by many. As for Jack's family members, neither his mother nor grandfather had been present. Myron had been playing a chess game, and Charlotte had been talking to Regan. Dr. Keegan had left the gymnasium, presumably to return to Speedwell, shortly before Jack had gone out.

When Matt returned to his office, he made a phone call. "Myron, will you be in town today? I need to talk to you."

The principal sounded peevish. "I had hoped to get some sleep, but with the phone ringing off the hook, I doubt that I'd manage it anyhow. Everyone wants to speak to Trudy, but she has gone off somewhere with your girlfriend. Something to do with the flowers back at the old house. It seems a strange time to be talking about flowers. I'll meet you at the school in half an hour. I need to get some things done there anyway."

Arriving just as Myron was inserting his key in the lock, Matt asked, "How many people have those?"

"Those? Oh, keys, you mean. Too many. Everybody that wants one, basically. Most of the teachers and coaches. They sometimes pass them out to students who need to be here after hours. What can you do?"

Matt followed Myron Hargrove down the hall toward his office. "Well, I suppose there's not much point to a school without kids in it."

Jiggling with the lock on his office door, Myron said, "If they were actually doing something constructive maybe." He looked owlishly at Matt through thick lenses. "But that doesn't seem to have been what they were up to, does it?"

He pushed into the office, heaving his scuffed briefcase onto the desk.

"Have the state police talked to you?" Matt asked, following him in, pushing the door shut, and leaning against it.

"About Jack? Yes. What did you think I was referring to?"

"And it didn't surprise you that your young cousin should have heroin in his locker?"

"*Nothing* surprises me about teenagers, Chief Olin."

"Not even one who grew up in the same house as you? I would think he might see you as a surrogate father."

"I wasn't interested in being a father. Jack has always spent a lot of his time at Speedwell. He hero-worships Howard Keegan. Much to Trudy's chagrin. She suspects Keegan of wanting to assume control of Speedwell. I imagine she's right about that."

"Then Keegan might have a reason for wanting Jack out of the way?"

Hunched over his briefcase, Mryon scowled. "Jack overdosed on heroin, Chief Olin. I don't know why you're trying to turn this into a mystery. I should think you had enough publicity over your last big case."

"Did you ever suspect Jack used drugs?"

"No. My cousin always had a good reputation in the community. Perhaps," Myron added dryly, "too good."

"What do you mean by that?"

"As if he were trying too hard. You have to consider his background. Illegitimacy, a crippled mother, no father. There had to be some cracks in the foundation. I think he's done pretty good to get this far before breaking down. Of course, he had Amos and Keegan to model himself after. He picked up on their charm, their way with people. Who or what the real Jack was..." Myron shrugged. "Perhaps we'll never know now. He couldn't live a part forever, any more than his grandfather could. There was a lot of pressure on him to become a doctor, continue the Speedwell tradition. Just as there was on Trudy to replace Vita."

Myron tapped broodingly on his blotter with the cap of a pen. "And look what it did to her. I've tried to point out to Amos that not all of us are interested in medicine, that maybe Jack would prefer to do something else. It didn't help, of course. Good men do the most harm. Did you know that, Chief? If Amos were a tyrant, Jack would have felt justified in rebelling. But, as it is, Jack would do anything Amos asked, so as not to disappoint the old man. Maybe the kid felt trapped."

"Where do you think he got the heroin?"

"I wish I knew. There have been rumors, of course. There always are."

"About?"

"Raven Scion. The name is so obviously fake. He's close to the school, and the problem did start getting worse after he and his daughter arrived."

"How has it gotten worse? How many of your students are involved? Besides Ken Fermin and his crowd, of course."

The principal shrugged again. It seemed a favorite gesture. "Who can tell? We find the capsules lying around. Teenagers can be very secretive when they want to be. And they don't tell on each other. I can't give you a nose count, chief, but I can tell you that you had better get busy and do something about it. Some TV reporters are going to be here later this afternoon to interview me. I'll try to downplay things, but they've already concluded that we have a crisis here. Let one more kid overdose, and we're going to have hysterical parents coming down on both of us. I would suggest you dump the whole thing off on the state police. I bet they're still smarting over being kept out of the Culver murder investigation." He leaned back in his chair.

"You do realize that if the national press gets a whiff of this, they're going to be down here again in droves?" he continued. "Alden Culver was a friend of Amos's, mentioned Speedwell pretty freely in his books. And a lot of those reporters still think they didn't get the whole story about Culver's murder."

Matt gave a shrug of his own. "The state boys have already insisted there's no more dealing around here than there ever has been. Less, actually, since they got a couple of felony convictions this summer. They were pretty indignant, insist it must be a very local problem."

He straightened wearily. "I suppose I'd better talk to Scion. Make vaguely threatening noises. Without proof, there's not much else I can do. We could start routine sweeps of the lockers, but then we would have the civil liberties people at our throats."

"Borrow one of those drug-sniffing dogs," Myron suggested. "That would limit the number of lockers you actually have to search. With any luck, maybe the parents will start insisting on the sweeps. Just so it doesn't seem to be our idea."

"But are you sure we won't be exaggerating the problem by all this? Lucerne insists it isn't that serious."

"That girl?" The principal raised his brows. "In the set she comes from, it probably isn't considered a problem. There has been some suspicion about her also. Much too mature for her years. Not to mention that she's seen buzzing all over town at odd hours. Why did her mother pack her out here to begin with? To get her away from some kind of trouble in the city, most likely. But a girl as sharp as that one is bound to be bored in a hick town. And she's a clever little actress, stars in community theater. She doesn't need the money, granted, but I can imagine her flouting any law she doesn't like just for fun. Can't you?"

Matt nodded reluctantly. He could.

■   ■   ■

Regan ran for the north windows but heard the cellar doors thud shut while she was only halfway across the floor. By the time she pressed her nose to a filmy pane, nobody was there. No point in pursuit either. Whoever it was would have reached the shelter of trees and brush by now.

She found the door that led from the hall into the living room, hastily upended the contents of desk drawers into her box, listening intently as she did so, then scurried, sneezing, back to the front door. She paused in pulling it shut behind her when she saw that Trudy was no longer alone.

Howard Keegan lounged on the ground beside the wheel-chair, watching Regan with a certain sardonic interest, hands interlaced around one drawn-up knee. He wore riding boots, jeans, and an open-necked shirt. A horse was tied to a low branch of the crab-apple tree.

Regan picked her way down the steps and across the drive. "How long has he been here?" she asked Trudy, even before she reached them.

"Too long," Trudy said. "Fifteen minutes or so. Why?"

"Somebody was in the basement just now. Whoever it was left by those outside doors at the back."

Keegan raised his eyebrows, got up, and ambled around the corner of the house. "Well, it couldn't have been him." Trudy seemed sorry to admit it. "He's been going at me for at least fifteen minutes."

"About what?"

"The same as usual. When am I going to start practicing medicine again. Dr. Sombriel is leaving in a few days, so Speedwell is going to need somebody else. The whole idea is ridiculous."

"Why?" Regan asked. "I won't say there are lots of handicapped physicians, but there are some. Actually, your disability would probably make you a better doctor. In the alternative medicine mode anyway. Help you relate to the patients."

Keegan returned from checking the basement. "Somebody's been hiding something down there. Drugs, from the looks of it. White powder residue here and there. Not a large amount, apparently, since he seems to have carried it off with him. I'll have to remember to bring a padlock up here for those outside doors."

"What are you doing here anyway?" Regan asked.

"He *says*," Trudy answered for him, "that he was riding on the trail up there." She gestured to her right. "And just happened to see our van. A trail did come out here from Speedwell, but I had thought it long overgrown. Seems he rides this way a lot. Likes to look at the flowers."

"Somebody should get some use out of them." He seemed more amused than perturbed by her skeptical tone. "I even pick some to take to my patients occasionally. They're not doing anybody any good up here."

"Like I'm not doing anybody any good, I suppose." Trudy was leaning back in her chair, eyes half-shut, features appearing even tighter than usual.

"Hey, you said it, not me." Howard moved behind her chair and dug his thumbs into the base of her skull. Trudy didn't object to this treatment but tilted her head back as he, keeping one thumb in the nape of her neck, reached forward to press his other thumb and forefinger into the hollows on either side of her nose bridge.

"Trudy," he said to Regan, "has never followed even the first of her father's dictums—accepting her illness. If she can't have things the way they used to be, she isn't going to have them at all."

He picked up her left hand and pinched the webbing between the thumb and index finger, holding it for a moment, then repeating the action with her other hand. "All right?"

"All right." She opened her eyes, looking more relaxed. "Headache," she explained briefly to Regan.

"Yes," Regan said. "I figured that was acupressure."

"You're too tight up here." Howard prodded her scalp with deft fingers. Trudy started suddenly as at a shock, raised both hands to her head.

"What was that?" Regan asked.

"Cranial osteopathy."

Moving away, he said to Regan, "Stand up straight. You're scrunching your liver. You might want to tell your fiancé about our little cache here, by the way."

Trudy waited until he was out of earshot to say, "Don't. They'll say it was Jack. He's the only one besides me who ever comes up here."

"Not the only one, apparently," Regan said, still thoughtfully watching Howard. "Dr. Keegan and somebody else makes at least two more. The person had only been in the basement. The dust was undisturbed in the rest of the house. He couldn't get up there without breaking a bolt or a lock. Apparently he didn't feel the need to. What is Dr. Keegan like?"

"Good with his hands," Trudy said. "I wonder how he did that last thing." She was still gingerly probing at her own scalp. "To do that, I've read, you have to be sensitive enough to feel a hair under several sheets of paper. Kind of like the princess and the pea. Howard is always trying new stuff. As long as it works, he doesn't have to know why."

"Would he feel the need for some extra money on the side?"

Trudy shook her head vehemently. "I can't feel anything," she said with a sigh. "*Except* hair. No, he's a bachelor, and he makes plenty; has invested a lot of it over the years too. If he wants Speedwell, it's not for the money. He's as opposed to recreational drug use as Amos is. That's one guy who makes his opinions very clear, believe me. I suppose he thinks that if he makes me mad enough, I'll have to prove something, and I'll start practicing again."

"And you still think he tried to kill you—after all this concern he's showing?"

Trudy smiled. "Oh, the concern isn't for me but for Speedwell. He wants to show me up, show Amos who should be running the place. And he can't win as long as I refuse to play the game. It's either beat me or kill me, so to speak."

"But *you* can't win," Regan pointed out, "as long as you don't. Was this *game*, as you call it, going on before you got pregnant?"

"Oh, I was never really any threat to him." Trudy forcefully propelled her wheelchair through the crackling leaves to the drive. "It's too bad Vita wasn't still around. She, at least, might have given him a run for the money."

"Maybe that was the problem," Regan said. "She gave her

husband too much competition. Some guys can't stand that, you know, from a woman. Especially guys who are weak in self-confidence."

"Howard has no lack of self-confidence, that's for sure." Trudy was rolling her chair onto the lift.

"And you've talked yourself out of any at all. You thought your job was to replace Vita—"

"Wasn't it?" Trudy wheeled herself into the van. Regan shoved in the box, slammed the rear doors, climbed in on the driver's side, and started the engine.

"Of course, that was impossible," Trudy said. "Because I wasn't beautiful, and I wasn't confident."

Don't let me say the wrong thing now. "You were not," Regan carefully navigated the curve onto the rough trail, as she tried to navigate around pitfalls in this conversation, "beautiful in the same way that she was. You are very attractive in your own right. Frankly, whatever his motives, I think Howard is better for you than Charlotte. He at least wants you to do things."

"Oh, I despise Charlotte too," Trudy said. "I'm really not a nice person. She's right about that. I hate being dependent on her. She insists on pushing my chair and talks about me over my head as if I were a child. So I snap at her, and I don't go out more than necessary. I'm not asking you to like me or to approve my lifestyle. What's that book you have there?"

"Vita's diary." Regan tried to hand it over, but Trudy refused to reach for it.

"No. You found it; you read it. I'll go through the box. You're the objective observer. If you decide that my father did it, I promise to accept that as final."

"You're putting entirely too much responsibility on me. When I'm done, I'll present you with what I've found, and that's all. I'm not going to draw conclusions for you. You have to do that yourself."

Their gazes clashed. Trudy was the first to look away. "I've already gone round and round with the story till I'm sick of it."

"So get off the merry-go-round. Go one way or the other, and don't look back. Because what your father was has nothing to say about you."

■ ■ ■

"So what do you think of God?" Lucerne asked.

Gabe stared. "What kind of question is that?"

"I'm trying to make conversation here," she said. "And small talk bores me. Frankly, I'd say you need to have it out with him the same way you did with Matt Olin."

Interested despite himself, Gabe came back with, "Oh yeah?"

"Yeah. Someday you're going to have to come to grips." Lucerne straddled a chair with her arms crossed over the back, resting her chin on those arms to stare at him. "What did you think of your father?"

"That's none of your business."

"You should know by now that I am not insultable. Another female would have figured that out already and quit trying. Is he the reason you have a compulsion to be first?"

"Think I'm going to beat you for valedictorian, don't you?"

"Probably. It won't bother me too much, but it would bother you too much if you didn't. I could tell you weren't joking about that the other night. People sense that driving compulsion in you. It's why they believe you wanted Jack's place on the team. You're still trying to please your father, aren't you?"

He ignored her.

She dismounted from the chair, strolled around behind him. "God is an easier parent. He doesn't demand that you be any more than human. Trouble is, you made a little mistake this morning when you threw down the gauntlet. If he comes through, you're going to have to do something about it."

"Which he?" Gabe said, tilting his chair back, right ankle cocked flippantly over his opposite knee. "Olin or God?"

"Both."

■ ■ ■

Matt didn't have far to go. The Scions had rented a little house on the far side of the high school athletic fields, down a long, rutted lane. No one had bothered to mow the grass from the summer months when the house had stood empty. Pine trees taller than the roof crowded close to the windows.

Betony answered the door. She didn't say anything.

"I'd like to talk to you and your father," Matt said. "Is he here?"

"He's probably around. He'll come if he sees the car."

She let him in, gestured toward the couch, and sat down primly herself on the edge of an armchair. "Is it about Jack?" The room was murky due to those evergreens.

"Kind of." A pile of teenage beauty magazines lay on the coffee table. They did not, he thought, seem to be doing Betony much good.

He caught a knowing look from her, realized that she had followed his glance and his thought processes. Shy maybe, but not stupid.

"What does your father do for a living, Betony?"

"Right now he's farming."

Matt refrained from a skeptical lift of the eyebrows. He had seen no signs of cultivation on this pathetic bit of acreage. Of course, it wasn't really the season for it. Except for wheat, most crops were planted in the spring. Perhaps Raven was waiting. But what was he living on in the meantime?

"Do you get public assistance?"

"Welfare? No." She didn't appear offended by the question, just disinterested.

Nothing for it but a head-on approach. "Does your father sell drugs?"

The muddy eyes regarded him dubiously through an under-brush of bangs. "Drugs?"

"Marijuana maybe? Heroin?"

"Oh. Illegal drugs, you mean. I don't know."

"You don't know?"

She shook her head. "Daddy is gone quite a bit. We don't bother each other much. We're not really very alike, you know. Here he comes now. You can ask him." A door had opened somewhere in the back of the house. "Daddy," Betony said, hardly raising her voice from its natural monotone, "Mr. Olin wants to talk to you about drugs."

Raven Scion appeared in the hall doorway, looking more Indian than ever in a heavily beaded leather shirt and jeans, head perilously close to the ceiling of the little house. He wore the sunglasses even in this gloom.

"Afternoon, chief. What about drugs? You don't mind a guy smokin' a peace pipe, so to speak, in his own wigwam, do you?"

Betony picked up a magazine and went past her father into the hallway. Matt heard a refrigerator door open. The kitchen must be back there. She was a strangely incurious child.

"I might," Matt said dryly, "if he was passing it around. So to speak." He wondered if there could be a practical reason for those sunglasses. Concealment of telltale pinpoint pupils, for example. "You do have a minor in the house, after all."

"Oh, Betony isn't interested in botanicals," Scion said. He raised his voice. "She isn't like her old man at all, are you, honey?"

"No, Daddy," Betony agreed. "Do you want lunch? I'll have to make soup. There isn't anything else."

"That's fine, sweetheart," Scion said heartily, and, in a lower tone, "A bit stodgy, my Betony. But it takes all types, right? And she's never any trouble. Looks after herself."

"Good cover, too, no doubt," Matt suggested. "Do you have a record, Scion?"

"Raven Scion has no criminal past."

"I can believe that. But how long have you been Raven Scion?"

"I adopted the name to suit my quest. Son of the raven. It is much more appropriate than the original."

"Which was?"

"That," the man said, "is behind me. It's irrelevant."

"I doubt that." Matt rose to go. These little games weren't getting him anywhere.

"If Jack Hargrove dies," he said, "somebody is going to be charged with murder."

Scion held up his hands, palms out. "I wasn't even there, Mr. Policeman. Honest."

"Your daughter was. Not only cover but also a courier maybe? I would advise you to be careful. The judges in these parts are quite capable of indicting a dealer for murder, whether he meant it or not."

"Hey, man," Scion said, "I told you. It wasn't me. Why aren't you out there bugging Vinson? Those fascists are the dangerous ones. And they have to have money to buy all their guns and hate books. Where does ol' Emmett get his? If I was you, I'd hustle on out there and show that guy what a police state is all about."

Driving away, Matt felt dissatisfied. Scion was, in his opinion, little more than a poseur, a middle-aged teenager wanting to look exciting and dangerous. Perhaps that explained his daughter's patient, almost bored, attitude. She had long ago seen through him.

Matt turned the patrol car up a hilly dirt road. Scion had a point about Emmett Vinson. There was always the chance that the bees and the heroin had been meant for Gabe.

Emmett's cabin drowsed in the autumn sun. No sound answered Matt's knock but the distant whine of a power saw. He tried the knob and found the door wasn't locked.

Not so surprising. Few people locked doors in Hayden, but somehow he had expected Emmett to be an exception.

The cabin only had one room with a stove and sink in a corner, a bunk in another. A dilapidated couch, a TV and VCR, a well-stocked bookshelf with more or less what was to be expected: *The Turner Diaries,* innumerable conspiracy theories on both books and tape. Most new looking and, as Scion had implied, probably not cheap. One must pay for one's paranoia. With what? Vinson had no job that Matt knew about.

He was pushing ethical conduct just by being inside the cabin without its owner present. He could not justify opening drawers without a warrant.

He went out to lean against his patrol car, tried to push his tired mind into a decision about what to do next. The warm air smelled of cider from apples fallen and rotting under a tree.

His thoughts jumped to a dark-haired woman in an orange sweater whose soft hands had smelled of bitter flowers as she came across the room to kiss him. He saw her again at the front of a classroom behind a battlement of plants, then sitting in a black dress at the other side of a crowded auditorium, and with the concerned crowd, crossed arms hugging herself against the cold.

The engagement had been a mistake. He could tell himself that quite convincingly as long as he wasn't with her. She had much more in common with someone like Keegan, who was a well-off naturopath like her father had been and, reportedly, extremely attractive to women. Matt had noted her beckoning glance at the doctor during the dance.

Matt had lived without her once. He could do it again. He had been sure of his rightness when he walked out. Had walked out, in fact, because he knew his own fatigue and frustration and was afraid of saying worse. He hadn't intended the separation to be permanent. But she had seemed satisfied with things as they

were, had made no attempt to speak to him. Leaving him to suspect that she had already been regretting their hasty engagement
and was relieved at its crumble.

Up to the time of her father's murder, Regan had always been
spoiled and protected. Granted, she had only been twenty-two
when she lost her mother, but that had caused Alden Culver to
safeguard his daughter all the more. Not that Matt could fault
him for that. *In my own few encounters with her before his murder, I did the same thing.* Regan's indictment for that murder
must have been a rude awakening for her, but she had proved
much tougher than she looked.

It had not taken her long to rebuild her snug nest. These days
she was an executive in a thriving company with her half-sisters
and niece around her.

Matt wasn't sure just why he resented all that. It couldn't be
that he preferred Regan in her fragile mode. He hadn't fallen in
love with her then—not until he felt rising in her a strength of
will to match his own. But now he felt himself to be somehow
extraneous.

Emmett Vinson's old truck jounced up the drive, a pile of
wood and a power saw in the back. Matt stayed where he was.

Vinson picked up something from the seat beside him before
getting out of the truck. It wasn't until he came around the front
of the cab that Matt realized the man was carrying a rifle.

Matt's relaxed stance did not change. In ten-plus years as a
cop, he had discovered it wasn't wise, or safe, to make an issue
out of everything. At the moment, the gun barrel tilted toward
the ground. As long as it stayed that way…still, his senses and
thought processes had sharpened. Leaves crackled with unnatural
loudness under Vinson's feet, the bustle and chatter of squirrels
had gone ominously silent.

Vinson wore a quilted red-and-black flannel shirt over
jeans and work boots. He might have been the quintessential

lumberman with his bushy, dark beard and mustache and heavily sloping shoulders. "What do you want?" he growled.

Matt looked straight at the man's shiny eyes, though he was preternaturally aware of the gun barrel's black hole. "I was just curious about where you were Friday night."

Vinson laughed, a rumbly, subterranean sound. "What business is it of yours? I wasn't at any hokey old high school dance, that's for sure. From what I hear, the kid injected himself with heroin. I suppose his well-heeled folks don't like that idea and are pressuring you to find a fall guy. You had better look elsewhere. I know you guys' methods. You won't get away with it with me."

"Actually," Matt said, "I was thinking that somebody might have mistaken Jack for Gabe Johnson. You were heard to make some comments about Gabe."

Vinson's big shoulders moved, in a shrug or a laugh? He was clearly enjoying himself. "It's a free country—last I heard. Let him stand up for himself, if he don't like it, instead of hiding behind that girl's skirts. Probably, he's the one who got Hargrove on dope to begin with. I don't have any use for the stuff, myself. You won't find any up here."

Matt shoved away from the car. "Does that mean I'm free to look?"

Vinson made a broad, encompassing gesture that brought the gun barrel up again. "Sure, why not? Just as long as I can watch to see that you ain't planting anything." He turned his back and started for the cabin.

Matt followed, dimly aware of the buzz of a motorbike in the distance. He was going to look like a fool, pawing through drawers under the sardonic eye of their owner. But maybe Vinson hadn't expected to be taken up on the offer. Matt left the door open.

The cabin smelled of an unpleasant combination of sweat and must. There were not that many drawers to paw through.

The man got by on the minimum as far as kitchen utensils, clothes, and furniture went. The only thing he had plenty of was his alarmist literature, most of it looking brand-spanking-new and cleaner than anything else in the place.

Preoccupied with what he was doing, Matt didn't pay any attention to the approaching motorbike until it putted into the drive. Vinson, who had been intent on Matt's hands, started and turned, bringing up the rifle.

Matt grabbed a flannel-clad arm and yanked it down, clamping a hand around a surprisingly thin wrist. "Give me the gun."

The shiny eyes stared defiantly into his for a moment, but when Matt applied pressure, Vinson let go. "Hey," he said. "No call for getting physical."

Lucerne Abiel had remained on her bike to observe this little altercation. "Itchy on the trigger finger, isn't he?" she observed.

Matt ejected the shell from the rifle, said to Vinson, "I'll leave it in your truck," and strode out. After clipping the rifle onto a rack in the vehicle's rear window, Matt searched the glove compartment, felt under the seats. Vinson made no objection, snarled at Lucerne from the doorway of the cabin, "What do you want?"

"Thought I'd inquire about your foot," she said with mock solicitousness. "Actually, I wanted to make sure you were being taken seriously as a suspect. I see I needn't have worried."

"Come on," Matt said to her, heading for the cruiser. "I'll give you a lift."

She rolled the bike back so he could hoist it into his trunk, went around to the passenger door.

"She's the one you should be searching," Vinson said, then added with a leer, "Do it for you, if you like."

■ ■ ■

"Don't you know any better," Matt asked Lucerne as they rolled back into town, "than to confront a paranoid like that guy alone?"

"Those types aren't brave except when they're in groups." The girl slouched comfortably in the seat, as if she rode in patrol cars every day. "Always talk bigger than they are. He probably wears those padded shirts to make himself look broader. When I see something that needs doing, I do it. Because usually nobody else is going to bother. There isn't much point in believing something if you don't act on it."

"That attitude could get you killed."

"Yeah, but at least I will have lived. I'll tell you a secret you probably won't believe. Before I came to Hayden, I was the timid, mousy sort. Like Betony." She grinned at his skeptical expression. "Really, I swear. I decided that this was my chance to change since nobody knew me here. So I just did the opposite of everything I'd done before. Now when I'm afraid of something, I go out and do it right off."

"So you're not bored here?"

"Bored?" She gave him an incredulous stare. "Have you been bored here this summer, chief? Run off your feet, more like. This Podunk hops. I swear, I can hardly keep up. In between all the murder and mayhem, I've joined everything in sight. You're looking at a member in good standing of the community theater, the League of Women Voters, and the historical society. Next year we are going to fire that cannon on the square."

"Over my dead body," Matt said.

"Okay." She winked. "If that's how it has to be."

As he pulled the car up in front of her place and she unfolded from the seat, she added, "By the way, chief, you and Miss Culver's studied avoidance of each other is being noticed and commented on. Not to mention that it's got poor Gabe worried. Of course, he may just be fretting about his championship, but he will think it's his responsibility to fix things, and who knows what horrors that will lead to?"

■ ■ ■

That evening, Harold Keegan came to call on Regan. "I'd like to talk to you, Regan," he said, having followed Diane into the living room. "Alone."

With a lift of her brows, Diane said, "I'll be in the kitchen." Regan's two half sisters, Agatha and Gina, had been away for several days helping a sick aunt, so Diane and Regan were on their own.

Keegan sat forward on the couch, hands dangling between his knees. In a denim jacket and jeans, he looked much younger than his forty-odd years. "I want to know what you and Trudy are up to."

A fire snapped and crackled in the fireplace, throwing flickering shadows over his bold features. Regan closed the diary she had been reading, crossed her hands over it. "That's direct enough. There's no secret about it, I guess. Trudy wants to know if her father killed her stepmother forty years ago."

"Why?"

Regan shrugged. "Wouldn't you? If you're into mind-body medicine, you must know some psychology too."

"I tell my patients that what their parents were is irrelevant now, that the present is their choice. I don't believe in living in the past. Trudy has done too much of that already."

Regan looked away to the bouquet on the mantel. The calendulas had already closed for the night. *Perhaps that's why they're considered a symbol of grief. Because every evening they appear to mourn the loss of the light.*

"The woman's son is dying," she said. "I thought helping to investigate was the least I could do."

Keegan shifted impatiently. "She's pinned all of her hopes on Jack. She has been on hold for eighteen years herself. Whether he lives or dies, she's going to have to continue."

"I understand that she keeps the books for Speedwell. What's wrong with that?"

"Nothing, if that's what you're meant for. Trudy isn't. She was a good doctor. Sensitive."

"Was she?" Looking straight into his eyes, she could tell why Trudy avoided them. The man was mesmerizing. He should include hypnosis in his alternative treatments. "She doesn't think so."

"That was her problem. Lack of confidence. But she would have gotten over it if it hadn't been for Lance Porter. That guy has a lot to answer for."

"I don't know," Regan said, tearing her gaze away to focus on the fire. "This is important to Trudy right now, for whatever reasons. I doubt that I'm going to find out anything new after all this time, but maybe I can gather whatever information there is. Was your father in love with Vita Dawson?"

"No."

"You were five or six at the time. Do you remember that day at all?" She was looking at his face again, avoiding the eyes, trying to figure out what it was that made him so attractive. He was never hesitant or tentative; perhaps that was it, not self-conscious either. And he kept all his attention and energy focused on whomever he was with at the moment.

"No," he said again. He apparently didn't feel the need to elaborate. "Let's concentrate on Jack Junior. There's still a chance to save him." He stood. Clearly, he had said what he came to say.

"Don't hurt her," Regan said quickly. "Trudy, I mean. I don't know you well enough to tell whether what she believes is possible, that you want her out of the way. But I can believe that what you want, you'll get. Dedicated sorts like you can justify your actions by saying it's for the greater good. But it's not necessary for you to own Speedwell to have it. I'm sure that you can figure out a better way."

He lifted a brow at her. "Trying to appeal to a killer's vanity?

Not a bad idea, if I were one. I'm a Christian, remember, and a healer. I don't do murder. Frankly, I don't care who runs Speedwell, as long as they run it along the lines Amos and my father intended. I think you're misreading who has the upper hand here. I love Trudy. After her accident, I asked her to marry me, but she wouldn't have any of it."

The corners of his eyes crinkled in genuine amusement at Regan's befuddlement. "Life just doesn't make sense sometimes, does it? But you have to admit, it's quite a ride." There was no trace of self-pity in his tone.

"Speaking of which, how's it going for you, Regan? No, wait, let me guess." His tilted his head toward the fire, the half-consumed cup of ginger tea on a tray beside her. "You're feeling the cold already, and your stomach is uneasy."

"I know," she said. "Nerves."

"Your father did say you were the strongest proof of the mind-body connection that he would ever need." Keegan sat again, leaned toward her. "Keep in mind, Regan, that your body believes whatever your mind tells it, whether your mind is right or not. A curse does sometimes work, if the victim believes it will. Tell your body it's going to die, and it will be happy to oblige. That's why," he said as his face hardened, "I get so angry at the doctor who pronounces a death sentence on a patient. To me, that's equivalent to voodoo. Of course, the converse is also true. What did Jesus always say to those he healed? Your *faith* has saved you."

He touched her hand. "You're like Trudy, much better at anticipating rain than sun."

He rose again. "She even considered my proposal just another try to get Speedwell. The woman does *not* like me."

"Of course she doesn't," Regan said shortly, getting up from her chair. "You warned her about Lance."

"But I was right."

"That was the problem." Regan led the way toward the front door. "I assume you didn't tell her your feelings before her accident?"

"I didn't know them then. I did know that my father and Amos were hoping we would marry. I was still in my twenties; I wanted to make my own decisions. Trudy and I had more or less grown up together. I didn't think of her in that way, or not until she took up with Lance. I admit, my opinion of him was tinged with jealousy. It provoked several scenes between Trudy and me."

Which drove her right into his arms, Regan thought but didn't say it. *And what woman is going to believe you want her, handicapped and disfigured, when you showed no interest before?* She turned on the porch to face him. "Eighteen years. I must say, Dr. Keegan, you are either a very patient man—"

"Or a liar?" His grin, under the stark illumination of the porch light, looked ambiguous.

"On the night Jack collapsed," she said, "when Trudy and I arrived at the sanitarium, I went in to get Amos. He sent one of the nurses to find you. Where were you?"

"Just coming in from out back. I'd been getting a breath of fresh air in the gardens. Why?" His hand closed around her forearm. "Something else happened that night, didn't it?"

A car was pulling into the drive. She turned to watch it, stiffened, squinting against the headlights. "A dummy," she said absently, "thrown in front of the van on the curve. Fortunately, Trudy was expecting it."

"And what, or who, are *you* expecting?" he asked. "Hey, what did I tell you? Chest up, and breathe!"

Her heart was thumping in an erratic and uncomfortable way as a car door slammed and there was the sound of footsteps on gravel.

"I *am* breathing," she said crossly.

"No you're not; you're whiffing." Keegan grabbed her upper arms from behind, pulling them back. "Better?"

"Yes," she had to admit. Her respiration felt freer, more confident, her pulse steadier, though still rapid.

"Any guy," he murmured, "who makes you shrink isn't worth it. Remember that." And louder, "Evenin', Matt. Any news about Jack?"

"No." The police chief stood at the bottom of the porch steps, regarding them in a cool, professional manner.

"I had better be going," the doctor said, releasing her arms. "I'll talk to you more about this later, Regan."

Matt turned his head to watch Keegan's exit, turned it back to say to her, "Gabe says you kept the note off that bouquet somebody left for him."

"Yes."

"I'd like to have it please." He hadn't moved from his distant position.

Warm with anger, Regan turned on her heel to flounce inside and up the stairs, leaving the door open behind her.

Diane, just coming out of the kitchen, started to say something. Catching sight of Matt, she desisted.

In her room, Regan jerked hangers about in her closet, making a satisfying clatter, until she found the dress she had worn for her talk on Friday. The scrap of paper was still buried deep in its pocket.

Diane had gone out on the porch to speak to Matt. She was having heavy weather of it. He was replying only in monosyllables.

Regan interrupted without ceremony. "Here you go." She stayed at the top of the steps, making him reach for it, knowing that she was being childish but not caring. *"Darling,"* she added in a sugary tone.

She had the satisfaction of seeing a muscle jerk in his cheek before he snatched the paper out of her hand and turned away.

"I am happy to see we are all being so adult about this," Diane said, as she followed Regan back inside. "What *has* gotten into you two?"

The warmth had faded fast. Regan felt cold—and bereft. "Actually," she said, "if it hadn't been for Dr. Keegan, I probably would have been conciliatory, eager to please. Whatever the doctor may or may not be, he talks to a woman like she's intelligent, an equal. He leaves you," she added wryly, "standing taller just for having been with him. It's a heady feeling. Why couldn't I have fallen for somebody like him?"

She returned to the living room. Diane paused to look down the empty drive before closing the door. "I would shape up fast if I were you, Matt," she murmured under her breath. "The good doctor strikes me as being one fairly dangerous man."

CHAPTER 7

And with him rises weeping...

Trudy would have agreed heartily with that assessment. She was alone in her living room, her wheelchair drawn up to her desk, sorting through the box of musty papers when the doorbell rang. The others had gone to bed already, worn out by the events of the past twenty-four hours. But Trudy had wanted to stay near the phone. She had insisted she would stretch out in her recliner if she felt tired.

Wheeling to the door, she squinted out the peephole that had been installed at her level. Of course, this gave her mostly a view of the caller's chest, but this chest was recognizable enough.

Caution struggled with curiosity, and curiosity won. She unbolted the door, pulling it open a few inches. "What do *you* want?" she said to Howard Keegan.

"To talk to you." He insinuated himself through the opening with ease. "I've just been to see Regan Culver."

"Snooping. It figures." She rolled back into the center of the room, set the brakes on her chair. "I suppose you charmed her into disclosing all."

"The part about the dummy anyway," he said, taking a seat

in her recliner. "What were you thinking, Trudy? Why didn't you report it?"

"Just to be told it must have been some kids pulling a Halloween prank? That's what they would have said, and you know it. That's what you counted on their saying if anybody survived."

"Why did you let me in, Trudy, if you think I'm a killer?"

"You would be a fool to try anything here with people upstairs. And you're not a fool."

"No? Sometimes I wonder. And sometimes I wonder if you really want me to kill you. You don't have a death wish, do you?"

She shook her head. "You adapt to an abbreviated life after a while."

"A life that you have abbreviated deliberately. You could be doing much more. Why won't you learn to drive a car with hand controls?"

She just shook her head again wearily. It was an old argument. "There aren't that many places I need to go."

"Strangely enough," he said, "you look better tonight than you have in some time. Because you're doing something. You have a purpose. Of course, green was always your color too."

She did not look down at her jade silk blouse. She did not trust his compliments either.

"Why do you want to know what happened to your father and Vita?"

"For Jack."

"How can knowing the details help him? Better to leave it vague, I would think. You don't know what kind of mess you could be stirring up."

"Are you afraid something might come out about your father?"

"My father? Don't bring my father into your dislike of me. It's best to leave it alone, Trudy. You don't want to hurt Amos."

Her eyes narrowed. "You devil! I suppose you're going to try to sneak in the fact that Amos had the best motive for murder. Both of them had life insurance policies with Speedwell as beneficiary. Two hundred thousand dollars all told."

His face was pale but stern. "Yes, that got Speedwell out of its financial crisis, but it wasn't what I meant."

"What *did* you mean? I've never known you to pull any punches. Why don't you just come out and say it? 'Your father was a killer, Trudy, and your son's either a junkie or a suicide. Deal with it.'"

"I won't say it, because I don't believe it." He was out of the chair then and bending over her. "But you do, don't you? You're afraid that somehow you weren't enough for either of them. That they didn't love you enough to live. But you aren't willing to drag that monster out into the light and take a good look at it, are you?"

She flinched away from him. "Why don't you just hit me? It would be much more humane."

"Do you really think so little of yourself as all that?"

She turned her face aside.

"Just as you believe that a man would only say he loves you to get what he wants. I am *not* Lance Porter, Trudy. Look at me. What do you really have against me?" He reached out to tilt her face toward him, but she kept her eyes skewed stubbornly away.

"You *are* beautiful, darling."

She did look at him then, reflexively. Hand still holding her chin, he said, "Why do you think Amos still wants to leave Speedwell to you? Not because he feels sorry for you. He wouldn't risk his precious hospital on a pseudo-emotion like that. It's because he knows you're the best person to run it. Why do you think I've waited eighteen years for you?"

Her chin came up. "I'm not one you can charm, Howard. You'll have to kill me."

"Is that what you really want?" He put both hands around her neck. "To be dead so you can be proven right about me? Well, it's not going to happen, and you know it. Or you would be frightened right now. It occurs to me maybe I've been too kind. I haven't pushed you enough. Nobody has pushed you. We all wanted to allow you time. We've allowed you too much time. No more! You've already cast me as your nemesis. I'm going to start playing my part. You're a doctor. I'm going to insist to Amos that you start acting like one. You had a contract with Speedwell, you know, a contract you never fulfilled. I'm going to bring that up. I'm going to point out that, if you're going to run Speedwell when he's gone, you had better start now. Because when the time comes, I'm not going to do it for you, missy, believe me!"

She jerked her head in a futile attempt to dislodge his hands. "And what happens," she demanded tearfully, "the first time I wet myself on the job?"

"You do what your patients have to do under the same circumstances. Clean yourself up and go on."

"Amos won't listen to you."

"Oh, won't he? I've been told I'm pretty good at bringing people around to my way of thinking. If all else fails, I'll threaten to resign."

Her eyes widened in alarm. "No, you can't do that to Speedwell! We wouldn't survive—"

"Oh, yes you would. If you wanted to badly enough. And I'm going to harry you to the point you'll *pray* to see the last of me. You wanted an enemy, sweetheart, and you've got one. It's gloves-off time. New game, new rules. From now on, you get treated just like everybody else. If you don't pull your weight, you're history."

He grinned at the alert pink in her face, her quick breathing. "*That's* brought you awake, Sleeping Beauty."

Her color came up in earnest then. She reached up to tear his hands away from her throat. "You're bluffing! You love Speedwell as much as Amos does. You would never leave here."

"I love other things more. If that's what it takes, that's what I'll do. You should never accuse a male of bluffing, love. That just makes him more determined."

"Don't call me that! Get out of here!"

"But that's what you are to me. Why shouldn't I say it? It's called honesty." He straightened, turned toward the door.

"I can't believe even you would be cruel enough to do this to me now," she said, "with Jack the way he is."

He looked back. "I think Jack should know his mother can go on without him. It's what he would want." The door closed with a decisive bang.

■ ■ ■

Diane was called away abruptly on Sunday evening. The aunt whom Agatha and Gina had been attending was dying. Standing beside the car, Diane said to Regan, "Are you sure you're going to be all right here alone? I'd feel better if you would come along."

"Your great-aunt has never met me," Regan said. "I would just confuse the poor woman. Besides, the kids are counting on me to sit with Jack tomorrow." She didn't add that Trudy was also counting on her to illumine a forty-year-old mystery.

"Well, be careful," Diane said, hugging her good-bye. "Whatever happened to Jack isn't your business, you know. Leave it to Matt. Speaking of Matt, if I could just know that he would be checking up on you..." She trailed off at Regan's expression. "All right. I'll drop it. I'll call you tomorrow morning about eight. If she dies, we'll probably have to be there for several days, until after the funeral."

The following morning, Regan breakfasted alone on the terrace with the portable phone beside her plate. In the garden below, purple asters and gold chrysanthemums poked up through drifts of fallen leaves. She had stirred baked apple and cinnamon into her hot oatmeal and, as she ate, tried not to think of anything but the cereal, the flowers, the sun already burning off the chill of night. It was going to be another unusually warm day. No frost yet. A heavy dew though.

The calendulas dripped with fat globules of water—like tears. They were just opening their petals to the sun and would turn their heads to follow it faithfully all day. That constancy would continue until the first snows, probably. Calendula was a very hardy flower, had received its name because in certain parts of the world it would be blooming at the *calends*—beginning—of every month.

She opened Vita's diary again to the last written page. Because Regan was also interested in gardening and alternative medicine, the journal had not been dull precisely. But neither had she found the writer attractive. *Perhaps it's just because I'm on Trudy's side, so to speak. I want to dislike Vita. But she seems to have only valued her plants and patients as a means of showing off her own cleverness.*

Vita had been more than pleased with herself over the final month, had made several cryptic references to October 26. In her last entry, on the twenty-fifth, she had written, "I daresay I will have much to report tomorrow night."

She had been up to something. This coyness as to what, though characteristic, was also aggravating. But what was lacking was any animosity toward her husband. She clearly considered her marriage a success. Whatever had caused her uncharacteristic rage must have disabused her of that notion. Could she have found out that Jack was having an affair? That might have done it, not so much from hurt love as hurt pride.

The telephone rang. Regan leaned back in her chair to speak into it.

"She died last night," Diane said. "A couple of hours after I arrived."

"I'm sorry." Regan didn't think there would be any heartrending grief over this death. The old woman was going in season after a long, productive life.

"The earliest we could schedule the funeral is Tuesday. Then we have to close up her apartment. We probably won't make it back until Wednesday afternoon sometime."

"That's okay," Regan said, looking down over her quiet garden. "I'm fine."

Diane put her mother, Agatha, on then. "Diane's been telling me about you and Matt," Agatha said. "Cut out this nonsense and call him! Your pride is going to be cold comfort, I can assure you."

Regan had to smile, remembering when she herself had delivered a similar lecture on pride to Agatha. Agatha had secretly suffered near destitution for years rather than ask her father or her hated half-sister for help. Things had changed drastically in the past few months. Relieved of her creditors and her constant worry, Agatha was almost a different person.

Oh, she was still abrupt, opinionated, and impatient. She would never be widely popular. But now she was truly a big sister to Regan—something both of them would have considered impossible before the summer's events.

"I know," Regan said. "But I don't think we can reconcile if I give in to him, Agatha. If he would demand that I sacrifice what is so important to me, how far would I have to go? What would be next? My career? I'm no longer sure he really loves me at all. Back when he was first attracted to me, he was angry at himself for it, you know. Because he thought I was a spoiled brat. Actually, when you compare my childhood to his, I probably was. He overcame that resentment for a while, but now I think it's surfacing again. It's too bad for him that he didn't discover me a year earlier. Back then I would have been easily convinced it was all my fault. Now I don't think so."

"Of course it's not your fault," Agatha said impatiently. "You can't help it that you were born well-off, and he can't help it that he wasn't. You two should have discussed this ages ago. But if I know you, you avoided the whole subject, tried to pretend that it didn't matter. Now somebody is going to have to make the first move. And whether it's fair or not, it will probably have to be you. The longer you let it go, the harder it will be. Grudges set, you know, like concrete, and then you're trapped."

The flowers blurred as Regan's eyes flooded with tears. She and Agatha both knew how hard grudges could set and the severity of the blow it had taken to shatter theirs.

"I'll think about it, Agatha. I'm still wearing his ring anyway. I'm not going to make it easy for him. If he wants to end the engagement, he's going to have to say so. I never thought that you approved of my relationship with Matt."

Agatha laughed. "Oh, I kind of like the guy. He doesn't let public opinion dictate to him. From what Diane tells me about this Hargrove thing, it sounds like he's putting people's backs up again already. And you two were bound to clash eventually. You're both strong-willed. Diane says Howard Keegan has been around. Anything doing there?"

"No. Honestly, Agatha, Keegan's a magnetic type, but I am not in love with him. Just a small crush maybe. Too bad he wasn't Jack's father. They have a lot in common. Maybe Jack modeled himself after the doctor, come to think of it. And Amos. They're all easy to like."

"And Matt isn't," Agatha concluded. "It's up to you, kid. Decide how much you really want the guy. Because it's never going to be easy between you two. Whatever you decide, we'll back you."

"Thanks, Agatha." Regan swallowed and smiled. "Though I

think there was a little bit of challenge in that last part. Like you're implying I could darn well make it work if I really wanted to."

"Hey," Agatha said, "best way to get people gung-ho about anything. Question their ability to do it and let pride kick in. Pride does have its uses. By the way, if you're determined to become mixed up with the unfortunate Hargrove family, watch your back. I was only ten or twelve when that doctor shot his wife, and I still remember how upset Father was at the time. He knew Jack Dawson and insisted there must be more to it than what they were saying at the time."

"I know. Daddy told me about it too. Do you remember them at all—Jack and Vita?"

"Father took Gina and me down to Speedwell a couple of times when we were children. We wanted to swim. Yes, I remember Vita. Pretty, energetic, charming."

Charm was something of an epithet to Agatha, who didn't have much of it. "You didn't like her."

"Oh, kids can take unreasonable aversions, you know. I was eager to get in the water, not make polite talk to an adult. She was smiling and asking us questions, but she wasn't really interested in the answers. Then again, most adults aren't. Do you remember Vita Hargrove Dawson, Gina?"

"Smug," Gina opined succinctly in the background.

"I knew she'd hit it on the head," Agatha said. "Here, I'll put her on."

"Smug," Gina repeated agreeably into the receiver. "The woman was smug. How are you doing, Regan? You're just being obstinate, you know. It's a family trait. You can rationalize it backward and forward and upside down, but you're peeved because he walked out on you, and you're going to make him crawl back. Except that I doubt he will. And then, like Agatha said, you're both going to be miserable. That doesn't move things forward, does it? Yes, Vita was self-satisfied. At least you're not that. Rather the opposite, actually. You know, you're just going to worry this whole thing with Matt around until you make yourself sick. So *do* something! Going back to Vita, I suppose she couldn't really help it. She had been indulged by her father. Good men make the worst fathers sometimes, you know. And she had never had anything nasty happen to her to smack her out of her conviction that she was the center of the universe. Until the murder, which was much too drastic to help."

I wonder if I was like that, Regan thought, stroking the black cat, which had just jumped up into her lap, smelling of sage. *Before my mother died. No, I was always a little insecure. Even as a child. Not pretty or gregarious enough to be that confident. Maybe that's more of a blessing than I realized.*

"What about her husband?" she asked.

"Ambitious," Gina said. "The most ambitious men are the ones who were deprived in childhood, you know. But nothing they attain is ever quite enough to make them sure they won't somehow slide back." Regan thought of the Speedwell road tilting toward dark water and shivered.

"And Galen was one of life's resenters," Gina concluded. "A lot of intellectual pride, but no confidence to go with it. We were down there quite often, you know, that summer before the shooting. About the only way we got to see Daddy was to ride along with him when he was going somewhere. Amos Hargrove was wonderful. He used to give us slippery elm to chew. Any anise smell like that always takes me back to summer afternoons on Speedwell Lake."

"I keep thinking of Thanksgiving, myself," Regan said. "Probably because Gato has been in the sage. We'll have to figure out what we're going to do for the holidays this year."

"I vote for staying home and taking it easy. I think we all deserve it after the year we've had. We'll hibernate, gather around the fire, and eat ourselves sick."

Thinking back over the past months—Agatha's bankruptcy, Diane's losing her teaching job, Gina's divorce, her own arrest for her father's murder, and their joining together to save the beleaguered herb farm—Regan had to agree that they did deserve some rest, some respite. But not yet.

"It'll give us something to look forward to," she said, "through all this other stuff. I'd better go now, Gina. I have to be at the hospital at nine."

She met Lucerne in the hospital parking lot, and they walked together through the sliding doors past the emergency room and toward intensive care. "Are you sure you don't mind missing your classes?" Regan asked. Unable to get hold of Gabe the previous evening, Regan had called Lucerne instead, and the girl had offered to take Diane's place.

"What do you think?" Lucerne fluffed up the hair that had been scrunched by her motorbike helmet and took off her goggles as they came into the dimmer light of the hallway. She gave Regan a sardonic look. "Besides, I was supposed to be Gabe's partner for biology lab today. He will finish the experiment much faster without me, and he'll also have the satisfaction of telling me off about my irresponsibility. Then when he gets quite done, I shall raise a tragic, misunderstood face and say, 'But Gabe, I was at the hospital with Jack.' After which he should feel ashamed of himself but probably won't."

Regan couldn't help laughing. "Well, you probably won't be the only absentee. This unnatural weather can't last—"

"Don't do that," Lucerne said. "Why do people, when things are good, always expect the worst? Why can't they just enjoy it?"

"Probably," Regan said with a sigh as they came in sight of the comatose teenager, "because a lot of times the worst happens. Good morning, boys."

Chris and Ken got up from their chairs on either side of

Jack's bed, stretched hugely. "I've never known six hours to go so slowly," Chris said.

"No change?" Regan asked, though the answer to that was obvious.

"No change," Ken said bleakly. "Here's the list of doctors and nurses who are allowed to treat Jack. Keegan was in, by the way, left a few minutes ago. He didn't do anything except talk to him."

Chris was already loping toward the door. "We'd better step on it if we're going to make the last half of first period."

"Hey," Ken objected, "we have a good excuse to skip, but you don't got the brains to use it."

Chris laughed and waved in return.

Lucerne had moved around to the other side of Jack's bed and was talking matter-of-factly to him. "Jack, kid, you're being a real pain. All of us want to get out of here and play hooky, but you're putting a damper on things. Come on; wake up." She clapped her hands sharply together, but the recumbent figure didn't stir.

Ken edged closer to Regan. "Where would Chief Olin be this time of day?"

Regan was careful not to appear surprised. "It's hard to say. Since there's not as much call for him in the morning, he sometimes doesn't come into his office until the afternoon. Then he usually works late into the evening. He doesn't really have set hours since he's on call all the time. I imagine he's already out and about today, though, with a case like this to handle. If you want to talk to him, your best bet would probably be to phone him. He has a beeper; he'll call you back."

Ken hadn't been looking at her as she talked. Rather, he had been watching Jack's lack of response to Lucerne's urgings.

"Yeah," he said with a grim air of decision. "I'll do that." There was still that bleakness there, though, as if he knew it was going to cost him.

He left the room, passing the elderly woman who was just coming in to sit beside her husband across the way. "Hi again!" Lucerne called to her.

"Good morning." The woman timidly approached the foot of Jack's bed. "Is he...?"

"No change," Lucerne said.

"Poor boy. I think those are the worst words in the language: no change. My husband..." She glanced back at the old man. Regan didn't hear the rest. She had gone across to a plastic chair by the window to set down the books and magazines she had brought with her. The window overlooked the parking lot.

She saw Chris driving away in an old blue clunker. Then Ken emerged, strode across to his Harley. He still looked resolute. He swung a leg over the seat, unhooked his helmet.

The flat cracking noise lifted the boy, slammed him forward over the handlebars where he hung for a suspended instant before uncoiling sideways to flop on his back onto the blacktop. A scream ripped Regan's throat; she whirled on an open-mouthed Lucerne. "Stay with Jack! Whatever happens, don't take your eyes off him! Don't let anybody near!" Regan ran out into the hall where others had frozen in place. "Call the police! A boy has been shot!"

It would take her too long to run around by the emergency entrance. Another door at the end of a short hall opened directly onto the parking lot. She had noticed it on that interminable first night she had spent with the Hargroves here. It had a sign that read, "Emergency exit only. If door is opened, an alarm will sound."

She ran at it, all out, dodged around a man who emerged from a room and tried to grab her arm, scarcely felt the bang of the push bar against the palms of her hands, scarcely heard the blat of the alarm above the uproar in her own mind. *Wait! Wait...*

The blacktop radiated warmth. A car window dissolved into splinters beside her and something stung her cheek. She disregarded it. She could not even feel the slap of her feet on pavement—just a burning in her chest, a gasping in of the bright, hard air.

When she dropped down beside Ken, his eyes seemed incredibly blue, reflecting the sky, the spreading splotch on his shirt a garish red. She put both palms over that stain and pressed hard, trying to push back the heat of young life that was running out through her fingers.

He smiled crookedly at her, even his teeth unbelievably bright. "Well, I was gonna do the right thing. Think God will—" He coughed pink froth. "Give me credit for that?" He finished on a gasp.

"Nobody gets any credit, Ken. Ask for mercy."

The blue was dulling, but his eyes remained fixed intently, desperately, on her face. His lips moved helplessly.

"God comes," Regan told him. "When you call him, he comes. You don't have to say it aloud. Just think it. Jesus Christ, have mercy."

The faltering lips framed the word *mer-cy.*

A car screeched behind them, stopped. Then Matt was kneeling across from her, his big hands holding hers down, pressing her ring painfully. "Hold on, Ken," he said. "You can make it."

The slightest of negatory motions, the crooked grin again. The kid knew.

"Who was it?" Matt asked then, quickly, urgently. "*Who,* Ken?"

"Jack." The word was barely audible. "It was Jack Dawson." Ken coughed and his head slipped sideways.

■ ■ ■

Regan had no sooner dashed from the room than Lucerne jumped up to grasp the old lady by the shoulders, to push her firmly into the chair on the other side of the bed. "Please," the teenager said in a tight voice, "sit there and help me watch him. It could be meant as a distraction. What's your name?"

"Estelle. Did somebody get shot?"

People were rushing past them to look out the window. Lucerne turned her back on it. "Yes," she said. "I'm Lucerne. It must have been either Chris or Ken. Probably Ken. He left last."

She put both hands on one of Jack's arms, shook it urgently. "It's Ken, Jack. Remember how you always worried about him? Wake up, Jack, please."

"I never dreamed this sort of thing could happen here," Estelle said, taking Jack's other hand between her gnarled ones. "TV, yes, but not really. Not here."

A nurse approached them. She looked calmer than the others, small, red-haired, and neat. "Time for his shot," she said. She wore a nametag that read Marie Armstrong. Lucerne glanced at the list, nodded.

The old lady turned also to squint up at the nametag much closer to her. Then one of those gnarled hands shot up to grasp the smooth round arm that held the hypodermic. "No! You, go away! You're not Marie!"

The nurse smiled patiently. "Of course I am, Estelle. You've just forgotten."

Estelle now had both hands around that arm, crying to Lucerne, "Don't let her! She isn't Marie!"

The nurse's tolerant expression said, *Old folks, you know. We have to make allowances.*

"Now, Estelle." Lucerne stood and edged around the foot of the bed. "Her name is on the list. We don't want to get paran—" Lucerne's long, purple-nailed fingers shot out like fangs into the nurse's wrist above the glove. Marie gasped and dropped the hypodermic. Lucerne caught it.

Young face implacable, Lucerne said, "Get out of here before I stab this into *your* arm."

The nurse said some words that caused Lucerne to move forward threateningly, hand raised and thumb on the plunger.

"Fake!" Lucerne screamed. "Fake nurse! Get her!" The false Marie scuttled out of the room. A few people turned to look, but the rest seemed too preoccupied by what was happening outside.

"I do hate bad language," Lucerne said. "It is so unimaginative. We can't chase her without leaving Jack. We probably wouldn't have any luck anyway. She'll ditch that red hair first thing. Probably the green eyes too. Tinted contacts. Nobody has eyes that green except a cat." Lucerne wrapped the hypodermic in a facial tissue, tucked it into her purse, which she placed on the edge of the bed in front of her where she could keep an eye on it.

Estelle was trembling. "I didn't think you would believe me. When you get older, people don't, you know. They just give you those indulgent looks, as if they were patting you on the head. It's so maddening!"

"Little kids don't like it either," Lucerne said. "I know I didn't. Temporary new rules for immediate crisis. Nobody but us gets within arm's-length of Jack no matter what the nametags say."

■　■　■

"He's slipping away," Matt said. "Listen, I'm going to put him over my shoulder, make a run for it. You have a cut on your face, but it looks shallow. Lie down right up against the car. If you don't move, you'll be all right."

Regan stretched out obediently on the warm blacktop. She felt his running footsteps and clenched her eyes and fists against the sound of shots she felt sure must come, must rip into that broad, uniformed back. Only when a door slammed did she relax, cheek down against the comforting heat.

■　■　■

When Regan returned to the intensive care ward, Lucerne was practically leaning against Jack's shoulder on one side, the old lady equally close on the other. They were holding his hands tightly and looked scared.

"Ken?" Lucerne said.

Regan nodded dumbly, sat down in a chair by the foot of the bed.

Lucerne's mouth tightened. "Bad?"

Regan nodded again, not trusting herself to speak.

"I never thought," Estelle said, "that it would come here. The drugs. The shooting. The young dying."

"But it hasn't," Lucerne snapped. "That's why none of this makes sense!"

Regan looked at her hazily. "It hasn't?"

"Oh, a few kids experiment. Any school anywhere is going to have that. But the drug of choice in these parts is still alcohol. And they're pretty careful about that. Half the guys in high school are either on the football team or want to be. And the ones who are know plenty of others are willing and eager to replace them if they get kicked off. When your coach is a police chief who pretty much knows everything that's going on, you just say no, believe me. Especially since Ken got the ax last year for smoking pot." Her face twisted momentarily. "Ken isn't a bad kid, you know. He's just wild, not mean. He'll straighten out eventually, given a chance. None of this makes any sense!"

She gestured toward the elderly lady. "They would have gotten Jack, too, if it hadn't been for Estelle here. A nurse came in to give him a shot. She had the right name, one on the list I mean, but it was the wrong nurse."

Estelle, face pale, nodded firmly at Regan. "I know what Marie looks like. She's been very kind to me. And that wasn't her. Marie is large with dark hair. So I made a scene. You know what they say, bad things happen because people are afraid to make a scene."

"That's wonderful," Regan said. "You're both wonderful. If

you hadn't kept your heads..." She shuddered then couldn't seem to stop.

"Are you all right?" Lucerne half-rose.

Regan waved her back to her seat. "Yes, I'll b-be—" She stopped as her voice shook, too, concentrated hard on her hands until they stilled. "I can smell the blood. I must not have washed my hands well enough. You're right. None of this makes any sense. When Matt asked Ken who shot him, he said Jack Dawson. It couldn't have been. Jack Dawson has been dead for forty years. Even if he weren't, he would have to be at least seventy by now."

Matt Olin came into the room accompanied by another police officer. "Miss Culver," the officer said, "I'm Lieutenant Woods of the Clearview Police Department. We're fortunate Matt happened to be on his way in here to see Jack and was able to get to the scene so fast."

Regan stood up, looking at Matt. His skin was gray. His uniform was damp and splotchy in places where he had tried to wash out the blood.

He shook his head. "Dead when I carried him in. They couldn't bring him back. They tried, but the doctor knew it was hopeless from the moment he saw him."

Lucerne turned her face momentarily against Jack's sheet. Regan let the words slide over her. She had known they were coming.

"A nurse was in here while I was gone who tried to give Jack a shot. She wasn't who she was supposed to be."

Lucerne reached into her purse to produce the hypodermic. "I took it away from her."

Woods accepted the syringe. "Forcefully, I assume." He was looking at her broken fingernails.

Lucerne wiped at her eyes with the sheet. "She'll have some scratches on her wrist. The only other thing I'm sure of is that she was small. The red hair and green eyes were probably assumed, but it's hard to fake short."

"Age?"

Lucerne and Estelle looked at each other. "Thirtyish?" Lucerne said.

"It's hard to say," Estelle finally decided. "She could have been in her twenties, but she looked more experienced than that."

"Or as old as forty," Lucerne said. "You can do things with makeup...I was concentrating on the syringe."

"Are you sure," Matt said, "that it was a woman?"

Lucerne and Estelle looked at each other again. Estelle nodded tentatively. "I think so. I didn't notice any strangeness. In the movies, when a man dresses up like a woman, you can usually tell by the way he moves. Of course, then they're usually trying to make it obvious, for laughs. I suppose a small, slender, fair man might be able—"

At that moment, Howard Keegan came striding down the ward toward them. "I don't have much time," he said. "I have appointments I don't want to cancel. But the administrator here called and suggested we move Jack to Speedwell. It would be easier to guard him out there. We're a smaller operation so strangers wouldn't be able to sneak in as easily. Trudy could move right in with him, if she wanted. They're willing to loan us any extra equipment we might need provided we take Jack off their hands. They're worried about the safety of their staff and other patients."

"And *you* aren't?" Woods inquired.

"We have more of a commitment to Jack than this hospital does. All of our nurses know and like him. Well?"

"That's out of my jurisdiction," Woods said. He looked at Matt. "You certainly don't have time to play guard, and we can't leave it up to the kids after this. Maybe if we asked the state guys to pitch in..."

"I'll call them." Matt started away, stopped to look at Keegan. "I hear you left the hospital shortly before Ken did, Doctor."

"I came in about eight-fifteen, stayed half an hour or so."

"What time did you get back to Speedwell?"

"I haven't been back yet. They called me on my cell phone."

"Where have you been in the meantime?"

The doctor steadily met his gaze. "I stopped at one of the Clearview churches."

"To do what?"

A slight smile touched the doctor's mouth. "To pray for Jack. If you're asking for an alibi, nobody was there but me—and God."

He turned to Lieutenant Woods. "I have Dr. Hargrove's permission to move her son. I'll scare up an ambulance. If you two"—he nodded at Regan and Lucerne—"will agree to ride along with him and stay until the police guard arrives, we'll see that you get back. If they can't provide a police guard, we'll hire some professionals from a security agency." And he was off again.

"A man of action," Lucerne sighed.

"Trudy must be torn," Regan said. "She wants Jack with her, but she doesn't trust Dr. Keegan."

"Don't!" Lucerne begged. "Don't tell me that he is going to be the villain of this piece. I won't believe it. Did you know that guy cured my migraines just by doing a little realignment of my skull plates? A guy with those kind of hands can't be a killer."

"He could probably snap your neck just as easily," Woods said.

■ ■ ■

"Howard was out to see me last night," Trudy informed Regan. "Fortunately, nobody else was there at the time. Why did you tell him about the dummy?"

A police car had been waiting in the driveway at Speedwell when the ambulance arrived. The trooper looked ridiculously young but alert. While Jack was being wheeled in, Trudy had motioned Regan aside.

"Why not?" Regan said with spirit. "If he did it, he already knew anyhow, didn't he?"

Trudy gave her a shrewd stare. "Don't let him get to you too, Regan. When he's with you, it's hard not to believe him."

"If you distrust him so much, why did you let him move Jack?"

"Because it's like he said, I can keep an eye on Jack here. And frankly, if Jack and I have to go, I'd prefer that it be together."

Regan felt a stab of apprehension. "Trudy, you wouldn't..."

"Kill myself? Oh, no. I considered it years ago after I had my accident, but I couldn't do that to Amos. If Jack goes, I'll have to be dispatched at the same time or soon after. There would be no point otherwise. Everyone will believe Howard brought us here to protect us, when actually it's just the opposite. He's good, you know. He's very good."

"Then why didn't he *dispatch* you, as you put it, last night?" Regan asked. "Why aren't you more afraid of him?"

Trudy shrugged. "Fear is a hard emotion to sustain. Live with it long enough, and it leaches out of you. I would feel it at the last minute, probably. I think I've always known that guy was going to be the death of me. One way or another."

"That guy" came striding up then with a handful of folders. "We're late for rounds, Trudy. We have three new patients today besides Jack. They're all yours." He dumped the folders in her lap. "Here are the preadmittance interviews I did with them. You'll want to give those a quick once-over first." He was off again then, leaving Regan open-mouthed.

"What did I tell you?" Trudy asked wryly, wheeling herself after him. "The man does get his way."

CHAPTER 8

> *These are flowers of middle summer,*
> *and I think they are given to men of middle age.*

Matt decided to set some inquiries in motion concerning Jack Dawson. He didn't think a dying teenager would lie. Still, Ken probably had never seen a picture of Dawson. He must have obtained his information some other way. And it might have been only a suspicion or a misunderstanding.

Matt doubted the shooter he was seeking was the original. Having heard the old story of the Dawson murder-suicide from his predecessor, Matt realized that forty years ago Jack might have simply staged his suicide then sought help from his family in Trafalgar. The Dawsons had been a shiftless, shady bunch. They would have delighted in smuggling their sullied white sheep away somewhere.

But why, after a successful disappearance, would Jack Dawson return to Hayden now? And assuming Ken's murder was connected with the attempt on Jack Junior, why try to kill his own grandson?

That's whom I'm supposed to be concerned with, Matt reminded himself, *Jack. Ken's murder is Clearview's problem.*

Still, his thoughts persistently circled back to Jack's namesake.

None of the guys seemingly connected with the case were old enough to be Jack Dawson resurrected. Most were, in fact, middle-aged, in their forties or fifties. A dangerous age, the experts claimed, when men often became dissatisfied and developed an increasing sense of urgency. An age which, at thirty-five, Matt was moving up on all too rapidly himself. Anyhow, the guys in question were all dark haired and dark eyed, while Jack Dawson had had blond hair and blue eyes. More likely this Jack was a relative of the original. Trafalgar was not all that far away. It was probably just a coincidence that one of the Dawsons should show up here selling drugs. Raven Scion and Emmett Vinson seemed the most likely suspects.

Matt called Trafalgar and spoke to the police chief, who was new, both to the office and to the town. He didn't know if any of the Dawsons were still around but promised to check. He took down a description of Raven Scion and Emmett Vinson and agreed to ask around about them too.

Myron Hargrove came into Matt's office as the chief was hanging up. "I just came down to see if you're making any progress," the principal said. "We've had counselors in to talk to the kids; they're taking Ken's death hard. I didn't think he was much of a loss, myself."

Matt looked at him sharply. "That's a callous attitude."

Myron shrugged. "I'm realistic. The boy was a troublemaker, always in my face about something. The other kids liked him for that defiance, of course. Even Jack seemed to find him amusing, perhaps too much so. Probably he's the one who led Jack astray. Ken was bright enough, could have done well if he had made the effort. But he wasn't bright enough to stay away from drugs."

Intelligence or lack of it was, thought Matt, always the conclusive factor in Myron's eyes. Myron was very bright, verging on genius, some said. He had taught before becoming principal.

But he had had an impatient attitude, hating to explain over and over what he found so easy. He had been moved up to principal, Matt suspected, simply to get him out of the classroom. He had not done appreciably better in the new position. His testy demeanor intimidated the students. Also, he spent too carelessly and had to be reined in by the board.

"About Jack," Matt said. "Would anybody profit from his death? Is he Amos's heir, for example?"

Myron raised his brows. "You're kind of stretching, aren't you? No, I get the house and the land on the western side of the lake. Trudy inherits Speedwell and the land on the east. She already owns that old house on the north end. Her father and stepmother left it to her. Jack will only inherit Speedwell if Trudy dies before Amos does."

"Jack has no life insurance?"

"A teenager?" Myron shrugged. "I don't know, but I doubt it. Jack Dawson and Vita did though. Trudy was talking about that last night. Strangely enough, it went to Speedwell. Not so strangely, I suppose, since they were essential to the running of the place—or thought they were. Their deaths, ironically enough, saved Speedwell financially. I've always wondered if Ian Keegan might have had something to do with that. He was not fond of Jack Dawson, you know."

Getting up, Myron shook his head. "Verging on slander, aren't I? Still, Trudy suspects the present Keegan of wanting her and Jack dead. Probably paranoia on her part, but I thought I'd better mention it. Don't tell her I told you. She probably wouldn't appreciate her spat with Keegan being overheard. Speedwell does go to Howard, if she and Jack aren't around. Did you talk to Raven Scion?"

Matt nodded. "He tried to pass the buck to Emmett Vinson. I don't find Vinson very convincing."

Myron looked interested. "How so?"

"For one thing, the literature and tapes he has up there don't look as if they've been used. Look almost as if they'd all been purchased at the same time. He isn't as big as those quilted shirts make him look either. I grabbed his arm, and it was scrawny. I think the whole militia thing is just cover."

"Maybe *both* of them are drug dealers. That would explain the extremity of the problem." Myron turned toward the door. "Good luck in sorting all of this out." From his tone, apparently he thought Matt was going to need it.

■ ■ ■

When Gabe approached the Clearview Library at about four-thirty that afternoon, he discovered Lucerne Abiel lying on one of the stone lions that flanked the steps. She was on her stomach, facing the library, with her legs twined casually around the lion's mane and a magazine resting open on its rump. She was making marks in the magazine with a pencil. "If you're looking for books and articles about comas," she said, "I have them all in my book bag here." She pointed with her pencil toward the other lion. "Have a seat."

"You get down from there," Gabe said, perching on the steps. "You aren't supposed to sit on those. What did the articles say?"

"They were universally depressing. A coma isn't like sleep, from which you can pop bright-eyed. Most people are confused when they come to, and many of them are so brain-damaged they have to learn everything over again. Of course, some of them never do. Emerge, that is. And some, only partially."

It was about what Gabe had expected, but it didn't improve his mood any. "I hope," he said, "that isn't one of the library's magazines you're writing in."

She raised her head then to look at him. "You are so stodgy, Gabe, it's a wonder Matt Olin ever had any trouble with you. Do you see any sign that says, 'Thou shalt not sit on the lions'? No, you don't, because there isn't one."

"That's because everybody else knows better."

"It's because everybody else has no imagination. Present company included. And this is my own personal issue of *Cryptic Crossword*. What's an answer for 'talk right, but wear your flowers backward?' Gabriel! Get it? *Gab* for 'talk.' *R* for 'right' and *lei* for 'backward.'"

"I get it," Gabe said. "But it doesn't make any sense."

"Cryptic clues aren't supposed to make sense."

"Yes, but the best ones sound like they do."

Lucerne gave a windy sigh. "You just absolutely have to spoil my fun every time, don't you?"

The library faced west and was spotlighted in the lurid yellow haze that preceded sunset. Raven Scion swaggered out of that haze like a rock star out of a dry-ice fog and looked up at them.

His sunglasses cast their own vivid reflections back in their faces. "Evenin', kids."

"Hello," Lucerne said coldly. "Move your legs, Gabe, so the man can get through. I, you will notice, am not in the way. That guy," she added after Scion had pushed through the doors into the library, the blackbird on his back glaring down at them, "gives me the creeps. I always thought *his* name sounded like a cryptic clue, actually." She stretched and wiggled into a sitting position against the lion's high-flung neck. "I'll see if I can make something of it."

"It's going to be dark in a few minutes," Gabe said. "I hope you didn't ride your bike clear over here."

"Of course I did. And, yes, I was going to ride it back in the dark until you graciously offered to take me. The bike does have a headlight, you know, and I always carry a cell phone for emergencies. Gabe, I think I have something here. What's the other name for 'blackbird,' besides raven?"

He frowned at her. "Crow? Grackle?"

She shook her head. "Keep going."

"Ouzel. Jackda—" The word caught in his throat. He jumped up.

"Right. Jackdaw. And we know what *scion* means—'descendant' or 'heir.' In other words…"

"Son. Jackdaw Son. Jack Dawson!"

Just then, the man of whom they were speaking emerged from the doors above them, smiling his constant smile, sunglasses turned toward them as he descended the steps. Lucerne opened her mouth to speak, but Gabe squeezed her arm in warning, standing in front of her and keeping his back to Scion so the man couldn't read either of their expressions.

"See ya, kids." Was the tone mocking?

"See you," Gabe said curtly, without turning.

"But it doesn't make any sense," Lucerne complained in a whisper as Scion swaggered away from them. "Why would he choose a name like that unless he wanted people to figure out…"

"Maybe he thinks nobody else is as clever as he is. He can't be the Jack Dawson that killed his wife though. Scion isn't in his seventies. We had better tell the chief."

"With all that hair and those glasses, who could tell?" Lucerne asked as she scrambled down. "Still, I have to agree with you. In his forties at most, I would say. But what good is it going to do Matt Olin? A word game isn't proof."

"Maybe it's a word game Ken figured out first. Ken didn't have time to say much. By using what he thought was the guy's real name, he pointed out something weirder is going on here than just drug dealing. That maybe a killer didn't kill himself forty years ago."

"And now he's back?" Lucerne shivered.

"Of course it could just be a coincidence," Gabe muttered. "We better not let it get around unless we're sure. People in

Hayden are in an ugly mood right now, and Scion has always been suspect. They're scared for their kids."

"I'm scared, too, Gabe." Lucerne looked up at him. "I don't understand any of this. Was the drug problem at school worse than I realized? Because I didn't see it."

People descending the library steps cast curious glances at the teenagers, standing so close together and talking in low, almost conspiratorial tones.

Gabe shook his head. "Neither did I. But what matters now is what people believe. The news has convinced them that Jack, whom they all trusted, was betraying them. They think that Matt Olin is protecting his most valuable player. They've even fit me into the picture." He grinned mirthlessly. "Some think I got the drugs for Jack through my connections in the city. We did go up there together once. I allegedly am blackmailing the chief into compliance by threatening him with a brutality charge. A few people are even looking askance at Speedwell. What kind of herbs do those people use, they're thinking."

"How about the other kids? You were at school today when they heard the news about Ken."

"It rocked them, but most are holding firm on Jack's side. They're looking to us for leadership though."

"*Us?*"

"Yes, us. I am not going to do this alone. You have plenty of brass. You had better get ready to use it. It's going to be us against them, you know."

"Them?" She winced. "The adults, you mean. That's a pretty big order, Johnson."

"Not all the adults. We at least have Regan and Matt on our side. She has clout these days, now that she could fire half the town. And Matt is still in charge of Jack's case, if not Ken's."

"Most of the old folks will stand behind Matt," Lucerne said. "I've met a lot of them this summer. They like me, once they get beyond the makeup and the motorbike. And they definitely like Matt. He looks out for them. Not to mention that they tend to be more indulgent toward their grandchildren than they were with their own kids. This is going to be very strange if it turns the old and young against the middle."

"Not so strange, maybe," Gabe said, "when you consider how little most adults trust teenagers. Even their own."

"Hey," Lucerne said, "no regressing to the angry young man attitude. We want to look like the reasonable ones here. They were teenagers once themselves. All we have to do is remind them of that—and that they weren't so bad. And hope," she added with a wry grin, "they weren't. Considering some of them were sixties kids, that may be a futile hope."

"It's a better idea than any I've had." He nodded toward the street, where a couple of men were climbing out of a parked car. One carried a video camera. "I told that reporter I would meet him here. He wanted to interview some of Jack's friends. I didn't want to do it at home with Aunt Lily hanging all over me. It's convenient that you're here. You're good at gab."

"Suspiciously convenient," Lucerne said, looping her arm through his and smiling sweetly at the reporter while she continued in a viperish, sibilant undertone. "Did you make this appointment *after* you had called my housekeeper to find out where I was?"

The reporter was smiling back in an open and friendly way. "Good evening, Mr. Johnson, Miss Abiel. Thank you for coming."

"I guess," Lucerne muttered, "that gives me my answer, doesn't it?" And her nails dug, very briefly, into Gabe's arm.

■ ■ ■

"We believe that Chief Olin is right," Lucerne Abiel said from Regan's television screen. "Heroin was planted in Jack's EpiPen and in his locker to kill him without making it look like murder."

"But why," the reporter asked patiently, "would someone

want to kill Jack if he had no involvement with the drug trade at your school?"

"Probably because he had discovered who was involved," Lucerne answered with spirit. "And he would have told; they wouldn't have been able to keep Jack quiet."

"Yet you still contend a drug problem doesn't really exist at Hayden High?"

Regan grimaced. That was what reporters did. They tried to mix you up in your own words. Gabe came to Lucerne's rescue. "She didn't say there *isn't* one. She said that it's no worse than you would find at most schools, that it has been exaggerated out of proportion. I think most of the other kids would agree with us on that."

"Would their parents?"

"Parents don't know," Gabe replied softly. "Do they?"

Regan thought he was getting mad.

"No," the reporter agreed quickly, "parents don't know. That's why they worry. But they have been around long enough to realize most people who talk about being framed—"

"Jack hasn't talked about being framed," Lucerne interrupted. "Because he can't. He can't say anything right now."

"Do you have any idea who shot Ken Fermin?"

Regan could imagine the fast thinking going on behind Lucerne's violet eyes. To mention Jack Dawson, she would have to acknowledge that Dawson was the present Jack's grandfather— and a killer. "No," Lucerne said. "But someone tried to murder Jack at the same time. A nurse who, it was later proved, had no connection with the hospital. I was there; I saw her try to give Jack an injection that he wasn't supposed to have."

This obviously was news to the reporter. Regan was sure the Clearview police wouldn't appreciate its being broadcast, nor would the hospital. Apparently, the reporter realized that too and remembered that in a small city like Clearview, it wasn't a good idea to antagonize two of your main news sources. He pursued the subject only indirectly.

"I understand Jack has been moved," the reporter said. "For his own safety?"

"Yes," Lucerne agreed unhelpfully. "For his safety."

Not, Regan thought, *that her silence about Jack's present whereabouts will accomplish much. Anyone with even the faintest glimmer of intelligence can guess where Jack is now.*

Since Lucerne obviously wasn't going to volunteer anything more, the reporter turned to Gabe. "It has been suggested the students at Hayden voluntarily submit to locker searches and drug tests. Do you think they would be willing to do that?"

Gabe considered the question. "Perhaps," he said finally, "but I'm not going to suggest it. I think things will have come to a sorry pass when the town starts to treat its kids like criminals."

That was where the reporter had chosen to end the interview. Regan switched off the TV and turned to the box of papers she had picked up from Trudy's van that afternoon. Gato, the cat, was curled up in her lap, and Regan propped the insurance papers up against him while she studied them. Speedwell was listed as second beneficiary on each, after the surviving spouse. The insurance company apparently had determined, to its own satisfaction, that neither spouse had survived.

Regan had decided to forget about method for the moment and concentrate on motive. Amos clearly had the best. It was all very well to assert that a man like Amos wouldn't murder his daughter and her husband to save his precious hospital. But good men had gone off the rails before, had justified their actions as the greatest good for the greatest number. That could apply to Amos as well as Howard.

It also could apply to Howard's father. Ian was reportedly as devoted to Speedwell as Amos. And he may have had a score to settle as well.

Galen had a motive too; he might have thought Vita's death would be the final blow to Amos that would convince him to sell. If he no longer had a family member willing to carry on at Speedwell, what was the sense in fighting financial realities?

Not to mention that it would leave Galen the only heir. In that case, Galen would have been unaware of the insurance policies.

What about Bennington? Jack apparently had known him from somewhere. What secrets might be hidden in that past? The man was evidently hostile to the whole idea of Speedwell. Why would he have bothered coming unless some pressure had been applied? A doctor like Bennington could have been involved in all sorts of unsavory practices—illicit prescriptions; abortion, which was still illegal in the fifties; the doctoring of research results. She would have to find out if Bennington was still alive.

Could Faye have fallen so madly in love with Jack Dawson in just a couple of days that she was willing to commit murder? Most murders did spring either from money or passion. *Madly* was the key word here. How sick had the girl really been at the time?

All right, so they all had motives of sorts. Even Jack, who could have wanted his wife's insurance money. But, in that case, why hadn't he made her death look like an accident or a suicide? Regan hadn't seen any suicide clause in the policy. There couldn't have been one, in fact, or the company wouldn't have paid on Jack's death. And why look for another motive for him when a fit of rage would suffice? Why, in fact, look for another murderer? For no matter who might have had reason to wish Vita dead, Jack was the only one in the room with her when the gun went off.

The only other possible solution was that Vita actually had retained possession of the revolver and turned it on herself in such a way as to implicate her husband. It was awkward to shoot yourself in the back of the head but not impossible. That act, though, would require hatred, malice, and despair of epic proportions, and after reading Vita's diary, Regan didn't think the woman capable of emotions that strong. Still, nobody had thought her capable of that kind of scene either...

The cat sneezed. Giving Regan a reproachful look, he crawled out from under the papers and jumped to the floor to wash himself. Regan got up also and paced. *I'm just grasping at straws here for Trudy's sake. It's all so open and shut. Or it was until Ken's final words raised the dead, so to speak. Is Jack Dawson alive, or isn't he?*

■ ■ ■

That was the question Matt had asked the law in Trafalgar, too, and he received no satisfactory answer. Chief Larkin had found a Merilee Dawson. She had admitted to being the wife of Jack Dawson's nephew. Her husband's name was John, a name that was, as Larkin pointed out, synonymous with Jack. Rose insisted that her husband was in prison in Texas; Larkin hadn't been able to locate him there.

"I have my doubts if a suicide actually occurred," Larkin said. He had looked up some old files. "There was never any proof of it except that Dawson's car was abandoned up on the bridge with his lab coat and the note inside. They searched the river in that area, but all they found was one of his shoes. Granted, it's a deep lake. But I would bet the guy simply ditched the car and skipped town, probably had help."

"If he had a nephew, he must have also had a brother or sister."

"Brother," Larkin supplied. "Chuck. A no-good type. Died in prison. His son seems to take after him. But Chuck was free enough in '57."

"Jack Dawson would be in his seventies today," Matt said, "if he's still alive."

"You have reason to think he is?"

"His name has come up in a murder investigation."

"You don't say. Well, considering his family, I'm not too surprised. Nobody's heard of those other two guys you mentioned. Of course, nobody knows where John Dawson is either. He could have changed his name. He was tall with dark hair and eyes, in his forties."

"He didn't have a daughter, did he?"

"No kids."

"Was he ever involved in any white supremacist groups or militia?"

"Not that I know of."

"Ever use a crow as his symbol?"

"That," Larkin said, "would be a bit colorful for him. From what I've gathered, he was just a common crook, went in for burglary mostly, was careful not to catch anybody at home. Not violent in the past, but you never can tell."

"No drugs?"

"Not that I've heard about. He wasn't a sociable guy. To sell drugs, you have to have connections."

That would seem to point more to Vinson. But on the other hand, a complete change of persona would be a more effective disguise. Vinson or Scion? A knock sounded on Matt's office door.

Gabe and Lucerne came in to answer that question for him.

■ ■ ■

A large number of high school kids showed up that evening to see Jack. Trudy had been about to have a glass of juice and retire early. She abandoned that plan to sit between her own bed and Jack's, watching.

The trooper was alert. He allowed them to approach Jack only one at a time on the side of the bed opposite to the officer so he could watch their hands. Even Betony was there, and she had brought her father with her. They were all awkward and unhappy, except for Raven, who seemed to find the guard amusing.

Howard came in and kept a frowning eye on things for several minutes and, later, Amos. Charlotte stood in the doorway, said, "He seems to have enough visitors for one evening," and went away again.

"Thank you for speaking up for my son," Trudy said to Gabe and Lucerne.

"A school-board meeting is scheduled for tomorrow night," Lucerne told her. "The word is that a lot of outraged parents are going to be there, along with the press. Things are bound to get nasty."

"You're going?"

Heads nodded all around. "We wouldn't miss it," Sylvia said grimly. "Don't worry, Ms. Hargrove. If anybody tries to blame Jack, we are going to point out that it wasn't Jack who shot Ken."

"We just have to remember to hold our tempers," Lucerne reminded. "If we start to yell, people are going to see us as a bunch of in-your-face kids."

"In your parents' place," Trudy said, "I might feel like they do. They trusted Jack, and they feel he has betrayed that trust."

"What good is trust," Sylvia demanded, "if it can't survive the tough times? They're the ones who taught us to be loyal and stand up for what's right."

When Jack's friends were gone, Trudy looked across at the young policeman. "There's going to be trouble. It's been a tough year; Hayden is already divided enough."

"Sometimes you can't avoid trouble," he said. "Sometimes the only way is not around but through."

"I guess. I'm going to bed now." She leaned to kiss her son's unresponsive face. "Good night, Jack."

His skin felt cool and swollen. As she touched him, he shivered. His feet were encased in high-topped sneakers to keep his toes from pointing.

"Do you need any help?" the trooper asked. "Shall I call a nurse?"

"No," she said. "I can manage." He had watched her hands too. She was glad of it. He wasn't taking anything for granted. He was a smart young man. He would go far. She had once expected to go far, herself.

She propelled herself out of the wheelchair onto the edge of the bed, drew the curtains around it while she changed her clothes. Was Howard right? Had she given up too easily?

The bed and its side table provided all the things she needed: a hanging overhead bar for pulling herself up, a catheter, tongs, the forgotten glass of cranberry juice. As she leaned to reach for the glass on the side table, she saw a small scrap of paper on the floor, half under the bed. She used the tongs to retrieve it, smooth it out. It was plain white paper; nothing was written on it. But some of the white came off. She rubbed finger and thumb together—powder.

She reached for the glass again and held it up to the light. It was hard to see anything in that deep maroon, but at the bottom lay a suggestion of silt, nothing that would have been noticeable under ordinary conditions. The taste would not, she thought, have been noticeable either under the tart overlay of cranberries.

Who would be surprised if a handicapped woman whose beloved son lay comatose took this way out? That was why the paper had been left where she could have dropped it. *You are such a clever man, Howard,* she thought almost admiringly.

The trooper would not have seen anything. He was concentrating on those near Jack. Besides, she had been between him and her bed, blocking his line of sight. What if she called out to him now, showed him this paper?

Did she really want to see her suspicions in the newspaper, on TV? One Speedwell doctor accusing another of attempted murder. It would make quite a sensation. It would also destroy the hospital. Even if she didn't accuse Howard directly, his motive would come out. And Howard Keegan *was* Speedwell in the public eye. But if he was also the one responsible for Jack's condition…

What would Jack say? He had liked Howard. *You have no proof, Mother. A lot of other people were here tonight. It could have been any of them. You can't wreck a doctor's reputation unless you're sure.*

"Are you ready?" the trooper asked. "Do you want me to turn off the overhead light?" He had been provided with a lamp next to Jack's bed.

She couldn't make such a decision quickly. "Yes, please," she said. "Turn it off." Not that it would make any difference. She wouldn't sleep tonight anyway.

In the morning, she got up early, wheeled herself out onto the empty porch, sat with a blanket over her shoulders, and watched the calm lake turn from gray to blue as the sun rose in a cloudless sky.

Howard came out and dropped onto the couch. "No change?"

He didn't show any surprise at seeing her alive and well. "No." There would be nurses in this morning to massage Jack, exercise the limbs he could not move himself, turn him to prevent bedsores.

"How did it go with your other patients yesterday?" he asked. "Any problems?"

"No. The girl with early MS wanted to try bee-venom therapy. I told her we would have to travel to the beekeeper's place to do it. It would be too risky to have the bees here now."

"Good. About that school-board meeting tonight, do you want to go?"

"No. I think I can trust Jack's classmates to look after his interests."

"Word is that Lucerne has talked her mother into making an appearance. That should be interesting."

"I don't see what Ruby Abiel can have to say about people she doesn't know."

"That's celebrities for you. Their opinion carries more weight, even when they don't know what they're talking about. Lucerne is cagey enough to realize that." He stood. "Let me know if you change your mind. I'll run you up." He looped an arm around her neck in a kind of half-hug then went away. She sat for a few minutes longer, looking at the water through eyes glassy with tears. When she returned to Jack's room, a nurse was just bustling out—carrying an empty glass.

"Morning, Trudy," she said. "I made up your bed for you while I was in here, tossed that warm juice. Decided you didn't want it, huh?"

She didn't wait to hear Trudy's quiet answer. "No, I didn't want it."

CHAPTER 9

I would I had some flowers o' the spring that might
become your time of day.

Regan stood in her garden the next morning and wondered if there was any point in taking flowers to Jack when he couldn't see them. She should also take some to the funeral home for Ken. Of course, he couldn't see them either.

These mums and asters weren't appropriate flowers for youth. A tea rose was blooming with pale lavender, almost steely flowers. It was different. She thought Ken would have liked it.

After she had dropped off the roses and a card at the funeral home, Regan drove to the library in Clearview. She found copies of both the *Hayden Herald* and the *Clearview Clarion* on microfilm. Regan asked for the issues from a certain week in October 1957.

Doctor Kills Wife and Self, ran one of the headlines.

Yesterday war hero and promising young physician Jack Dawson shot and killed his wife, Vita, after an argument in the second-story bedroom of their rural home. Guests and family members rushed upstairs but were too late to intercept Dawson, who escaped down an outside stairway and fled in his '57 Continental.

Police discovered the car several hours later, abandoned on a

bridge overlooking Blue Lake near Trafalgar, Dawson's birthplace.
He is believed to have returned there to take his own life in remorse
over his crime. His coat and a suicide note were discovered in the
car, but his body was not found.

Both Jack Dawson and his wife worked at Speedwell
Sanitarium, which was founded by her father, Amos Hargrove.
There had been, Hargrove reports, no prior signs of trouble with the
young couple, who had been married for thirteen months and were
expecting a child.

Surviving are Vita's father, Amos, and brother, Galen, also Jack
Dawson's daughter, Trudy, from a previous marriage.

The article was not long. Perhaps the editor of the Hayden
paper had been a friend of Amos's and had not wanted to sen-
sationalize the tragedy. The Clearview article was longer and
more dramatic but had little more information.

Vita's horrified family and friends looked down from the win-
dow of the murder room to see the panic-stricken young doctor
scrambling into his car, etc. At that distance, Regan thought
dryly, it would be hard to know whether he was panic-stricken
or making a cold-blooded getaway.

A photograph of Jack Dawson in military uniform appeared
with the article. Regan sat back, squinting at it, trying to age it
in her mind, to see similarities to somebody she knew. The
resemblance was there, but pointed only to a teenager.
Charlotte was right. Jack Hargrove looked very much like his
grandfather.

Though Jack Dawson, Regan thought, didn't seem to have
had the warmth and humor that animated his young namesake.
Not that he looked like a monster either. Just a practical, ambitious young physician.

■ ■ ■

Lucerne came to see Regan that afternoon, bringing sketches,
which Regan enthusiastically approved.

"I suppose you've heard about the board meeting tonight," the teen said. "Are you going to be there?"

"Should I be?"

"I think so. Chief Olin is likely to take a beating. Probably Myron Hargrove, too, but we're not all that concerned about him."

"They would probably consider my opinion of the chief prejudiced."

Lucerne arched a brow. "For or against?"

Regan ignored that. "I hear your mother's coming."

"Yes, if something else doesn't arise at the last minute. I played on her guilt. She's ashamed that she doesn't spend more time with me."

"Maybe she should be."

Lucerne shrugged. "I'm the one who asked to come to Hayden. You have a lovely house and gardens. Do you think I might come up sometime to draw?" They were sitting on the terrace.

"Any day," Regan said. "Even if I'm not here. I don't usually lock the gates."

"Such great weather too," Lucerne said, "if we could just enjoy it. But worry and sadness make you feel all cramped and locked down inside, don't they?" She picked up the portable phone that was lying on the table between them, studied the number in the plastic sleeve for a moment. "Flowers."

"Pardon?"

"That's how I remember phone numbers," Lucerne explained. "I try to make up an appropriate word from the letters above the numbers."

"Good idea." Regan took the phone to refresh her memory as to which letters went with which numbers. "If you can't get me here, try 'florist.' That'll be my car phone. Now, how would you like to go riding? This is the best time of year for it. Crisp and clean and no insects. Gina's horses could stand the exercise."

They didn't talk much as they rode at a brisk canter along leaf-crackling trails and galloped over fields thick with late clover.

"That was great." Lucerne sighed as their mounts jogged back to the barn. "I feel wind-scoured."

Regan smiled. "There's nothing quite like it for lifting the spirits. Maybe being literally lifted up helps."

Lucerne had dismounted first, and Regan found herself looking down on the top of the girl's head. Light-colored roots showed up plainly against the coal-black hair. Lucerne must really be a platinum blond. Why would she want to cover that up?

Regan felt vaguely uneasy as she rubbed down her mount. She liked Lucerne but had to admit she actually knew very little about the girl. Until Lucerne had come to Hayden, Regan had never heard that Ruby Abiel had a daughter. The artist was not exactly a conveyor of respectability either.

After Lucerne had gone, Regan went back to the box of musty papers from Vita's desk. Receipts, invitations, advertisements. One was for a bomb shelter, and Regan smiled at the naiveté of its claims. People had learned to live with the threat of nuclear annihilation, didn't appear to even think about it much anymore. A mass form of denial. Trudy had said a person couldn't live in fear forever.

Regan glanced at the clock. She would have to eat supper soon and change her clothes if she intended to go to the board meeting. Only a large manila envelope was left to look at. It contained a sheaf of papers. Another insurance policy? She pulled the papers out, sneezed, and squinted at the first one through watery eyes. No, it looked more like a manuscript. She began to read.

The grandfather clock began to bong as she laid down the last page. She automatically counted the strokes as a counterpoint to her disjointed thoughts. *One, it was an, two, accident. Three, that*

*explains, four, yet doesn't. Five, why run? She, six, might not, seven,
have been dead.*

Seven! The board meeting started at seven, and she had virtually promised to be there. Regan tore up the stairs, shedding
her riding clothes en route, yanked open the closet door, and
grabbed the first dress she saw.

Still, she was fifteen minutes late as she tried to slip, unnoticed,
into the back of the meeting room. Lucerne, whose neck was
craned toward the door, looked relieved and hissed, "Miss Culver,
over here!" The school-board members were still self-consciously
conducting routine business. Some of them glanced up at Regan,
and the impatient audience turned as one to stare at her. A man
who was down on one knee at the front, wielding a video camera,
aimed his lens briefly in her direction. Gloom deepened on several faces. Many, she suspected, were weighing their outrage
against their desire to return to their jobs at Thyme Will Tell come
January.

As Regan slipped into an aisle seat beside Lucerne, the
woman on the other side of the teenager whispered, "*I* should
make such an entrance!"

Regan smiled, leaned to shake hands silently. Ruby Abiel was
at least six inches shorter than her daughter and looked no older
than twenty-nine. She must, Regan knew, be at least in her forties. Ruby wore dangly earrings in abstract copper and pewter
and a geometric dress in a similar bronze shade. Her hair was, at
the moment, red, and she was stunning. Beside her, Lucerne
looked over-tall and gawky.

The school-board president raised his head and cleared his
throat. "Now is the time," he said unhappily, "when we usually
allow visitors to address the board. We had better place a five-
minute-per-person limit on these speeches, or we'll never get
out of here. Who wants to go first?"

The reporter with the camera, who had been looking bored,

perked up and stood. An awkward moment of silence followed the announcement. Then a man who worked in the shipping department at Regan's company shot a defiant glance in her direction and got up. His tone was nervous and restrained, almost subdued. What they all wanted to know, he opined, was why the school administration and the police had allowed things to reach such a desperate point that the star of the football team was dealing drugs and another student was cut down in cold blood.

Although laced with clichés, his concern obviously was genuine, and he didn't mention any policeman by name. The woman who followed him was not so discreet. "If the principal and the police chief were really unaware of the depth of the drug problem here, they are, at best, incompetent. If they looked the other way to spare Hayden's oh-so-important football program, then they are criminally liable. Either way, I don't think they're fit to hold their offices. Why isn't Chief Olin here to face us in person?" She went on in that vein until Myron Hargrove said, "Time."

She was not finished. "If the wealthy element thinks it can dominate this town and corrupt our children, not to mention get away with drug dealing and murder, I think it's time for us little people to stand up and be counted."

Many of the teenagers had been twitching in their seats, but they apparently remembered Lucerne's warning and didn't speak. When the woman finally subsided, Ruby Abiel stood up. "I agree that *little* is an apt description of you, madam. I also believe that most of what I have just heard is slander and will become libel, if any of these reporters choose to print it. I hope you are financially equipped to deal with lawsuits."

The belligerent one, who had been looking smug, wilted.

"Fortunately," Ruby continued in a husky drawl, "I doubt that many here take you seriously. I am in a unique position, myself, being both a parent and enough of an outsider to be more objective. My daughter says this high school has not had a significant drug problem in the time she has been here. I believe her because my daughter has never told me lies. In fact, I think that as parents and teachers, you are to be congratulated for raising children who have a sense of loyalty and fair play. I understand that most of you liked and trusted the young man in question. When doubt is raised, it's all too easy to assume the worst. Not only of Jack but also of your own teenagers. This is a cynical generation. It's easier for us to think bad than to think good. But you might take an example from your children and wait until Jack Hargrove can speak for himself before you condemn him. I believe," she concluded, "that we have with us tonight a woman who has experienced what it feels like to be convicted without a trial." And Ruby bowed slightly in Regan's direction before sitting down.

Regan hoped her face didn't show her panic. She was always careful to be well prepared before making a speech, and she was not prepared tonight. But all faces were turned expectantly toward her.

Standing, Regan said, "Yes, Ms. Abiel is right. I know what it feels like to be the object of condemning looks. I was fortunate that Chief Olin looked beyond the obvious to discover the real guilty party. Connie Denton must also be grateful that our chief is not the type to jump to conclusions."

An uneasy ripple moved through the crowd at the mention of an old incest case involving a former town council president and his daughter. "I know that Matt is at times controversial," she continued, "but that's because he doesn't accept the easy answer; he goes deep to discover the truth. The truth may be painful, but it is, I think, what we all want."

Her questioning gaze challenged any of them to deny that. No one cared to.

"Now," she said, "I think we should hear from one of the

students." She looked at the row of teenagers, and they all looked at Gabe.

He got up, reluctantly. "I think Miss Culver"—he cast her an approving glance—"and Ms. Abiel"—his look was noticeably less approving—"have said most of what needs to be said. We know Jack wasn't a drug user or pusher, and you must admit, we are the ones who *would* know. Ken, our friend who was killed, said the same thing. There have been some rumors that Jack was corrupted by me. I hope my skin color isn't the only reason for those suspicions. I'm willing to submit to a drug test, if that will help. I don't know what else I can do to convince you. I'm proud that Matt Olin is my coach. He has taught us that being just is more important than being popular." Gabe sat.

The mood in the room had perceptibly shifted. An elderly man in the rear said, "I don't think that test will be necessary, son. We've all been a little hasty, I'm afraid. This isn't really a school-board matter anyway."

"Finally, a sentiment I can heartily agree with," Myron Hargrove snapped. "If you have complaints about Olin, I suggest you take them to the mayor or the town council." He didn't allude to the complaints about himself. Perhaps it stung that no one had stood up for him as they had for Matt.

The board hastily adjourned the meeting. As the teenagers huddled, Ruby said to Regan, "Gabe disapproves of me, I'm afraid. Probably because I leave my daughter here alone. Actually, I kind of like him for that. I've been enduring your praises from Ja—" With scarcely a pause, Ruby corrected herself. "Lucerne, I mean. She should have had a mother like you."

Regan shook her head. "For her to turn out the way she did, you must have done something right. What is she hiding?"

Ruby shook her head in turn. "I do know better than to tell my kid's secrets. He *was* here, by the way."

"He?"

"Big guy in a cop's uniform, standing just to one side of that open door back there. I could see his shoulder patch. Lucerne says there's some kind of trouble between you two. What is it? That old thing about the too-successful female?"

Somehow, Regan didn't resent this nosiness from Ruby; it was so open and unabashed. "Partly, I guess."

"I can relate. Most guys don't hold up too well under that one. If he can't deal with it, tell him to take a hike. If he can't be happy for you, he doesn't love you."

"It was all too fast, really," Regan said. "Our whole romance, I mean. There wasn't any foundation."

Ruby looked skeptical. "Love is not architecture. It doesn't have to go by the blueprint."

"God's way of showing us we aren't the ones in charge?" Regan suggested.

"Something like that. Of course, letting him suffer a bit won't hurt. I hate to say it, but guys seem to prefer women who treat them badly." Ruby winked. "I should know." Looking beyond Regan's shoulder, she said, "Why would any woman make herself look that plain?"

Regan turned her head enough to see that the artist was indicating Betony. "I doubt she does it on purpose."

"I beg to differ. She couldn't be that bad *unless* she did it on purpose. Who is she anyhow?"

"A senior, like Lucerne."

"You have to be kidding!" Ruby was frankly incredulous. "I would have said she was thirty, if she's a day!"

As some of the teenage girls approached Ruby deferentially, she reached to shake hands with Regan again. "I like you. I'm leaving tonight, but I'm counting on you to keep an eye on my kid. Drop in and see me when you're in New York."

Lucerne tugged at Regan's sleeve. "I think that went pretty well, didn't it?"

"Better than I expected, actually. What town did Betony and her father come from, do you know? I notice he's not here tonight."

"Smart of him," Lucerne said. "Vinson isn't either. They were probably afraid of getting lynched. Betony is from Trafalgar. Speaking of which, there's something I forgot to tell you this afternoon. Do you do cryptic crosswords?"

At Regan's confused nod, the girl added, "Pretend Scion's name is a clue." Lucerne watched the other's expression until she saw light break.

"But none of this makes sense," Regan objected. "I found some new evidence tonight. I haven't had time to think about it yet, but it seems to indicate that whole thing forty years ago was an accident. Jack Dawson was—or is—not a killer."

■   ■   ■

The next morning, Regan dug out a computer CD that contained all the phone numbers in the U.S. Only one Reuben Bennington was listed, in Boston, but no medical initials appeared after his name. She dialed the number.

A man answered.

"Reuben Bennington, please," she said.

"Speaking."

"Is this the Reuben Bennington who was a surgeon?"

"I'm retired."

"Did you visit a clinic called Speedwell in the autumn of 1957?"

Silence. "Who are you?" he asked finally. "A reporter?"

"No, my name is Regan Culver. I run an herb company, actually. But at the moment I'm looking into the murder of Vita Dawson at the request of her stepdaughter, Trudy."

"What's the point of looking into it? There was never any mystery about it. Does Amos approve of what you're doing?"

"You remember Amos then."

"What do you mean, *remember* him?" He sounded amused. "I may be old, Miss Culver; I'm not senile. I had lunch with him only a couple of months ago. Amos is one of my oldest friends."

"But I thought...somehow I had the idea you weren't much impressed with Speedwell and the people there."

"I'm always initially skeptical about any business in which I might invest. But I knew even back then that Amos and people like him were going to become necessary in the medical community. Progress always seems to harp on the strictly mechanical, as if man were a machine. You must be Alden's daughter."

"Yes," Regan said. "You knew my father?"

"I attended his funeral. You probably didn't see me. You were in no state to take in much of anything."

"You're right. I'm sorry; I don't remember. Were you surprised by Vita Dawson's murder, Dr. Bennington?"

"I'm a man who spent his career trying to preserve life, Miss Culver. Murder is always odd to me. I wasn't surprised that Vita could aggravate a man to the point of violence. She was not a likable woman. Obtuse, I would call her. Not stupid. She was intelligent enough. But she did not take seriously any opinion besides her own. She constantly misread people and circumstances in her own favor."

"She thought you were a chauvinist," Regan said.

He chuckled. "That's typical. I suppose my dislike was clear enough so even she couldn't miss it. No, I am not a chauvinist, Miss Culver. My wife was a doctor too. Knowing the difficulty she had getting through medical school and finding a good post, I was prepared to be sympathetic to Vita Dawson. But I suspect that Vita did not have trouble. She would have played the game. If she thought they wanted the fluttery, helpless female, that's what she would have given them. She had those kittenish, Marilyn Monroe looks too. No, I doubt she had to face the hostility my wife did."

"Manipulative."

"Quite. But like I said, insensitive. She read the world the way she wanted it. It would not have occurred to her that anybody could have a good reason to dislike her. I thought she and Jack made a good couple, though, because he wasn't perceptive enough to see through her. Stubbornly ambitious but not nearly as observant as someone like Ian Keegan, say. Ian didn't like her either."

"He didn't? There was some gossip he wanted to marry her."

"Now that," Bennington said, "would really have annoyed Ian. I got to know him fairly well after the tragedy. Speedwell didn't need my money after the insurance settlement, so the decision was made to keep it all in the family, so to speak. But I did refer patients to them now and then. Ian never got over his first wife, I think; he never married again. Died in a plane wreck down in Brazil, '78, if I remember the date correctly. Must have taken a real smash to kill Ian."

"Dr. Bennington, do you think Vita would have been angry about staying home that day instead of accompanying the rest of you to Speedwell?"

"No. If she thought me a chauvinist, she would have considered it the smart thing to do, I imagine."

"Didn't you think that fight between her and Jack was a little out of character?"

"Of course it was—for both of them. According to their characters as I had read them anyhow. But unlike her, I can admit myself wrong on occasion. I would have thought anger beneath her."

"Did it ever occur to you that it might all have been theater?"

"Theater?"

"Her brother wrote plays, remember?"

There was silence from the other end except for the rap of fingernails on wood. "You know," he said finally, "you could be right. And what happened? She handed him the wrong gun?"

"Do you think that's possible? Say they had been given a blanks gun that looked similar to his revolver."

"Any soldier should know better than to leave a loaded gun lying around, especially with a kid in the house. Still, I admit it's intriguing. He might have panicked and run. Are we just speculating here, or do you have proof?"

"I found the play."

Silence again. Then, "That does put a different complexion on things."

"What I don't understand is why Galen didn't say anything. He must have known it was an accident."

"Oh, I can explain that." Bennington was peremptory. "He was scared that he would be blamed. It was probably his idea. It's the sort of trick he would find funny. I've just had a thought. What if he deliberately gave them a gun that was supposed to have blanks in it but didn't?"

Regan considered. "From what I've heard about Galen," she decided, "I don't think he would have taken the chance. He could have no guarantee that the shot would be fatal or that Jack would run if it was."

"Yes, you're right," Bennington conceded. "Galen wasn't one for taking chances. If you could find the other gun, you could probably convince Amos and Trudy anyhow. I doubt that anybody else would care, after all these years."

"Jack might. Jack Hargrove, I mean. Amos's grandson. Have you heard what's happened to him?"

"No."

Regan explained.

"As if Amos hasn't had enough already," Bennington said. "With Vita and Galen both dead, Trudy paralyzed..."

"Do you think it's possible Jack Dawson is still alive?"

"You're getting me punch-drunk," Bennington complained. "My brain doesn't work as fast as it used to, you know.

Is it possible? Yes. Is it likely? I don't know. I think he probably did commit suicide. It would be hard to act rationally after you had done something like that. Whether he shot her by accident or on purpose, his career would be as dead as his wife. I can see his ending it all under those circumstances. That's the most likely aspect of the whole case, actually."

"What aspects did you consider unlikely?"

"I thought we should have been able to save the baby, but that may just have been professional chagrin. Also, I would have expected her to be facing him. But, if she was getting into her acting, she may have turned her back as a gesture of contempt. I guess that's why she wanted us home early; so they could run through their little production before dinner. Then what? They come out and say 'Gotcha'?"

"Probably. It was a cruel joke, actually. It would have alarmed Amos. She wouldn't have minded that?"

"Not if it gave her a chance to show off another talent. The woman thought she could do anything."

■ ■ ■

After some tedious calling around, Matt discovered John Dawson had been in a Texas prison until his parole six months ago. He apparently hadn't bothered to tell his wife about his release. Where he was now was anybody's guess because he had skipped out on that parole. The Texas police faxed Matt a mug shot, which was too grainy to be much help. Dawson had been tall and dark.

With a beard, he might be Emmett Vinson. Or with long hair and sunglasses, he might equally well be Raven Scion.

Matt walked down to the funeral home. Few mourners would be there for the afternoon calling hours, and he wanted to talk to Ken's mother. When he opened the door, he saw Regan standing at the other end of the plushly carpeted hall, signing her name in the book. Laying down the pen, she glanced back, and they stood for a moment, staring at each across the hushed space. Then she said, "Hello, Matt," and moved on into the viewing room.

Mabel Fermin was a small woman with bewildered eyes and worn hands. She did housecleaning. She sat in a straight chair near the casket, with Lucerne Abiel beside her. The room smelled of wax and autumn flowers.

Regan stopped for a moment beside the coffin to look at Ken's face. The boy was dressed in a motorcycle jacket and jeans with his helmet nestled beside him. His pallid lips seemed to curl in a half-smile.

Matt heard Regan take a deep breath. Then she turned toward Mabel.

"Here's Regan," Lucerne said, helping the woman to her feet. "Regan Culver. She's the one who tried to save Ken's life."

Mabel made a small movement with her hands, stopped. "That's all right," Lucerne said. "Go ahead. Hug her. She won't mind."

When Mabel seemed frozen, Regan leaned awkwardly to put arms around the smaller woman. At once, Mabel clung and began to cry. "Ken wasn't a bad boy," she said through her sobs. "Not like they say on TV. He was always good to me."

"He was brave," Regan said. "He wanted to help Jack, and that's why he died. For his friend, like it says in the Bible. Don't listen to them. He was right at the end, and that's what matters." She helped Mabel back to her seat. All three women dabbed at their eyes, looked uncertainly around at Matt.

"There's Chief Olin," Lucerne said. "He's the one who carried Ken into the hospital. I expect he wants to ask you some questions. We'll wait right over here, okay?" She led Regan farther down the room.

Matt sat down in the chair Lucerne had occupied. "I'm sorry for your loss, Mrs. Fermin," he said. "I liked Ken. He was on his way to tell me something when he died. Do you have any idea what that might have been?"

She simply stared and shook her head.

"Do you know any reason why somebody would want to kill him?"

Again that silent negative.

"Do you know who his closest friends were, who he ran around with?"

She did speak finally. "He went out a lot. He knew I like to be quiet in the evenings, so he didn't bring people back. He was always considerate like that. Not like some teenagers. I never had any trouble with him." She looked hopefully toward Lucerne, who came to join her. Regan had slipped out.

Matt tilted his head toward the doorway, and Lucerne followed him into the hall.

"Is she going to be okay?" he asked in a low voice. "Ken was an only child, wasn't he?"

"Yes," Lucerne said. "Don't worry. I'm going to fire that lazy slob I have for a housekeeper, and Mabel's going to come and stay with me. As long as she has work to do, she'll be all right."

He smiled. "You're an extraordinary person, you know that?"

Lucerne flushed. "You had better believe it!"

Regan was waiting for him at the end of the walk, looking resolute. "I just wanted to tell you," she said in clipped tones, "that Jack isn't the only one in danger. Trudy didn't want me to say anything, but I'm not going to risk her ending up in there too."

■ ■ ■

At Speedwell, Trudy was trying out the new hand controls Howard had ordered for her van. She proceeded at a jerky stop-and-start pace around the parking lot. Since the driver's seat could be swiveled, it hadn't been too difficult to transfer herself into it. Howard was slouched in her wheelchair. After brief directions at the beginning, he had made no comment.

"Okay," he said abruptly. "I think you have the hang of it. Let's go for a drive."

"On the road?"

He grinned. "That's what it's for."

She was, she reassured herself, perfectly safe as long as she was known to be with him. He wouldn't try anything then.

"Left?" she asked hopefully as they reached the end of the drive. Left led into town, but it was infinitely preferable to that curve above the lake.

"No," he said. "I think maybe we had better stick to the country to begin with. Not as much traffic. Besides, it's prettier."

Trudy didn't notice the prettiness as she maneuvered the van out of the drive and turned right. Blue sky, afternoon sun, and the tattered remains of autumn leaves had no meaning for her as the van crept into the curve. All she saw were her own white-knuckled hands on the wheel and the tar-black road. More blue than black, she thought, pulse jumping in her throat. Almost purple really. Funny how they called it blacktop when it wasn't.

The sickening tilt. For a frantic instant, a memory reeled across her eyes. A dizzying roll in darkness, crazy headlights glancing off tilted trees, a bone-snapping crunch, then a slow-motion release and slide…

She blinked and was back to a serene, sun-drenched October road. Howard still slouched in the chair with sleepy, half-shut eyes. He must know how risky this was. Didn't it occur to him that she might rebel, turn the wheel, and take him with her down that slope?

He looked unworried; he didn't even have a hand out to catch the wheel should she make a mistake. That infuriated her. How dare he have more confidence in her driving than she did? She came out of the curve, moved shaking fingers to the accelerator. "Are you really sure I'm ready for this?"

"The only way to learn is to do," he said. "Let's go up to Snakeskin. We'll walk out to the rock." Snakeskin was a trail they had hiked often in their early teens.

"Need I remind you," she inquired savagely, "that I *cannot* walk?"

He shot her that grin again. "No problem. I'll carry you. You're small, and the rock isn't far."

At several points along Snakeskin trail, all he would have to do was hold her over the edge and let go. She pulled into the gravel turnaround at the head of the trail. What was the use? All she accomplished by this dithering was to ruin whatever time she had left.

He jumped down and came around to the driver's side of the van. She held out her arms, and he lifted her easily, setting off up the slope. "Not so well-worn as it used to be," he said of the trail.

"Maybe kids these days aren't as energetic as we were."

Trudy watched almost forgotten landmarks swim past. The huge oak that dated from the days of the Indians had cracked open to reveal a hollow core. A section of old rail fence was now only a slight bulge under the fallen leaves. "Don't you ever come up here anymore?"

"It isn't as much fun alone," he said. They were now on a flat section of the trail that ran straight along the upper edge of the valley. Here and there through the trees they could catch glimpses of the house, the lake, and Speedwell beyond.

Leaves crunched underfoot. Closing her eyes, with the sun on her face, she could almost imagine the easy stride was her own.

"Remember this?" She opened her eyes to find herself inches from a tree. A slow flush warmed her skin. There at eye level were the initials H. K. + T. H. She had carved those herself, hadn't been aware that he knew about them. She had made them deliberately small so as not to draw attention. But the years had, as the beech grew, expanded and spread the initials into something impossible to miss.

She refused to look at his face, knowing he was grinning at her. "You must have liked me at one time," he said.

"I was young." And foolish, her tone implied.

He walked on. She thought of a gawky twelve-year-old in braids, scrambling worshipfully after a dark and handsome teenager. He had been kind, she had to admit, and never had implied by word or look that she was a nuisance. Just as he would never imply now, by as much as a stumble or pant, that she was a burden.

They had arrived. The trees thinned and fell away, and before them lay the large, flat slab where they had often sat looking down on their valley, their future. Neither of them had had any doubt that they would work and live where they had grown up. Neither of them had wanted anything else. It had been a secure feeling. Her eyes stung.

He set her down carefully on the boulder, dropped down beside her, and put a supporting arm at her back.

They sat so long in silence that the squirrels and chipmunks began to scurry about again. The rock was warm; she could almost imagine that she felt that warmth all the way down her useless legs. She could almost imagine that nothing had changed.

"Do you remember," Howard said finally, "what I asked you after your accident?"

She nodded without shifting her gaze from the placid scene below. The hospital room had been dim. She had wished they had taken her to Speedwell instead. The rooms were never dark there.

He had stood by the window with his back to her, only his white lab coat showing up well. On the TV screen, soap-opera characters moved and mouthed silently. She had been watching them indifferently; she had cut the sound when he came in. Soon a nurse would bring the baby. The baby was the only thing to live for.

"Trudy," he said, wheeling on her almost aggressively, "will you marry me?"

It was as unreal as the dramatics the actors were playing high on the wall.

Just pity, she decided. He thought she needed somebody to take care of her. Still, she was tempted. Didn't she deserve something? "No," she said.

She had considered it pity before she had had time to think what else it could be.

Now he said, "Will you answer me differently today?"

What should she say? Would he spare her and Jack if she agreed to be his wife? Speedwell would be virtually his then. Would that be good enough?

Howard, Howard, she thought, *if you only knew how easily you could have had me anytime. I only turned to Lance because you weren't interested. I could have been persuaded. Even now. That little pigtailed girl is still here, Howard. She never really learned. Jack wouldn't stand in your way either. He loves you as if you were his father.*

She thought of how as children she and Howard had laughed at the story of Rumpelstiltskin, laughed that any woman would agree to marry the king who had threatened her life. Of course, with kings you didn't have much choice.

If you don't spin my straw into gold, you will die.

"I'll think about it," she said finally.

She felt his laughter again. "Not as romantic an answer as I'd hoped for," he said, stroking her hair, "but better than the last one anyway."

A silent wave of longing shook her. How easy it would be to

turn and put her arms around him, say the words he wanted to hear.

What use is your resistance, when your family and friends betray you by not realizing, not believing, when your own heart and body betray you?

She had stiffened against his touch. He said, "Time we were getting back, I expect. It gets dark early these days."

Though sun lingered on the rock, the woods were already shadowy as they started down. She drove back without worrying about the curve, the unfamiliar controls. "But I don't even have a driver's license," she said to Howard as they got out.

"So you don't," he said with a wink. "Better apply for one, don't you think? You'll want to buy a smaller car eventually, too, instead of this bulky thing—and a lighter wheelchair. One you can just toss into the backseat." Eventually.

Regan was waiting on the hospital porch. When Howard had gone inside, Trudy said to her urgently, agitatedly, "Regan, you have to hurry. I can't hold out against him much longer."

CHAPTER 10

O, these I lack,
to make you garlands of, and my sweet friend,
to strew him o'er and o'er!

"You love him, don't you?" Regan said quietly. "Your determination that he was a killer had something of disillusionment in it."

"He never paid any attention to me," Trudy replied, "until after the accident didn't kill me. He asked me to marry him then. Howard is like that. If one method doesn't work, he won't waste time harping on it. He'll just try something different. A crippled wife wouldn't hinder him much—and he would have Speedwell."

In the lounge people were laughing and talking. They seemed far away to the two women on the porch, the timeless lapping of water more immediate.

"I thought I was over all that," Trudy went on. "I haven't seen him much in recent years. He seldom came over to the house. I would go for weeks, months, without setting eyes on the man, and it didn't bother me. I haven't been miserable, you know. I was content enough."

Regan smiled strangely. "You sound like me several months ago. I thought I was happy enough too. You and I are," she continued, looking out over the water, "very alike in some ways,

Trudy. Because we are afraid of disappointment, we don't expect much. When something good does happen, we mistrust it. We look at it from all sides. We feel there must be some catch to it. And because we take that attitude, we often lose it. Then we feel justified in our cynicism. And the whole wretched circle goes on. Sometimes we're right. But sometimes we're wrong too. It is much more likely Howard didn't realize how he felt about you until you almost died. That abrupt proposal was typical of him, I think. He isn't the type to beat about the bush. You have said yourself, if he wants something, he goes for it with none of our female fluster. And if he doesn't get it, he isn't the type to hang around and sulk."

The ruddy glow of sunset was on Regan's face as she turned her head to look at Trudy. "I can't believe that if he intended to kill you, he would dive in after you without waiting long enough to make certain you were dead. I know you think there is no other possibility. You didn't read this, did you?" She indicated a manila envelope on her lap. "When you were looking through that old stuff from the desk?"

Trudy gave it a puzzled glance. "Galen's play? No, I didn't. I'd read some others of his and never been very impressed."

"You need to read it. It implies, to me at least, that Vita's death was an accident. Nobody saw any alternative to murder at the time. If they were wrong then, you could be wrong now." She placed the envelope in the other woman's lap, stood up. "I told Matt about the dummy. I felt I had to. He's in there now; he was waiting to talk to Howard. There isn't much Matt can do about it. He doesn't think the state police will want to contribute any more men. We don't, after all, have any proof your life is in danger. He is going to suggest, I think, that Speedwell hire somebody."

Trudy shook her head. "We can't turn this place into an armed camp. That would sabotage everything we're trying to do here. Besides, I couldn't stand having somebody following me around all the time. When you're guarded, you're a prisoner."

"I was afraid you would say that. Be careful then. Stay in the same room with Jack's policeman as much as you can. Ask for angels."

■ ■ ■

Howard Keegan leaned forward in his chair, elbows on knees. "Is that a warning?"

"I'm only reminding you," Matt said, "of what Regan says she has already informed you. Trudy's life may be in danger. If you're innocent, you should want to protect her. If you aren't, you should be aware I know whom she suspects."

"So if something happens to her, I'll be in the hot seat? But I am already, aren't I?"

"You are one among a number of suspects. You left the dance shortly before Jack did. I saw you go myself. According to the time your nurses say you arrived back here, you must have dawdled a bit on the way."

"And I was in a nearby church alone when that shooting occurred in the hospital parking lot."

"Not to mention that you were out walking alone when that dummy was thrown in front of the van. You were also at the bee-venom lecture. You do seem to get around, Doctor."

"What can I say?" Keegan turned his hands palms up. "The job I do, I need my dawdling and praying and walking time to refuel. I am grateful you haven't mentioned any of this to the press."

"Last I heard, you're not guilty until I can prove it." Matt stood. "And I can't figure any good reason for a guy with your reputation to risk it all."

"Why do people on high places feel a strange urge to jump?" Keegan rose, grinning at Matt's expression. "I'm not saying that I do. I'm saying that I understand it. Being in a position of responsibility gets lonely. Haven't you found that so? You also," he added, smile fading, "have a lot farther to fall. Whatever the problem is between you and Regan, don't let it drag on too long. Being right is, I can assure you, not much consolation when you're also alone."

■ ■ ■

Driving home, Regan realized Trudy didn't need a solution to the forty-year-old mystery so much as she needed a solution to the current one. *I'll drive up to Trafalgar*, Regan decided, *after Ken's funeral.* All she knew of the town was a gray photo of a raw-looking lake. The place had turned up too many times, in the old case and in the new one, to be irrelevant. She should search the old house for the blanks gun, but that wasn't urgent. Not like the present situation was. Thus far, the murderer had been unlucky. But it was only a matter of time.

She found her foot pressing urgently at the accelerator. If she packed an overnight case, ran up there now, she could get an early start in the morning. It would mean missing Ken's funeral. But if she waited, there would be the ceremony itself, then interment, and probably some sort of dinner afterward. The afternoon would be spent by the time she got away. She could almost see Ken's flashing grin, hear his, "I'm *dead*, Miss Culver. It ain't going to make any difference to me whether you're there or not. So go already!"

She left the Land Rover on the drive in front of the porch and ran upstairs to throw a few small items in a carry-on bag. In her bed-and-breakfast directory, she found a Blue Lake Inn just outside of Trafalgar, made a phone call. Yes, they had a room available.

An hour later, she was eating a late dinner in an elegant but empty dining room. Apparently hers was not the only room that was available. It was October 30. The fall foliage season was over; the holidays yet to come.

The waiter approached. "We have," he said in the firm tones of one who is going to brook no refusal, "some excellent pumpkin flan."

"That will be nice," Regan replied weakly. She wasn't at all sure what flan was.

"A quiet night," the waiter commented as he placed her dessert in front of her.

Life, Regan decided, and flan were both peculiar. This morning she hadn't had the slightest notion that come nightfall she would be alone in a tasteful but overpriced inn, hovered over by a bored waiter.

Life, she discovered with almost the same surprise, was also good. As good as the nutmeg-tinged custard, the warm flutter of candle flame, the hot crackle in the nearby fireplace. In spite of death and danger and fracturing love.

As the poet Ruth Pitter had put it, "All life is strange:...all mantled in mystery of perpetual change..."

"I suppose," Regan said to the waiter, "you're much busier in the summer."

"Much," the waiter unbent to agree. "The families up at the lake, you know. Come down around Memorial Day, go back to town about Labor Day. But most return on weekends right up through October."

"So Trafalgar is a tourist town?"

The waiter's brow furrowed. "Hardly. With Trafalgar virtually a private lake, we are spared the riffraff. Mr. Norville's development company owns it all. They put in a lot of plush, secluded vacation cottages. Well, hardly cottages, but that's what they call them. We only get the best people these days. It's done wonders for the town. All the old shops have been restored into little art and antique stores. The British name gives us a certain cachet too, you can guess."

Regan could. All in the best taste, but good taste carried to extremes could be stifling. Where had she heard the name Norville before?

"Speak of the devil," the waiter muttered and she looked toward the door to see a handsome, expensively suited gentleman of forty-odd years with his coat draped over his arm.

"Evenin', Gene," the gentleman said. "I know I'm late, but will it still be possible to get a meal?"

"Certainly, sir." The waiter hurried to take the man's coat and ushered him to a table near Regan. "I was just telling the lady here about our lake. Miss Culver, this is Mason Norville."

Norville bowed slightly in her direction. "I am pleased to meet you, ma'am. Have you traveled far?"

"I'm from Hayden."

"You don't say?" Sitting down, he turned invitingly toward her. "My father originally hoped to make Speedwell Lake the site of his development, but it was not to be. He was close friends with Galen Hargrove, but Galen's father refused to sell, I'm afraid. Do you know the family?"

"Oh, yes."

"I've always had hopes of succeeding where my father failed. I've thought that Speedwell, with its fine reputation, could be turned into a world-class spa. With development similar to what we have here. I invite Galen's son, Myron, and his wife up a couple of times a year just to keep my oar in. The grandfather is getting up in years, isn't he?"

"Yes," Regan said. "He was a close friend of my father's."

"Really? You must be Alden Culver's daughter." He half-rose in his seat, as if hoping to be asked to join her.

"That's right. Somehow I don't think that Amos or his daughter will be amenable to your plan, Mr. Norville." She ignored his movement, and he subsided reluctantly.

"So I understand. Myron will inherit the eastern side of the lake, but of course, half a pie is no good to us. Our customers enjoy their privacy, you see. Perhaps you could speak to Amos for me, Miss Culver. We would be quite open to retaining the staff at Speedwell. Look at our town here and imagine what we could do for Hayden. I'd be happy to show you around, if you like."

"That's nice of you," Regan said, gathering up her purse. "But I'm afraid I have some inquiries to make that will take up most of my time. Do you know a family named Scion by any chance? Or Dawson?"

"I don't know any Dawsons," Norville said, "but the Scions were one of the town's founding families, I understand. They experienced a tragedy this spring, actually. Teenage girl fell off her horse and died. Really promising girl. Everybody liked her. What was her name now? Something like Betty…"

"Betony," Regan stated more than suggested.

"You're right. That's what it was. Betony Scion."

■ ■ ■

When Amos came into Jack's room that evening, he paused to put a hand on Trudy's shoulder. "What are you reading, my dear?"

She shuffled together the yellowed pages and handed them to him. "I think you had better see this."

The old man took the papers and sat down to peruse them under the curious stare of the guard. "I see," Amos said quietly when he had finished, passed the manuscript to the policeman to whom he added, "Though you won't, probably. It's an old story."

And to Trudy, "So now you think it was an accident?"

"Don't you?"

"I hope so. I really hope so."

■ ■ ■

Regan lay on the four-poster bed in her room and stared up at the canopy. It hadn't been easy getting away from Mason

Norville. He had been disappointed in her. The waiter had been disappointed.

Although she had designed gardens for many of the wealthy, Regan had never been comfortable in that world. Her own home could, she supposed, be called upper middle class. But her mother, Rosemary, had spent her first thirty-some years in virtual penury. As a result, Rosemary had, for the rest of her life, practiced economies that were ridiculous.

Partly, Regan supposed, out of habit. Partly, to avoid any implication she had married Alden Culver for his money. Regan herself felt some guilt about the cost of this room, even though it was only for one night, even though she had inherited several hundred thousand dollars from her father.

You taught me well, Mother. Regan purchased many of her own clothes at thrift shops. She had a good enough eye for style and quality that most people would not have guessed her wardrobe's source. *I got the money from Dad, and my guilt about it from you, Mother.*

Of course, those economies might become necessary. Regan had plunged a large percentage of her fortune into expansion of the herb farm. If it failed…she turned her head restlessly. *You know there isn't any point in harping on that. Why do you do it? Of course, there would be one advantage to bankruptcy,* she thought wryly. *Matt Olin would probably be much happier about me if I were broke.*

She should be thinking about what she was going to do tomorrow. She should have realized that the Betony Scion now in Hayden, if a fake, would have needed some school records to transfer. How better than to steal those of a dead student?

Hayden was far enough away that nobody there was likely to have heard, or cared, about the accident. Say Raven Scion was Trudy's cousin. Was it possible he believed he could inherit from her? In that case, he would almost have to contest her adoption.

He might be able to do that, she realized, if Trudy's father, Jack, had not really been dead at the time of the adoption. You would surely have to have the natural father's permission for that.

As for the rest of the plan, it might have worked if Amos and Trudy had died in the same van crash. Regan seemed to remember that when two people died together and there was no way of telling who had gone first, it was legally assumed that the legatee had outlived the benefactor. Trudy would have inherited, and what she had inherited would have gone to her son. If that son were already dead, as he was supposed to have been, it would have gone to any other of her heirs. Howard would not have gotten it unless Trudy and Jack's deaths preceded Amos's.

Would Trudy's cousin have murdered on the chance he might be able to make a case for himself as Trudy's heir? If he knew about Norville's desire for Speedwell, maybe. A man might risk a lot for a chance at several million dollars.

Regan found a phone book on the bedside table. Only one Dawson was listed, a woman, Merilee. She did not sound merry when she answered the phone. She had a hoarse smoker's voice and the tone of one who didn't expect much joy from any telephone call.

"Ma'am, my name is Regan Culver. I'm investigating the murder of Vita Dawson forty years ago and the disappearance of her husband, Jack. Are you related to Jack Dawson?"

"My husband is. I don't know anything about it. My husband isn't here now. He's in prison."

"I would like to talk to you anyway, if I might. Will you be home tomorrow morning?"

"Where else?"

"And where," Regan glanced at the listing again, "would Hyde Lane be?"

"Hidden, where else?" Merilee barked a humorless laugh. "It's behind the feed mill. Don't come before nine. I like to sleep in."

The following morning Regan had a leisurely breakfast in the empty dining room, paid for her stay, and returned to her room to pick up her bag. It was almost nine.

"Mornin', Mason," someone was calling outside. Regan tugged back a heavy lace curtain to peer out. Norville had just pulled up to the curb in a dark BMW. He waved to somebody across the street and advanced purposefully toward the inn's doorway.

Regan remained in place, biting her lip, after he disappeared. She wasn't surprised when the phone on the bedside table began to shrill. She allowed the curtain to fall back into place, swung her bag over her shoulder, and crept out into the hall, turning away from the front staircase toward the smaller one at the back that led down to the lounge and thence to the garden. As she descended, she heard the cheerful voice of the innkeeper coming up the other way. "Her car is still here," he was saying, "so she should be too. Unless she's gone for a walk."

Regan strode across the lounge, a comfy room with shelves of books, chintz, and fresh flowers. Too bad she wouldn't get to use it. The innkeeper was knocking up above. "Miss Culver, are you there?"

Regan ran lightly down some steps into the garden, trotted along a dew-damp brick walk. They had, she noted with approval, that most favored of the English dahlias, Bishop of Llandaff, with its scarlet blooms startling against dark maroon foliage. She yanked open the Land Rover's door and hurled her bag into the passenger side. A window was thrown up somewhere. "Miss Culver!" the innkeeper persisted. "Please wait! Mr. Norville is here."

Regan gave no sign of hearing him, slammed the door and started the engine to cut off the importuning voice, navigated the drive that looped around to the street. As she paused to check for traffic, Mason ran toward her from the inn's front door, waving.

She waved blithely in return and pulled out. In her rearview mirror, she saw him shake his head in frustration and dash to his car. While his back was turned, she swerved into a side street and took several more turns until she was sure she had lost him. She sat in the vehicle at a crossroads, debating which way to go. To her right was a long, low brick building with a curving drive at the front and athletic fields at the back. Almost certainly the high school. She decided she might as well stop there first.

Just in case Norville was cruising around looking for her, she parked in a lot behind the school. It wouldn't take Norville long, she suspected, to cover a small town like Trafalgar. Inside, she approached the area marked Offices. A long counter closed it off with only one swinging gate for entrance or egress. A fiftyish woman with tight, waxy skin and a sweater set said, "May I help you?"

"I hope so. I wanted to inquire about a girl who used to be a student here. Betony Scion?"

The secretary's expression turned wooden. "She's dead."

"Yes, I've been informed of that. I was surprised to learn it. You see, a girl calling herself Betony Scion attends Hayden High School now. And she claims to have transferred from here."

"That's preposterous." Red spots burned high in the other woman's sallow cheeks. "We've only had one Betony here. She was a lovely girl. It was a great loss. How anyone would dare—"

"I assume," Regan said, "that this false Betony must somehow have had access to your records. To transfer them, I mean."

The secretary's lips thinned. Without a word, she turned on her heel, plucked a ring of keys from a tray on her immaculate desk, and advanced on a bank of filing cabinets along the back wall. She crouched down on her heels to reach a lower one.

Regan edged to one side so she could watch the woman's hands. The hallway was quiet but for the distant drone of a teacher's voice.

Competent, short-nailed fingers flicked swiftly through file tabs, paused. "They're not here." The secretary shoved the door shut and locked it again, stood to look almost defiantly at Regan across her desk.

"Who would have had access?" Regan asked. "Who is allowed back there?"

"Staff members come in to pick up their mail." The secretary gestured toward a wall of cubbyholes on her right. "The principal's office is behind mine."

"Were any staff members here last year who aren't here now? There is," Regan explained, "some suspicion that this student is actually older than she claims to be."

The woman thought, tapping her nails on the back of her desk chair. "The nurse," she said finally. "Miss Bumpkiss."

"Do you have a photo of her?"

The secretary plucked a yearbook from between bookends on her desk, carried it across to the counter, and began to leaf through the pages. A man came out of the office behind her, headed for the gate but hesitated as he saw Regan. "Good morning."

Both women looked at him. "Good morning," Regan returned politely. When the secretary made no attempt at introduction or explanation, he shambled away down the hall.

"Principal," she explained shortly. "New. Incompetent. Wouldn't know anything. No point in asking. Here."

She shoved the book across, pointing. The picture was overbright, but the nurse was short and rather attractive with an impatient twist to her smile. Regan, about to shake her head, stopped and considered that twist. "Maybe," she murmured. "She doesn't wear any makeup now, and her hair is straight with bangs, but she does have that same bored air. Yes, I think it could be she. Why did she leave?"

The secretary smelled of soap and pencil erasers. She closed the yearbook. "There was some suspicion she might be dispensing more than aspirin. She left before it could be proved. What are you going to do about it?"

"I would like you, if you would," Regan said, "to call the police chief in my hometown and tell him what you've discovered. I'll write down his name and number. I have some other things to look into while I'm here, but I think he should know right away. We've been having some drug problems at our school too. Will you do that?"

"Certainly. I never liked Amy Bumpkiss. And I did like Betony. Everybody did. Why is it always the good ones who are taken?"

Regan didn't know what to say. Two teenagers gone, and another close to death. Of course, with Betony it had probably been just an accident. But any extinguishing of youth must seem an unnatural death.

■ ■ ■

Merilee Dawson's place turned out to be a beauty shop, a white, peeling one-storied building with living quarters in the back. "Mason Norville phoned," Merilee said when she came to the door. She was heavy with dark hair, hollow eyes, and a knowing smile. "Offered me cash if I would call him when you showed up."

"What did you say?"

"Told him the only thing I sold was hairdos. Want yours done? Might as well, while you're here."

"All right. Nothing permanent though. No cutting or dying. I like it long. It does need to be washed."

"No problem." Merilee snuffed out her cigarette, pointed to a chair in front of a basin. "All the high muckety-mucks say no woman should have long hair after thirty. What do they know? Yours is nice." She unpinned it deftly. "Needs a bit more pizzazz, though, if you want to impress the guys. Guys aren't subtle, you know. They go for the obvious. Wear red or black, I say—and the shinier the better. Of course, you can't be doing too bad if you have Mr. Moneybags sniffing around."

"It isn't me he's courting," Regan explained, relaxing under the influence of warm water and massaging fingers on her scalp. "I know somebody he wants to do business with."

"You have scales," Merilee said. "Stress, I expect. I'll put some vinegar in the rinse. I can always tell when my customers are having a bad week. What do you want with John?"

"Just to know where he is, mainly. A man is hanging around Hayden we can't identify. Some think he might be the Jack Dawson who disappeared, but he seems too young for that."

"Last I knew, John had been shipped to some prison down in Texas. You know how they shuffle them around these days. Of course, he might not tell me if he was getting out. Always was a secretive cuss. The expect-me-when-you-see-me sort. You married?"

"Engaged. At least, I *think* I still am. To the police chief in Hayden."

Merilee laughed. "He's one of the touchy types, huh? Steer clear, I say. Those ones have got a warp somewhere. Worse than buying a car when the frame is cracked. Of course, we females never learn. We're the fix-it sex. You can't fix people, sweetheart. I learned that a long time ago." She patted the excess moisture out of Regan's hair with a towel. "I think we'll put some big curlers up top for volume, some smaller ones at the bottom to give you some bounce. So you're helping your guy out, huh? Trying to sweeten him up a little?"

"Actually, he doesn't know I'm here. You probably aren't old enough to remember Jack Dawson, are you?" Regan asked.

"I'm fifty-two and don't look a day over forty. I would have been twelve or so when he was supposed to have killed himself. He came back here first after the war, you know. I don't remember that but did hear my mother talk about it later. This town wasn't good enough for him anymore. We could have used a doctor, actually, but he had other plans. Trafalgar wasn't much to look at in the fifties. Tell you the truth, I liked it better then. Almost everybody was poor so it didn't matter. We helped each other out. Most of us were honest too. Except the Dawsons. They had a bad reputation. Nobody expected Jack to make anything of himself, were surprised when he did. Maybe that's why he left. Of course, when he killed his wife, they all said they had known it couldn't last."

Merilee continued to swirl Regan's hair around the curlers. "I felt sorry for John. And a high school girl is more attracted to the wolves than the sheep, you know. John didn't need my sympathy. He's not really the sensitive type. The slights didn't bother him any. He's always been nice enough to me when he's around. Doesn't drink, doesn't beat me up. I can't complain really."

"Is he intelligent?" Regan asked. "Could he get away with pretending to be somebody else? Does he like word games, for instance?"

"No." Finished with the curlers, Merilee rolled Regan's chair across to an old hood-type dryer. "John's smart enough about some things, but that would be too fancy for him. He just robbed houses when nobody was home, got away with it for a long time. He was careful; they had a hard time proving anything. Always told me he was a traveling salesman. Well, he *did* travel. And he sold *me* a bill of goods, all right. I'll turn this on and see if I can find a picture of him."

Regan closed her eyes under the roaring warmth of the dryer. John Dawson didn't sound too promising. Of course, a man who could fool his wife about his daily activities might also fool her about the scope of his intellect. How much could you really read another person, even those intimate to you, under what they chose to show? Love was a gamble against long odds.

When someone touched her on the arm, she started, came awake. "Everybody snoozes under there," Merilee hollered above the roar, placed a photo in Regan's hand.

Regan studied it long and carefully. John Dawson leaned back in a porch chair with his feet up on the railing, grinning in a lazy sort of way. Medium build, receding hair, and a distinctively small, full mouth. Peeking up at Merilee, Regan shook her head. The woman appeared relieved. Maybe she wasn't as indifferent to her husband's activities as she appeared.

Raven Scion's mane could be a wig, Regan thought. But she would have noticed that mouth.

When Regan's hair was dry, Merilee began to take out the curlers. "Is it all right if I keep this?" Regan asked her. "I'll need to prove to some people that it isn't he."

"Go ahead. I must admit, you had me worried. After Chief Larkin came around yesterday."

So Matt *had* thought to check with the local police. He wouldn't, she was gloomily certain, appreciate her horning in on the investigation. What else had she planned to do while she was here? "Is the bridge still open to the public?" she asked. "The one across the lake, I mean."

"Yep. It's about the only part of the lake that is. Most of us common types have to do our fishing from there these days. It's why I'm none too fond of your friend Norville. The town is prettier now, I'll grant you that. But all this country style is a put-on with them, if you know what I mean."

"Contrived," Regan suggested.

"And how! It all looks like a stage set. And the real country kids aren't happy here anymore. Granted, most of them probably would have left anyway. But when they have to look, day in and day out, at what all of them rich kids got…We had a few well-off families to begin with, of course. But people like the Scions didn't put on airs. They didn't put on anything. They were folks just like the rest of us. Betony used to sit in this chair all the time; she didn't like that French guy uptown. I think her dying was the end. She was the Scions' only kid. They aren't the same anymore; nothing is." Finished combing out Regan's hair, Merilee handed her a mirror. "Sorry to be such a gloomy Gus. I'm not usually."

"That's all right." Regan's hair was now parted on the side instead of the middle. It looked fuller, curled under at the shoulders, bounced. "It's beautiful." She handed the mirror back, climbed out of the chair. "I'm just glad that Norville's father didn't come to Hayden as he originally had planned. Your loss, our gain. Thank you so much, Merilee." Regan pressed a twenty into the other woman's hand. "If you ever decide to move, consider Hayden first, won't you?"

"Will do." Merilee looked gratified. "I wouldn't mind the upper crust so much if they was all like you."

"That's because I'm not really upper crust," Regan said. "I run an herb company. That makes me a glorified farmer."

Looking out the door to discover Norville's car parked by her own, she added, "But who has a pitchfork when she needs one? I guess I'll just have to be rude. I was trying to avoid that."

"Want me to do it?" Merilee asked helpfully.

"No, that's okay. I spent most of my life avoiding confrontation until a few months ago. I don't want to regress."

Regan straightened, took a deep breath, opened the door, and started down the cracked walk.

"Miss Culver!" Norville was out of his car before she was halfway to her own. "I've been looking all over for you—"

He had started eagerly forward before her cold stare stopped him. "I mean, that is, I—"

"I thought I had made it clear," Regan said, "that I was going to be very busy today."

"Well, yes, I know you said that, but I assumed—"

"That my business wasn't important?"

"No, no. If you would just let me show you around, I know you would be—"

"Impressed? I haven't been thus far. From what I've heard, your development has spoiled this town's real character. People were here when your father arrived. What happened to them? It looks to me as if they've gradually been squeezed down or out. I don't want that for my town, thank you."

"But people should be grateful. We brought increased employment. Land went up in value."

"So that only the elite could afford it? Forget it, Mr. Norville. Healing people is what Amos Hargrove does. Seriously *ill* people, not debutantes who want to shed a few pounds in a pampered atmosphere. Frankly, I would consider your plan for Speedwell the end of everything it has ever stood for."

Norville was getting angry. "That end, as you call it, Miss Culver, might be closer than you think."

"You don't say? Do you know something about the attempted murders of Amos's daughter and grandson?"

Norville paled. "I had nothing to do with that."

"Just as your father had nothing to do with what happened to Jack and Vita Dawson? Jack was an ambitious man, and he came from this town. He could have known your father. Was his marrying and killing Vita part of a plot to discourage Amos from keeping on with his clinic? Killing off its future, as it were?"

Norville glanced nervously sideways at an attentive Merilee Dawson. "I will thank you, Miss Culver," he ground out, "to remember the laws about slander."

"I wasn't making a statement," Regan said sweetly. "I was asking a question. As I'm sure Merilee here will testify. Doesn't it seem strange, Merilee, that Jack Dawson would return to a town he hated to commit suicide? Much more likely, don't you think that he came back to meet somebody? To collect his pay, maybe?"

"I would be very careful, if I were you," Mason Norville snapped, striding to his car.

"Don't pay any attention," Merilee advised. "That one's all bark. His father was a different story. Do you really believe what you were implying there?"

"It doesn't seem to fit with the latest evidence I've collected. But it does mesh nicely in several other places." Regan sighed. "That old crime looked obvious on the surface but turned out to be much more complicated than I thought. For a few moments there at the school I thought the new one was going to prove easy after all. But if Raven Scion isn't your husband, who *is* he? You would have met Amy Bumpkiss. Did she have a brother, a boyfriend, a husband?"

"Not that I know of. She struck me as a pretty cold fish. Send me a photo," Merilee suggested. "If the guy's from around here, I bet I can identify him. May I say that, for somebody not good at confrontation, you don't pull any punches."

Regan smiled ruefully. "That's probably why I always avoided it. Once I get going, I don't know when to stop. And I call myself a Christian too."

"Hey," Merilee said, "from what I've heard, Christ could be plenty direct at times. At least you didn't call Mason a pretty grave full of rotting bones. Although," she added thoughtfully, "it's probably an appropriate description."

CHAPTER 11

■ ■ ■

What, like a corse?

Regan stood on the bridge over Blue Lake, wondering if Jack Dawson's bones lay moldering somewhere under the pretty water. The bridge was wide with pull-off areas allowed on both sides. Two or three retired men fished silently, leaning against the railings.

It was not a long fall to the water. A man would have had to be pretty determined to die here. She did not think the plunge would have killed Jack—stunned him, perhaps, and allowed water in the lungs to finish the job. But in that case, wouldn't his body have surfaced eventually? She looked down the lake at the cottages in their vernal settings.

An elderly man walking an Irish wolfhound paused beside Regan. "Nice view, isn't it? You should have been here two weeks ago. It was breathtaking then."

"I can imagine. How long has this development been here?"

"Close on forty years, I think. Norville started it in the fifties. Hank, that is. The old man. That's his place there." The old man nodded at the nearest house. "Next came, I think, the Cordells."

Regan jerked her head around to stare at him. "Faye's parents?"

He looked uneasy. "They had a daughter named Faye, yes. They're both dead now. Faye is in an institution. Her brother has the cottage."

"I know Faye's son. I had thought I might stop and see her when I was up this way. Do you know where this institution is?"

He inclined his head west. "Over in Inglenook. Next town. The asylum is called Green Meadows. I don't think I'd bother, if I were you. It's a depressing place."

Looking across the bridge in the direction he had indicated, Regan wondered if this was where she should stop. It was better surely for Trudy to believe that her stepmother's killing had been accidental, or even an impulsive act rising from a sudden rage.

What if we come to the end only to find our worst fears realized, not only about Jack Dawson but also about his grandson? And maybe Howard Keegan too? Not to mention the horrible possibility that every believer must deal with, that we may come to the ultimate end to find nothing there, to discover that God was all in our minds. Ruby is right. Cynicism would be easier.

But even as she wondered, Regan knew she would go on. "Where is the truth that will inform my sorrow? I am sure myself that sorrow is not the truth." Ruth Pitter's verse had been a mainstay to Regan as she mourned for her father. Because underlying the Christian poet's most melancholy passages was a steely hope.

Our continual searching is necessary, isn't it? Because by it we show faith that there is something, someone to be found.

■ ■ ■

Green Meadows didn't look depressing when Regan stopped her Land Rover at the big, wrought-iron gates. It looked, in fact, like a converted country estate. A guard came to open the gates for her. "Who were you planning to visit, ma'am?" he asked politely. When she told him, he relayed the message over a hand-held radio, listened intently to the return crackle. "All right, ma'am. You can drive on up. The parking space is to the right of the drive. An orderly will meet you on the porch."

She continued over neatly raked gravel to the mansion. Here and there, people walked on velvety lawns or knelt in flower beds. But it seemed, for an institution, too quiet. Her tires crunched loudly. The slam of the door, when she got out, echoed off the building's gray stone. A young man in white lounged in a wicker chair on the porch, photo ID pinned to his shirt pocket. He got up. "Ma'am?"

"I wanted to see Faye Cordell. If that's all right." His silence caused her to babble on. "My name's Regan Culver. I don't know her really, but I'm looking into an event that occurred forty years ago. I thought she might be able to help me."

"This way, ma'am." He led the way down the steps to a sidewalk that curved away to the right. "She's been here a long time. When her father died, he left a trust fund for her keep; so I expect she'll stay until she dies."

"How is she doing?"

He shrugged. "Most of our patients seem content enough. Her original doctor thought she wasn't willing to face up to something, that her illness was a kind of protection for her, a retreat. We get some like that. They don't usually get better. You can't change unless you want to."

They had come to a row of small cottages built from the same stone as the main house. "I'd better warn you," the orderly said, "that she's the histrionic type. They tend to overreact to everything. So don't get concerned if she starts yelling. Also, when she's really worked up, she tends to skip words. Impressionistic speech, we call it. You have to fill in the blanks."

He approached a door and rapped. "Miss Cordell, you have a visitor." Apparently Faye had gone back to her maiden name. He led the way inside without waiting for a response. Faye sat in an armchair near the window, although the curtains were drawn. She didn't seem to be doing anything except looking at the clock over the mantel.

Faye was still an attractive woman. Although she must be seventy, she appeared younger. Her hair was cropped in a short, almost faddish style. Her face was carefully made up. She wore an artsy necklace of dichroic glass. She had been quite still, but after Regan sat down, the woman's hands went nervously to her pendant, her dark eyes moved restlessly, focusing on anything but her visitor.

"My name is Regan Culver. I know your son, Myron. He lives in Hayden like I do." No response. "I also know Trudy Hargrove. Do you remember Trudy? She probably would have been a child the last time you saw her, about three years old." Regan thought that the fitful gaze was narrowing in, that somewhere behind it Faye was listening warily. The orderly waited in the background.

"Trudy has asked me to look into her stepmother's death. You remember Vita and Jack? Jack was supposed to have shot Vita and run away. Run away up here, to Trafalgar. Your parents had a vacation house on Blue Lake then. Did Jack hide there? Were you two lovers? Is that what Vita was angry about?"

Faye laughed shortly. "Jack was hidden all right. By water."

"He did drown then?"

The dark eyes blinked craftily. "I didn't say that."

"But he is dead?"

"Yes."

"You're sure?"

"Yes."

"But how? His daughter wants to know how he died. Can't you tell me?"

No answer.

"It's been forty years, Faye. Surely it doesn't matter if you tell now."

"He said it wouldn't matter either. That it would be over fast, and we would have the money." Her voice had started out low and gradually escalated in volume. "He said easy. But real not easy. Like horse, takes bit, won't stop. No money—all for nothing!" She was shrieking now, leaning forward to glare into Regan's face. The orderly edged closer. "Whole life all for nothing!"

"Which he?" Regan asked. "Jack?"

Faye sank back exhausted. "Stupid, stupid woman. All stupid except Ian. Ruined everything. Wrong ones died. Should have been Ian. Ian important one. Any woman knows that. Real not like plan. Goes quietly, you feel safe, then bolts."

"What was the plan, Faye? To make Amos want to sell Speedwell? Was that it?"

A wily glance. Faye still had some sense of self-preservation.

"You got sent there on purpose, didn't you? You were part of the plan. Why was it necessary for you to be there? It doesn't seem like you did much."

Faye's pride was piqued. "Couldn't have done it without me."

"Done what?"

Faye tossed her head, puffed up her chest, made a prissy patting motion that implied a fuller mane, a fuller figure. Faye must have been, Regan realized, a good actress. "Vita, complacent cow. Too dumb to live. Who misses her?"

"And Jack?"

Faye looked sly again.

"Can't you tell me straight out, Faye? Did Jack kill Vita?"

"They say." Faye smiled. "Witnesses. Argument."

"But that argument was part of a play. It wasn't real. Didn't Galen tell you?"

Faye's eyes widened. Then her head snapped back against her chair. Staring at the ceiling, she began to croon wordlessly.

"Was the gun supposed to be loaded with blanks?" Regan persisted. The crooning amplified. Faye began to writhe against the chair back.

"Might as well give it up," the orderly said. "You must have hit too close to home. That's what she does when she's had enough. Sometimes I wonder if she's really mad at all—whether it isn't all just an act."

Outside, he said to Regan, "What was all that anyway? You think she witnessed a murder?"

"Or helped commit it," Regan replied. "Though I must admit I can't figure how she was necessary, except to provide Jack Dawson a place to run. And she wouldn't have had to be there for that. I guess I'm not cut out to be a detective. The further I go into this case, the more snarled it becomes. Do you think there would be any point in my coming back another day?"

The orderly shook his head. "If she's taken a dislike to you, she'll start that tuning out when she sees you coming. Used to do it to her father. She blamed him for not encouraging her acting career."

"She is good, though, isn't she?"

He nodded. "She could have been. But she's one of those people who can't carry through on anything. I've heard she idealized her husband at the beginning, hated him by the time she came here. Was an enthusiastic mother the first year or so, indifferent now. The type you can literally call unstable. Are you a private eye?" He studied her face. "Haven't I seen you somewhere? On TV maybe?"

Regan got that reaction a lot these days. Her father's murder had made the national news for only a couple of days before another, juicier scandal eclipsed it. So people only vaguely remembered her face and seldom her name.

"Actually," she said, as she crossed to her Land Rover and shot him an enigmatic smile, "I'm a farmer."

■ ■ ■

Matt hung up the phone, scowling. The caller had been a secretary at the high school in Trafalgar. She had been asked to contact him but couldn't remember the woman's name who had made the request. Dark hair, almost Spanish looking, wore an antique brooch.

Regan was fond of brooches. But what was she doing in Trafalgar? Pursuing suspicions about Betony, apparently. And what was he supposed to do about it? He could arrest Betony, or Amy, as her real name seemed to be, for stealing those files and for impersonation. But what was the point of that impersonation?

Drug dealing seemed the most likely answer. But who was the guy? There had been no guy in Trafalgar, as far as the secretary knew. And in a small town, she would have known.

He had asked the secretary for the name and number of the real Betony's parents, put in a call to them, finally located the father at the bank he owned. Scion was flabbergasted, then furious. It might, Matt thought, be good for him. When the man had answered the phone, he had sounded flat, mechanical, like someone just going through the motions.

Scion wanted the impostor prosecuted and would drive down to Hayden himself, if necessary. No, he knew no one named Raven Scion, didn't recall anyone he knew leaving Trafalgar at the same time the nurse did. He had known the nurse, in fact, only distantly. She had kept pretty much to herself.

Matt called the new principal, who knew nothing, and the old one, who knew little more. He didn't recall that Miss Bumpkiss had had any male friends, few friends at all, actually. Not hard to see why. She acted aloof, superior. He thought maybe she had come to Trafalgar in hopes of snaring a rich husband and wasn't going to be satisfied with anyone less. No proof, of course, just a thought.

Matt tried the courthouse in that county. There was no record of an Amy Bumpkiss applying for a marriage license. He phoned the state police and had them run her name through their computer. No record of an Amy Bumpkiss wanted any-where. That probably wasn't her real name either. If Regan was going to do his job for him, she might at least provide more detailed information.

His phone rang. It was a hairdresser in Trafalgar, John Dawson's wife, in fact. She too had something to tell him. Regan Culver had said straight off that John Dawson could not be Raven Scion.

"Do you know where your husband is, Mrs. Dawson?" Matt asked.

"No," she replied sweetly. "Do you know where your fiancée is?"

A definite hit. Matt swallowed his temper. "Did she say where she was going next?"

"She wanted to look at the bridge where Jack Dawson's car was found forty years ago. One of our local millionaires was pursuing her—Mason Norville."

Matt sat up. "What did he want?"

"What does any guy want from a good-looking woman? She claimed he only needed her to put in a good word for him with the guy who owns Speedwell Lake. But I think she's selling her-self short. I bet Mason desires more than just the lake."

Matt frowned. "This guy wants Speedwell? How badly?"

"To the tune of several million, I would say. I wouldn't underestimate him, if I were you. Money talks, and he has enough to make quite a speech."

Big money, Matt thought after he had hung up, made much more sense as a motive in this case than drugs did. But it all depended on who thought they were going to get what. Trudy might have a point after all. Maybe Howard Keegan would like to retire as a rich man. Not that he was poor at the moment, but a few million as a cushion wouldn't hurt. People weren't very rational when it came to large amounts of money, as evidenced by lottery fever. Many these days had a sense of entitlement. More than most, Keegan might be justified in that belief.

If this Norville wanted it all, Myron wouldn't be able to sell his section until whoever owned Speedwell was willing. And until Trudy agreed to give up the portion that had belonged to her father and stepmother. And if Raven Scion was really a Dawson...

All of this might, of course, have nothing to do with Jack Hargrove's collapse or Ken's murder. It might all go back to narcotics and an unscrupulous nurse. Nurse. Amy had been a nurse. And it had been a nurse who had tried to give Jack an unauthorized hypodermic. Woods had had that hypodermic tested. It had contained a massive dose of heroin. She had made her attempt at the same time somebody else was shooting Ken. That meant she wasn't in it alone. That meant Raven Scion.

Matt glanced at the clock. Eleven. He had a good idea where Raven and Betony would be this afternoon, along with almost everybody else in town. Ken's funeral was at one.

■ ■ ■

But Raven Scion wasn't there. Matt arrived late, just as people were leaving the funeral home to climb into flagged cars and limousines. Betony, in a long-sleeved navy dress, turned toward an Escort at the end of the line.

Matt was not alone; Lieutenant Woods accompanied him. "Might we speak to you for a moment, Miss Scion?" he said. She turned, seeming neither surprised nor fearful.

Lucerne had been about to get into the limousine with Mabel Fermin, Myron Hargrove, and several of the teachers. Now she turned and walked back toward the policemen, her heels ringing loudly in a sudden silence. Everywhere, people got out of their cars again and stood watching.

I am going to look an awful fool if I'm wrong, Matt thought.

"Would you," he asked Betony, "be willing to raise your right arm for us?"

She frowned at him, seeming genuinely puzzled. "Raise my arm?"

"Yes, just put your hand up, as if you were volunteering in class."

She shrugged and complied. As she did so, the navy sleeve slipped down, revealing half-healed pink scratches on the underside of her wrist.

"You!" Lucerne said. "It was you!"

Betony finally comprehended. "Those don't prove anything. I got caught in a bramble."

"Maybe not," Lieutenant Woods admitted. "But the red wig and green contacts we found at your place do. Amy Bumpkiss, alias Betony Scion, I am placing you under arrest for the attempted murder of Jack Hargrove on the morning of October 29 at Clearview Hospital. You have the right..."

When he had finished reciting the Miranda warning and was snapping handcuffs around her wrists, Matt asked, "Where is the man who has been posing as your father, Miss Bumpkiss?"

She merely smiled, looking beyond them to where Mabel Fermin had climbed out of the limousine and was saying to everybody and nobody in particular, "Was it her? Did she do it?"

"She couldn't have killed your son," Lucerne said, raising her voice. "She was occupied elsewhere at the time. It must have been Raven or John Dawson or whoever he really is."

"*Not* John Dawson." Nobody had noticed the Land Rover arrive. Regan Culver had come quietly up on the far side of the group. "I've just been to Trafalgar to see his wife." She extended a photo to Matt, and he accepted it almost reluctantly. "The shape of the mouth is all wrong."

"It might be more to the point," Myron Hargrove said, "to find Scion first and figure out who he is afterward. I suggest we leave that to the officers and get on with this interment."

"Come on." Lucerne turned to Regan. "You can ride with us in the limousine and tell us all about it."

"I'll take her out to the cemetery," Matt said. It was not so much a suggestion as an order.

Lieutenant Woods hustled his prisoner away.

With icy politeness, Matt held the passenger door of the patrol car for Regan. He remained silent as he pulled in front of the limousine, switched on his revolving light to lead the procession. They rolled through Hayden, which basked in simulated serenity under the autumn sun. Then they started the climb toward the cemetery on the hill.

"What were you doing in Trafalgar anyway?" he asked. "Did you think I needed some help?"

She swallowed what would have been an equally snappish response. "I went to Trafalgar because of the older mystery. But I figured that as long as I was there, I might as well check up on Betony."

"And it never occurred to you to mention what about Betony had aroused your suspicion?"

"It was just something that Ruby Abiel said. She thought the girl was older than she claimed to be. It wasn't enough to take to the police."

"So that's what I am to you—the police?" They were rolling into the narrow, shaded lanes of the old cemetery that overlooked the town.

"Have you tried being anything else lately? Perhaps not talking is the best thing for us right now, if you're going to be like this." They had rolled to a stop not far from the raw earth of a newly opened grave. Regan shoved open her door and climbed out without waiting for him. He came around the car and offered her his arm. There was no way to refuse without having everyone see and note it.

"I should be happy," he said in an undertone, "that you're off flirting with the jet set?"

She shot him an exasperated look. "If you spoke to Merilee, she should have informed you that I told Norville off—royally. Can we forget this until later please?"

In any case, they would have to. The minister was beginning to read. "Jesus said unto her, I am the resurrection, and the life: he that believeth in me, though he were dead, yet shall he live: And whosoever liveth and believeth in me shall never die.... For he that is dead is freed from sin. Now if we be dead with Christ, we believe that we shall also live with him: Knowing that Christ being raised from the dead dieth no more; death hath no more dominion over him."

The teenagers had held up well thus far. But now some of the girls began to cry softly. The dominion, Regan thought, was the only part evident here, the finality of a hole in the ground and the young life shortly to be dropped into it. Her fingers tightened on Matt's arm. He put his hand over hers, his bleak gaze on the coffin. He was wondering, she realized, if he could have prevented this. If he had been a better cop, a better coach...

"For this corruptible must put on incorruption, and this mortal must put on immortality...then shall be brought to pass the saying that is written, Death is swallowed up in victory. O death, where is thy sting? O grave, where is thy victory?"

Mortal, she wanted to say to him. *You're only mortal, Matt. You can't do it all.*

The minister closed his Bible. Lucerne circulated with a basket, passing out sprigs of rosemary as the coffin was lowered into the grave. "These stand for remembrance," she kept saying. "Take two. One to give to Ken and one to keep. It means we will never forget him." She pressed the sheaf that was left into Mabel

Fermin's hands, led the mother around to the opposite side of the hole from which they could face the rest of the assembly.

One arm around Mabel and looking down at the coffin, Lucerne began to recite a paraphrase from Fra Giovanni. "We salute you, Ken. You were our friend, and our love for you goes deep. There is nothing we can give you which you have not got now. But there is very much that we can take."

Lucerne raised her head to look at her audience. "No heaven can come to us unless our hearts find rest in today. Take heaven! No peace lies in the future, which is not hidden in this present little instant. Take peace! The gloom of the world is but a shadow. Behind it, yet within our reach, is joy. Take joy! Life is so full of meaning and purpose, so full of beauty, that you will find earth but cloaks your heaven. Courage then to claim it, that is all!"

She looked down to the grave again. "And so we greet you, Ken, with profound esteem and with the prayer that for you, now and forever, the day breaks and the shadows flee away."

She touched Mabel's arm. The woman dropped her bunch of rosemary onto the burnished mahogany and her bewildered expression dissolved into knowledge—and tears. Lucerne led her away.

■ ■ ■

Matt drove the patrol car farther back into the cemetery, parked under a spreading tree. "Now," he said, "is there anything else you found out you haven't told me?"

"I'm not sure." Regan toyed with the piece of rosemary she had retained, remembering a time when she had done the same while sitting beside him with her hands in cuffs. "I've been looking into Vita's death for Trudy. I don't know that it has anything to do with what's going on now, but I suppose I'd better inform you—just in case."

She talked while Matt looked out over the old graves to

where a couple of men were filling in the new one. When she had finished, he said, "So was it an accident? Or did he marry her with the express intention of killing her?"

"It could be a combination, I suppose," she said. "Perhaps he had intended it to look like an accident, planned to say that he thought blanks were in the gun. But then in the actual circumstance, he panicked and ran."

"And you think Norville's father might have been involved?"

"He had a reputation for ruthlessness. And he must have known Faye and her family well. Perhaps she brought Jack Dawson into it."

"But she married Galen?"

"She says that Jack is dead. Maybe Norville didn't want any witnesses to what he had done."

"Then wouldn't she have been disposed of too?"

"Well, she was, wasn't she?" Regan asked. "In a way, I mean. It was only a couple of years later that she went into Green Meadows. Something must have sent her over the edge. Fear perhaps?"

"Or guilt." Matt drummed his fingers thoughtfully on the steering wheel. "The murderer can hardly be the same, but the motive might be. Norville millions. Maybe Trudy has been right all along. Howard Keegan. Raven Scion is seldom around. If Scion's hair isn't real and the sunglasses hide his eyes…"

Regan finished. "He could be somebody local. Somebody whose occasional absences wouldn't be noticed. But not Howard."

"Why not? He's gone fairly often, isn't he? Speaking engagements, TV appearances."

"Yes, but Howard has a certain something that Scion doesn't. I don't know what you would call it exactly. Charisma. Dynamism. All right," she concluded irritably as Matt's expression chilled, "sex appeal maybe. Whatever it is, Raven doesn't have it."

"Maybe," Matt suggested, starting the car, "Keegan only turns it on when he wants something. It's a possibility you might keep in mind."

When he pulled up at the funeral home where her Jeep was parked, she said, "Why are you really angry at me, Matt? This can't all be about the house."

"You want things to stay the way they've always been with a husband tacked on as a kind of bonus." He leaned across her to shove open her door. "It doesn't work that way." For just an instant they were very close, and he averted his gaze to say hoarsely, "Go on, get out. I can't think straight when you're around."

Numb, Regan drove herself to the church where the funeral lunch was to be held. In the basement community room, many of the teenage girls were still crying. Most of the guys sat apart from them, silent and miserable.

"I never liked Betony," one of the girls was saying, "but Lucerne was always friendly enough with her."

Regan went down the hall to the rest room where she found Lucerne in front of the mirror, holding one eye open with the thumb and forefinger of her left hand and advancing the forefinger of her right. "People who wear contact lens," Lucerne said in a preoccupied voice, "should never cry."

Regan smiled past a jolt of alarm. The contact on Lucerne's finger showed up well because it was not clear but blue. So those violet eyes were also artifice. Were they "just vanity" like her dyed hair?

■ ■ ■

In the community room, Trudy had saved a chair for Regan, who, when she returned from the rest room, seemed morosely preoccupied. Myron and Charlotte sat with them at one of the long tables—also Howard Keegan. Amos had returned to Speedwell so a doctor would be on hand there.

People were restless, Trudy noticed, only nibbling at their food or letting it sit while they pushed their way through the narrow aisles between folding chairs to speak to friends. The room, with its cement floor and pillars, did not echo with the reunion-like chatter often common at funerals. Today fear and conjecture kept the tone down to a mutter.

Regan came out of her brown study long enough to tell Trudy about her trip to Trafalgar. Several of those sitting nearby turned to listen.

"I suppose I'd better apologize to the guy on the school's behalf," Myron said of Betony Scion's father. "Before he decides to sue. Though how anybody can expect us to do background checks…Come on, Charlotte. You're better at soothing ruffled feathers than I am. Maybe the pastor will let us use his phone."

Howard Keegan had been sitting with arms crossed, staring, heavy-lidded, at the table. A few minutes later, he rose abruptly, almost knocking over his empty teacup, and went out into the hall too.

Now that they were virtually alone, Trudy said to Regan, "I take it your talk with Matt didn't go so well."

Regan shook her head. "About as badly as possible, actually," she said in an unsteady voice, pushing away the ham sandwich she scarcely had touched.

"You're exhausted," Trudy said. "And so is he. When you're in that state, everything looks harder than it actually is. At least he doesn't seem to have asked for his ring back. Why don't you go home and take a nap? You'll feel better."

"I don't like to leave you alone here."

"I'm hardly alone." Trudy nodded wryly toward the subdued crowd. "The others will be back shortly. You go ahead."

Regan didn't leave by the hall but, as most were doing, by the exit door to a flight of outside steps that led up to the parking lot.

Despite herself, Trudy did feel rather alone then, with empty chairs on all sides of her. But Sylvia Laird came across almost immediately.

"This is awful, isn't it?" the girl said, sitting down in Regan's abandoned seat. "Ken would never have believed how some of them are carrying on."

"'But I had smiled,'" Trudy quoted, "'to think how you, the dead, so curiously preoccupied and grave, would laugh, could you have heard the things they said.' Dorothy Parker," she added in explanation.

"She was a cynical poet, wasn't she?" Sylvia appeared thoughtful. "But I think she's right. Ken would have laughed at some of them. It's the ones who disliked him who seem to be the most emotional."

"Perhaps I should have been quoting Eliot instead. 'It is only when they see nothing that people can always show the suitable emotions—and, so far as they can feel at all, their emotions are suitable.' People thought Regan was cold because she didn't cry publicly for either of her parents. Those people can't begin to comprehend how she has suffered."

"And you, Ms. Hargrove?" Sylvia asked softly.

Trudy gave her a crooked smile. "I think I can get a glimpse of it. Maybe you had better become a stoic, kid. Buffer all your affections. You'll probably be better off."

"But then joy would be distanced, too, wouldn't it?" Sylvia said sensibly. "No, I think I'll take my chances."

Myron and Charlotte came back then. "Scion is steaming," the principal said. "I think I'd better go out there and try to calm him down, if we don't want a lawsuit on our hands. We had been invited out to Mason's this weekend, anyway, but had turned him down due to recent events here. Now I'm sorry we did; he may have given our room to somebody else."

"Regan said the inn was empty," Trudy remarked.

"Maybe that's the best solution," Myron agreed. "We've been

there before, so the guy knows us. I think we'll go back to the house now, pack some overnight stuff, and head out. We'll take the car so you can have the van. I asked Howard to see you back. He's out in the hall. He looks rather beat, so I suppose he'll be wanting to leave soon."

At her reluctant nod, Myron added, "Tell Amos where we've gone. He can call us at the inn if, God forbid, anything new comes up."

"That," Trudy said dryly when they had gone, "provides a good excuse for them to scuttle off to their fancy friends."

Sylvia looked concerned. "You didn't seem happy about going back with Dr. Keegan. Would you like me to give you a ride?"

Why can't I come up with some devastatingly clever quote about Howard? "No, but thanks for the offer. I'll be all right."

■ ■ ■

The lumpiness of her own hands under her back got through first to Trudy, even before she was fully awake. She never slept on her back. She shifted over onto her side, tried to bring her hands up to her pillow, to snuggle down. But there was no give anywhere. Her hands remained behind her, the bed was unyielding, and she had lost the pillow. Her head hurt, and her mouth was dry. She hadn't had a headache since Howard did that stuff to her skull days ago. Howard. Hadn't he been there when…Her hands must have gone numb from lying on them. She flexed her fingers. They tingled, but she still couldn't pull her arms forward. Horror enveloped her. This was what she had always dreaded—that the paralysis would progress, and she would lose the use of her hands.

It was irrational, she reminded herself. Paralysis could not progress. It was or it wasn't. Not unless there had been another accident.

She opened her eyes. The orange light of late afternoon filtered into the room, illuminating a calendar hanging on a door. A blond little girl holding a collie puppy. *You are three years old. You have just awakened from your nap. A man and a woman are arguing in the next room—your father and your stepmother. You get up and walk across the floor.*

Trudy twitched as if to give action to the words, but neither her arms nor legs would cooperate. No matter. In her mind, she was already taking the necessary steps, reaching up for the knob. This was where the dream-memory had always faded before. But now she felt the knob turn under her hand, pulled the door toward her far enough to peer into the room beyond.

■ ■ ■

The policeman had had his supper. When the nurse came to clear away the tray, he asked, "Where's the kid's mother? She's usually here by now."

"She called around three," the nurse replied. "Said she had stopped off at home and was going to stay there a few minutes. Probably needs some time alone, actually. She's gotten quite good at driving herself, you know. Don't worry. I imagine she'll be back before bedtime. She won't leave Jack for long. It's sad, isn't it? He could stay this way forever."

"Keegan here?"

"He hasn't come back," the nurse said.

After she had gone, the policeman got up and began to pace uneasily. It was after five now. Quiet because many of the patients were down in the cafeteria. It would soon be dark. Of course, when people said a few minutes, they didn't always mean a few minutes. He found the Hargrove number in the phone book and dialed it. Nobody answered. The woman in the wheelchair was not his charge. He stopped and stood, looking down at Jack.

Where are you, kid? he wondered. *And what's it like there? Do you dream?*

Behind him a splintering crash, then shards of pain in his back. Something hit the bed rail, shattered onto the floor. A buzzing from the wreckage.

"Help!" the policeman bellowed. "Bees! Come help me!" He grabbed the sheet that was folded back neatly under Jack's arms, jerked it free and over the boy's head, climbed on top of the flaccid young body, holding down the sheet as tightly as he could, feeling a crawling on the back of his neck. Exclamations and screams.

"The cop's bleeding! Has he been shot? Get Dr. Keegan!" someone was yelling.

"Where is he?"

"He's not here."

Hands tugged at the policeman, who hung on grimly.

"No! The man knows what he's doing. Don't move him until we get these bees out of here. Epinephrine. Somebody get the epinephrine!"

Watch, the cop wanted to tell them. *Watch and make sure nobody's in here who isn't supposed to be.* The voices were going away from him. *Watch, somebody, watch...*

■ ■ ■

Trudy lay for a long time, half up on her shoulder, staring at the calendared door but replaying the forty-year-old scene a little girl had witnessed in the room beyond it. There were no arguing voices in the present, nothing but a deafening silence. But it was getting darker. The lurid sunset glow was fading. If she was going to do anything, she had better start.

Her hands, she realized now, were tied behind her. A cloth was stuffed into her mouth. Not that it was necessary. Nobody was close enough to this place to hear screams anyhow. They hadn't bothered to tie her feet. It might have helped her if they had. The limp limbs were easier to deal with if they were lashed together.

She had been at the church, wheeling herself down an empty corridor, looking for Keegan, when she had felt somebody come up behind her, touch her. "Howard?" she had said—and then nothing.

If steady pressure was applied to a certain point on the neck, unconsciousness could be induced in seconds. There wasn't much point in going over what had happened; it was much more urgent to determine what was intended. They couldn't realistically expect her to die of starvation or thirst before she was found. So they must have something else planned. Whoever they were.

From its roughness, she suspected the cord was some kind of jute. Easier to cut than nylon anyhow, but they wouldn't think her worth more than that. How much, after all, could a cripple do?

And what of Jack? Had they gotten her out of the way first so they could...The policeman would still be there. But policemen were, like other men, vulnerable to violence or to deception.

The door was open; they hadn't bothered to close it. Beyond that door, one of the rails that surrounded the stairwell leaned out of sync with the others. Where a spindle was askew, there might be an exposed nail. She flopped over onto her stomach, attempted to continue onto her back. It was not like rolling down a green lawn as a child. Then she could hold her arms in close to her sides. Now, her elbow got in the way. She had to rock over it just to have all her weight come down hard on her bound hands. Then the process had to be repeated with the other elbow. Then she crashed down on her stomach, chin banging the floor. She lay, breathing hard, staring at the boards so close to her face. There might not even be a nail. If there was, what about the stairs? It was possible to go downstairs on your fanny, feet first, but much harder than going up. The legs always got in the way. She set her shoulders and rocked again.

■ ■ ■

Gabe felt restless that evening. Ken's funeral had brought home all too clearly the realization that a person might not be given time to prove himself.

Lucerne is right, Gabe thought. *That's what my whole life is about. Proving something to myself and everybody else. But what if it had been me on the receiving end of that bullet? What would I have to show?*

He suspected Lucerne would say that wasn't the point. But what if you didn't have any other point? His aunt was sewing in her room. Gabe left the TV news on to cover his exit, grabbed a coat, and went out. He drove over to Lucerne's place. Mabel Fermin answered the door.

"Uh," he said, "is she here?"

"No," Ken's mother said. "She's gone over to the school. Something about some prints she was doing for Miss Culver. I told her I would be all right."

"Oh," he said, and after an awkward pause, "*are* you? All right, I mean."

"Yes. I'm used to being alone, you know. Ken was out a lot. I don't mind."

Gabe got back in his car and drove to the school. By the time he arrived, he had worked up a good head of steam. Granted, it was good of Lucerne to look after Mrs. Fermin, but then to abandon her on the night after the funeral...not to mention that the idiotic girl was still sallying around town on her own after dark just as if no murder had happened. No sense of responsibility. No sense, period.

Her motorbike leaned in the shadow of a bush. She must have been given a key because the main door was open. No lights were on in the foyer where the offices were located, but one of the corridors at right angles was illuminated. He eased the door shut behind him so it only clicked faintly, padded on rubber soles across the foyer tiles, and made the turn into the lighted hallway. He didn't want her to hear him coming. If he gave her a good scare, maybe she would learn her lesson.

The door of the farthest locker down was open, and somebody was standing on the other side of it. He knew whose locker it was. Ken's. Surely she wouldn't have the nerve to...but of course she would. That thing about having to go to the art room had only been an excuse. He padded faster. He was almost there before he decided the legs were much too prosaically clothed to be Lucerne's.

"Hey!" he said.

The element of surprise was all that he could have wished. An elbow banged against the locker door, and for an instant, a face peered around it. Raven Scion minus the sunglasses. Then the lights went out. Too late, Gabe remembered the switch was at that end of the hall.

He could hear nothing now, though Scion must be within yards of him. He should turn and run. Whoever Scion was, the odds were that Gabe, a receiver in training, could run faster. But where was Lucerne? The art room was on the opposite side of the hall from the lockers. No light was on in there either.

He edged to the left, felt for the wall, groped along it. His hand found the doorway. The door was standing a little bit open. He slithered inside. A hand closed on his arm. He grunted, jerked the arm to bash whoever it was into the wall.

But the someone was pressing too close to hit. Female, definitely female, and a whisper that was little more than a faint stirring of the air against his ear. "It's me. What do we do?"

"Get out," he whispered in return, grasping her shoulder, pushing her toward where the windows were a slightly grayer line in the blackness.

She felt her way. A hand came back to grasp his free one, to place it against metal. The press. They edged along, around it, his hand still on her shoulder. She kicked against something. He felt a swaying, grabbed with both hands. Thin wooden uprights. An easel. He set it carefully to the side, reached for her again, found nothing, and lurched forward. She must have turned to wait for him because he tramped heavily on her foot.

A choked gasp. So eloquent were the swirls of air in front of him that he could envision her dancing on one foot and clutching at the other. There was no time for that. Pushing up beside her, he found the crank for a window. It creaked in starting. He whipped the handle around till the pane was at its full stretch, scooped up Lucerne and fed her, feet first, through the space. He felt her touch ground, then a scuffing as she dropped on hands and knees to crawl away to the left behind the juniper bushes.

It was a tighter fit for him. His too-wide shoulders stuck at the sides, and he banged his nose against the slanted glass. The lights blazed on in the room behind him. There was hurried movement and a raised arm. He threw up his own arm to protect his head. Something smashed down, and he felt bone snap in his forearm. His vision swirled with pain-shot darkness. He slumped and slipped through the window to fall facedown into the sting of juniper needles.

■ ■ ■

It was completely dark by the time Trudy had worked herself over to the doorframe, her elbows raw, her hands numb. She suspected her legs would be bruised, too, from the constant knocking against each other. It had been hours since she had used the catheter. *Wetting yourself,* she thought, *is the least of your worries.*

She had been straining her hearing all along for the sound of a car engine, but it was as if she and the house were encased in a vacuum. The only sounds were those she made herself: the creaking of boards under her, her puffing grunts and groans.

She would have to be careful now. There was only a narrow hallway before the rails. If she rolled into the loose one, she might keep going—the fast way down. She didn't want to add a broken neck to her broken back. So she inched forward face-down, raising her shoulders and wiggling her stomach until her head touched a rail. Then, she shimmied to the left until she lay parallel to the edge, eased herself onto one shoulder with her back to the spindles, and began to feel at their bases one by one with her bound hands, pushing herself along on an elbow.

When she found one that gave at her tug, she stopped thankfully, sucking in air. Cold air. The house was chilling quickly now that the sun had gone. She pushed the spindle to one side, felt it slip out and fall away into the darkness below, hitting with a rolling clatter.

She clenched her teeth and felt around where she thought the base of the spindle had been. A sharp prick to a forefinger. Pain had never been so welcome. She eased her bound hands toward it.

■ ■ ■

Gabe wasn't completely unconscious, but he couldn't move, and the urgency in his mind had been smacked into languor. The window above him creaked shut, the rectangle of light around him clicked into darkness. Footsteps scurried, and a door banged. An engine purred somewhere.

It sounded much louder when it pulled up onto the grass verge beside him, almost roaring. He felt hands under his arms as he was dragged upward, his back scraping, onto the floor of a vehicle.

He remembered Lucerne and reached around vaguely with one hand but could locate no other body. Maybe she had gotten away then. Or maybe she was in on the whole thing. She could recite the benediction at his funeral too. He tried to laugh at that, but the blackness, as if released, swelled and almost overcame him. He had to concentrate to beat it back, millimeter by millimeter. Gabe knew he was in serious danger but couldn't seem to translate the thought into any real alarm. As a child, he had never expected to live this long anyhow.

"You thought your father would kill you, didn't you?" The voice was only in his mind, but it was one he recognized well enough. He had heard it off and on his whole life. In his torpor, he was not surprised at the question.

Yes. He would kill me. Or you would. You're the one responsible for putting me there. And here.

"Am I? Did I force you to drive out to the school tonight?" The voice seemed sad. "Your choices put you here."

But not there. I didn't choose to be that man's son. You can't put the blame on me for that.

"And you think I'm like him? An arbitrary punisher? Did your father ever make himself helpless like you were, Gabe, experience your pain?"

Fat chance!

"Did your father ever die for you?"

The voice was gone as suddenly as it had come, leaving him feeling cold and alone. The van turned onto gravel. He thought he could hear the lapping of water. Then the vehicle began to rock and claw its way over rough ground. He was slammed repeatedly against the steel supports of a seat. That pain jabbed him back again and again from the darkness that drifted to the sound of waves. He tried to put out a hand to ward off the metal, but the hand itself felt as immovable as a lead weight.

Where did you go? You might at least stick around till the end, put a big mark on Scion's debit sheet. He's going to roast for this, right? My life should be worth that much at least. Say something! Are you going to let me die alone?

It was then that he remembered the Good Friday scream. "My God, my God, why have you forsaken me?" And shuddered. *All right. I'm sorry. I was way out of line. You do know what it's like. Just don't leave me alone with this maniac. Please?*

"I haven't gone anywhere, Gabe. I never do, you know. Not unless you ask me to. It's part of that choice thing."

Okay, if I have a choice, I'll stick with you!

"All the way, Gabe. All the way."

The van had finally careened to a stop. Scion was tugging at Gabe again, not having an easy time of it either. Then Gabe's broken arm flopped against the ground, and the darkness drowned him.

He didn't feel himself scraped up wooden steps and along a hall or feel the fusty cloth that dangled finally in his face before he was dropped on lumpy things that smelled of rubber.

The door slammed behind him. Even when a sharper, cleaner smell penetrated his dusty prison, he did not stir.

■ ■ ■

Trudy's hands and wrists were no longer numb. They burned with a score of pricks and scratches. It was only a stub of a broken nail, and the rope kept slipping off it. So instead of a sawing motion, she had to do a series of catches and pulls. She thought that the jute was giving, though, its tiny strands snapping one by one. It felt looser.

But there was a different sound now, an outside sound. A vehicle in the distance, drawing closer.

Just a few more minutes. Please!

But it came on and on, relentless, louder. Her frantic efforts now slashed only at her wrists. She stopped, breathing hard and shivering, her eyes clenched shut.

Why did you let me get this far? Why did you let me hope?

More slowly now, resignedly, her hands went back, the rope caught, plucked. They were on the porch. She yanked fiercely, and the rope relaxed, began to slither, like a snake over the edge.

She caught it with free hands, pushed herself hastily back

from the edge as the door crashed open, and a person came in dragging another. The reflection of headlights shining on the porch was the only illumination, but she caught the glint of mirrored glasses, a dangling of hair on the upright man. The skin of the other was dark. Gabe.

Was he alive? She stared hard, edging forward again so she could keep them in view as they paused at a closet door almost directly beneath her. She thought she saw a brown arm twitch just before Gabe was tossed inside. Scion switched on a flashlight, went into a room on the right, returned with a dinner knife, did something to the doorframe. Trudy couldn't see what, but she could guess. With the blade stabbed into the crack between jamb and wall, the haft would hold the door against any attempts to open it from inside.

Trudy edged back from the railing. Would he come and check on her? The flashlight beam flicked upward, paused for an instant that seemed suspended in eternity. The missing spindle! Surely he would notice that.

She couldn't see him now but tried to envision his face as on previous occasions. Who was behind the big glasses, the dramatic hair? But she couldn't remember the rest of his face at all. It was the obvious that one noticed and remembered. A man invisible because he was so loud. The beam drifted away. Something splashed, and the sharp, resin smell of turpentine sliced through the must of years.

Dear God, he's going to burn us alive! Oh, Gabe, I'm sorry. You saved Jack's life. You deserve much better than this. If I had only kept the spindle up here, I could at least have had a try at braining him with that. Why is he killing our children? Gabe, Jack, Ken...

Hey, Ken's irreverent voice seemed to remind her, *it ain't over till adipose Annie sings.*

A scratch and crackle came from the back of the hall—a faint glow. Then Scion was going at a trot toward the front. Another rasp, and flame ran along the floor toward the foot of the stairs. The door slammed.

All right. I'm not going to make it down those steps in time. But I do have a rope. She grabbed at the spindle next to where the loose one had been, tried to shake it. Firm. Working as quickly as her quivering fingers would allow, she knotted the rope around it, pushed herself forward into the hole, looked down on the open stretch of floor luridly lit by the flames to either side.

Go. Grasping the rope with both hands, she slid as far forward as she could, but her legs wouldn't come. She wiggled and writhed desperately, hanging half out in a waft of rising hot air. She remembered what Regan had said. Ask for angels.

Push me. Her legs fell free, and the floor zoomed closer, the rope ripping between her palms. She caught herself with a jerk, continued hand over hand until she was on a level with the knife, let go with one hand to yank it out, came down the last few feet hard. It could, she thought, sometimes be a good thing to have no feeling below the waist.

Still holding to the rope with one hand for support, she reached as high as she could with the other, turned the handle, pulled the door toward her, edging backward. She had to let go of the rope then and propel herself forward on her stomach like a soldier wriggling under barbed wire. The flames were climbing voraciously, the hall filling with smoke.

"Gabe!" she cried above their manic cackle, tugging at his shoulder. "Gabe, wake up! We have to get out of here!"

There was no response.

She felt for his throat and found a pulse. "Gabe, for Jack! We have to do it for Jack—before they get him too. Gabe, can you hear me?" There was a swelling on the back of his head.

He turned his head only slightly. "Mommy?" he said plaintively. "Mommy, don't leave me in here. It's dark. Daddy hit me again. He hates me. Can't we go away?"

Trudy struggled to a sitting position against the back of the closet, lifted Gabe's head into her lap. "I won't leave you," she said steadily, the reflection of the flames in her eyes. "See, it's getting much lighter now. Yes, we'll go away, Gabe. We'll go far away."

CHAPTER 12

■ ■ ■

No; like a bank for love to lie and play on;
not like a corse.

Regan couldn't settle down to read. She picked up the TV remote, but the sitcoms were jangling. Finally, she was reduced to tinkering with the radio.

"Are you lonesome tonight?" a young Elvis sang, and she switched stations quickly only to be met with "I Will Always Love You." She spun the dial irritably.

"You would think these people could sing about something else," she said to Gato, who was her only company. "I used to *like* being alone."

The cat looked skeptical. "Okay, so maybe I've never really been alone more than a few days in my whole life. Daddy was usually around, then Sasha, now Diane, Agatha, and Gina. I wish they would come back. Six months ago, I couldn't imagine wanting them around. Now they're my family."

"Like fun they are!" the radio snapped, and she jumped.

"Oh, a lot you would know about it!" a female voice jeered.

It was, Regan realized then, some kind of radio drama, surprising because it was so rare these days. But for a moment, the voice had seemed actually to speak to her. Her eyes widened as her hand reached automatically to cut the switch. She stared at the blank screen of the TV as if she could see pictures there.

The telephone rang. She rose slowly, still distracted, to answer it.

The tone of the girl's voice on the other end snapped her back to the present. "Miss Culver? This is Sylvia. Do you remember? I'm a classmate of Lucerne's." Sylvia's voice was even, but precariously so, as if she were struggling against panic—or tears.

"Yes," Regan said. "I remember; you were homecoming queen this year. What's wrong? Is it Jack?"

"Yes, but he's all right now," the voice reassured quickly. "Somebody threw another jar of those bees through his window tonight. But the policeman was quick. He covered Jack up with his own body. The policeman got stung, but they don't think Jack did. Amos had them give him a shot of that epinephrine just in case."

"They gave Jack a shot?" Regan demanded sharply.

"Yes, but it's okay, Miss Culver. I was watching. I had come to visit Jack. I got here just when the policeman started to yell. I went in right away and watched very carefully. The nurses got the epinephrine out of the cabinet the policeman had been guarding. But what I called about, is Trudy or Dr. Keegan over there with you, by any chance?"

"No. They're missing?"

"I'm afraid so. I spoke to Trudy after you left. Then she went out in the hall to look for the doctor. He was supposed to bring her back here. Around three, she called and spoke to one of the nurses, said she was going to stay over at the house for a little bit. She isn't there now. Dr. Keegan never came back either. I don't think she really wanted to go with him."

"Is Chief Olin around?"

"Yes, the state cops called him in. Do you want to talk to him?"

"Not now. I'll come over. I suppose they have checked that curve above the lake?"

"Yes, nothing went in there."

I should have insisted that she have protection, Regan thought on her way out the door, *if I had to hire a guard for her myself.* On the way to Speedwell, her thoughts flew back and forth between Jack Dawson's disappearance forty years earlier and his daughter's now. If her new revelation was right, Jack was in the water, but not up at Trafalgar. And that was, she realized sickly, the easiest, the most likely way somebody would dispose of Trudy too.

Her cellular phone rang. She picked it up. A girl's voice again, but this one panting, distraught. "Miss Culver, do you know what Matt Olin's number is? I can't remember!"

"Yes, of course I know. What is it, Lucerne?"

"Raven Scion has Gabe. I was at the school, and Gabe came looking for me. Scion got him and took him away in a van. I followed on my bike with the headlight off. He turned in up by the Hargrove place, but he went on to the back where there's this rough trail—"

"Yes, I know where it is, Lucerne. I'll call Matt. He's just across the lake at Speedwell. I'm on my way there. Where are you now?"

"I wrecked my bike, so I'm running. Scion's coming back! I can see the lights. Shall I try to stop him?"

"No!" Regan said sharply. "Get off the trail and hide. It won't help anybody for you to get hurt too. Matt and I will be with you in minutes."

She cut the connection, dialed quickly again. "This is Regan Culver. Give me Chief Olin, please. It's an emergency."

When he came on, she said, "Matt, Scion has Gabe. Lucerne followed him into that trail that leads to the old house. She says he's coming back now. I'm betting he took Gabe there, maybe

Trudy too. I'm on my way. Wait for me. The Land Rover will get over that rough ground faster than your car will."

All of the time she was speaking so tersely, another small voice in her was crying imploringly over and over, *No, no, no...*

When she swung into the Hargrove drive, a police cruiser was pulled up on the lawn. She barely had braked before Matt was scrambling in, saying, "All right. Go!"

She shifted into four-wheel drive, aimed the jeep at the hole in the brush. "Where are the state cops?" The beams of the headlights bounced crazily over bare branches.

"They had all left to prowl around the roads before you called. Except the one guarding Jack. I gave him my radio, and he's calling for backup. They're going to have a rough time getting in here though. How did Scion get Gabe?"

"I don't know. It was apparently at the school. Lucerne didn't go into detail. There she is."

The girl was running down the middle of the trail toward them, face even whiter than usual in the glare of the headlights, carrying a flashlight that seemed dim by comparison. "He went back!" she gasped as she scrambled into the rear seat. "Didn't you see him?"

"I must have just missed him," Matt said. "But we think he might have left Gabe at the old Dawson place."

"Is that what this goes to?" She leaned against the back of the seat, her breath coming in great gusts. "It was a nightmare. I kept falling down. Almost went into the lake once. Dropped my phone somewhere too. Are you sure they left him?"

"It's our best hope—" Matt began when Regan grabbed at his arm.

"There's a glow in the sky, and it can't be lights," she said. "There's no electricity."

His face tightened the way it had at Ken's funeral. He

grabbed up her phone, punched out a number, and began to speak in tight, clipped syllables.

"Fire?" Lucerne faltered. "Scion set the place on fire?"

The Land Rover lurched around the final turn, scrambled up onto the lawn. Everybody tumbled out, Regan, at the last moment, grabbing up the phone Matt had thrown down and shoving it in her coat pocket. He had pounded up onto the porch, put his palm against the front door, shook his head, and ran around the east side toward the back, stumbling and almost falling in places where his foot went through the porch floor's rotting wood. By the time Regan caught up to him, he was returning from the back.

"Both doors are hot," he said. "That's where Scion will have set the fires. How do I get in?"

She didn't try to argue with him. She knew it wouldn't do any good.

"This way!" She ran around toward the west, gasping an explanation as she went. "A shutter is off on the front room over here. You can break the window. It'll be close to the fire though. If you go through into the room behind it, a door opens onto the end of the hallway, and another door catty-corner leads to the back stairs."

He stripped off his leather jacket, wrapped it around his arm, and punched his fist through the glass. A gust of heat surged out to greet them. "You two get away from the house!" He disappeared into the smoky gloom. The two females looked at each other. They could hear him yelling, "Gabe! Trudy!"

"If they're both in there," Regan said, "he's going to need some help. Give me the flashlight and get down on the lawn, Lucerne."

"Like fun I will," Lucerne said. "After you, Miss Culver. You're the one who knows the place."

"Ruby told me to take care of you." Regan stepped gingerly

over the sharded sill. "I don't think she would approve. Stay close."

"My mother should learn," Lucerne said, "that there are worse things than dying. Lead on, Macduff."

"Down on your knees." Regan dropped to her own by way of illustration. "We're going back, then around. Don't lose sight of me."

"I'll hold your coat hem in my teeth," Lucerne suggested. "Okay," she added in a cloth-muffled tone. "Ready."

Regan crawled forward into the fug, her knees chafing alternately over rough wool and varnished wood. She came up against books. Too far over. She groped to her right. More books. To her left. A space there. She edged in that direction around the shelf, found the doorframe. A tug on her coat assured her that the girl was still back there.

Now the living room. She could hear the fire's mutter in the far wall. *Keep as close to the south wall as possible. That's where the door is.*

She felt her way along the baseboard, around the desk. A gust of hot air and white ash drifted down onto her back.

More baseboard. Open space. He had found this door then. She crawled forward, heard voices, and picked up speed.

"He must have been hit pretty hard," Trudy was explaining to Matt. "He can hardly move."

Regan bumped into Matt from behind, and he shone his torch over his shoulder into her face, found Lucerne's beyond. "Are you guys crazy?"

Lucerne spat out Regan's coattail. "Nope, you are," she said calmly, "if you think you can carry two people out by yourself. I'll take Trudy piggyback. I've done it with my mother, and Trudy isn't any bigger. There are some advantages to being a great, gawky girl."

Matt picked up the broken banister spindle. "Give me the

belt off your coat," he said to Regan and, when she complied, began to splint Gabe's arm. Lucerne helpfully handed over a gaudy silk scarf she had been wearing around her neck.

"Get on his other side," Matt said to Regan when he was done, and handed Lucerne the flashlight. He pulled the splinted arm over his shoulder; Regan took the other. They stood up into a pall of smoke.

"Move your feet, Johnson!" Matt bawled, and Gabe managed a shuffle. They followed the foggy glow of the flashlight.

Lucerne had stopped, aiming the light ahead, Trudy like an oddly shaped bundle on her back. "No way through here."

The living room now crawled with flames. Regan felt rather than saw Matt look at her through the hot, swirling haze. Just as the smoke clouded sight, the increased roar of the fire dimmed her hearing. She wasn't sure if he had spoken or not.

"Basement!" she screamed as loudly as she could, pointing toward the door diagonally across from the other. "Through there!"

Lucerne felt the panel. "Warm but not hot!" She turned the knob and shoved the door, jumping back as she did so. When no gust of flame leapt out, she moved through. Matt and Regan staggered after her with Gabe sagging between them. They came into the smaller hallway that connected dining room with kitchen, and the basement door was just opposite them. Lucerne already had it open and was descending slowly, groping each step with her foot. It was less smoky down here. The beam picked out a dirt floor, a low-beamed ceiling, ranks of empty canning jars.

Matt used the arm he had had around Gabe's waist to pull the door shut behind them. Gabe's feet slipped on the stone steps, and his weight pitched toward Regan. She fought for balance.

Matt's hand shot out again to grab her waist. They swayed for an instant with Gabe between them before regaining equilibrium.

"Better put him on my back," he said, voice loud in this quieter space.

Lucerne set Trudy down on the dirt floor and came back to help. Matt went down a couple of steps, bent, and together Regan and Lucerne pushed Gabe up as far as they could so his arms dangled on either side of Matt's neck. Matt reached back to lock his elbows around the back of the boy's knees.

"'He ain't heavy,'" Lucerne quoted, as she followed him down. "'He's my brother.'" She handed Regan the flashlight and crouched down for Trudy again.

"This way." Regan turned north. "There's a way out here."

A crash shook the floor above them, and they all froze for an instant, heads tilted upward. Dust from the beams sifted down into their eyes.

"Here it is! Hurry!" The light had picked out another flight of steps ascending to slanting doors. Regan ran up the stone treads, hollowed in the center from years of use, a bursting exultation filling her chest. They would make it after all. She laid the flashlight down on mossy rock, pushed at the inclined panels. They were as immovable as the rock under her feet. She shoved harder, and the swelling joy burst like a punctured balloon.

They saw it in her face as they came up. Lucerne's grin faltered only slightly as she turned and knelt to lower Trudy onto the steps. "Oh, well, we knew it couldn't be that easy, right? Maybe if we all try…"

But even the concentrated strength and determination of all three able-bodied members of the group could not budge those doors.

"Howard," Trudy said suddenly. "Remember, Regan? After somebody was in here that day, he said he would put a padlock on these doors. He must have done it."

"A male who does what he says he will do," Lucerne said,

dropping wearily down beside her. "Usually commendable but annoying at the moment." There was a tremor to her flippancy.

"We'll be safer here than anywhere else," Matt said. "This is out from under the house, and it has earth on three sides. I shouldn't have left that radio behind."

Regan stared at him for a moment. "I'm an idiot!" She reached into her coat pocket to pull out the cell phone, began matter-of-factly to punch out a number. The others watched in mute fascination.

"Let's hope Howard got back. Dr. Keegan, please," she said. "Quickly. This is an emergency. Howard, we're trapped in the outside basement stairs at the old house, and the house is burning. Yes, Trudy is here. All right."

She handed the phone to Matt, explaining. "He says he can make it in a few minutes on horseback. He's leaving now, but one of the state cops is back and wants to talk to you."

After another of his clipped conversations, Matt handed the phone back. "A police car crashed on that rough lane in here, and they have to get it out of the way before the fire trucks can come in. Some of them are trying to come in on foot, but whether they'll get here on time...I guess Howard, his horse, and his key are our best bet."

"It can't be long," Regan responded. "A fast horse can do thirty miles per hour. It's quicker than taking a canoe across, as I'm sure Faye Cordell knew."

"So you figured out she was in the house that afternoon?" Trudy said.

Regan nodded matter-of-factly. "You remembered?"

"When I woke up from my nap that day, I heard my father and Vita arguing and, still half-asleep, stumbled over to open the door. It didn't make any sense at all because my father wasn't even in the room. Vita was lying across the bed sleeping, and a woman was standing near the dresser, with her back to me, wearing

Daddy's coat. I must have thought I was dreaming, closed the door, and went back to bed. I felt so groggy, and even a child of that age can tell what is rational and what isn't."

A strange peacefulness permeated the basement. There was a surreal quality about this conversation that proceeded steadily despite the crashes and cracklings overhead.

"I suppose you had been drugged like Vita was," Regan said. "You're lucky Faye didn't see you, or Jack Dawson might have shot more than his wife that day."

Something snapped at the far end of the basement. Broken boards and flames rained, hissing, onto the damp floor. The monster was back.

"Don't let me die in suspense," Lucerne said, raising her voice. "How could Vita have an argument when she was drugged?"

"The radio," Regan said distractedly. "Galen wrote plays for radio, and he convinced his sister and her husband to act in one. That's why she wanted everybody back at five. To hear her debut. It was supposed to be a surprise, I expect. This isn't really important now, is it?"

"Hardly." Matt put his arm around her and pulled her close. On his other side, Gabe's eyes were fluttering. "Daddy?" he muttered, peering up at Matt, half-scared, half-defiant. "I tried, Daddy. I really tried." There was no hope of being believed in his voice.

"I know you did, son." Matt put his other arm around Gabe. "You did great. I'm proud of you."

Lucerne nestled up to Gabe's other side then, and Trudy completed the circle with one arm around her, the other around Regan. "Thank you for what you did for me," she said. "You were right. I should have believed."

"Even though," Regan asked quietly, "Howard hasn't come?"

"Even though." Her voice was steady. "You can't let one person, any number of persons, deprive you of hope."

That was when something clinked above their heads, and the doors were thrown open on the wide, black, cold, wonderful night. They came up and out in a group, a unit, feeling as if their feet had never touched the steps. A horse huffed in the background. Men were running out front somewhere, yelling. Howard scooped up Trudy and glanced at his illuminated watch. "Five minutes," he said in a voice that shook only a little. "Even Secretariat couldn't have beaten that."

"It seemed much longer," Trudy said. "I think Gabe has a concussion or something, Howard, and a broken arm. You had better look at him."

Fire trucks were pulling in then. "I'll see what can be done about an ambulance," Matt said and jogged toward the front of the house.

Howard said, "Let's move up on the bank here, out of the way."

They backed into flowers and sat down. The flowers smelled bitter and wonderful. Howard knelt to probe gently the lump at the back of Gabe's skull.

Gabe opened his eyes, looked straight ahead at the burning house, then at the people around him. "What—"

"Well may you say what," Lucerne said tartly. "We had to haul you out of there bodily—with little help from you, I might add."

"You all got me out?" He looked at Keegan.

"I wasn't here."

"The chief carried you," Lucerne said.

"But how did he know where I was?"

"Lucerne followed you," Regan explained, "on her bike. She called me, and I called him."

"All of you went into that burning house after me?" He shook his head dazedly. "You shouldn't have."

"Of course we shouldn't have!" Lucerne snapped. "The

whole thing was your own fault. If you hadn't come stomping out to the school to read me one of your loathsome lectures—"

"But I was right." Gabe pointed out. "You have *got* to be more careful. If you hadn't—"

"I knew you would find some way to blame it all on me!"

Trudy raised her eyebrows at Regan, mouthed, "Shock?"

Regan shook her head ruefully. "Actually, I think they're back to normal."

"In fact," Lucerne was blazing on, "I don't see how you dare talk to me about being careful when I was the one lying low and being quiet. He never would have seen me. But you, you sneaked right up to this weirdo who was looting Ken's locker and said 'Boo!'"

"He didn't!" Trudy said.

"Except for the boo part. I think what he actually said was 'Hey!' Scared Scion half to death."

At Gabe's bulldog-sullen look, Trudy began to laugh. Howard and Regan joined in. The teenagers eyed them doubtfully.

Matt came back with a pile of fire department blankets and one of the engines trailing him like a huge dog. "Glad to see you're all having such a good time. They're going to have to take him out on the truck here, don't think they can get an ambulance through. No stretchers either. Think he can walk a few steps?"

Keegan raised an eyebrow at Gabe. "How are you feeling, kid? Any dizziness? Sleepiness? Blurred vision?"

Gabe shook his head. Holding onto his blanket with his uninjured hand, he said, "I'll be okay." He tried to stand. Matt rushed to support him, and Lucerne moved in on the other side.

"Lean on me," she began to sing in an exaggerated falsetto. Regan and Trudy promptly joined in. "When you're not str-r-ong."

Matt said to Keegan, who had scooped up Trudy again, "Is that hysteria?"

"We're not hysterical," Lucerne said. "We're happy. There is a difference."

Matt went with Gabe in the truck. Regan said to the others, "My Jeep is at your disposal."

"I'll take you up on that," Keegan said, "seeing that my mount apparently has taken himself home again. He does that sometimes when I forget to tie him."

The doctor staggered slightly as he finished speaking, and Trudy looked up in alarm.

"Are you okay?" Regan asked him.

"I'm still recovering from what I suspect was a healthy dose of barbiturates," Keegan explained. "I started to feel groggy at the funeral dinner and left the room, thinking I must be coming down with something. I recall Myron asking me to take Trudy home. But shortly after that, I felt so drowsy I went into the lounge and lay down on the couch. The next thing I knew, the pastor was slapping me in the face with a wet paper towel. The police had called him, asked him to look around. He drove me back to Speedwell. Apparently, somebody put something in my tea at the dinner. It would have been easy enough with everybody up, moving around, and pushing past my chair from behind. I seldom get that tired during the day and never just black out like that."

A moment of awkward silence followed his explanation. The three women were thinking about how the police would view this story. That Keegan could just as well have been gone from the church for most of the afternoon and evening, returned shortly before the pastor found him, and faked his inertia. The lounge was somewhat removed from the community room, and the couch had its back to the door. It was highly unlikely anybody would have seen him there. On the other hand, nobody would be able to prove he wasn't there either.

"You're lucky it wasn't something stronger," Lucerne said. "These people seem to have a taste for narcotics."

Maybe we should wonder why it wasn't stronger, Regan thought, some of her elation draining away. *These people don't seem to have much respect for human life, after all. He has to be either the villain or an intended scapegoat.*

When they were all crowded into the Land Rover, following the fire truck, which proceeded at a snail's pace, Trudy broke the strained silence. "Maybe now we can talk about what happened to my father, Regan. Where do you think he is?"

Regan inclined her head in the direction of the lake. "In there. I don't think he ever made it back to the house that afternoon."

"Maybe you'd better explain it all," Trudy suggested. "Just what you think happened that day. From the beginning."

"All right." Regan settled down in the driver's seat for the long haul. "The clinic wasn't doing well financially. Galen tried one last time to convince his sister to side with him on the sale of Speedwell. Actually, selling would have been the logical thing to do at that point. But nobody really listened to Galen. They never did. That was at least partly his fault, granted. His wasn't an attractive personality. But the life of any type of artist is difficult because it's seldom financially rewarding. He is often reduced either to taking a job that doesn't interest him and giving up, for the most part, his true calling or living on the charity of relatives. I don't think Galen was really lazy; he turned out enough plays. They weren't all that good, but given encouragement, he might have improved. His family's attitude, though, was one of uninterested tolerance. Faye had the same problem, and she *was* good. The two probably met at Trafalgar when Galen visited the Norvilles, though they would later pretend not to know each other when Faye arrived at Speedwell."

Regan paused. "I am *not,*" she emphasized, "condoning what they did. I'm just trying to explain it. A contributing factor was,

I believe, Galen's experience of what his life could be like if his father would just give up this, to Galen, strange and unprofitable preoccupation with Speedwell, and sell. Because Galen did, through Faye and Norville, experience how the leisured live."

She looked around at their absorbed faces and asked, "You can feel, can't you, his frustration? With money, he and Faye both could pursue their respective careers without having to make a living at them. Your ordinary criminal mind, of course, simply would have killed Amos. But Galen knew that the police would suspect him; he had motive. Besides, it was his sister whom I believe he secretly hated. She was the favored, the good one, the success. She felt superior to him, and she showed it. For all her looks and intelligence, your stepmother was," Regan said, looking at Trudy, "not much liked, I'm afraid, by anybody except her father and husband."

"Who was more ambitious than perceptive," Trudy finished for her.

"Unfortunately," Regan continued, "Galen was not any better. He was more sensitive but just as vain and self-centered as she was. His needs came first, no matter what. He did give Vita a final chance to change her mind. Even then I think desperation impelled him to the final act. In his thirties, he felt life was passing him by, and this was his only chance. He knew his father was depressed and anxious. Galen thought Vita's death would end all of Amos's hopes for the future of Speedwell. Galen was sure that then Amos would finally give in and sell."

Regan looked around at her listeners again. "You know, it *should* have worked. Without that life insurance, which Galen apparently didn't know about, it probably would have. When Vita, as usual, didn't take him seriously, Galen's mind was made up. He already had set his plan in motion. By appealing to his sister's vanity, he got her and Jack to record parts in a play for him and to keep it a secret until the day of the broadcast. Though not enthusiastic about her brother's work, Vita was as excited as most of us would be over being on radio. She had proved yet again that she could do anything, and springing the play, full-fledged, on everyone would have appealed to her. Galen read his sister much better than she read him. Does anybody know, by the way, what their mother was like?"

"According to my father," Keegan said, "only Amos was unhappy when she died young. And nobody cared to talk about her afterward."

"Perhaps that explains some things," Regan continued. "Galen would be sure to pick a time when no one else they knew would be likely to listen to the radio. Probably when an extremely popular program was airing on another station. That's the type of time slot he would have been given anyway. And it was just right for his purposes."

She plunged on, as if eager to get the next part over quickly. "Anyway, I imagine Galen disposed of Jack in the lane, shot him, and dropped his weighted body into the lake."

"So Jack Dawson *has* been dead for forty years after all," Lucerne said, "and he *wasn't* the promising young man turned killer."

"No, the only thing Jack was guilty of was trusting his brother-in-law."

"And he never suspected a thing?" Lucerne persisted.

"I would like to believe he didn't," Regan said, "that there wasn't time for fear for either him or his wife. Galen would have been smart enough, I think, to get Jack out of the car on some pretext before killing him so there wouldn't be any stains. He must have also removed Jack's shoes, since one of them was found later up at Trafalgar. Meanwhile, Faye had waited until the men left in the canoe to provide herself with an alibi of sorts, then rode one of the horses to meet Galen at Jack's house.

I imagine she just turned the animal loose to find its own way back. At Speedwell, they were used to her leaving the horses saddled and sweaty outside the barn."

Regan watched the fire truck bump slowly down the lane ahead of them as she continued. "Somewhere along the line, Vita and Trudy received heavy doses of barbiturates, probably in that cider she served to the men for a mid-afternoon snack. Vita told her husband she felt tired, remember, and that was as unusual for her as it was for you, Howard. Maybe Galen would have just let her sleep it off if she had agreed to help him, but that didn't happen. When he and Faye met at the house, they probably rearranged Vita on the bed to make it look like she had fallen there, and brought in her baskets of herbs to suggest she had been up and about after the others left."

The truck had stopped. Matt got down, gestured to those in the Jeep to stay put, and walked forward to talk to somebody.

Watching flashlights dance like fireflies ahead, Regan went on. "Galen was in the front room to meet the other men when they arrived, but Faye stayed in the bedroom with Vita and the gun. Faye would have had her watch carefully set to know just what time to turn on the radio to miss the preliminaries. And voilà!" Regan gestured, as with a wand. "A full-scale argument between Jack Dawson and his wife, with the wife in a drugged sleep, and Jack not even present. At the prechosen, appropriate spot, Faye turns off the radio and fires the fatal shot. It all depended on the audience arriving on time, of course, and they had promised to be prompt. Still, I imagine it was a tense few moments for the plotters. Galen also would have had a bad moment when Ian reached for the knob of the downstairs radio. Can you imagine the effect if the audience had heard the argument overhead being duplicated on the airwaves?"

"Marital discord coming to you in stereo sound," Lucerne murmured.

"As soon as Faye had fired the shot," Regan went on, "she ran. That was the most dangerous part of the plan. If someone had thought to head her off...But as the plotters had presumed, everyone dashed upstairs, and she was going down on the outside while they were coming up on the inside. She lingered beside the car just long enough for Galen to call attention to her from the upstairs window. She was a tall, thin woman, remember, with short, dark hair. At that distance, and wearing Jack's coat, she would look enough like him to pass. People see what they expect to see anyway. Then Faye simply drove to Trafalgar and left the car on the bridge with Jack's coat, note, and gun inside," Regan concluded. "She tossed his shoes in the water and walked the short distance to her parents' vacation cottage where she had her car stashed. Then she drove back to Speedwell. She was always coming and going; nobody would have paid any attention."

"And the suicide note?" Trudy said.

"I imagine it was written out while they were rehearsing or taping the broadcast. The play calls for the man to write a suicide note, reading it aloud to himself as he does so. There was no actual murder in the play, incidentally. Its character proved too conscientious, or in Galen's opinion, too weak, to kill his wife. Besides, they wouldn't have wanted the play to be too much like the real thing, lest one of the few other listeners notice the coincidence. It was an imaginative, convoluted crime that depended a lot on the acting abilities of its instigators. Maybe Galen should have taken to the stage himself instead of writing for it. But its complexity was what made it solvable."

Lucerne nodded understanding. "They say the hardest murders to unravel are the simplest ones. Drive-by shootings, for example. With no witnesses and no known enemies, there's nothing to get hold of. Good job," she added to Regan, and to Keegan, "You don't seem surprised."

"I'm not," the doctor said simply. "My father figured it out shortly after it happened. He had an eye for detail, like any good doctor, and he noticed a few odd things. Trudy's lethargic condition, for one. Also the position of the body. He thought it unlikely that Jack and Vita would have an impassioned argument in the narrow confines of that space between the bed and the dresser. Finally, he didn't think the argument sounded like Jack and Vita at all, and my father had strong faith in his own opinions. When he got back to Speedwell, the gardener was complaining that Faye hadn't even bothered to tie her horse when she brought it back this time. And Faye herself was nowhere around even though her car was supposed to be in the shop."

Regan saw in the rearview mirror that Keegan was watching Trudy as he spoke. "Of course, everybody at Speedwell had heard about the tragedy by that time. They were all subdued, wondering how they could have missed signs of trouble between Jack and his wife. One patient mentioned that, coincidentally, he had been listening to a play about marital discord at about the time it must have happened. He had found it depressing and had turned it off. My father probably wouldn't have made the connection except he had just picked up a newspaper Faye had left on the porch and found that particular show marked on the radio schedule. He had never believed anything was wrong with Faye, had believed she was up to something from the beginning. But, of course, he had never imagined anything as extreme as murder."

"Probably thought she was in love with him," Trudy commented dryly.

Keegan grinned. "Maybe. She was the flirtatious type. Anyhow, Faye didn't return until after seven. She claimed she had walked into town to pick up her car from the repair shop. That seemed unlikely too. She never walked, and the garage would have been closed that late on a Saturday. The owner disclaimed ever seeing Faye or her car when Dad called. He talked to Elaine then, the woman with polio who was lying on the beach, remember, and she reported seeing Faye take off in the direction of the stables as soon as the canoe left the dock that afternoon. Remembering Vita's insistence that everybody arrive on time, Dad could guess what had been on the radio show—and who had scripted it. He confronted Galen and Faye the next day."

Everyone was silent, waiting for Keegan to go on. "My father was pretty rabid on the subject of Speedwell though. Much more so than you accuse me of being," he said dryly to Trudy. "And he was also fond of Amos. He was convinced a lurid public trial would finish the hospital. Not to mention devastate its founder. I mean, losing a daughter was bad enough for Amos; you can imagine what it would have done to him to learn her brother was the killer. Dad told the unhappy couple that if they agreed to clear out of these parts and stay away, he would keep quiet. I remember coming on the scene—I was only five or six at the time—and being scared to death. I had never seen my father like that. It's no wonder he intimidated them. I lit out and didn't hear the whole story from him until I was grown. He told them he would obtain a tape of the radio show and hang on to it. If they ever came back, or if something suspicious happened to Amos, my father would take the whole thing public. They believed him, and did what he said. Up to a point."

"But Galen *did* return," Regan breathed, easing her foot off the brake as the fire truck lurched forward again, "at just about the time Trudy had her accident." They all looked to the side at the police cruiser, which was slewed half off the trail, its nose pointing downward at the lake, its front bumper crumpled against a sapling.

Howard nodded somberly. "After my father died. Galen

wouldn't have dared before. Yes, I always thought Galen was the one who caused Trudy's accident. Because he knew she had replaced him in Amos's affections and would probably inherit Speedwell. I didn't know that Galen was back—I was away just then—until I returned on the very night of the accident. If I had known, I would have informed him that my father had passed on the evidence to me and that there is no statute of limitations on murder."

With a shrug, he added, "All I could do was confront him after the fact. That's what I was doing when he had his heart attack. I wasn't my father; I would have told, and he knew it."

"And you never," Trudy said in icy tones, "told me any of this. Not even when you knew that Regan and I were trying to find out for Jack's sake."

Howard met her accusing gaze steadily. "I did not think any good could come from disclosing it all now. Galen is dead. Faye is institutionalized. But Amos can still be hurt. Do you want to tell him his son killed Vita and crippled you?"

She turned her face away.

"If I get a vote," Lucerne said, "I agree with Dr. Keegan. I don't think Jack would want this made public just for his sake."

Regan sat up straight. "Jack! I forgot!"

"Yes," Keegan said. "There's something else I haven't told you, Trudy. Something that happened tonight."

As her frightened gaze came around to meet his again, he said, "Jack is okay. But somebody threw some bees..."

CHAPTER 13

■ ■ ■

Or if, not to be buried,
but quick, and in mine arms.

Regan drove back to Speedwell as rapidly as possible. When they entered the building, lights were burning, but the nurses' station was empty. Keegan, looking worried, transferred Trudy to a wheelchair, and they all trotted down the corridor toward Jack's room. They could hear voices as they approached and, reaching the doorway, stopped short at sight of the crowd.

Patients in nightclothes stood or perched on chairs and on the edge of Trudy's bed. Nurses bustled among them, handing out crackers and juice. Sylvia sat, beaming, beside Jack's bed. Behind her, the policeman stood with crossed arms, keeping an eye on everyone. But he, too, grinned from ear to ear.

A nurse looked around and cried, "Here they are!" The chatter stilled. Those standing parted to either side like the Red Sea to reveal Jack sitting up in bed.

"Hi, Mom," he said matter-of-factly.

Trudy closed her eyes tightly for a moment, and when she opened them, tears streamed down her face. Keegan wheeled her forward so she could put her arms around her son. She wasn't the only one crying.

"Isn't it great?" Sylvia sniffed to Regan. "I was sitting here, and all of a sudden, he just opened his eyes, looked at me, and said, 'Hi, Syl.' Just like that. No confusion at all. Then he glanced around and said, 'Uh-oh, those bees did get me, huh?' He was a little surprised to see the officer though. I had to explain that."

"I think it was the extra adrenaline we gave him just in case," one of the nurses opined excitedly. "Snapped him right out of it."

"What's been going on?" Jack was asking his mother. "Why do you smell like smoke? No one would tell me where you were."

"Because they didn't know," she said. "It's a long story, Jack. I'll tell you later. All that matters now is that you're back. You've been out for almost a week, you know."

"No wonder I feel so rested. Did I miss anything important?" A pained silence fell. "I see," he added quietly, "that I did."

"Ken's funeral." Keegan sat down on the edge of the bed. "He got shot. And somebody's been trying to kill you too, Jack. You had better know that right off the bat so you can take precautions. Do you know why?"

Jack slowly shook his head. "I'm sorry. I have no idea."

"Did you know anything about who was distributing drugs at the high school?"

"I thought Ken was doing it. I didn't know where he was getting the stuff though. Ken was the type who would try anything once. He didn't seem to be addicted. I tried to warn him how dangerous it was. But I didn't persist because I knew it wasn't a good argument with him. He got his kicks out of danger. I thought if people didn't put up a fuss, he would probably get bored with it. I guess," he finished haltingly, "I should have persisted."

"Hey," Lucerne said, "Ken wouldn't have wanted to be the damper on any party. He was okay in the end. Miss Culver here was with him. She can tell you. He's probably looking down on us right now and saying, 'Lighten up, people.' To Ken!" Lucerne held her juice glass high. "Thanks, buddy! Make heaven hop!"

■ ■ ■

The following morning, the phone's ringing awakened Regan. She gave the clock a quick glance as she bounced out of bed and ran out into the hall to answer. Eleven o'clock. They had all sat up late the night before, unwilling to leave the scene of their miracle.

"I thought we told you to be careful!" It was Agatha's voice. "For future reference, plunging into burning houses does not qualify."

"Oh," Regan said, "did we make the morning news?"

"And how! We're coming back today. I know what my aunt would say, 'Chuck my stuff to the Salvation Army and skedaddle back there before that gal gets herself killed.' Do they really not have any idea who's doing this, or is your boyfriend just playing dumb?"

"They don't know. Except for Amy, alias Betony, of course. And she's not talking. Matt thinks she's probably the one responsible for putting the bees in the costume, but he doesn't think it was her idea. And he can't prove it. That's why he let the Clearview police have her. There is at least proof for the murder attempt at the hospital. I think I agree with him that she's shrewd enough about some things, but not highly intelligent. She should have known what he was up to when he asked her to raise her arm. That's how he found out she had scratches on her wrist without actually having to search her."

"I presume," Agatha said, "that all this means you two are talking again?"

"Minimally," Regan replied. "Which is more than Trudy is speaking to Dr. Keegan. We did manage to solve the old murder though. I'll tell you all about it when you get back. I've missed you, by the way."

"We've missed you, too, strangely enough. We'll try to get home before dark."

Regan was smiling when she hung up. "And I think to myself," she sang, as she headed back into her bedroom to change, "what a wonderful world!"

Gato, still curled up in the blankets, shot her a blearily resentful look.

"Hey," she said to him, "I'm happy. Deal with it."

■ ■ ■

Matt was not as chipper, suspecting that the real brain behind this crime spree was still loose. Raven Scion remained among the missing, as did, for that matter, Emmett Vinson. They were not going to be easy to find. Leaning back in his desk chair, he thought, take away the long hair and sunglasses on Scion or the beard and quilted shoulders on Vinson, and what did you have? Tall males with dark hair. Scads of men matching that description were around, including Matt. A sudden thought struck him, and he let the chair down slowly.

■ ■ ■

"Jack," Trudy said, "it might, you know, be Howard who is behind all this." She had just finished telling her son, in entirety, what had taken place while he was unconscious.

"Mom, that's crazy!"

"Is it?" She turned her head toward the police guard. "If Jack and I are both dead, Dr. Keegan inherits Speedwell. What do you think, officer?"

"You might have something there, Ms. Hargrove. The doctor always seems to be among the missing when something peculiar is happening. I've heard some millionaire is itching to buy this place too. Money is still the number one motive for murder. That or sex," he added as an afterthought. "You got any disgruntled boyfriends, ma'am?"

Jack was trying to catch her eye. "Mom, Howard loves you. You know that."

Interested, the policeman asked, "Does this guy have any reason to be angry with you, ma'am? You turned him down maybe?"

"Yes, I did," Trudy said defiantly. "He asked me to marry him eighteen years ago, just after my accident. Don't you find that surprising? I did at the time."

The cop raised his brows. "Not really, ma'am. You're an attractive woman, if you don't mind my saying so."

"I was a *cripple*," Trudy said sharply, color rising in her face. "He tries to blame that accident on Galen now, but I'm not convinced. The man is good at hiding things. He knew who killed my father, and he never told. I have some doubts about that too. There's no proof Ian Keegan wasn't behind the whole thing. He didn't like my father or Vita; everybody says so. Their deaths allowed him virtually to take over at Speedwell. Galen and Faye were weak. Doesn't it seem more likely to you that a stronger personality was in the background? Remember what Regan said Faye told her. 'Ian was the important one.'"

Jack was looking beyond her toward the door. "I don't believe that, Howard. She doesn't either, really."

Trudy turned her head quickly to see Keegan standing, with crossed arms, in the doorway. "Doesn't she?" he said, meeting her startled eyes. She had never seen him quite so grim. He turned away.

She bowed her head, fighting back tears.

"Don't let him intimidate you, ma'am," the cop said. "You very well may be right."

"Don't you see?" Jack retorted fiercely. "She doesn't want to be right."

■ ■ ■

When Regan stopped in at Speedwell that afternoon, one of the nurses said to her, "Oh, Miss Culver, Dr. Keegan said he would like to talk to you if you came in. In fact, it looks like his patient is just leaving. He's free after that. What beautiful flowers. Are those for Jack?"

"Yes, they are," Regan said. "Would you mind carrying them down to his room? Tell Trudy I'll be in after I talk to Howard."

Keegan was standing in his office doorway, chatting with a tall, attenuated-looking young man. As Regan hesitated, the doctor waved her over. "Joe," he said, "meet Regan Culver."

The young man's face brightened. "Not..."

"Yes, she's Alden's daughter. Joe," Keegan explained to Regan, "is here because your father mentioned Speedwell in his books."

"It's great to meet you, Miss Culver." Joe started to extend a hand, pulled it back. "I have AIDS. You might not want..."

Regan reached to take the hand. "My father was a doctor, remember? I know how AIDS can be passed—and how it can't. You're going to be staying here then? Dr. Keegan has had some very good results with AIDS cases."

"Yes," Joe said, as if having just made up his mind, "yes, I am."

When he had gone, Keegan led Regan into his office to a cluster of comfortable chairs. "First thing my father taught me," he said. "Don't hide behind a desk and pretend to be the knowledgeable one." He looked more drained than she had ever seen him.

"'In the doctor-patient relationship,'" Regan quoted, "'the patient is the expert, the one with experience of the symptoms. That should put him on an equal level with the doctor, who has only head knowledge to contribute.' End quote. My father," she explained taking a seat opposite him.

"That's why I wanted to talk to you," he said. "You know a lot of people in the natural-health field. Who do you think would be the best doctor to replace me here?"

"To replace..." She leaned forward. "Howard, you're the best naturopath around. *Nobody* could replace you. What are you talking about?"

His face relaxed into a genuine grin at that. "I would like to believe you. But nobody's indispensable. Carot is the best of the young doctors, in my opinion. Do you think he would be interested in coming on staff here? I happen to know he's looking for a rural location."

"He would probably jump at it. But why?"

"Trudy's frightened of me. I never realized how much until today. I guess I just didn't take it seriously before. Having to work with me under those circumstances would stress her unduly. And I do want her to continue to work."

"Give her some time, Howard. Once they catch this murderer—"

"No, I think she will always suspect my motives. Her peace of mind is important to me. But I don't want to leave Amos in the lurch without a replacement. So Carot, you think?"

"Howard, I wasn't kidding. This place needs you. What's going to happen to all the Joes out there otherwise?"

He sighed. "Joe didn't think we would accept AIDS patients because this is a Christian clinic. That's a sad commentary on the church, isn't it?"

"And it's why you have to stay. This place was never intended to be just a hospital. It's also a ministry. And what do you know about Carot's beliefs? Not all of these people can be healed. Some of them need to be prepared for death."

"As if any of us can be." Keegan shook his head. "It's bound to be hard, the tearing apart of the soul and body, the division of what wasn't meant to be divided. I never tell them it's going to be easy, just as I would never tell them following Christ is easy. Because we know differently, don't we?"

"But it has its moments," Regan said, remembering Jack's return to life. "It definitely has its moments."

■ ■ ■

"Trudy," Regan said sharply, as she came into Jack's room, "what have you been saying to Howard? He's talking about quitting."

Trudy, hunched in her chair like an old woman, blanched. "I'm sure he wasn't serious."

"He was as serious as I've ever seen him. And at a time when we all should be ecstatic." She smiled at Jack. "You are a miracle, you know."

His response was worried. "I know. By all accounts, I should at least be brain-damaged. Howard isn't really going to go, is he, Miss Culver?"

"I don't know. But I do know he won't be dissuaded once he makes up his mind about something. I didn't mean to snap, Trudy," she relented, sinking into a chair. "I know what you've been through in the past few days. And I can't imagine what it's been like to have to live with suspicion for so many years. No one is going to have any real peace until whoever is behind all this is caught."

"She has to learn to trust him *without* proof," Jack said. "She's never really learned to trust God either. I suppose she thinks he failed her, too, because of the accident."

Trudy irritably shook her head. "I'm not the sort to say, 'Why me?' Why shouldn't it be me? I messed up; that wasn't God's fault."

"And you've never forgiven yourself," Jack said. "You thought the accident was a punishment, didn't you? That's why you accepted it so stoically. Is that what you really believe God is like? Don't you understand he loves you, loves you even more than Amos or I ever could?"

Trudy looked confused. "Which he? God or Howard?"

"Both. You just have to put yourself in his hands."

"And let whichever one we're talking about do whatever he likes with me?" Trudy concluded bitterly.

"Yes. That's the only way."

"And what if you're wrong about him?"

It was Jack's turn to say, "Which him? Either way, it's a risk.

We give our devotion, our lives to a God who isn't proven. It's an enormous risk."

Amos appeared in the doorway then. "What's an enormous risk?"

"Love," Regan said.

"You're right about that." He pulled up a chair beside her. "I want you to tell me the rest of what you discovered about Jack and Vita's deaths."

To their suddenly closed faces, he said, "Galen killed them, didn't he? Don't try to protect me. I've always said people have a right to hear the truth."

Regan told him then, as tersely as possible. Her words plopped like relentless stones into serene water and seemed to leave that serenity unruffled.

"After Trudy showed me the play the other night, I thought it must be something like that. Don't all of you look so unhappy. This means I hadn't misread my daughter and son-in-law as badly as I thought I had. Of course, Vita was never any match for you, Trudy, as a doctor or as a person, but I loved her. It's the unlikable ones, such as she and Galen, who need the most love, I think. But love wasn't enough for my son. Nothing ever would have been enough for him."

He circled the bed to put one hand on Trudy's shoulder, one on Jack's. "And God gave me back, like Job, much more than I had lost. Don't any of you ever be afraid of love or the truth. Both of them will hurt sometimes, but the pain proves you are a living soul. And a living soul, like a living body, is capable of healing."

■ ■ ■

Matt phoned the Blue Lake Inn in Trafalgar. "Good afternoon," he said. "This is Chief Matt Olin of the Hayden Police Department. I'm making some routine inquiries. Can you tell me if a Myron and Charlotte Hargrove stayed there last night?"

"Yes, they did." The innkeeper sounded guarded. "Is there some problem?"

"Just routine, like I said. We have to know everybody's whereabouts for a certain time period yesterday afternoon and evening. What time did they arrive?"

"About four."

"Did they go out again?"

"Not last night. They had supper up in their room."

"You're sure they didn't go anywhere?"

"I was in the back all evening, and their car didn't leave the parking lot. Myron came down to watch a TV movie with me about nine."

"Did they come in together when they first arrived?"

"No, they parked in the back, and Charlotte came through by herself to register while he was carrying in the bags. They have been here before quite often."

"So the first time you actually saw Mr. Hargrove was at nine?"

The innkeeper sounded annoyed. "I didn't *see* him before that, but—"

"That's all I wanted to know. Thank you."

As Matt hung up, Gabe came into the office. He moved more tentatively than usual and wore a forearm cast.

"So they let you out?" Matt said, rising and circling the desk to perch on the edge of it. He shoved a chair out with his foot. "Here, sit down. You still don't look too good."

"They said I had a hard head." Gabe slumped into the seat.

"I'd like to ask you something," Matt said. "Think carefully before you answer. Have you ever seen Raven Scion and Emmett Vinson together?"

Gabe stared dully down at his cast while considering, shook his head. The question didn't seem to interest him. "If they're co-conspirators, they must be discreet about it."

"That wasn't quite my point." Matt grinned to himself.

"I don't see what you're so happy about. I'm not helping if you're trying to make a case against those two guys together."

"'Together,'" Matt said, "is the operative word. United. Indivisible."

"Sorry. I'm not in the mood for games."

Matt, swinging a foot, looked at him sharply. "I thought you would be happy with the news about Jack. What's the problem?"

"Lucerne said I should come down here and thank you."

The foot slowed. "No problem," Matt said curtly. "I owed you, remember?"

"That's what I told her, but she said life isn't a ledger. And if it was, I was on the debit side where you and God are concerned. We got better than we asked for from him, actually. We would have settled for just having Jack back, no matter what condition he was in. You're a Christian, aren't you, chief?"

"I try to be."

"I think that's what Lucerne would call a cop-out." Gabe made a face at his own pun.

"That girl," Matt said, "can be annoying at times."

"And how! Inconsistent too. She yelled at me last night. But this morning she came along to the hospital to apologize, said it was all her fault, which it wasn't. A few days ago she told me I would owe God big-time if Jack got better. Now she says God doesn't call in accounts, that he does what he does because he cares about us." Gabe made another face. "She's provoking all right, but she does make other girls look kind of dumb and boring by contrast."

"I know how that goes." Matt's expression was distant, bitter. "Watch your step."

"Anyway, there's something I want to tell you." Gabe looked down at his hands again. "I didn't spend all of my childhood in the slums. I was born in a suburb. My dad was a policeman."

"I see," Matt said.

"Do you? He was a pretty violent guy. Nobody quite came up to his expectations. Not just at home. Some people, when they get a little power, go crazy with it. He eventually was thrown off the force. My mom and I had moved out by then. According to Lucerne, I said some pretty wild things last night. Just thought I should explain. I guess I mistook you for my father."

"It's not the first time," Matt said, and Gabe's head came up. "Never mind. Under the circumstances, I don't blame you for not liking cops. I didn't know my dad. Maybe I got off lucky."

"Lucerne was right. My view of God goes back to my view of my father." Gabe stood. "Maybe you have the same problem."

Matt looked at him coldly. "What did I just tell you? I never knew my father, never wanted to either."

"And how well do you know God?" Gabe grinned and moved toward the door. "I won't be able to play football for a while."

"With you and Jack both on the injured list, we'll have to do some major reorganizing," Matt agreed. "I'm not worried. This team has already proved itself to me."

Gabe hesitated. The question came out of his mouth as if compelled. "Why *did* you do it?"

"What?"

Embarrassed, as if he would now prefer to retreat, Gabe said truculently, "Why did all of you go into that burning house after me?"

Matt rose slowly to face him. "For the same reason God does what he does, I expect. Because we cared about you. It means you don't owe *us* anything either."

■ ■ ■

That evening as Jack lay sleeping, Trudy said to the policeman, "I'm going out onto the porch for a while."

"Are you sure you want to do that, ma'am? You know I can't go with you when the boy is here."

It was a different policeman, so he wasn't alarmed when she said, "I don't want you to, officer. I need to talk to Dr. Keegan."

She was grateful for the wool throw around her shoulders because it was so cold outside she could see her breath. The distant stars glittered like ice crystals. The full moon, which would have risen orange, now shone like alabaster, bleaching the grass and flower beds. It was finally going to frost. Tomorrow morning those flowers would glisten as if with stardust, the final enchantment that would cause them to sink and shrivel under the touch of the sun.

She was warm enough, huddled in her wool. Some of the old-time doctors had thought that cold air, if the patient was otherwise well wrapped, was good for the system. Bracing.

Perhaps they were right. She had never felt more alive. *Maybe Jack is right, too,* she addressed the distant stars silently. *I never trusted you. I never realized until today how much of an insult that is. I just thought of it as sensible caution, I guess. Or, as Regan says, I never expected much because there are fewer disappointments that way. I've just realized that there's precious little joy either. All right. I'm going to change. Send Howard out here, and I'll prove it to you.*

Almost at once, she heard the nurse at the front desk say, "Good evening, Dr. Keegan."

"Evenin', Susan. I'm out for a breath of fresh air."

"That air's more than fresh," the nurse responded. "Fresh from the freezer, more like."

The door creaked, and Trudy tensed. She had not decided what she was going to say.

When he saw her, he didn't come across or touch her as he usually did. Instead, he walked to the porch rail, turned to lean against it. "Good evening, Trudy." His tone was polite, reserved. "Does my being here bother you? Do you want me to go away?"

She didn't know if he meant for the present or for good.

Both, probably. With the moonlight behind him, his face was in shadow.

"No," she said. "I was just thinking that I would like to go out on the dock and look at the water. Will you take me?"

She thought she had, for once, succeeded in startling him. He knew how she felt about the lake ever since her accident.

"All right," he said finally, circling behind her wheelchair to push. He went silent then, and that silence chilled her more than the autumn night. He had never been reluctant to speak to her, to touch her, before. Rolling down the ramp to the walk with him behind her, she could imagine herself alone under the moon's cold luminescence.

"Aren't you afraid?" he asked finally, almost harshly, as the wheels rattled over the rough boards of the pier. "I could push you right off the end, you know."

"I know." She didn't add to that simple statement right away. But when he reached the edge and stopped the wheelchair beside the bench bolted there, she said, "Lift me over to that, please. I want to talk to you."

He complied, though his touch seemed impersonal, the fire that usually animated him, banked.

"What do you want from me, Howard?" she asked straight-out when they were side by side on the bench.

"A wife," he said. "A partner."

"Are you talking about a platonic relationship—a marriage of convenience?"

"No!" He turned to face her more directly. "I am *not* talking about a platonic relationship. I don't know why you should imagine I would be."

Her face warmed, but she did not look away. "And if I marry you, you'll stay?"

"Never mind now, Trudy." He rose to put his back to her. "I don't want a wife who is afraid of me."

The scene was black and white, symbolic, like an allegory. Did God sometimes do this? Was there a point in his long pursuit of man at which he said enough? Was that what hell was all about? Not flames but the pale chill of being finally left alone?

I will not have an unwilling lover.

"I was *always* afraid of you," she said and saw his broad shoulders wince. "Even before my accident. But it wasn't fear for my life. You had a hold over me that I couldn't shake. I found that frightening. I only turned to Lance to prove to myself that I could do without you."

"So that's why you were angry?" he said. "If not for me, your accident never would have happened."

"I *wasn't* angry. How many times do I have to tell people that?"

He turned. "Your accident," he repeated doggedly, "never would have happened if—"

"All right," she said in a shaking, furious whisper. "My accident never would have happened if you had deigned to pay any attention to me! Are you satisfied?"

"That's better," he said, sitting down again. "I was twenty-something at the time, Trudy. My father had just died. I was having to take on more responsibility than I'd ever imagined, and I was scared to death. A guy's entitled to be something of a jerk in those circumstances, don't you think? I was insanely jealous. That's why I stormed at you about Lance. I didn't realize that myself at the time, of course. I just thought I was being eminently reasonable, and you were cracking up. Until I saw your car flip into the water that night. Then I went a little crazy myself. So what is it?" He reached to touch her hand, and she didn't pull it away. "Are you still carrying a torch for Lance?"

"Don't be ridiculous. I can't even recall his face. He was never important. Remember what Faye said about your father? 'Ian was the important one. Any woman would know that.' Faye settled for second best too. Don't you see, when you first asked me to marry you, I thought you were sorry for me. That was unendurable. I hated you for it. But I had to find some other reason for that hatred. To justify it."

"Did you really believe I would hurt you?"

"I could convince myself when you weren't around. But I knew my weakness. That's why I always avoided looking at you, for fear of giving myself away. If you had ever said one word about love, I would have buckled."

He looked puzzled. "I didn't? I must have assumed you knew. Not to insult your intelligence, but"—laughter kindled in his eyes—"why else does a man propose?" The humor flared into something warmer, from which she could not turn away. He cupped the side of her neck, stroked the line of her jaw with his thumb. She shivered, but her gaze didn't falter. "Cold?" he whispered, gathering her to him and covering her mouth with his, that radiant energy of his seeming to beat in her blood like fire.

She yielded at once, small, eager hands pressing against his strong back. He raised his head to say unevenly, "I should have done that long ago. Action beats words any day. I love you, woman. Do you believe me yet?"

She saw it then in his face—a miraculous, preposterous vulnerability. The reality that one so strong and confident adored her, a cripple, was awesome and baffling. In a blinding flash, she realized God was like that too. The source of all power had chosen to make himself weak and unprotected against the slights and malice of feeble man. He also bled when distrusted and rejected.

Her face glowed with the moon's reflected glory. "I think," she said to both of them, "that I will take you up on that partnership thing after all."

CHAPTER 14

Come, take your flowers.

Matt drove out to Speedwell early on Saturday morning with a warrant in his pocket. He was in time to intercept the young trooper who was just going off his shift. "If you don't mind," Matt said to him, "I'd like you to accompany me on a search. I want a witness to what I think I might find."

"Sure," the trooper agreed. "I'll follow you. Is it far?"

Matt looked across the gray lake at the Hargrove house. "No, it's not far."

When the two emerged from that house half an hour later, Matt carried a bag with several tagged items inside. The trooper was excited but puzzled. "What does it all mean?" he asked.

"Impersonation on a massive scale," Matt said. "Or perhaps that's the wrong word for it. You can't impersonate somebody who doesn't exist."

■ ■ ■

Regan arrived at Speedwell later that morning to find Trudy sitting on the porch, beaming almost brightly enough to make up for the missing sun. Clouds had moved in late the night before. "We've been spared frost one more time," Regan said, mounting the steps. "Agatha, Gina, and Diane returned last evening. I hated to leave on their first day back, but next week is supposed to turn drastically colder. I thought I'd better take a look at Vita's flowers while I have the chance. Do you want to come along? You seem much happier than you did yesterday."

"I'm engaged," Trudy said.

Regan laughed and leaned over to hug her. "I don't need to ask who the fortunate man is. I'm glad you two have got that settled. Would you rather stay here?"

"No, I'll ride along. We doctors are supposed to have weekends off. We can do that since we don't handle emergency cases. But Howard had to go into the city this morning to address a conference."

At the end of the torturous lane, the once elegant house was a heap of ashes, the thick grass crisscrossed with ruts. "In a way, I'm glad it's gone," Trudy said when she had levered herself out of the car into her wheelchair. "I can let them go too, finally. They were happy, after all. They weren't what Galen's play tried to make them. I think he *wanted* that marriage to be a sham."

Regan regarded the remains thoughtfully. "Or perhaps he only foresaw what was to come. We've agreed he was a good judge of character. Maybe he saw what it could lead to and precipitated matters." She shook herself. "I'm being a real downer, aren't I? Never mind. It wouldn't have happened. Jack Dawson wasn't a touchy type. We've agreed on that. He didn't carry his past like a millstone into the relationship."

"Vita probably wouldn't have noticed if he had." Trudy wheeled herself over ruts toward the flower beds.

"I think I'm just going to make a list," Regan said, following with a clipboard and the package of photos. "A layout with descriptions. Then I can spend a blissful winter trying to figure out what all these things are. It's getting late to be dividing perennials now, and I don't want to risk losing any of them. We might gather some seed though. Where are you and Howard going to live?"

"Here, I think. We'll build a new foundation, lay a smoother road."

Looking at the long slope of flowers, Regan said, "I'm reminded of something Sasha said to me once." Flinging up her hands, she recited in a childish treble, "'So many flowers. You've got enough flowers for a hundred people.' I think I told her what I told Matt when he brought me a bouquet. 'You can't have too many flowers.' But I wonder..."

"Is that his problem?" Trudy asked. "He thinks you have plenty and don't need him?"

"Maybe." Regan stood with her head tilted, considering. "Even more than most men, Matt must associate love with being needed. He raised his little brother, you know. Then his football players needed him, as do the townspeople he protects. But since I have been cleared of murder, I don't appear to need him anymore."

She turned up her palms and shook her head. "How do I convince him otherwise? How can I make him understand that a love I choose must be more genuine than one I require? It's not something you can explain to someone; it's something they have to *know.* Get married right away, Trudy. If Matt and I were husband and wife now, we would feel obliged to work it out. As it is..." She shook her head again.

"In Bible times," Trudy said, "a betrothal was just as binding as a marriage. It *is* a promise, after all."

Regan looked blindly at her. "That *has* occurred to me. So there's going to be no backing out for you? Happily ever after doesn't come with the ring, you know."

"I know, and if anyone ever had equivocal feelings about a man, it was me. But like Jack says, you're either in all the way or not at all. I'm going to go for it."

■ ■ ■

At Speedwell, Jack said to his guard, "Will you call Chief Olin for me, ask him to come out here? There's something I have to tell him."

After speaking to his resurrected quarterback, Matt left the clinic around half past one. Things were coming together. A midmorning rain had caused the temperature to drop, and a sharp wind harried the dingy clouds.

Matt had reached Speedwell's parking lot when Charlotte Hargrove caught up with him. Bundled up sensibly against the cold in a hooded coat and gloves, she carried a potted yellow chrysanthemum.

"Chief Olin, I was wondering if you might give me a ride up to the cemetery. Myron has taken the car."

"Sure." Matt gestured toward the passenger side. "I have a few questions I'd like to ask you anyway."

As he started the car, he said, "You just got back from Trafalgar?"

"Yes, a couple of hours ago. I thought I might take this up for Ken's grave. Those funeral arrangements will be wilting about now, but I can set this right in the earth."

"You stayed at an inn out there, I hear," Matt said, waving to Lucerne who was buzzing cheerfully into the drive as he was pulling out. Apparently the motorbike had suffered no serious damage. Charlotte had her head bent over her flowers.

"Yes, the owner said you had been making inquiries. I suppose that's routine after what happened to Gabe and Trudy. Myron wasn't with me when I registered, by the way. I'd dropped him off at Mason Norville's."

"And when did you see him again?"

"It must have been close to nine when Mason brought him to the inn. At least, I assume it was Mason. I didn't see the car."

Matt pulled into the narrow lane of the cemetery, coasted to a stop beside the raw earth and damp, drooping flowers that covered Ken's grave. "I don't think you can be telling me the truth, Mrs. Hargrove. I'm pretty sure Myron was still in Hayden around four o'clock yesterday, driving Trudy's van."

When she just looked at him without speaking, he added, "Did you know that your husband was having an affair with that girl, Amy Bumpkiss? Jack saw them kissing in the principal's office on the night of the homecoming dance."

"That would have worried Jack, all right," Charlotte said. "Did you really think I didn't know? Look at these flowers, Chief Olin."

It had just occurred to Matt that she wasn't carrying a trowel. How had she expected to plant anything? Something round and dark poked out from the yellow petals, the business end of a gun barrel.

"You thought I was just a patsy, didn't you?" Charlotte said. "The loyal, unsuspecting wife. Amy was *my* idea. I told Myron to find a mercenary and not-too-bright little trollop and make love to her. I imagine he enjoyed that part of the plan. She was attractive enough until she made herself over to look inconspicuous. She doesn't even know I was in on the plot; she thought he was going to divorce me and marry her when the whole thing was finished. But of course, he would have to push it by kissing her at the school that night. The risk excited him, I suppose. I guess we're luckier than we know that Jack collapsed before he could say anything. It didn't look like luck to begin with. We had intended those bees for Gabe, to play up the racism issue and point a finger at Emmett Vinson. Then Myron was going to send Jack out to look for Gabe in hopes that Jack would get stung when he tried to help his friend. Jack's involvement would have seemed accidental. It didn't work out the way we had planned, but by all rights, Jack still should have died that night." She sounded aggrieved.

"Apparently you haven't paid much attention to your family's philosophy. The body is linked with the mind, and the mind can be stubborn about living."

"Don't start with that Pollyanna poppycock," Charlotte snapped. "Just wait and see how much good positive thinking will do you against a bullet. They're not my family anyhow, and I should have known better than to link up with a narcissist like Myron. He's no more effective than his father was. Intelligent enough and a good actor, I'll grant you, but weak."

"He fades in the home stretch?" Matt suggested.

"That's one way to put it. He never would have made it this far without me. His father raised him on hate, of course. Drummed into him that the family fortune should have been his. That may have been true enough, but a sense of entitlement doesn't get you anywhere. Just makes you impatient and careless. I was the one who taught him to bide his time until the circumstances were right."

"Not to mention creating a few of his own." Was she planning to shoot him, or was she waiting for her husband?

"Some of them were created *for* us. That marijuana scandal out at the herb farm made people uneasy about narcotics, not to mention that your romance with a murder suspect made them mistrustful of you. All we had to do was introduce the drug element a little stronger, play it up to be much worse than it actually was, and stir in a bit of racism. It's amazing what a few carefully planted rumors can do. I was going to kill you here, make it look like suicide, but I've had a better idea. Drive. No tricks. I don't have anything to lose at this point."

Matt followed the cemetery's circular path back to the gate again, slowly, to avoid jolts. Amateurs were notoriously nervous with their trigger fingers. "Why did you think people would believe suicide?"

"Everybody knows how glum you've been lately after your

fuss with your fiancée. You might have considered Ken's death your fault too. You're the feel-guilty type. Turn left."

Leaving the flower on the seat, she edged cautiously down onto the floor, still facing him, hiding herself from any passing motorists.

"And you're obviously not."

She smiled. "You've got that right. I've spent almost twenty years in this hole. I think I've paid my dues. You're also the go-it-alone type. You'll have kept most of what you know to yourself, I expect. Like the wig, sunglasses, and beard you found in Myron's briefcase. He's visiting your fiancée right now, by the way. She'll provide his alibi. That's a good touch, don't you think?"

"Myron is good at covering himself, I'll grant you that. Whether it requires cowering behind his wife's skirts or getting some teenagers hooked on heroin."

Although he was furious, Matt was thinking clearly and quickly. *That eager young trooper who accompanied me on the search will have something to report if I turn up dead. And if I have to die, I must make very sure it doesn't look like suicide. Whether or not Regan still cares for me, she would blame herself. The town would blame her too. They would say that movie was right, that she used me then dumped me.*

"It won't do you any good to try to turn me against Myron," Charlotte was saying with amusement. "I already know what he is, remember? We're going to Raven Scion's place, by the way."

"One of the suspects you created out of whole cloth just as you did your circumstances. I'd been realizing all along that most of the guys involved in the case were tall and dark, as compared to Jack Dawson, who wasn't. It suddenly hit me that most of them could be one guy. Myron only had to add a long wig, sunglasses, and flashy clothes to transform himself into Scion or a beard and flannels to be Vinson. People who wear thick glasses are hard to recognize without them. I suppose that was why Raven always stood so close to people; Myron had a hard time seeing *without* those thick glasses. After I shoved him out of Regan's class that day, I suppose he changed his disguise and attended the bee lecture as Scion."

"He was there," Charlotte said impatiently, "but I stole the bees. Myron's job that afternoon was to leave the bouquet. He hadn't planned to make a scene during Regan's talk, but when Gabe sat down next to him, it was too good an opportunity to miss. He returned as Scion after the talk was over to do the bouquet. He didn't think you would let Vinson back in. Then he changed again and made it to the last half of the snake thing to harass Gabe some more. I knew that improvising of his was eventually going to get us into trouble, and it did—yesterday. I thought we should just dump Trudy in the lake. It was the easiest way. But he wanted to try for an alibi, and he thought they would be able to tell when a fire started. He was supposed to give me an hour to reach the inn before setting the blaze. So he dropped Trudy off at the old house and walked up that horse trail to Speedwell to throw the bees through Jack's window. Then he went back for the van and drove out to the school to pick up the heroin we had stashed in Ken's locker after you searched it."

"Why did you have to kill Ken?"

"He was too smart. As were you. That's another of Myron's weaknesses. He never gives anybody else credit for having brains. Ken guessed the whole Raven persona was a disguise. He kept bugging Amy about it—she was the one who sold him the drugs—until she admitted that Scion was Jack Dawson. That old case was supposed to be brought in as another red herring eventually, but not until later, not until the Scion disguise was abandoned. But Amy jumped the gun. Ken got curious, rode up to Trafalgar, chatted up some of the kids there, and found out that the real Betony Scion was dead. He taunted Amy with that;

he hadn't found out who she was yet, but he would have eventually. Until Jack got hurt, it was all a game to Ken, but then he got serious—and threatening. He even suspected Amy of killing the real Betony Scion, which was ridiculous, of course.

"After all," Charlotte continued dryly, "Amy was not very good at arranging accidents. She flubbed up with the dummy, though she didn't do too bad at planting the bees in that costume. And at least she knew enough to cover her tracks by picking up the EpiPen after Jack collapsed and the dummy after that part of the plan failed. Everything went downhill from there. The whole thing was just too complicated. I told Myron that. I also told him we should get rid of that heroin, flush it or something, but he thought it was too valuable for that. So what happened when he went to get it? He took off those sunglasses so he could see better indoors. Then he was afraid Gabe had recognized him."

"Gabe didn't."

"I thought it unlikely myself after one glimpse in a dim hallway. But of course Myron panicked. Then not to even realize the girl was there too!" Charlotte's peevish expression seemed to invite Matt to share in her disgust over her mate's blunders. But the precise barrel of her little gun never wavered.

"He should have taken the disguises with him to Trafalgar. But he was pretty sure the police would be looking for Trudy's van by then, and he didn't want to risk having that stuff with him if he was pulled over. So he stopped at the house to drop it off and change the license plate on the van. He was in the garage, incidentally, when you drove your car up on the lawn. That gave him a few bad minutes until he saw Regan arrive and both of you go back down the lane together. I should have insisted he be the one to go to Trafalgar. But that trip was a last-minute decision, and I can't be expected to think of everything. Who knew that Trudy and your fiancée would go poking around that old house to begin with and almost stumble on the drug stash? They *said* they were just going out there to look at the flowers. It's a good thing I was watching them to make sure." She raised herself on her knees. "All right. We're here. Turn."

Matt veered into the rutted lane, slowing to a virtual crawl. "You don't think that Amy will keep quiet forever, do you?" He would, he thought, have his best chance when they got out of the car. If, that is, she wasn't going to shoot him where he sat. He was careful not to glance toward any of the mirrors.

"Yes, I do. The woman has a strong sense of self-preservation, and she believes Myron shot Ken. She's not going to risk the same fate herself. And don't think I'm not aware that Lucerne Abiel was behind us. If she knows what's good for her, she'll keep going. Yes, she just passed the driveway."

Charlotte's attention swung back to Matt.

"Emmett's truck, by the way, is stashed in one of the out-buildings here. Apparently you didn't search far enough yesterday. Drat, the girl's turned around and come back."

"You don't have to hurt her," Matt said. "She doesn't know anything. I'll send her away."

"I wasn't born yesterday." As they pulled up beside the sagging house, Charlotte leaned closer, eyes intent. "You are going to unbuckle your gun belt, get out, and stand beside the car door with your hands on the roof. Don't look at her. Remember, at this range, I can't miss."

He followed her instructions. He thought he would have his chance when she was on the other side of the car. But she didn't go that way. Instead she kept her eyes and the gun barrel trained on him while she eased his revolver out of the holster, moving the gun up to replace her small one, which she slipped with her left hand into a pocket. Then she slid over into the driver's seat. The sputter of Lucerne's bike grew louder. He was remembering a similar scene at Vinson's cabin, another gun. Charlotte's husband had been easier.

"Did you know," he asked, "that Galen killed Jack Dawson?"

"Of course. The dummy trick that crippled Trudy was Galen's idea, too, but Myron carried it out. If not for Howard Keegan, it would have worked that time. That's why we decided to try it again."

The sputter died. Lucerne, who couldn't see Charlotte, said, "Hi, what's up?"

Matt didn't answer, still looking down into Charlotte's cold eyes, waiting for her attention to flicker. Lucerne got off her bike and came forward to peer at the woman on the seat. "Mrs. Hargrove? What are the flowers for?"

Charlotte's left hand came out of her pocket thrusting toward Matt's stomach. It wasn't the same weapon she had put in. In the seconds it took to kick in, he had time for a flash of recognition—stun gun!—before his body convulsed with a surge of electric heat, and he dropped, writhing, to the muddy ground.

Lucerne gaped, wheeled to run. Charlotte lurched out of the car, spilling the flowerpot and the stun gun on the ground, and wrapped her left arm around the girl's neck. "You might come in handy after all, my dear," she said, pressing the revolver into Lucerne's hand and holding it there. "People will be all too willing to assume you were part of the gang. Shoot him!"

Gagging, Lucerne fought with revulsion to get her hand free of the metal, but Charlotte's grip was implacable. She tightened her arm. "I'm sure you've heard what a choke hold can do," she said. "It's him or you. Pull the trigger, and I'll let you live. Of course, I'll deny I was ever here, and I think I'm the one who will be believed. If you're smart, you'll say it was self-defense. Everybody knows about overaggressive cops. Otherwise, I'm going to have to shoot you too."

■ ■ ■

When the doorbell rang at a quarter to two that afternoon, Regan found Myron Hargrove on her porch. "Good afternoon, Miss Culver. I thought we had better discuss those plantings you promised us."

Regan blinked. When Thyme Will Tell had first offered to do some free landscaping for the school, Myron hadn't been overly enthusiastic. Regan had thought the whole idea forgotten.

"All right," she said. "I suggest we go over to the school, then, so I can point out what I had in mind."

He seemed taken aback. "Can't we just do it here?"

"Hardly. I'll have to show you where I think the flower beds should go. Just a minute; I'll get a notebook."

She followed him to the school in her Land Rover, wondering what had caused his change in attitude. Despite his wearing one of her carnations at the dance, she didn't think he was really a flower lover. When had he gotten that carnation anyhow? Neither he nor his wife had been at Regan's lecture. Perhaps Jack or Trudy had passed the bloom on to him.

At the school, some teenage boys were hanging around their cars in the parking lot, including Gabe with his cast. Chris came up to her window. "Hi, Miss Culver. You don't know where the chief is, do you? He's late for practice."

"No," she said. "Sorry."

A car pulled up on her passenger side, a police cruiser. Lieutenant Woods and a subordinate. "Afternoon," the lieutenant said. "Olin here?"

On receiving a negative answer, he looked puzzled, scanned the empty athletic fields. "He asked us to meet him here. Wait a minute. Isn't that him?"

They all looked where he was pointing to see a cruiser lurching up the rutted lane toward the Scion place, a motorbike trailing it.

They saw Matt, small in the distance, get out and stand with his arms on the top of the car.

"That doesn't look natural," the lieutenant said, scooping up a pair of binoculars and training them on the scene.

Gabe didn't wait to hear more. "Come on, guys," he yelled, tucking his plaster-encased arm into his side as if it were a football and charging onto the field. "We need a warmup anyhow."

The lieutenant, face suddenly grim, jumped out of his car. "I think they have the right idea. It'll be faster cross-country. Jeff, you go around by the road. Be careful. There's a woman with a gun. Now, Miss Culver, if you don't mind—" And the lieutenant scrambled into the passenger's seat of the Jeep and fastened his seat belt.

Regan was already yanking the vehicle into four-wheel drive. Myron jumped into the back just before she gunned it forward over a curb and onto the field.

The lieutenant had the binoculars up to his eyes again. "Olin is down. The woman is struggling with the girl over the gun, looks like. Fortyish woman. Faded looking. Know her?"

"Yes." Regan fought to breathe against an invisible weight of hopelessness on her chest. "In that case, I think—"

Myron Hargrove reached over the backseat to snatch the lieutenant's gun from its holster. "She was about to say it's my wife. Stop the car!" The last to Regan.

She ignored him.

"I said stop—"

Regan stomped on the brake, jerked the wheel violently to the right. The jeep spun sideways, and Myron catapulted against the door behind her. The lieutenant clicked his seat belt off and dove into the back.

Regan did not look around at them. Having fought the wheels straight again, she drove on. The maneuver had cost her some time. But the football players were running well, Gabe out in front.

■ ■ ■

Although Matt's body couldn't move, his thinking was crystal clear. The shock would wear off in about five minutes, but irreparable things could happen in five minutes. Lucerne was gasping for air, but she had managed to keep her scrabbling fingers free of the trigger.

She's young and foolhardy, God, but you're surely not going to let her die in this ridiculous way. I'm not asking anything for myself, but—

"Why not?" The answer came quick and sharp before he had finished. "Because you don't believe in asking for help, do you? The woman is right. You have to do it all yourself."

Risk is my job. I'm not complaining. I was stupid about Charlotte. I'll take what I've got coming, but—

"Do you think what happens to you is only going to affect you? What about Regan? What about your team? What about your town?"

"Weak!" Charlotte raged. "Must I do everything myself?"

She jerked the gun out of Lucerne's grasp and leveled it at Matt's chest. Lucerne grabbed feebly at her arm, pushed it up.

"Will you people just let it be?" Charlotte shrieked, yanking back against Lucerne's throat until the girl shuddered and went limp. Charlotte heaved her to the side, wrapped both hands around the butt.

All right, God. You win. Help me.

Gabe jerked open the passenger door of the cruiser, came in a long flying tackle across the front seat, wrapping both arms around Charlotte's waist to bring her crashing down on top of Matt. Then Gabe simply raised his fist and hit her across the back of the head with his cast. She went slack.

"That should hold her for a while," Gabe gasped, crawling across to Lucerne. Chest heaving, he put fingers to the base of her throat.

Then more teenagers were spilling around both sides of the car, and the Land Rover slued in behind it, Lieutenant Woods jumping out, pistol at the ready.

"Stun gun, huh?" he said, seeing it lying on the ground. "You'll be okay in a few minutes."

Regan, who had started forward, white-faced, heaved a sigh and turned to Lucerne.

"Check her, will you?" Gabe panted, craning his neck to look up. "I can't feel a thing except my own pulse."

Regan knelt and turned a cheek close to the girl's nose and mouth, felt a soft warmth. "She's breathing."

A few minutes later, Regan crossed to Matt. Lucerne was showing signs of regaining consciousness. The two other policemen had radioed for an ambulance and were putting Myron and Charlotte into the backseat of their car. Matt was sitting up now and leaning forward, elbows propped on drawn-up knees, head dangling. Regan crouched down beside him on the cold and muddy ground, placed a hand on his arm and felt him stiffen, though he didn't look at her.

"I think you need some time, Matt," she said in an undertone. "I'll wear your ring till June." She moved the hand to his shoulder. "I still love you. I didn't realize how much until I thought she had killed you." He didn't answer, but one of his hands came up to catch hers briefly, to squeeze her fingers tight around the ring.

■ ■ ■

Later that evening, Gabe drove to the hospital in Clearview, took an elevator to a third-floor room. When he came in, Lucerne was alone, her face turned toward the wall.

"I'm getting awfully tired of this place," he grumbled. "Here, brought you something." He tumbled a bouquet of roses onto her pillow.

"Oh," she said in a stifled tone. "How nice. Red roses."

"Burgundy," he said, "to be exact. You look different."

She buried her face in the flowers, as if to avoid his gaze. "Must you stare at me?" she said crossly.

"You know something?" he said. "You actually have more color than you usually do."

"That's because they washed my makeup off!" she wailed.

"Well, you needn't blush about it."

"I'm not blushing," she said. "This is the way my skin always is."

He sat down to regard her, frowning. "Sunburn easily?" he hazarded. "Your eyes look different too. Almost...pink."

"They took my contacts out too." Lucerne sat up finally, defiantly, dropping the flowers into her lap. "I'm an albino, Johnson."

"A what?"

"A fluke of nature!" she flashed. "An aberration. My hair is white. My eyes are pink—and sensitive to light, I might add. That's why I'm more comfortable at night. Weird, huh?"

He didn't say anything.

"Of course, albinos are often morons too. At least I escaped that!" She tried a shaky laugh. "My mother did her best to protect me. She kept me hidden away at a discreet private school. But the kids there knew a freak when they saw one. My name only made matters worse."

"What's wrong with Lucerne?"

"It isn't really Lucerne. That originally was my middle name. I changed that when I came here too."

"So what *is* your real name? If," he added at her silence, "you don't mind telling me."

"Why not?" she said, shrugging in resignation. "It's Jade."

"That's pretty."

"Don't act the innocent with me, Gabe Johnson! My mother was thinking of the stone. As you can tell, she's fond of green. It isn't what anybody else thinks of when they hear the word."

"As a slang term for a prostitute," Gabe said, "it's rather outdated."

"That didn't keep my classmates from delighting in it. I spent my first seventeen years keeping as low a profile as I could. But I got sick of it. So…" She gestured widely. "A new start. Where nobody knew what I was. I swore I would never be that little wimp again. And I haven't."

"Yes, but by hiding behind makeup, you're implying that the real you is defective."

"Aren't I?" she asked in a small voice.

He got out of his seat to perch on the edge of the bed. "Lucerne, I'm the last person to feel sorry for you because of your skin color. The last person to mock you for it either. How do you know the kids here would be the same as at your other school? Give us a little more credit, can't you? Look how everybody pulled together for Jack."

"They *like* Jack. They don't like me."

"Of course they do. In fact, I came early to warn you that a bunch of them are heading over here at eight. So if you want to get ready…"

Looking steadily up at him, she shook her head. "You're right. I'm through hiding."

"Atta girl. Though I must say," he added with a teasing glint, "I was unusually perceptive when I said you were too darn white."

She hit him with a pillow.

"And I'd think you would have learned your lesson about chasing cars after the other night."

She hit him again. "You wouldn't be here if it weren't for me and my motorbike, I'll thank you to remember, buster! I just thought it strange that the woman ducked her head when she saw me, like she didn't want to be recognized. So I just waited till the police car drove out of sight, followed along until I saw it parked in the cemetery, then hid and waited for it to leave. Good thing I did too. I swear, you males shouldn't be allowed out without a keeper!"

Regan came in after the other teenagers had arrived, said to Lucerne, under cover of their jubilant high jinks, "I see that he found some burgundy roses."

"Gabe wanted that color in particular?" Lucerne looked suspiciously over at him. "Why?"

"The meaning, I expect," Regan said. "The language of flowers, remember?"

"And what do burgundy roses stand for?" Lucerne demanded gruffly. "Pest? Capricious idiot?"

"Not quite." Regan smiled. "Unconscious beauty."

Catching Gabe's eye, Lucerne blushed in earnest.

■ ■ ■

That night, an emotionally exhausted Regan sat up in bed reading her well-thumbed volume of Ruth Pitter's poetry. Coming upon a poem called "Sinking," Regan felt a flash of recognition.

Pitter was talking about a swimmer who, far from shore, has no more strength to go on and concedes that she must go down. Regan had always thought it an unusually heavy poem for Pitter, a poem about defeat. But as her gaze dropped to the last lines, Regan felt a shock of comprehension:

> Whether in sleep, or love, or death you must
> drown;
> Cease then your striving, sink and go down.

I've been trying desperately to stay on top of life and love, to keep some control, but that's impossible. Amos was right. Yielding to you, love incarnate, is not resignation, is worlds removed from resignation. It's what the Old Testament meant by choosing life. It means I can't design my own future, but then I never could, really. It means embracing instead of fighting the adventure, the uncertainty,

the danger. All your writers from the apostle Paul on have talked
about the life that only comes through death. Why didn't I ever see
that before?

"Because," the answer came at once, "you told Matt you
loved him without expecting anything from him in return. You
can only see by doing."

That night when her sleeping mind again struggled in dark
waters, she gave in and slipped beneath the surface to where iri-
descent fish played in the coral forests, and where the seabed was
strewn with treasures beyond any pirate's wildest fantasies.

■ ■ ■

In the end, Charlotte and Myron turned against each other.
Ironically, Amy was the only one still not talking.

"He killed Ken," Charlotte said.

Matt didn't buy it. "You said, if I remember correctly, that Amy
believed Myron had done it, which would imply he hadn't. Besides,
he has an alibi; he was at the high school all that morning."

"But why Keegan?" Woods asked, when they had finally gotten all the statements they needed and retired wearily to a
Clearview restaurant for a late supper. "Why did they settle on
him for a scapegoat? What had he ever done to them?"

"What he *prevented* them from doing would be a more
accurate description," Matt said. "Ever since the original
attempt against Trudy eighteen years ago, Keegan had been
getting in their way. Actually, I think his being close to the
scenes of all the crimes was just coincidence at first. But a
coincidence they eventually decided to use. Since it didn't
seem likely they could arrange the deaths in the right order
again, he would stand in the way of their succession to
Speedwell. The original plan called for Amos and Trudy to die
together after Jack did. Which, if I have it right, would have
left everything to the only surviving relative, Myron. But if
Trudy and Jack died before Amos, the hospital was to go to

Howard. Also, he wouldn't be too happy about losing the woman he loved and the kid who was almost a son to him. And he was no small opponent. I think they were a little afraid of him and didn't want to have to deal with him directly."

"So at the funeral dinner," Woods contributed, "they drugged him and let it be known he was going to take Trudy home. That was very iffy. Someone might have found him and revived him a lot earlier."

"It was a desperate patching together of a plot that was failing pretty drastically all around. And I suspect there might have been a bit more to it on Charlotte's part. She is about the same age as Keegan, you know, and she has made it quite clear her own husband never overly impressed her. Could be that Myron was her second choice, just like Galen was Faye's. A woman scorned..."

"History repeating itself." Woods stirred his coffee thoughtfully. "In more ways than one. People don't learn. Myron's plot depended heavily on theater, just like his father's, and the motive was the same. You know, this whole thing makes me kind of glad I don't own property worth millions, or," he added with a grin, "the Keegan sex appeal. Charlotte is right, you know. The plan *should* have worked. In fact, if Jack had died on schedule, it *would* have. Human nature being what it is, people were ready, almost eager, to be disillusioned about him."

"Or if Regan hadn't asked Lucerne to make some prints for her," Matt said, "even the patched-together version of the plan probably would have succeeded. Keegan definitely would have been the prime suspect. Galen and Faye's plot forty years ago should have worked too. All of this leaves me to believe that somebody else was weighing in. Somebody neither pair took into their calculations."

"Somebody," Woods agreed, "who wanted Speedwell to carry on."

■ ■ ■

Six weeks later on a cold December afternoon, Matt and Gabe sat together on a bench. The final game for the state championship was about to go into overtime. Gabe's cast had been removed only a few days before.

"So," Matt said, "decide what you're going to do after you graduate?" He had been, Gabe noticed, carefully refraining from looking behind him at the section of the stands where the Hayden contingent was sitting.

"Yeah." Gabe blew on his hands, tucked them into his armpits. "I'm going to Barlow College so I can commute. That way I can still work part-time at the farm."

"Good. I was afraid you might decide to go back to the city."

"Not much for me there," Gabe said without malice. "You and my mother made sure of that."

"Oh, so you knew?"

"About her calling you in when she was dying? Making you promise to keep me out of trouble till I graduated? Yeah, I got it out of Aunt Lily, finally."

"Your mother wouldn't have had such confidence in me if she could have foreseen how badly I would mess up with Ken."

Gabe gave him an incredulous look. "Yeah, chief, you're a failure all right. In one year, you've been responsible for two solved murder cases, a fire rescue, and taking your team to the finals for the third time. Not to mention convincing the most eligible woman in town she is in love with you. But that's not enough? Ken would say that somebody needs to cuff you up the side of the head."

Matt managed a grin. "You want to try?"

"Hey, it worked once, didn't it? Besides, if you're fixing to break my boss's heart, I figure you deserve it."

Matt looked away. "You'll learn, Gabe, that love isn't always enough. Marriage is difficult for couples from similar backgrounds; with Regan and me, it would be doomed. I think I knew that from the start, but I wanted—" He stopped to correct himself bleakly. "—*want* her too much to let her go easily."

"So I'd better not try for anything more than just friends with Lucerne?" Gabe asked.

Matt shot him a sharp glance. "I didn't say that."

"Yes, you did. And you're right. It would be asking for trouble. Lucerne and I don't even have a skin color in common. Much better to be realistic. Anything for a quiet life, huh?"

From the corner of his eye, Gabe noted with satisfaction that the chief had opened his mouth to object but appeared stymied. *I got him that time.*

"Wipe the gloat off your face," Matt said finally. "I know you don't believe a word of that. But you've made your point. What are you going to take at Barlow?"

"I don't know. What," Gabe asked, looking away, "do you need to be a cop?"

Silence. "I took pre-law myself," Matt said finally. "Of course, you aren't required to have a college education to get into the academy. You after my job, Johnson? I thought you didn't like cops."

"Yeah, but I figure it has to be a cushy job, sit around the diner and drink coffee all day. I mean, nothing much happens in these small towns, right?"

He dodged the mock blow aimed at his shoulder just as the team jogged off the field to surround them for the final timeout. Jack rubbed his palms together. "What's it going to be, Coach?"

"I'm taking hands off of this one," Matt said. "You guys are already winners in my book. You proved that by the way you hung together in October. It's your call."

Seeing the half-embarrassed but exultant grins around the circle, Gabe thought, *Thanks, Chief. You don't know what that means to some of us.* Then, recalling that Matt had been father-less also, *Or maybe you do.*

"What do you say?" Jack asked, looking around at all of them. "Do we put Gabe back in now?"

Gabe shook his head. "No way is my arm ready. Wait a minute though. They don't know that. If I go in at the last minute like this, they'll be expecting you to throw to me. Pretend you're going to do that, which will pull them right, then give it to the halfback, and let him go wide left."

"Me?" Chris looked overwhelmed.

"Sounds good." Jack's glance swept the circle. "Okay? Let's do it!" Their hands joined briefly, fell apart, and they strutted back onto the field.

The crowd went wild.

"Gabe, Gabe, Gabe!" Lucerne was yelling behind Regan. Her chant was taken up by the other teenagers in the stands and by the cheerleaders down in front.

Sitting between Trudy and Diane, with the frosty air nipping her cheeks and the bleachers vibrating to the rhythm of stomping feet, Regan thought again how wonderfully strange life was. They were on the lowest row, which was most convenient for Trudy's wheelchair, almost on the field. Lucerne and her friends had scrambled in just behind them, and Lucerne was now pounding happily on Regan's back in time with the chant.

Trudy grinned. "Maybe we gave these kids a little too much hot chocolate."

Regan laughed. "Right now, I'm pretty charged up myself, but I don't think it's the caffeine. Who knew football could be this much fun? It always looked kind of boring on TV."

"I guess you have to be out here where the action is," Diane said.

"That's the secret," Trudy agreed softly. "Being out where the action is."

The Bobcats took their positions. Regan imagined them grinning with a kind of cheerful ferocity at their opponents across the line. The ball was hiked to Jack; heavy shoulders smacked against heavy shoulders. Jack jogged right and, looking at Gabe, raised his arm. Gabe, fading back fast, held up his hands and went down under a barrage of bodies. The announcer's voice had risen to a shriek. "Colby's all in the clear. Look at him go! They are not going to catch him! There is no way in heaven or earth anybody can catch these guys tonight!"

Regan came to her feet with the teenagers and screamed just as loudly as they.

Across the goal line, Chris hurled the ball down so that it bounced higher than his head. Then he was surrounded, boisterously embraced, hoisted onto the shoulders of his teammates.

The announcer was continuing hysterically in the background. "What a comeback! Everybody said the Bobcats didn't have a chance with their two best players laid up for most of the season. But did they let that stop them? Remember, these are the guys who defied public opinion to stand up for their quarterback, and now they've done it again. This, ladies and gentlemen, is what team spirit is all about!"

When the Bobcats streamed from the locker room, the Hayden contingent was there to greet them. Although Amos and Howard had stayed at Speedwell, they and their patients would be crowded around a TV set about now. In the wintry atmosphere of the football field, most of the group was shivering, laughing, and crying at the same time. All of them were remembering another night and another football field.

A lot of hugging was going on too. Regan was whirled down the line of players and ended up in the arms of the coach himself. Looking up at him, she said, "Great job, Matt."

For an instant his arms tightened hungrily around her, his searching gaze dropped from her face to the ring on her finger.

Then he let her go.

Regan found herself standing beside Sylvia. Jack still did not, she recalled, treat Sylvia any differently than his other friends. The two women looked at each other in perfect understanding, heads up, undaunted. Although they had no promise of a happy ending, they were not sorry they had loved. Faith, after all, was hope with no guarantees.

"This," Sylvia vowed, "is just the beginning."

If you would like to receive a complimentary subscription
to Thyme Will Tell,
Audrey Stallsmith's quarterly newsletter,
please write her at:

Audrey Stallsmith
Thyme Will Tell
P. O. Box 1136
Hadley, PA 16130

THE THYME WILL TELL MYSTERIES

BOOK #1:

ROSEMARY FOR REMEMBRANCE

If you missed book #1 in the series, *Rosemary for Remembrance*, (ISBN 1-57856-040-3) be sure to ask for it at your local bookstore!

To save herself from jail, Regan must find her father's killer—before the killer finds her.

Regan Culver's beloved father has been killed—poisoned, apparently by his own daughter's hand. Now, following his sudden, tragic death, Regan finds herself not only parentless but horribly and unbelievably accused of the murder. The evidence against her is overwhelming; she is Alden Culver's primary heir—and the one responsible for bringing him a cup of poisoned tea on the last night of his life.

Now Regan's only hope is to find the killer herself—a quest that will lead her from the mysteries of the past into the perils of the future. For within the gardens and herb farm her mother Rosemary once loved, there lies a secret, a secret that drove somebody very close to Regan to an act of desperation—a secret that may once again lead to murder.

■ ■ ■

THE THYME WILL TELL MYSTERIES, BOOK #3: *Roses for Regret* (Available June 1999)